Blank Sheet

ERIC DILWORTH

PAGE PUBLISHING, INC.
New York, NY

First originally published by Page Publishing, Inc. 2018

The writing in this novel will contain detailed graphic actions. Violent behavior and a variety of acts of degradation are also encased in such reading. Some may not be suitable for the less mature. Due to the direction I attempt to take you, it has to be extreme therefore—extremely detailed. However, it is a read that can be appreciated by all due to the journey one can take with it.

ISBN 978-1-64298-843-7 (Paperback)
ISBN 978-1-64298-844-4 (Digital)

C O N T E N T S

PREFACE

A SERIES OF UNUSUAL murders have occurred. All have taken place in a public setting. On the surface, it would appear as random acts of violence. But they actually have one distinct connection. Given the severity of the case, two FBI agents are assigned to it. As they dig deeper into their investigation, a rather interesting revelation is discovered. The information found pertains not only to the case but also to their own personal past.

ACKNOWLEDGMENT

FIRST AND FOREMOST, I would like to thank my Lord and Savior, Jesus Christ, for being the Truth, the Way, and the Light. For only through Him, I may see the Father, the very reason I am able to do what I can and treat others the way I do. He is my guideline, my taskmaster, my authority. My source of strength, compassion, mercy, and proactivity.

CHAPTER 1

MOTION

I T WAS A cool, breezy, and clear morning with no sign of fog. Though it did not rain the night before, the ground was still wet with dew from the chilled air. Reflections of the sun bounced off the windows and mirrors of cars. Drivers headed up and down the road as the slick sound of tires sped over ground. The smooth, low rumble of the engine was heard intermittently during the change of channels on the radio station.

Two men by the names of Walter Fray and David Brice rode along the highway. Walter sat back comfortably with his left elbow resting on the door panel and his right hand on the steering wheel of a pearl-white hard-top two-door 1993 Ford Mustang (classic). The charcoal-gray-colored interior was spotless. At first glance, it would appear the car was brand-new despite the 102,125-mile reading on the odometer.

Black freshly vacuumed floormats, black leather shifter covering, black leather steering wheel cover, and a charcoal-gray dashboard all showed no cracks or any other signs of wear. The front seats matched the flawless charcoal texture as the back seats. The letters spelling out the word *push* on the seat belt latch also showed no wearing marks on either side, front or back.

The smooth and steady cruise enabled very little bouncing from the suspended yellow car freshener hanging from the rearview mirror. All notable accessories were of stock quality. Everything from the wheels, radio, sound system, window tint to the rear spoiler and a single-tone paint job were all right off the lot.

David also sat back slightly twisted in Walter's direction with his right arm resting on the door panel, as he glanced out the window at the scenery. From time to time, he reached for the cup holder, taking long sips of his fairly large soft drink after finishing off a bag of Cool Ranch Doritos.

Walter threw back handfuls of Skittles in his mouth as he peered forward, checking each off-ramp sign, going about fifteen miles above the speed limit on a freeway. There wasn't too much traffic to deal with, but they still seemed to be headed somewhere with a purpose as he shifted gears, changing lanes, enjoying random bursts of speed from the five-speed manual transmission.

One thing's for certain: the two men apparently made a stop at a gas station or convenience store of some kind to collect their snacks. They appeared to be good acquaintances due to the friendly nature of respect they showed each other while having a rather spirited debate about a sports-related topic, boxing in particular.

Shaking the contents in his left hand, making a small rattle, Walter spoke in between chewing. "So are you telling me that if they both fought in their prime, Tyson could take Ali?"

A crooked smile appeared on the face of David, as he responded, "No question about it. Tyson was a wrecking machine. An absolute beast of the first order."

"A wrecking machine indeed," Walter replied. "But don't act like Ali had no punching power. Out of fifty-six wins, thirty-seven were by knockout!"

Still glancing out the window of the passenger side, David responded, "Yeah, okay. But out of Tyson's fifty wins, forty-four were by knockout." He shrugged haplessly. "Numbers don't lie."

At a steady speed with no need to shift gears on the open highway, Walter reached his right hand over and grabbed a bottle of water to chase down the sugar. After a few swigs, he responded in kind, "But he didn't fight anybody. Can you name how many world champions he beat?"

"Now that's a separate argument." David waved a dismissive hand as he continued. "It's not his fault he had no competition equal to him. I'm not taking anything away from Ali and his greatness. I'm just saying, if they had ever fought prime for prime, I'm taking Iron Mike."

Glancing over his right shoulder while his hand was on top of the steering wheel, Walter arched both eyebrows while responding, "You can't be serious. Reach advantage, Ali. Combinations, Ali. Defensive strategy, counterpunching, footwork . . . Ali."

Finally, turning toward Walter, offering his full attention, David responded. His tone of voice suggested that he was now very interested in continuing the debate. "Mike had good footwork too. And great combinations. But Ali dropped his left too much. Mike kept his guard. And at the first sign of dropping that left against Tyson, it's a wrap."

No longer leaning against the door, Walter then shifted his weight in his seat from a left-side lean to the right-side lean. Switching hands on the wheel, with his right hand, he pointed a finger in the air as he addressed the remark just made. "See, that's where you got it wrong. Ali only dropped it to read. He would bring that left up just as quick to parry anything coming, especially a hook. Which is what we know was Tyson's best punch. To be honest, most of the hits he took were the ones he wanted to."

"But no one *wanted* to take shots from Tyson though. And the same would go for him. If the first few didn't put him down, they would have made him think about feeling them again." David added a little chuckle at the end.

"Tyson was undersized, so he had to lunge with his power shots. It's hard to lunge when you're getting jabbed all night."

With both palms facing up, his eyes wide and shoulders held in a high shrug, David protested, "Yeah, and? He was undersized against everybody he fought and still dropped forty-four people. They tried to jab him too. But I never seen a fighter jab while he's on his back. You?"

"People only see the hand speed Ali had and forget he was a great defensive fighter. He had tremendous parry skills and always knew to clinch when things got out of hand."

"But how do you parry and clinch a freight train? And don't give me that rope-a-dope stuff either. Two body shots alone would've buckled his knees."

Tilting his head toward David, Walter's eyebrows went up again. "You clearly underestimate the timing Ali had on his punches and his ability to evade. Plus, he would have got a couple hard shots in. More than a couple. Then Ali just would've grabbed him and frustrated him like he did Spinks."

David offered his rebuttal. "You forget how crisp Tyson was when he would weave. And he would have had majority of those jabs right on his gloves or right past his ears. I mean seriously, the guy could move his body side to side like this." He held his arm up at eye level. He mocked, moving only his wrist freely, flopping it back and forth. It made the hand look independent of the arm. He was describing how Tyson could move his body.

"Ali would have jabbed his body just the same as his head. We saw how Mike fought when he was frustrated. Last time we saw that, he went all cannibal and bit another man's ear, for crying out loud."

"I'm just saying. A tad bit overrated as far as being called the greatest of all time, if you ask me."

"What! Overrated!" Walter nearly jumped out of the driver's seat. "You need to be drug tested!"

The conversation turned from friendly banter to a heated debate. The radio was completely drowned out by the events taking place in the car between these two. Walter began to raise his voice as he banged his hands on the steering wheel in disagreement.

David obliged him in the debate as he raised his voice as well. He sat his drink down in the cup holder and spoke vigorously as he clapped his hands together in between sentences.

It was a heated exchange. Both tried to talk over the other one while in the middle of making his point. To the outside eye, it would appear this conversation was going to escalate into something. However, neither showed any indication of it leading to a physical altercation. It was a common occurrence among most men when discussing sports opinions.

Walter still kept good control of the car as they cruised around seventy-five miles per hour down the highway. Even though he banged the steering wheel, he did not swerve. The windows fogged up a little from the debate, but he was still able to see clear.

David addressed his pet peeve regarding different eras. "I think that if they switched eras, Tyson would have been considered the greatest, hands down. That's the reason why Ali gets the nod. There were more people besides him that wore the belt. But Tyson was undisputed. Let us not forget the psychological play. Tyson had dudes scared before they even walked to the ring. In my book, that makes Tyson the greatest. Nobody was scared of Ali. He had to talk his hype up. Mike would just show up."

"Now wait a second! First of all, Ali would have dominated Tyson's era of boxing even more than his own. And second of all, he was undisputed in his first reign until that draft situation. But the belt was held by Frazier and Foreman, two Hall of Famers considered by many boxing aficionados."

"I'll tell you this much. I remember Foreman himself, said he would've hated to fight Tyson. Plus, Mike would have crushed Frazier. I know he was tough and all, but I would have given that fight three rounds tops."

"You didn't say that. Tell me you didn't just say that," Walter remarked.

"Oh, I did say that."

"Based on what?" Walter's voice raised an octave or two.

"Well, based on skill for one. I'm telling you. Mike was nice, man. Real nice," David retorted.

"Smoking Joe Frazier is also one of the all-time greats. Tyson never beat an all-time great. As a matter a fact, every time he fought credible challengers, he lost. Buster Douglas, Lennox Lewis, and Evander Holyfield twice. I mean, really. Who has Tyson ever beat?"

David went on, dismissing Walter's point, "But Ali never faced anybody with the force and torque of Tyson though."

"Did you forget how powerful George Forman was? The guy was a beast! Not the smiling, grill seller, but the physical freak that pummeled Smoking Joe."

"Mike would have dropped George too!"

"Just like that, huh? He would have just dropped George Foreman?"

"Well, George might have lasted about three rounds."

"You're completely bias." Walter shook his head. "There is no objectivity in you at all. I can't have this conversation with you."

"What do you mean?" David turned his hands up in a gesture of questioning. "We are having this conversation. You think Ali was the greatest. And great he was. But he just wouldn't have matched up well with Tyson. It's just my opinion. I'm entitled to that."

"Yes. Your opinion belongs to you. But you're wrong in your opinion."

"How can I be wrong in my opinion? My opinion is my opinion. If you don't agree that's your problem, not mine."

"Well then, I don't agree."

Walter appeared agitated with the conversation. Being the big boxing fan that he was, he enjoyed the back-and-forth with another knowledgeable fan. However, provided his own bias for the great Muhammad Ali and all that he did in the ring, he couldn't look at it objectively himself. All in all, he never passed on an opportunity to get into a verbal skirmish with someone regarding boxing.

The same could be said for David. He seemed to enjoy stoking the fire a little bit. They stopped at the first light after getting off the freeway. Walter and David didn't have much to say at this point. But neither was actually upset.

They were just quiet for the moment. David picked his drink back up and finished up the very small amount left inside. The music was eventually turned off during the debate. The sound of slurping occurred, then he sat it back down as they sat and waited for the light to change.

The red light turned green, and they made a right toward their destination. They continued down the street; all the while, Walter was checking the GPS. Conversation began to start up again between the two. This time it was less confrontational and on a completely different subject. This time it was regarding where they were going.

David kept looking out the passenger side window as he spoke. "It should be right up here, right?"

Walter was doing a scan himself, leaning on the steering wheel with both hands to get a good look at street signs. "Yeah. At least that's what the address says."

"Ever been around here before?"

"No. You?"

"No."

David rolled down the window, resting his right arm on the door panel. He leaned into the side mirror, reaching up to scratch his nose with his left hand. Walter caught notice of a glare from the sun bouncing off David's watch.

"Now that's a fine watch you got there."

Turning his arm to look at it himself, David smiled with pride. "Yeah, I got it on vacation in Mexico two years ago."

"Mexico, huh?"

"Yeah. I got this *and* got lucky. Quite often in fact. Best two-week vacation I ever had."

"Did you get that at a store, or did you get a great deal at a marketplace somewhere?"

"Oh no, I went to the mall for this bad boy. Cost a pretty penny, but I couldn't pass it up."

"How much did it run you?" Walter asked.

"More than a few car payments for a brand-new Mercedes."

Walter gave a low whistle. "Besides the look, what else sold you on it? I mean, that's a lot of money for a watch."

"It tells time in every zone. Any country or continent. As soon as I enter a different time zone, it automatically switches to that zone and also links up with the astrological calendar."

"Well, what time do you have for this zone?"

"A quarter to eight."

The GPS told Walter they reached their destination. "This is the place right here."

"All right. How long did it take?"

"About twenty minutes from where we left."

David looked at his watch again. "We're still pretty early. You want to get some food?"

"Yeah, let's go."

The parking lot was empty save for a few cars. They headed into a restaurant called Pots-N-Pans for breakfast. It was the type of diner that allows one to seat themselves. The server came over, took their orders, and served them as normal. They received their meals and proceeded to eat with no conversation. After they finished eating, they sat for a while and resumed conversing.

David started the conversation, leaning back with both hands outstretched on the table, sighing in a manner of satisfaction. "That was probably the best French toast I've had in some time."

"I used to date a chef. She knew how to keep the bread crisp and used colored powdered sugar. You should have had some of hers."

"Colored powdered sugar? I never heard of that."

"Yeah, she would never tell me how she got it to color, though. But she always gave to me when it was piping hot and crisp."

"Were the flavors different with each color? You know, like red was cherry, purple was grape, and green was apple? Thank kind of stuff?" David asked.

"That's exactly how it was. Flat out amazing. The added part is, the bread was a bronze color. It was never burnt. I mean, never. I didn't even need syrup or butter."

"A chef. Man, how did you mess that up?"

"She was from Cuba. Her mother got sick, so she went back to help her."

"Man, I wish I would have dated a chef. Where did you meet her?"

"I met her at a mixer. A friend of mine wanted to fix me up. She thought it was time for me to settle down and stop playing the field. She's like a sister to me, so she introduced us."

"How about after her? Seeing anybody now?"

"No one exclusively. I had one I was talking with for a while. We got pretty serious. Even moved in together. But it fell apart months ago. That was my last relationship. How about you?" He started drinking his water as he awaited David's answer.

David paused for a second. "Well, I used to be with a bodybuilder."

Walter nearly spit up his water as he was drinking. "You did what? You like women that are built like Tarzan and look like Jane?"

"She wasn't Miss Olympia or anything like that. But she was nice and toned, had a very pretty face and a soft voice. She had a nice personality, so I said why not."

"Let me guess. You met her at the gym, right?"

"No. The post office. She was in a tank top and shorts with flip-flops. Other guys were in there looking at her but were intimidated. I, of course, was not."

"I like women with athletic figures too, but a bodybuilder?" Walter remarked.

"Actually, I've always dated girls that were a little on the plus size. So I thought, let's try something different."

"Plus size?" Walter smiled in joking amusement. "So you got a thing for big women, huh?"

David gave a sly smile. "I do. And I'm not ashamed to say it. Something about a big woman just does it for me."

The look on Walter's face was quizzical. "Just how big are we talking here? Just curious."

David maintained the smile. "All I require is a pretty face, great personality, and the ability to get off the floor on your own."

Walter leaned his head back and bellowed out a laugh. "So this bodybuilder was more of a curiosity fling then? Because she clearly didn't fit that criteria."

"No. We were married for two years."

Walter put the glass of water down on the table in emphasis. "Whoa, you were married? What happened?"

The smile left David's face as he looked to the side in memory. "We had, how you would say, philosophical differences that could not be resolved."

"So you got divorced. How long ago?"

"Last week."

A look of comprehension came over the face of Walter. "I see. What time do you have now?"

"Nine forty-five."

"All right. Let's go."

Walter went to pay the bill. David took his watch off and left it on the table before leaving first. Walter left a big tip to the server of fifteen hundred dollars. When David stepped outside, he took in a deep breath and held it for about two seconds. He then let it out, simultaneously stretching out both arms in the air. Walter soon followed out of the restaurant with a toothpick in his mouth.

He stopped right next to David, checking his pockets for his keys. Both men looked each other in the eye, and in unison, they stepped toward the car. No more words were exchanged at that moment. Walter unlocked the doors with the automatic button and entered the driver's side. He grabbed the empty bag of Skittles he had, his bottle of water, the empty bag of chips, and the cup that had David's drink in it. He then went to the trash and tossed them. While he was heading over to the trash can, David slid the passenger seat forward, getting out a bottle of all-purpose cleaner and paper towels from the back seat. He started to wipe down the inner door handles, door panels, steering wheel, and seats. The dashboard, arm rest, and shifter also received a good cleaning.

He even wiped down the inner windows, rearview mirror, windshield, and back window. Walter made his way toward the trunk to open it. He grabbed two sets of hand wraps out. The entire time, no words were exchanged. There was no sign of demonstrative body language, no disgruntled grunts, and no unsavory looks at each other. They both moved to their tasks as if they were on assignment.

David finished his part, then took his wallet and put it in a bag they had gotten from a convenience store. He started to walk toward the trash can to throw it away with the paper towels and cleaner. Walter made a clicking sound with his tongue then tossed David his wallet.

David turned without pause, still walking. He caught it with one hand, as if it was a play that a quarterback and wide receiver worked on for years. Walter put the keys in the outside driver's door.

Both wallets were thrown in a sewer drain close to one of the stores in the parking lot instead of the trash can. On his way back to the car, Walter tossed him a set of hand wraps he had grabbed from the trunk. They both began to wrap their hands, all while not saying a word.

It was now ten o'clock. The grand opening to the much-anticipated store called "The All Store." The store was petitioned by the patrons of the neighborhood to city officials. It was meant not only to provide a service of necessities but to also quench certain leisure desires some people may have in terms of hobbies, such as boating, fishing, golfing, camping, hiking, hunting, and various other outdoor activities. Typically in this area, one would have to travel a little distance for such items. And not to be forgotten, this store opened up plenty of job opportunities in a community sorely needing it.

The thrift store was large enough to house forty-five apartments, if it was a housing unit. Food, household appliances, children's toys, office equipment, bill pay centers, music instruments, entertainment, apparel, gardening essentials, electronics, arts and crafts, and many more diverse objects were to be found in this store. This particular area was seriously in need of such an asset. People began showing up as early as nine fifteen.

The parking lot filled up quick. Long lines formed at the doors and down the sidewalk. Multiple conversations began to consume a once-quiet parking lot as the public waited patiently for the doors to open. Meanwhile, Walter and David continued to move to their purpose, wrapping their hands.

They alternated slamming one fist into their own opposite hand, the same as a fighter does to check the impact of a hit or the comfort level of the wrap before a fight. The hand-wrapping jobs were finally finished to their satisfaction. David placed one hand on the rim of the lifted trunk, while the other scratched the left side of his goatee.

Walter rubbed both of his hands over the top of his head back and forth, as if he was removing lint. They looked at each other and nodded. Walter spoke first. "You ready?"

"Yeah. By the way, what's your name?"

"Walter Fray."

"David Brice."

CHAPTER 2

THE LOT

T HE TWO FIST-BUMPED as David shut the trunk closed. Then, simultaneously, they each threw arguably the hardest punch one can muster at each other—both direct hits. The impact was so loud it grabbed the attention of the people in line. Immediately, David was busted open above his left eye, pouring blood. Walter sustained an unmistakably broken jaw. His left cheekbone appeared to have caved in.

Both lost their balance and bearings from the hits on each other. Walter stood at five feet, eleven inches, weighing 219 pounds. David stood at six feet two inches, weighing 234 pounds. Being the bigger of the two, he was the first to come to after the hit.

Completely ignoring the rush of blood running on the left side of his face, he then delivered three punishing blows in succession to the side of the Walter's head. The combinations of straight rights and lefts were as strenuous as they were devastating. He held his breath and bit his lip as he threw each hit. Massive knuckle knots began to form on the side of the head of Walter, as if he were hit with a baseball bat.

Walter tried to get his faculties about him, but David didn't let up. He continued to pummel without mercy. Four more punches followed. In most fights, some punches slip. They don't hit with complete accuracy. The impact isn't as grand as it should be. But that's most fights. In this one, all of David's punches were direct hits.

Walter struggled to stay conscious. He had one knee down and one hand on the ground. The other hand tried to block whatever punch he could. David attempted to put everything he had behind the fifth blow, an overhand right, with brutish momentum. The force in which he came down with could potentially shatter a man's skull, possibly killing him.

At this point, Walter could see three Davids. Dazed and half-conscious, Walter moved ever so slightly to evade the anvil being thrown at him. It could have been instinct, slight recognition, or being completely off equilibrium that allowed him to move. Nevertheless, the sudden swerve of the head did the trick.

David put so much force behind the punch that he fell to the ground shoulder first, bumping his head on the pavement upon the miss. That was the opening Walter needed, but only if he could capitalize. Moving on sheer instinct of survival, Walter crawled over to David lying on the ground and dealt up a faint hit to the side of the head, causing a slight thud of David's face hitting the ground.

The punch didn't have tremendous power behind it on account of Walter's dazed condition but was enough to gain an edge. The hit compounded with the fall sent David into a state of weariness, providing Walter with the window he so desperately needed.

Parking lot patrons were in a state of complete shock at what they were witnessing. It was one of those strange moments that even if you hate fights, you can't seem to take your eyes off it. Call it curiosity. Call it intrigue. Or call it simply an opportunity to watch something out of the norm. But with the impact in which these two men were throwing at each other and connecting with, no one dared to get in the middle to break it up.

Walter threw two bone-crunching hits to the ribs, followed by two more to the back of the neck. You could clearly hear the snap and crack of the ribs with each hit. David began to cough up blood, as Walter went on.

The only thing that stopped Walter from continuing to finish him was the fact that he was getting weak and dizzy due to the over-exertion and blood loss. David managed to throw a wild elbow to the other side of the eye of Walter, which threw him off of him.

Both struggled to breathe and see due to the blood dripping in their eyes. David held his ribs with one arm, crossing himself, as he continued to cough up blood. The other hand held the back of his neck. The look on his face suggested he never felt pain like that before.

Walter's face was a red crimson mask, and his nose was so disfigured it could literally point in the direction of both east and west simultaneously. Both struggled to get to their feet, using the car to climb up on.

Some onlookers had their camera phones out, recording the encounter. Some put their cameras away because the live visual was too brutal. Some of the more queasy types turned their heads, wincing with each crushing blow. Others were crossings themselves, saying prayers, because these two were literally beaten the hell out of each other.

They got back up, and David charged like a bull, springing off his feet like a javelin, spearing Walter with his left shoulder. The explosive charge lifted Walter clean off his feet and backward into a metal light post. Walter fell back first against the post, nearly wrapping around it like a shoestring.

He fell on top of David like a folded chair. David rolled out slowly onto his stomach, coughing vigorously, trying to find a way to get some air. The hit that Walter took would have finished off a normal man. So it was clear he'd been in a fight or two before. He stirred around, getting to his hands and knees.

The hit didn't burst the back of his head open, but a knot was forming quickly. He managed to get a foot planted, trying to get back to his feet, only to stumble and fall forward into a shopping cart rack in the parking lot. David got up slowly, holding his ribs, and headed over toward the shopping cart rack to do more damage.

At this point, every move David makes was a slow one. Still clutching his ribs with one arm, he reached down with the other one hand, grabbing Walter by the hair. With great effort, he got Walter to his feet. In an unexpected quick burst of adrenaline, Walter swiftly kicked him in the groin, forcing David to hunch over. The follow-up was immediate. He grabbed David by the back of his head with both hands and delivered a powerful knee to the face.

David tried to fall backward, but Walter wouldn't let go. He then applied two more powerful knees, one to each rib while continuing to hold his head. After the last knee to the ribs, he used momentum to fling him to the side like a sack of potatoes. David rolled uncontrollably like a log downhill for about eight feet and stopped lying faceup.

Walter raced over, leaped up in the air, and landed on David with a crushing elbow to the center of his chest. Blood spouted from David's mouth like a fountain. The sequence took quite a bit out of Walter. He dropped to the ground and rolled on his side a half of a foot from David so he could still keep an eye on him. Both men lay there on the ground, coughing, bleeding, and writhing in pain.

From a distance, it appeared as if David was lying there motionless, his limbs unmoving, his breathing extremely slow and even. Only slight convulsions from his chest would occur, giving off the impression of nothing other than him being hurt badly. Walter stirred around, but not swiftly. He got to his feet and crouched down over David—his intention, to ground and pound.

He bent his knees, squatting down, preparing to sit on his chest. Upon the first swing, David put everything he had into one strike directly into that broken nose again. The hit snapped Walter's head back, standing him up completely, forcing him on his tiptoes. The hit was so hard and sudden it caught Walter's voice where he couldn't even cry out in pain. His hands went to his face to cover the injury, as blood ran through his fingers like water.

David got to a knee, holding his ribs and coughing. Then, like a raging bull, he roared, charging into Walter like a Mack Truck. This time he picked him up, holding the back of his legs with his shoulder leading into his chest. Walter slammed against the passenger side of the car, shattering the window with his back. The impact was "car crash" strong. It lifted the car up on two wheels about three inches off the ground.

The crowd gasped as the sound of broken glass and a smashed indoors resounded in the midst of the ring of silence. It was a considerable distance from the car to the people in line. But more than a few drops of Walter's blood made its way to within a foot from the curb the crowd stood upon.

Being so disoriented in the charge, David caught a bad break as well. The top of his head hit the car door as Walter's back. Blood-coated body prints smeared the side of impact as the two slid down slowly on top of each other.

Disturbing. Frightening. Mortifying. Surreal. Just a few words that describe the scene. The sounds of broken bones and the visual of blood pouring from both men. And yet, neither man showed signs of conceding. It appeared to be a fight out of rage. Normally, some verbal indication would reveal the origin of such a brutal encounter.

But there was none. Witnesses saw an opening to where the two men were too weak to fight anymore. Two men began making their way over to break them up. Provided that David was on top, they grabbed him first, pulling him away from Walter.

David, ever so slowly, reached toward his ankle. He pulled out a six-inch blade from a strap under his pants leg. The two good Samaritans dropped him like a hot skillet and sprinted back toward the line. Walter reached for his knife of equal size in his ankle strap, as he uncurled himself from the fetal position. They moved toward each other, using the car to pull themselves up.

Walter used the rear bumper and trunk to climb up. David started going the other way first, clearly disoriented. Realizing he was going the wrong way, he gathered himself to head toward Walter. He used the front tires and hood to get to his feet. Blood hand prints covered the passenger side of the car as they scaled it for balance, making their way to each other.

The once-pearl-white Mustang was completely defaced with blood smears and spatters on the hood, trunk, passenger's side, front and back windshields, front and back bumpers, the white wall rims and tires. A few spatters managed to make it to the roof as well.

It was near impossible to tell what Walter looked like at this point. Blood poured from his face like a broken faucet. There was no more white in his eyes, only red. Prior to the fight, he had a short low-cut hairstyle, the color of black. Various knots on his head and the steady flow of blood made identification extremely difficult. He used his formerly white and now blood-soaked shirt to get it out of his eyes. But the flow was just too great. It's a wonder how he was even still awake, let alone trying to stand.

David looked no better off. Struggling to grab a painless breath, he found himself unable to stand up straight due to the broken ribs and possibly a broken neck. His outfit was virtually identical to Walter's. His shirt, once the color of white, found itself crimson as well. Long streams of red ran down the front of his shirt from all the coughing-up he had done. His hairstyle was once a curly dark brown at around medium length. It was no longer stylish, now laid over in blood, stuck like it was doused with syrup.

They made their way toward each other until they had two feet of distance between them. Murmuring was finally heard by the two gladiators. Walter took a slow glance at the crowd like a punch-drunk boxer as he wiped the blood from his eyes. He grimaced in obvious pain due to the fact that he had to brush a hand across his already-mangled nose.

David glanced over at the crowd as well. The big powerful man, now reduced to a shell of his physical self, locked eyes with a young kid around the age of eleven or twelve. He attempted a show of pride and tried to stand up straight. He dropped the left arm clutching his ribs, pulling his shoulder back, sticking out his chest. Blood continued to run down his face from his eye sockets as he gained control of his breathing.

The young kid stood in front of his mother with his eyes locked wide-open. She held his hand, frightened, covering her mouth in shock with her other hand. David gave the young kid a slight wink of the eye as he attempted to maintain posture and breathe. But to no avail. He coughed up spatters of blood and immediately bent back over, clutching his ribs with his off hand.

After these brief few seconds, the two men turned their attention back toward each other. They were now close enough to touch each other. With knives in hands, they simultaneously thrust their blades into each other's stomachs.

They pulled their knives and repeated the thrust two more times at the exact same time. Apparently, both had the same idea. Both mustered whatever strength they had left and thrust a knife into each other's chest for the finishing blow. They both fell backward from the impact, lying flat on their backs, dead.

Onlookers were frozen in shock by the sheer horror they were seeing. The police and ambulance showed up right after the final blow.

Women and small children were in tears. Those that were not crying were in complete silence with their eyes and mouths wide-open. Two cops showed up, turning the corner, just as Walter and David stabbed each other. They both jumped out with guns drawn in typical standard fashion.

They sprinted toward the two men as they saw them fall, calling out for them to freeze. Quickly realizing they were too late to do anything, they lowered their guns as they advanced. Complete silence covered the parking lot. No birds chirped, no winds gushed. No voices spoke.

One could hear a pin drop on a rug as if they were in a small room with no windows. The police and medics found it hard to look at the brutality these two men displayed. One cop actually excused himself to the side to keep from vomiting.

Both men were lying on their backs on the ground with each other's knife embedded in their chests. Blood continued to ooze slowly from their heads, faces, and chests. Walter's body twitched a few times, giving off the false impression that he might still be alive. The medics rushed over to help him, only to find out there was nothing to help.

The store manager rushed to the front door, nearly dropping his keys in excitement. It wasn't yet time to open, but he was anxious to get business rolling and decided to open the doors fifteen minutes early. Seeing the crowd outside his windows brought a huge smile to his face and dollar signs to his eyes.

Grinning from ear to ear, he opened the doors. Spreading his arms in a dramatic welcoming fashion, he spoke to the backs of the crowd. "Welcome, everyone, to the All Store!" He closed his eyes, smiling, expecting a rush of people like water with the floodgates opened. But it didn't happen.

None entered or even turned around. The store manager opened his eyes while the huge smile faded. The look of bewilderment replaced the previous look of excitement. He noticed the crowd was facing the other direction. He couldn't help but notice the looks on the people's faces from their side profiles. Some were crying. Some were in a state of shock.

He stepped through the crowd to observe what had everyone's attention. He saw the police and ambulances, as well as blood spatters and puddles in multiple areas—the cart rack for the store, a light pole in front of the store, plenty of areas on the ground, and all over a white Ford Mustang. He made his way down the sidewalk to get a better look at what was the cause.

He saw the bodies of Walter and David near the car. Both men were brutalized, with knives in their chests. The police began taping off the area as a crime scene. Murmurs broke out. A few people began to dry heave and run away. Others used each other as crying pillows. Many decided to return home. The opening was not so grand anymore.

The store manager took it all in and fainted.

CHAPTER 3

THE CRIME SCENE

NEW ARRIVALS OF patrons showed up to bear witness to the carnage these two men inflicted. More police arrived, putting up yellow crime-scene tape and proceeded to hold the crowd back. The medics attempted to remove the knives but were unable to pull them without maximum effort. The force these two used to stab each other was so powerful it could have killed a bear.

The knife that Walter had in his chest stuck to such a degree it required two medics to pull it out. One medic bent down over Walter's body, holding the knife with both hands. The other one held him down by the shoulders, kneeling over his head.

The medic wiggled the knife with two hands, then heaved in one motion upward. Like water spouting out of a broken sprinkler, blood gushed out of Walter's chest in a small stream. Both medics jumped up to avoid the stream. More moans, gasps, and dry-heave noises came from the onlooking witnesses. Many even turned their heads and winced, covering their faces.

Police placed the knife in an evidence bag and headed over to David's body. With David being the bigger and stronger of the two, the impact of his stab was more intense. However, the intensity of stab caused by Walter was nothing to sneeze at. It took several attempts in the same manner as the previous body to pull it free. The knife was finally retrieved after three tugs. The evidence was given to the queasy cops that first arrived on the scene.

A federal mandate was instituted a year past that public displays of extreme violence ending in death was considered a federal offense, just as kidnapping and tax evasion. Granted, this wasn't a case of mass murder, but it was a public display with well over twenty witnesses. As a result, a call had to be made by the police department.

A jet-black four-door Lincoln Continental with tinted windows and stock quality wheels turned the corner with government plates. On the scene arrived two federal agents—lead field agent investigator Kyle Frazier and his partner, Norman Wiley. The tall, slender-built Norman Wiley was in his early thirties.

He stood around six feet two and was clean shaven. With his short-cropped hair, he looked like the typical popular high school quarterback in a letterman's jacket. He was buttoned down, wearing the standard outfit—black slacks, white dress shirt, black tie, black shoes, and a black blazer. He was a cop for five years before joining the bureau as recently as two months ago.

Frazier, on the other hand, was a cop for twelve years and an agent for fourteen. He stood nearly the same height as Wiley. Not quite lean, he also wasn't lumpy and out of shape. He was somewhere in the middle. The salt-and-pepper five o'clock shadow indicated a rough estimate of his age. He was in his midfifties. His black trench coat made him look more like an undertaker than an FBI agent.

He threw the standard operating procedure book out ten years ago. Given his seniority and impressive record, he had been granted freedom to conduct his investigations as he saw fit. He was one of the few field agents that requested to take on the most complicated cases. Though he was tops in his department, he preferred to be in the field rather than in the office. Being the senior investigator, Frazier had Wiley drive him around like a chauffeur. They pulled up to the scene, and Wiley exited the car first, eager to get started on his first case. Frazier sat for a while in the car, chewing on the licorice root.

Wiley went over to the officers on the scene, identifying himself as a special agent of the FBI. In classic rookie with power that doesn't know how to use it with fashion, he started throwing his weight around to the local police. He pulled out his notebook, investigating the visual evidence and asking questions.

"Special agent Wiley, FBI. All right, so what do we have here?"

One officer responded, "Looks like a double murder."

"Sir," Wiley asserted.

"What?" the officer asked.

"Looks like a double murder, sir," Wiley corrected him.

The cop didn't look pleased with the remark at all, especially since he was at least seventeen years older than Wiley. He gritted his teeth. "Looks like a double murder, sir."

"A homicide," Wiley remarked.

"What?"

"It looks like a double homicide, not a murder. I would think you would know to use the right terminology, Officer."

"Yeah, well, I know you're an ass," retorted the officer.

"What was that, Officer? Does a beat cop with too many years on the street with a failure to move up in life have something to say to me?"

The officer looked as if he were about explode. He pointed his finger at Wiley and took a half step forward. He was immediately stopped with a hand on his chest by his partner, who stepped in to speak. "Forgive my partner. My name is Officer Bill Green. This is Officer Tom Burns. We were first on the scene."

"Good for you. Now tell me what happened here."

"Honestly, sir. We just arrived on the scene half an hour ago. We called it in to our CO. She told us to call you guys. We pulled the murder weapons and bagged them for evidence. We sealed off the scene, as you can see. We didn't allow anyone to leave."

"You tampered with my evidence, put tape around a scene, and held these people like schoolkids in detention? And didn't even have the wherewithal to ask a few questions? Banged-up job, Detectives. Do you have anything worth your salt for me?"

Officers Green and Burns looked at each other for a second. Then Green looked back at Wiley. "As matter a fact, we have a crime scene and a case to give you, Special Agent. Have a nice day." They both got into their car and tipped their hats in a mocking gesture as they drove off smirking.

Wiley didn't handle that well at all. He thought, because of his position, they would cower from him. He was rude to people he needed help from, and it cost him possibly two people that he might need help from down the line. Standing there holding his notebook, not sure what to do next, he turned to see what happened to his partner.

Frazier sat in the passenger seat, observing the manner in which Wiley handled things. "Loser," he muttered, shaking his head disapprovingly. When Wiley looked at him and threw his hands in the air, Frazier turned his head to look away from him. He scanned the crowd of witnesses, observing them quietly.

Typically, there's a high degree of noise in crowds such as this. People are talking and talking over each other so they can here themselves. Normal body movement also causes noise, such as pants rubbing together, hands clapping, toe tapping in shoes, and other forms of gestures. But this crowd was silent.

After a quick gloss over of the crowd, he narrowed his interview search to a few possible. He took note of a married couple, holding each other. The wife buried her face in her husband's chest, with her hands gripping his shirt. His arms circled her, with his left hand rubbing her back soothingly. The matching wedding bands confirmed his assumption. The man was clearly attempting to console the woman, trying to suppress a look of horror on his face. These were clear indications of witnesses to the whole thing that may be able to shed some light with details.

There was also a young man between the age of twenty and twenty-five. He appeared to attempt to hide himself in the crowd, glancing down toward something in his hand. He attempted to hide his facial expressions by placing his hand in a balled-up fist, pretending to clear his throat. He was also using other body gestures, such as scratching the back of his neck and rubbing his face. All this while he continued to glance nervously toward the police and at other people around him.

Frazier exited the car and walked right over to the people at the scene behind the yellow tape. He didn't bother to look at the scene just yet. The entire time, he was being very cordial with them. He cracked light jokes with the remaining officers regarding what type of coffee and doughnuts he liked from across the street. He believed that bringing levity to a terrible situation relaxes people a little. And when people are relaxed, they can give information a lot clearer.

He worked his way down the line of people behind the tape, assuring them they would get to the bottom of this. Many people were calling out scenarios of what happened. All of them sounded different from each other.

He commissioned a couple of officers to take their statements and give them to him later. He continued this until he approached the married couple he spotted from the car. This strategy was all designed to get to them. He walked up to the couple and introduced himself.

"Morning. I'm Kyle Frazier. Were you two here to witness the whole thing?" Still chewing his licorice root, he made it a deliberate point to leave out the word *good* when he greeted them. He just left it at *morning*.

The husband answered first, realizing he was FBI. "Yes. We were the first in line for the opening."

"And who am I speaking with, sir?" Frazier asked politely.

"My name is Doug Callahan. And this is my wife, Shelly."

Frazier offered a sincere smile and a head nod to both of them. "By any chance, do you recognize either of the two gentlemen involved?"

"No."

"Can you tell me a little of what happened here? Before the fight?"

"Well, we were already standing in line when I turned around and saw the two men walking toward the car. I didn't think anything of it at all. They looked normal enough."

"Did they say anything that grabbed your attention?"

"No. I just looked at them like anyone else then started talking to my wife here."

"How about you, ma'am? Did you notice anything suspicious?"

She gathered herself enough to come out of her husband's arms, to speak. "I did notice they looked like they were cleaning the inside of the car."

"Cleaning?" Frazier asked with a raised eyebrow.

"Yes. They started cleaning the inside of the car. They had paper towels with some kind of all-purpose cleaner."

"What makes you say that?"

"Because they were using it on everything. On the steering wheel, door panels, seats, even the windowsills."

Doug Callahan chimed in, remembering something. "The thing that caught my attention was when one tossed the other a set of hand wraps."

"Hand wraps. How did you know it was hand wraps?"

"I used to box in the military. I can spot them a mile away."

Frazier and the husband appeared to be close to the same age. Frazier might have been a little older. He took a chance at bonding with the man. "Hooyah."

"Hooyah!" The man smiled at the kinship bond they suddenly shared. "You served in the army?"

"Yes, sir," Frazier replied cheerfully. "Paid for my schooling. Paved the way for getting into law enforcement."

"I was stationed in Georgia. You?" Callahan asked.

"Alaska."

"Oh. Sorry about that."

"Probably not as sorry as I was."

A smile broke across the face of Frazier with that remark. Not many people could develop inside jokes with people they just met. But Kyle Frazier had that unique ability. They were clearly making reference to the climate difference between the two regions. Shelly suddenly seemed to calm a little with the levity between the two.

"How did you know I was in the army?" Doug asked him.

"I'm very good at what I do," Frazier replied with a semiserious look.

The husband nodded in response. Frazier returned the nod and went back to questioning. "What happened after they pulled the hand wraps?"

"They started wrapping their hands, like they were about to have a championship title fight. Or in this case . . ." he paused and glanced around, "a death match."

"You saw all this too, ma'am?"

"Not that part. But one of them slammed the trunk real hard. That grabbed my attention. Then they did the little"—she did a mock motion forward with her fist a couple of times—"fist thing. And then . . ." She started sobbing at the memory and fell back into her husband's comforting embrace.

Frazier offered a sympathetic yet firm response. "I know it's difficult, and I appreciate your cooperation. But I need to know what happened."

The husband picked up the rest of the pieces. "They bumped fists as if it was a spirited contest and introduced themselves to each other. And then they—"

"Whoa, back up. They introduced themselves? To each other? Are you sure?"

"Yes, sir. I found it a little strange myself, considering they were in the same car. They didn't talk much to each other though, but I never got the impression that they were strangers just by looking at them."

A look of true curiosity was shown on Frazier's face. "Please, go on. What happened next?"

"Then they simultaneously knocked the hell out of each other. One overhand right. One a piece," Doug remarked.

"At the same time? They threw a punch that connected at the exact same time?"

The man nodded, and his wife started crying a little louder. He rubbed her back gently. "They began to fight like they were ordered to kill each other. It wasn't a very long fight, but it was a brutal one." He gestured an open hand toward the carnage.

"The report we got said they stabbed each other. Who stabbed first?"

"It's was simultaneous. Once they beat themselves half to death, they got up to finish the job."

"I see. Well, thank you for your cooperation. Here is my card. I'll need you to come by my office and make that statement official."

"Sure thing."

"I'm sorry you had to witness this, ma'am." Frazier offered a consoling hand her shoulder. She turned slightly, nodding her thanks. He shook hands with the husband and walked off.

He then made his way over to the young man he noticed while in the car. The young man saw Frazier coming. He quickly pulled his keys out of his pocket and dropped them on the ground with his camera phone in his other hand.

Already knowing the police would take it for evidence, he tucked the phone away in his sock and stood up with his keys in his hand. Frazier continued to chew on his licorice root as he saw the whole failed attempt of sleight of hand. He found it amusing, offering a smile when he spoke to him.

"How are you doing this morning, young man? I'm Kyle Frazier. I would like to ask you a few questions if you don't mind."

"I don't know anything. I just got here about five or ten minutes ago," the young man protested quickly.

"Well, that's a big difference." Frazier cocked his head.

"What is?"

"Five or ten minutes. People think it isn't because it doesn't sound like much. But in real time, it's a real big difference."

"What are you talking about?" The young man's face frowned in confusion.

"Well, it only takes a minute to commit a crime. And it also takes that same minute to witness it. If you got here five minutes ago and the crime took pace eight minutes ago, then you missed it. But if it was ten minutes ago, you caught the whole thing. So which is it, five or ten minutes?" Frazier spoke to him like a professor schooling one of his students in class.

"It was five minutes ago. Because I didn't see anything different than what you see right now."

"You are sure of this? Your clock read five minutes, and then we showed up?

"Well, yeah. It was about five minutes ago."

Frazier pulled out his phone and tapped it a few times with his finger. He stood staring the young man in the eye, still holding the phone. He didn't say a word for twenty seconds, then tapped his phone again abruptly with his finger.

"You see that?" Frazier spoke. "I just clocked twenty seconds of silence. I bet you couldn't count the number of different thoughts that went through your mind during that time. You may have even played out multiple scenarios."

The young man licked his lips nervously.

"Twenty seconds," Frazier went on. "Twenty seconds of things happening in your mind. And yet, here you stand, telling me that even in the three hundred seconds you were here, you have nothing at all to tell me."

"Three hundred seconds?" The young man lost his nervousness to confusion.

Frazier went back into his professor tone. "Well, sixty seconds is one minute. Multiply that by five, and . . ." He spread his hands, anticipating the conclusion to sink in.

The young man nodded his understanding and dropped his head in shame. Frazier patted him on the shoulder. "It's all right, kid. I'm not trying to give you a hard time. Just doing my job."

He turned and walked toward his partner. Along the way, he stopped and told an officer on the scene to confiscate the camera from the young man for evidence and bring him over to FBI headquarters for questioning. He would meet with him later.

Frazier finally made his way over to the scene and began to observe. He saw blood on the shopping cart rack, the side of the car and trunk, the hood, the wheels, the small puddles on the ground in different spots, and the light post, all within a fifteen-foot radius. He then looked at the bodies on the ground, where the knives used to be in their chests.

"Who pulled the knives?" Frazier called out to the officers and medics on the scene.

Two medics raised their hands nervously. They were young. They had to been around the same age group as the uncooperative young man Frazier was just speaking with. Being the first case of his FBI career, Wiley continued to handle things poorly. He stepped right next to Frazier and spoke to the medics.

"So you two are the ones that tampered with my evidence? You do know that's a crime and, in this case, a federal offense."

Frazier rolled his eyes but said nothing as he chewed his licorice root. One of the two medics spoke with a shaky voice.

"We gave it to the police. They told us to do it."

The arrogant look left the face of Wiley, as Frazier shot him a side glance. But in typical "big man on campus" fashion, he rallied his arrogance. "That's no excuse. This is a federal investigation, and you tampered with evidence." He pulled out his notebook. "Give me your driver's licenses."

Frazier reached over and pushed the notebook down. "That won't be necessary. What are you going to do, lock them up?" He turned back to face the medics. "How long have you been doing this job, gentlemen?"

One of them responded, "I've been doing this for three months, sir. Today is my partner's first day. My partner before him retired last week."

"And under whose word did you remove the knives?" Frazier asked.

"Officer Green, sir. He said they needed them as evidence. So we pulled them out and gave it to them."

Wiley reluctantly put his notebook back in his pocket. He gave a heated glance at the side of Frazier's face, opting to just stand there quietly and listen, something he should have considered doing from the beginning.

Frazier went on, "It's a long shot to ask, but I have to. You fellas didn't happen to see anything, did you?"

"No, sir. But we were close enough when we got the call. That's why we got here so fast."

That response made the veteran smile. The young man just answered the next question he was about to ask. Frazier motioned with his licorice root. "Go on, fellas, get out of here. We got this now."

The two young men couldn't have moved quicker. They nearly ran to their truck and left. Frazier turned toward the scene, observing, chewing his root in thought.

"Man, this was some fight. I kind of wish I was here to see it."

"Looks like we got a double homicide. I wonder who would do this to these guys," Wiley commented.

"It's a dual homicide. These two killed each other. Therefore, it's considered a dual homicide and not a double."

"You think they did this to themselves?" Wiley asked. "What makes you think that?"

"The witnesses make me think that. You know, the people who were actually here to see the whole thing."

"I spoke with the officers on the scene. I figured they already spoke with the people, if they were doing their job right. But they gave me nothing."

"Well, you clearly didn't do your job right. You were hell-bent on running those two officers down with your authority. You never know if you may need them later down the road. Now they think you're a prick. They'll never want to help you."

"I need *them*? For what? I'm a federal agent. We have access to unlimited resources."

"Don't kid yourself. It's not that unlimited. Let's say you need to locate someone who's in hiding. The case is a headache from top to bottom. And those guys have an informant that can help you locate said person. However, they are not going to be inclined to help you after the way you treated them."

"But if they have someone that knows something and they refuse to help a federal investigation, they're breaking the law themselves," Wiley asserted.

"Not exactly. They have the right to protect the identity of their informants. And trust me. As long as those two have been doing this, they have more than a few informants."

Wiley sighed and nodded as he responded. He had been on the scene for less than ten minutes, and he had already done a number of things wrong. "Okay, you're right."

"Of course, I am. Word from the wise, kid. Exercise some humility. It'll go a very long way."

Wiley fought the urge to give snappy comeback by saying, "It's word *to* the wise, not word *from* the wise." Instead he tried to begin his latest exercise, humility. "Noted. Anything you can tell me about where we start this investigation?"

Frazier took the root out of his mouth and answered, "Rule number one. Whenever you arrive on a scene, observe. Take in the entire scope. Play it in your mind. Then look to the witnesses. Compare and contrast what they report with what you notice. That's how you investigate, my little young upstart."

"Rule number one?" He scoffed. "And what's rule number two?"

Frazier put the root back in his mouth. "Don't piss me off." He walked away from Wiley to get a closer look at the bodies, with his partner following. He stood in the middle of where David and Walter lay. Using his licorice root as a wand, he pointed at them when he spoke.

"Now look at these guys. What do you think happened?"

"Looks like two guys really got into it, probably over something personal like money or women." He quickly felt out of place as he looked at Frazier for some kind of confirmation on his assumption. "Right?"

Frazier said nothing. He simply tossed the wilted root he had on the ground and pulled out another from his pocket, walking away without a response. He then squatted down and observed the hand wraps. They were both bloodied and still tightly wrapped. Most hand wraps tend to unravel after a while. Theirs didn't.

Each hand of the two were covered with a blood pattern of the other's face and head wounds. Though he already got some information from the witnesses, the patterns were consistent to what a fight of this magnitude would be. The knives in their chests had been jammed in at an upward angle. He told Wiley to check them for identification and made his way over to the car.

Shaking his head, Frazier muttered low, "What a goddamn shame."

Wiley walked close enough to hear him and respond, "I know, these guys really did a number on each other."

Frazier looked at him, slowly nodding his head. "Yeah, that's a shame too. But I was talking about them messing up such a classic right here." He pointed at the Mustang.

Wiley just looked at Frazier expressionless. "Two people lie maimed and dead with a crowd of people watching, and you are talking about a car?"

Nodding his head, Frazier had the look on his face that said he clearly didn't give a damn if anything offended Wiley. He walked away from him again, over to the driver's side.

Using the key that was already in the door, he unlocked and sat in. It smelled of fresh lemon all-purpose cleaner, just as Shelly Callahan said. The inside was spotless. It was as if it was brand-new, except the odometer read one 102,126 miles. There were no seat covers. The seats were made of normal leather. Even under the seat was clear. Typically, a car with this kind of mileage would have food crumbs of some sort on the floor.

He put on his white gloves and ran his finger across the dashboard, then looked at his finger again. Nothing. No dirt whatsoever. So far, everything the witnesses reported were spot on with what he saw. The side compartment between the driver and passenger was empty. There were no papers, receipts, manuals, or forms of any kind in the side slots of the door panels. The back seats looked as if they were never sat in.

He opened the glove box. The only thing there was a two-by-six-sized blank sheet of white paper. The same kind of paper one would find on a memo pad. Under normal circumstances, such sheet of paper would be discarded, which was exactly what Wiley was intending to do when he walked over and observed the investigation process Frazier was proceeding in. He reached for the paper without a glove, and Frazier quickly knocked his hand away. He took the paper and put it in an evidence bag.

"Never use your bare hands at a scene."

"It's just a sheet of paper. I just figured it was left behind."

"Look at this car, Wiley. Everything is neat and clean. Almost too neat and clean. There is no trace of anything here. Not even a car manual. Just this sheet of paper. Doesn't that strike you as odd?"

"At first, no. But now that you mention it . . ."

"This is evidence. At a crime scene, everything is evidence."

"Got it."

"Any ID on them?" Frazier asked.

"No. Nothing in their pockets. No gum, loose change, not even a freaking Chapstick."

"What about the trunk?"

"Also empty. Not even a spare tire."

Frazier got out of the car and went to stand over the bodies. He wondered just who these guys were and what they did this for. Frazier had a habit of going into an investigative trance when he was on the scene. He could go up to one minute straight without saying a word or even moving a muscle. This was when he not only gathered his thoughts but also attempted to put himself in the situation he was investigating.

He began to go into that very trance while on the scene. Thirty seconds went by with him being in a comatose trance while standing. Wiley tried to get his attention, calling his name over and over. But he got nothing. Frazier's breathing stayed even as he blinked slowly but rarely.

"And you thought I was a prick," Wiley muttered under his breath.

Frazier snapped out of it on the thirty-first second and decided they should head back to the office. Frazier made it to the car first, leaving Wiley in a state of bewilderment. He stood there holding his notebook, ready to do some more investigating.

The abrupt decision to leave baffled him. "Wait. Don't we have more investigating to do?" he called out.

Frazier said nothing. He simply buckled his seat belt and rested his arm on the passenger-side door. Wiley dropped his arms in exasperation and walked to the car. Frazier continued to look off in deep thought as they drove off.

CHAPTER 4

THE INVESTIGATION

FRAZIER AND WILEY rode back to headquarters, puzzled over the murder scene. Frazier had the fingerprints lifted from the knives and ran through a database. They found out virtually everything about the two victims/assailants, including who they were, where they lived, and a lot of their backgrounds.

> Walter Fray: Walter Fray had no legitimate criminal record. He was caught shoplifting once as a kid twenty years ago from a clothing store. That record was expunged for community service as a math tutor in high school. He lived in a hotel suite near LAX and worked as an independent financial consultant for a chain of banks. He was single with no children, an only child of two retired lawyers. His estranged parents lived in the Bahamas and had no connection with their son. He made a good living, with a yearly salary worth over a quarter of a million dollars. He was a former Olympian in track and field for the long jump. He withdrew from competition when allegations of enhanced drug use started to surface around his track team.

Frazier and Wiley went to his home to investigate. The name of the hotel was the Starry Night. Fray lived on the thirty-ninth floor of a fifty-floor hotel. They arrived to speak to the manager with a search warrant.

Standing behind the counter was a short, portly man with beady eyes, a double chin, and a bad hair toupee. He wore a white dress shirt tucked into black slacks that looked like it screamed to hold together at the buttons over his potbelly. He just finished berating a bellhop when he saw the agents walk in. His mood changed from belligerent to cheery. "Hello, gentlemen! I was informed you were on your way. I'm Harvey Newman, the manager here of the Starry Night." He extended a hand that was accepted by Frazier.

"Hello, Mr. Newman. I'm Kyle. This is special agent Norman Wiley." Upon release of his hand, Frazier looked at his hand, aware of a dampness. He rubbed them it off on his coat. Wiley did the exact same thing, but he did it right on Harvey's shirt. Harvey stayed cheery about it.

"Oh, sorry about that. Get the sweaty palms from my mom." He chuckled until he saw the unimpressed look on the faces of the two FBI agents. He quickly stopped and cleared his throat. "Well, I won't waste your time then. Let's go check the room. Follow me please, gentlemen."

On their way to the elevator, Wiley asked a few questions. "What do you know about Walter Fray?"

"I didn't know him very well," Newman responded. "But what I knew of him through my staff was he was decent enough. Didn't cause problems. Never late on rent. Hardly ever here."

Harvey thought to make small talk on the elevator, then thought better of it. The agents didn't appear very talkative. They exited the elevator and walked the long hall to the room. For a man of his girth, he walked surprisingly fast, each arm alternately extending far in front of him as he walked, almost acting like a row propelling him forward as his leg trailed along.

He went to unlock and open the door, only to find that the door was already unlocked. The two agents followed standard training and drew their weapons, telling the manager to stay back in the hall.

They entered the room one after the other, with Frazier entering first. Frazier hand gestured to Wiley that he was going right and Wiley should go left. They covered each side of the room. The room was massive. It had a balcony that stretched over twelve feet, providing plenty of walk room with a fantastic view overlooking the beach. There were four bedrooms, two bathrooms, a kitchen, a fireplace, and a massive living room.

It had two refrigerators, one for food, one for liquor. Central air conditioning vents were situated in the high walls right below the ceilings. There were two empty Jacuzzis. The larger one was on the balcony, and the other was in the master bedroom. The agents searched every one of the six closets in the suite. They found nothing. Absolutely nothing.

They lowered their weapons and took notice. There was no furniture, no clothing in the closets, no food or liquor in either of the refrigerators, no computers, no televisions, no sound systems, no beds, no hanging artwork on the walls. Not even small pieces of trash in corners on the floor that some people leave after they move. The place looked as if no one ever lived there. Wiley called the manager in and asked, "Did Walter Fray ever actually live here?"

"Yes, he did," Newman responded with obvious shock in his voice, looking around.

"Are you sure? When was the last time you saw him here?"

"I came here to speak with him in this very room last week."

"What was he doing? Was the place empty like this?" Wiley continued.

"On the contrary. It was quite furnished. Like regular living quarters. He had a little gathering here. It may have been about thirteen people here."

"What were they doing?"

"Just hanging out. He had people in the Jacuzzi, some were watching the football game, and some were playing poker right over there, near the fireplace."

Frazier jumped in to take over the questioning. "Who was playing?"

"What?" Newman and Wiley both questioned in unison.

"The football game. Who was playing?"

"I . . . I don't remember. I'm not a sports fan," Newman responded.

"What did you come up here to say to him?" Wiley grilled.

"Well, I asked if I could join in."

"Join? Do you fraternize with all your tenants?"

"No. Only a select few."

"What made him so select?"

Newman smiled. "Well, I heard he was throwing a hell of a party."

"I'm sure people throw parties here all the time. Why did you ask to join this one?"

"There were some of the most beautiful women I ever seen here." Newman beamed at the memory.

"Oh, I get it. Strippers," Wiley grumbled.

Harvey gasped in astonishment. "No, they weren't. They were gorgeous women with real legitimate careers—high-paying careers."

"So you were looking on hitching a ride with a big fish, or should I say, fishette, huh?" Wiley made no effort to keep the mockery out of his tone.

"Now wait a minute." Newman took great offense. "I'm the manager of this place. I do pretty well for myself. I don't have to hitch a ride with anyone."

Wiley laughed a little. "You're just a cog in a wheel. Not the owner. They could get another manager in here faster than that button can burst." He pointed to Newman's protruded belly.

Frazier left them to their banter while he searched the rest of the place. He looked in kitchen cupboards, under the sinks, in hall closets. Completely empty.

But the medicine cabinet in the master bathroom had something of interest in it—a blank sheet of paper. An identical type of paper found in the car earlier. He called out to Wiley, pulling out his gloves and evidence bag from inside his coat.

"Wiley! Get in here!"

"What is it?"

"Check this out. Does this look familiar?" He lifted the bag, showing him the paper inside.

"Looks like the same blank sheet of paper we saw on the scene."

Frazier nodded, reaching for his phone that just went off in his pocket.

"What do you think this means?" Wiley asked.

"Not sure. Ballistics just left me a text of the residence of David Brice. Let's go check it out. My guess is we'll find another blank sheet there too."

The manager stood scratching his head and frowning, turning around in a circle with a frown on his face. For the life of him, he couldn't remember when all the furniture could have been moved. Frazier stopped in front of him, grabbing his attention. He held up the bag with the paper it. "Does this mean anything to you?"

Looking confused by the question, the manager responded with uncertainty. "A bag with a blank sheet of paper in it?"

"What was Fray doing when you saw him in here?"

"I'm not sure I understand the question."

"What do you remember *seeing* him do?" Frazier clarified.

"A bit of everything. He watched the game for a while, mingled, served drinks, played cards, and then got into the big Jacuzzi with three women."

Wiley assumed the suspicious role again. "You sure know a lot about exactly what he was doing. Is there something you want to tell us?"

Being questioned so hard by the FBI would make anyone uneasy. Harvey started thinking what exactly they had on him that he should confess to. What if they knew he was cooking the books, skimming some off the top? But if they didn't know and he told them, they might let him off easy for cooperation. But if he lied and they already knew, he would go down for sure.

The tall, slim Wiley towered over the short, portly man. As if he didn't have a sweating problem already, the tension and intimidation made him damn near develop a puddle of sweat dripping from his hands on the floor. He finally worked up the nerve to confess. To everything. He let out a sigh and was stopped by Frazier.

"Thanks for your cooperation, Mr. Newman. I'm sure you have much to do, managing a hotel and all. We'll see ourselves out."

Harvey couldn't hide his anxiety, then excitement from the assist he just got. Wiley was grilling him like a summer barbecue. He was all too happy to be dismissed. "Yes, sir. You're right. I have much to do. If there's anything you ever need, just ask."

"Thank you, Mr. Newman. We appreciate it," Frazier replied.

Wiley stared a hole through the man as Harvey cautiously and uncomfortably turned his eyes away from him and left the room. "I don't trust him. I had him. He knows something," Wiley muttered.

"Honestly, kid, did you pay any attention in class on how to interview a person?" Frazier asked.

"I was taught to go with my gut. And my gut says that guy is hiding something."

"No doubt he's hiding something. Everyone on the freaking planet is hiding something. But he's got nothing regarding this case. That much is clear. What also is clear is that we need to get to Brice's place and see what we might come across. I already have a feeling what we're going to find there."

Frazier pulled the info from his email on David Brice, from his laptop, while they drove to his residence.

> David Brice: David Brice was a father to a two-year-old boy of whom he never met. The child was the product of a one-night stand he had while on vacation in Mexico. Brice had a few hiccups on his record, one count of aggravated assault. Apparently, he took part in a bar fight and emerged the victor. His reward was a few nights in prison. He also was arrested for drunk and disorderly, public intoxication, and indecent exposure.
>
> He accumulated over two thousand dollars in parking tickets. But they were all paid. He did four months in prison for assaulting a police officer. It was actually a fistfight that the cop insti-

gated and initiated but lost. So he pulled the assault card to save face. The problem was, the entire thing was video recorded. He was exonerated under the purpose of self-defense.

He owned a security firm for local entertainment venues. This included sports events, concerts, plays, and all manner of entertainment serving a mass crowd. Both of his parents were doing twenty-five to life in prison for drug smuggling.

Despite their horrible life choices, David kept a close relationship with his parents. He visited his mother once every over other month. The month in between, he visited his father. Suffice to say, David was the only one of their children that hadn't written them off.

His reckless nature could have been contributed to his bloodline. Provided that his parents were drug lords that ran a small criminal operation, it would be hard to speak against it. However, his two older sisters that virtually raised him debunked that theory.

His eldest sister was Katherine Brice-Hollis, a suburban housewife and mother of four: Kenneth, age seventeen; Grant, agent sixteen; Penelope, fourteen; and Cheryl, age twelve. All straight A students. Her husband was James Hollis, a military pilot in the United States Air Force.

His next sister, Elizabeth Brice was a human resource manager for a marketing firm. She never married but was in a long-term relationship with the father of her infant son, Edward. Neither one of these two ladies had a criminal background or anything close to it. They spoke to David regularly, but not their parents.

David lived in a duplex apartment downtown near his job. Frazier and Wiley contacted the landlord about a warrant they had to search the premises. But the landlord left a voice message on his phone that he was on vacation in Europe. Provided the warrant was sanctioned by the courts, they decided to enter anyway. Wiley motioned to kick the door in until Frazier stopped him.

"Wait a minute."

"What's the problem? We have clearance right here?"

"Right, but you don't kick down a door unless there's imminent danger. We clearly know that isn't the case, provided that the tenant is already dead."

"We don't know that. His parents were smugglers. The apple may have not fallen far from the tree. He might have some people in there."

"I seriously doubt that."

Wiley threw his hands up. "Then what do you want to do?"

"We're going in. Just no need to be dramatic about it with kicking in doors, especially when his patio door over there isn't locked."

"How did you know that?" Wiley asked.

"Never developed your 'cop eye,' did you? Always at least glance at your primary target. In this case, it was the door. Survey everything else first, then head toward it."

"Is that what you were doing at the crime scene?"

Frazier didn't say another word. A faint yet devious smirk cut across his face as he turned and walked toward the patio. He climbed over the railing and slid the door open. Wiley drew his weapon and followed in. Already noticing a pattern of some sort, Frazier never drew his weapon.

Upon entering, Frazier's theory was correct. The place was completely empty. The hardwood floors were waxed. The closets were empty. The cupboards were bare. The walls appeared to be freshly painted. The only telling sign of a resident was the small scratch marks in the floor. The light shone through the windows, bouncing off the finish of the floor, revealing some small semblance of movement. It appeared a television stand or bookshelf was in that spot.

Wiley began to do a walkthrough of the place, while Frazier headed directly toward the bathroom, expecting to find another blank sheet of paper. He headed right for the medicine cabinet and opened it. Much to his surprise, there was nothing there. He looked in the bathtub, under the sink, and even bent down to check behind the toilet. There was no blank sheet. He rose up, scratching his head in a state of wondering.

The two-bed, two-bath apartment had two entrances. One led from the front door, and the other led to the back rooms. Wiley headed toward the back rooms and noticed a rather tall closet. He pointed his weapon at the door, stalking slowly toward it.

With his free hand, he slowly reached for the handle and ripped the door open quickly. No one was in the closet. His anxiety receded as his shoulders slumped in relaxation. Upon gazing down, he noticed a blank sheet of paper leaning against the lower half corner and the bottom.

"Found it!" he called to his partner, holstering his weapon.

"Where?" Frazier asked excitedly.

"Right in this closet. Sitting at the bottom."

"Does it look like the exact same?" Frazier was still walking over from where he was as he said it.

"Yeah, it does. I'm going to bag it." He pulled out the plastic bag and shook it open.

Frazier got there and stopped him with a hand on his wrist. "No, wait. Let me have a look at it."

Frazier put on his glasses, eyeing the paper with an observatory eye. He pulled out his gloves and evidence bag, then pulled the paper carefully from the small crevice it was in. Wiley appeared to be a little confused as to why he wasn't allowed to bag it. *He didn't find it,* Wiley thought to himself. *Why is he the one to always do it?*

Frazier zipped up the bag and left the apartment without a word, deep in thought. Wiley raised his arms and dropped them in exasperation. He then followed him to the car, and they headed back to headquarters.

The ride was a quiet one. Holding up both bags of evidence in the light, Frazier sat there studying the evidence, chewing on his licorice root. Wiley was a bit disturbed as he glanced back and forth from looking out the driver's side window and watching the road. He wanted to say something but chose against it.

Once back at headquarters, Frazier sat down at his desk while Wiley sat at his desk across him. Both men were stumped with the investigation thus far. On the surface it looked as if Brice and Fray planned out this public display for the purpose of giving off a "wow factor." That clearly wasn't the case. However, Frazier believed it had to be something else that drove them. Plus the blank sheets didn't add up.

Into their office came a middle-aged man wearing dark gray slacks, a sky-blue white-striped shirt, and a matching gray tie. The rough-featured-faced man known as Director Art Russell came over to them inquiring on an update with the case.

"So where are we on this thing?" he asked.

Wiley played the part of the eager new guy wanting to impress the boss by trying to answer every question. "We checked the homes for both these guys, sir, and found the same thing."

"What's that?"

"Their places were emptied and swept clean. Just like the inside of the car they were in at the parking lot. But we've yet to find anything linking them to each other."

"Nothing?" Russell's face frowned in confusion. "Did you check their phone records, chatrooms, emails?"

"Yes, we did, sir. And found nothing."

"What about a seminar they may have attended together? Or a focus group?"

Wiley shook his head. "Nothing, sir."

"What about—"

During the exchange, Frazier was typing something on his computer. It appeared to be a long-drawn-out document. He appeared to pay no attention until he decided to chime in, cutting Russell off in the middle of his question, still typing.

"You know me better than that, Art. I had everything about them checked out for familiarities. From a pickup game of basketball to attendance at a strip club. And no, they didn't attend the secret retreats."

Russell nodded in acceptance. He turned back to Wiley. "What else you got?"

"We spoke to the hotel manager at Fray's place, the Starry Night. He said there was a party and the game was on. Said that he attended the party Fray had last week. He went on and on about—"

"Who was playing?" Russell cut him off.

"Sir?"

"The football game. Who was playing?"

He suddenly felt deflated at not having the answer. "I asked him that question, sir. He said he didn't know because he isn't a sports fan."

"So who was playing?" Russell pressed.

"I don't know, sir," Wiley stammered.

Director Russell put one hand on his hip and pointed a finger with the other hand at Wiley like a mentor teaching an apprentice. "A good field agent exploits every detail. It determines if the source is lying or not. There's police work, and then there's federal agent work. We have to know every detail there is." He looked over at Frazier, still typing out his report. "Kyle, who was playing?"

"The Alaskan Eagles versus the Tennessee Snappers. At Tennessee." Frazier continued typing without ever looking up at Russell.

Russell's demeanor changed, an urgent look on his face. "Who won? What was the score?"

Frazier stopped tying and looked over the rim of his glasses at Russell. "Had some money on this one, did you?"

"I'm in third place right now in the tournament pool. The records update next week. Mason held second place, but his team lost last night. I just need the points on Cunningham and Baxter. Then I vault to the number one spot." His eyes grew hungry with anticipation. "So?"

"Twenty-four to seventeen." Frazier sat back in his chair, letting the anticipation build. "Snappers."

Russell pumped a fist in approval. "Yes! I told that little momma's boy Cunningham I was coming for him."

Wiley never saw this side of Russell. He always saw him as the stern boss, responsible for the infrastructure. He clapped Wiley on his shoulder, no longer appearing interested in the case. Then suddenly, he went back to asking questions about the case.

"What day in the week was the game? What time was it? And who was at home?" Russell asked.

"I . . . I don't know, sir," Wiley stammered.

Frazier came in with the save, still typing and not looking up anymore. "It was a Thursday night. The game started at six o'clock. And I already said who was at home. It was at Tennessee."

Still looking at Wiley, Russell responded, "That's right. He did say the game was at Tennessee. But you weren't paying attention to that, were you? You see, special agent, every bit of information in an investigation is vital. Ask the hard questions, find the elusive evidence, and listen to everything. That's investigative work."

"Yes, sir. I understand, sir."

Director Russell walked over to the window. "What about Brice? Anybody around to vouch for his proof of residence?"

Frazier finished his typing, then leaned back in his chair to answer. "We called his landlord to let him know we have a search warrant. But he was out of town. So we went in."

"Sir, why are we taking this case and not the local police?" asked Wiley.

Still facing the window, with his hands behind his back, Director Russell answered, "Criminal justice passed a law two years ago stating that homicides that occur in a public setting with more than eight witnesses is a federal matter. We are responsible of the infrastructure, special agent."

Wiley nodded.

Russell went on. "Now, about the homes of Brice and Fray. Were there any neighbors to speak with?"

Sitting up from his leaning position in his reclining chair, Frazier spoke on the matter. "No. All we found in both places were these."

He slid the evidence bags of blank sheets across the desk for Russell to see. He turned around and picked them up. He studied them with an examining eye, turning the bags over several times and holding them up to the light of the window. He looked directly at Frazier with his eyebrows frowned.

"Blank sheets of paper. These are blank sheets of paper."

Frazier responded, interlocking his fingers behind his head, still leaning back, "Yes. They are."

"What's the connection?"

"That, I don't know."

"When do you think you can crack this case?"

"That, I also don't know."

"What about you, Wiley? What do you think this means?"

"I have no idea, sir. But we will get to the bottom of this," Wiley answered.

Russell looked back and forth between the two agents, then back to the contents in his hands. He set them down on the desk in front of Frazier and let out a sigh of cluelessness.

He glanced up and saw Cunningham make his way past. Russell threw his hands up. "Well, good luck to you. This is the damnedest case I ever seen." He rushed off, heckling Cunningham as he made his way over to him about the game.

A uniformed officer brought in the married couple Frazier spoke with in the parking lot. They were brought in per his request to make the formal statement for documentation. Another officer brought in the young man Frazier knew was hiding something but didn't know why.

He was handed to an agent, then placed into an interview room. Seeing them enter through his glass wall, he jumped up and went out to warmly greet the married couple. He sent them to the administrator Victoria Kendall to sign the necessary paperwork per their statement.

Then he and Wiley headed into the interview room to meet with the young man who was already seated at the table. He was wearing a green and black hooded sweatshirt. Wiley entered the room first. The young man's attention perked, not knowing what this was all about.

Frazier walked in shortly after, and he suddenly knew exactly what it was all about. He rolled his eyes and folded his arms, assuming a defensive position. He tried his best to appear unaffected, but that slowly waned when the two FBI agents took up chairs opposite him, staring in silence.

Frazier, ever the cool and collected, pulled out a licorice root and chewed on it. "So you didn't see anything, huh?" he asked.

"I didn't get there quick enough to see anything happening. I already told you that. I saw them on the ground like everybody else." He found it hard to meet their eyes.

Wiley decided to go all "tough guy" on him. He slammed a fist on the table. "Don't play games with us, you little shit! Not only can we lock you up, but we can beat your ass for wasting our time. We are the federal government, not the local city police."

He couldn't help but let the disdain drip from his words when he mentioned the local city police. Much to his surprise, the young man didn't flinch. Didn't budge. He continued to look away from him like he never said anything. He scoffed.

Wiley looked as if he were going to leap across the table and make good on his threat. Frazier put a restraining hand on up and spoke calmly.

"What's your name, kid?"

"Derek Cooper."

"And how old are you, Derek?"

"I'm twenty." He turned his head toward the double-sided mirror on the wall. "Is the boss watching behind that two-way mirror? Your partner here must be the pride of your department."

After two knocks on the door, a man walked in and handed a file to Frazier. Frazier's eyes never left the young man. He reached his arm back and received a file in his hand, keeping a grin on his face. Wiley continued to stare a hole through the young man as Frazier tossed a file on the desk. A thick file.

No longer sneering, the young man's eyes followed the file as it slid to a stop in front of him. "What's this?" he asked, pointing at the file on the table.

"Oh, this?" Frazier pointed a lazy finger at the file. "This is you. It's everything about you, your *real* name, your *real* age, your aspiring occupation, your first fight, which you lost, your first girlfriend, who dumped you publicly in a mall and never even kissed you, the embarrassing nickname you earned in the Boy Scouts, your failed athleticism, your shoplifting record, even which hand you favor in your . . . private times."

Wiley managed to crack a small smile out the side of his mouth, still looking at him. Frazier continued his grilling. "It is a crime to obstruct justice, as I'm sure you already know. That's a bad thing to do that to the police. Can you imagine the backlash headed your way from lying to the feds three times?"

"Whoa, whoa, what a minute. What do you mean three times?" His voice raised to a high pitch with anxiety.

Frazier held up a fist, peeling off numbers with each finger. "Your real name is Lane Norris. You are twenty-three years old. And you lied about seeing nothing." He pulled out a laptop from one of the drawers. He typed in a code then pressed Play. He spun it around to show Lance. It was a timed snapshot of Lance standing right behind the Callahans, when Brice and Fray were walking to the car.

"We pulled this from one of the cameras at the All Store. Unfortunately, the cameras that had the angles for the fight weren't in operation yet. Three lies, kid. Three pointless lies. Provided this is a federal investigation, we have the liberty to do certain . . ." Frazier shrugged, "unethical things to you for impeding our progress."

"What do you mean, unethical?" Panic rose to a fever pitch.

"Well, I don't share the same superior disdain for local police as my hot-tempered companion here." He threw a thumb at Wiley. "But he does have a point. We are the tops of the top. We could erase your identity, your past, your present, and have a very strong effect on your future."

The gleam in Frazier's eye as he leaned forward to make his point drove it home. The smug nature dropped from Norris's demeanor quick, fast, and in a hurry.

"Y-you . . . you can't do that. You can't do that," he stammered.

The smirk dropped from Frazier's face in response. He twirled the root in his mouth as he grabbed the file and leaned back. "Suit yourself, kid." He gestured to Wiley for them to leave, turning to get up.

"Wait, wait. All right, all right. I saw everything. It was insane. I saw them when they walked out of the restaurant." He was hysterical. His voice raised four octaves. He started talking fast. Real fast. Not stopping to take a breath. It was impossible to make out what he was saying, save for a few words.

Frazier turned back, putting up a calming hand. "Slow down, kid. Take a deep breath and just go slow. Go back to when you saw them come out of the restaurant. What caught your eye about them?"

"They just stood out to me a little bit."

"How so?" Frazier pressed.

"I never used the recorder on my phone before. I was just recording the restaurant. I was about to stop recording until I zoomed in on the taller guy. He was standing outside first, but something seemed off about him. He had a look on his face that said he was on a mission."

"What happened next?" Wiley jumped in.

"The other one came out and stood next to him. They walked to the car side by side, looking straight ahead. Usually when you walk with someone, you casually look around or at least speak to each other. But these two didn't. They just walked with their eyes forward. One guy threw his wallet in the gutter, then the other one tossed his to him to do the same thing. They were moving like they had a purpose. Then they started cleaning the inside of the car."

"Keep going." Frazier had stopped chewing on his licorice root. Being the first time Wiley heard any of this, he no longer held the sharp gaze on Lance. Instead, he looked at him like a kid listening eagerly to a scout leader telling a story.

Norris continued to sing like a canary. "Once they got rid of everything, they went to the trunk and started to prepare . . ." He trailed off.

Wiley chimed in, mostly just to hear himself be a part of the investigation. "Prepare for what?"

"I think it's quite obvious by now what the preparation was for." Norris's tone in his response was a flippant one again. He still had the nervous look on his face.

Frazier smiled at the wise crack. The kid was spot on with the timing of that remark. "And you have all of this on the video?" he asked.

"No. It stopped recording midway through. The damn thing started roaming."

The same man that gave the file to Frazier came back in and handed him a phone. Frazier slid the phone across the table to Lance, and Lance caught it clumsily, stopping it from falling on the floor.

"We know. And we appreciate your honesty. Not sure what you planned on doing with the footage of them prior to the fight. Nevertheless, we had it wiped from your phone and the URL address you were sending it to. We even had it seized from the cell provider."

Norris looked nervously back and forth between the two agents.

Frazier continued. "We know you're creating a website for reality events. The concept could earn you a lot of money but also a lot of enemies. Some you really don't want to tangle with, kid. That's why you were at the store. You were there to check out some hardware parts and software programming protection."

Norris looked truly nervous. "How, how did you know that?"

Frazier shrugged. He didn't bother to answer, just sat back in his chair, twirling his root. Wiley took the opportunity to drive the point home.

"Because we're the goddamn federal government, that's how. We own your ass. There's nothing we don't know about you. We *will* make an example out of you."

Frazier rolled his eyes. The young man gulped in fear.

"The only example we worry about is the one we set. This is a teachable moment." He motioned his head toward the door. "Get out of here, kid."

With no waste in motion, Lance got up fast, rushing to the door. He nearly hit himself in the face as he swung it open. He speed-walked right out of the bureau headquarters without so much as a second look from anyone around.

Frazier sent for Director Russell to come in and watch the footage he keyed up. The footage caught not only the part Norris told them about, but it also caught them walking into the restaurant, a detail he must have forgotten in his intimidated state.

For two hours, video analysis and fingerprints had been run on the blank sheets. Each time, Fray and Brice were the only prints to come out.

There was no pressure from their families. In fact, there was no contact from family members. There was no uproar of injustice, just the news itself of the occurrence. With nowhere else to go, Director Russell decided to write the case off and close it.

CHAPTER 5

FOLLOW UP

WILEY SAT AT his desk, continuing to complete the necessary paperwork required for closing a case. Frazier disagreed with the idea of the case being closed, simply because they didn't have all the facts yet. He and Russell debated for a while privately in Russell's office about it. Wiley remained at his desk, typing away.

Frazier walked over to him. "Stop that. This case isn't closed."

"That's not what I heard Russell say."

"But this is what you're hearing *me* say. Stop that. Leave it open."

Wiley ignored his words and continued. Frazier came closer to stand behind him. He fixed him with a hard glare, with his arms folded. Wiley looked over his shoulder and scoffed.

"Is this supposed to intimidate me?" he asked.

Frazier said nothing. He looked at him like an elephant in the wild noticing a band of tourists nearing too close to the baby of the herd. Not one to back down, Wiley spun around in his chair, returning the look.

"Do you want to stare at each other all day? Because I can do that," he commented. Still, Frazier said nothing. Wiley stared right back, his stare attempting to match the one he was receiving. He wasn't afraid of this man. Or at least he thought he wasn't.

The glare was stone hard. There are times when a look or demeanor alone can tell a story. Clearly, the look Frazier was giving was telling a novel. Fifteen seconds of stare-down went by.

"What the fuck are you looking at?" Wiley asked. His tone was annoyed, hostile, and a little fearful. Still, Frazier said nothing. His breathing was even. His eyes were freshly sharpened daggers. And his face would have won a big hand at poker.

The young agent didn't scoff this time. He slowly turned back around, reluctant to lose eye contact. He attempted to finish his report but couldn't, for reasons he couldn't explain or understand. He found himself unable to work his thoughts to his fingers. A wave of understanding washed over him. Chain of command.

Wiley didn't exactly answer to Frazier. But he was learning from a clearly respected veteran agent. That was evident by the way he spoke so freely and commandingly to the director of the FBI. He suddenly realized something. Russell told them to close the case. Frazier wanted it left open for reasons of his own.

Why should he be the one to stand in between these two? If Russell approached him, he could simply pass the buck to the veteran. And as much as he would never to admit it, the intimidation was slowly setting in. He turned to look over his shoulder again with a different demeanor.

He highlighted the long, drown-out document. He turned a little more to face Frazier, with his finger hovering over the delete button. Frazier stood as stone as he was at the beginning, never moved a muscle. His salt-and-pepper five o'clock shady gave off a look of serious conviction.

Behind Frazier's desk, myriad of achievements covered his wall. From the visual of the laminated recognition awards and plaques, Wiley figured Frazier was untouchable. Finally deciding to concede, he slammed a heavy finger on the delete button.

He picked up the file on his desk and handed it to the seasoned agent. Frazier took it, the only voluntary movement he made. He went back over to his desk without a word. He put the file in his drawer and slammed it shut. With that slam, a complete change in attitude occurred, almost as if nothing ever happened.

"You hungry?" Frazier's voice was slightly cheery.

"What?"

"Food. Are you hungry?

Wiley blinked. "Are you serious?"

"What I am is hungry. Come on, let's get something to eat."

"You can't just act like that then brush it off like nothing," Wiley nearly shouted.

"Well, I'm hungry. You don't have to eat, but I will. All this investigating business has really worked up an appetite. So, as your mentor and senior agent, I'll be in the car."

Frazier walked off, holding a bag in each hand. Feelings of confusion mixed with anger came over Wiley as he snatched his keys off the desk and yanked open the first drawer. He grabbed his sidearm and slammed it in its holster behind his back, aggressively. It was a good thing the safety was on. Or he would have gotten a butt shot for sure. Like a petulant child, he slammed the drawer shut, mumbling, then stormed out after him.

Wiley got into the car to find Frazier looking at something on his laptop, pointing in a southeast direction. He took it as the direction he was intended to drive. Still too upset to speak, he drove in that direction. Stopping at the first red light, he couldn't hold his tongue anymore.

"So are you going to tell me where we're going?" Wiley asked aggressively.

"The same restaurant David Brice and Walter Fray went to."

"Why that place?"

"Because they have food, and I'm hungry."

Wiley gritted his teeth at that comment. The sharp tone in his voice cut like a knife in response. "We could eat anywhere is what I'm talking about."

Frazier paid no attention to the rising anger directed his way. He shrugged nonchalantly, not even looking at him. "Well, that's the only reason."

"I find that hard to believe."

"Believe whatever serves you."

"What's that supposed to mean?" Annoyance was in Wiley's voice.

"It means I'm ready to eat. Make a right over here then take the back street, residential areas. I like to look at the homes other there."

Wiley thought, frowning, *What the hell is this all about? Driving him to get something to eat? What am I, the chauffeur now?*

Wiley had the sudden sense that Frazier wasn't just simply giving him some rookie treatment the way he was acting toward him. He felt there was something deeper going on. But given the prestige Frazier had reached in his career, he opted to not confront him on it. Yet.

The homes on the back street were nice, the type of neighborhood that implied the residents worked very hard and took pride in their homes. The streets were wide enough to allow two cars to travel in opposite directions at the same time comfortably, as well as parking in front of homes.

The block was extremely green. Every single home had beautiful landscaping. Some houses had picket fences the colors of white, green, tan, or dark brown. Some had enforced security gates. Some had open walkways up to the front door. Some driveways had cars parked.

A few people were even washing their cars. Unattended basketball courts were raised in some driveways. Dog walkers conversed as their animals frolicked. A ball rolled into the middle of the street. Such a thing usually has a child following behind it. And as sure as water is wet, a child darted out to get the ball.

It was a good thing Wiley was going slow enough to stop on a dime. The kid looked unafraid as he snatched up his ball. He simply smiled at the two agents, and Frazier smiled back. Wiley was a little worse for wear. But he quickly shook it off when the child went back to playing with his friends like nothing ever happened.

They reached the corner and made a left into the side entrance of the parking lot. They exited the car and made their way to the restaurant. Wiley received a text from his wife and began to read and respond while still walking. Frazier entered first through the glass door entrance, the type of door one has to push open. He walked through not bothering to look behind or hold the door open.

Still absorbed in his text, he never bothered to look up. The door swung back, smacking Wiley right on the forehead. The phone was knocked right into his chest, then ultimately fell. Frazier made no notice of the sound, fixing his attention on the scenery. After gathering himself, Wiley walked in, intending on confronting Frazier, but he was interrupted by the hostess.

"Hello, gentlemen, welcome to Pots-N-Pans," the hostess spoke in a warm greeting. "How many in your party today?"

Wiley glared at Frazier's back then moved to pull his credentials and identify himself when he was quickly cut off by Frazier. "Miss, I'm Special Agent—"

"Hello. My name is Kyle, and this is Norman. It'll be just the two of us dining. There's a specific table we are looking to sit at today."

"Sure, which one?" the hostess asked.

"We would like the one facing that northeast window over there." Frazier pointed directly to the seat Fray and Brice sat earlier.

"I'm sorry, sir. There is a couple sitting there already."

Wiley kicked right into form, assuming there was some legitimate reason Frazier requested that seat. "This is a federal matter, miss. We need that table."

Her eyes widened. Feeling uneasy about routing a patron from their seats when they already had their food was one thing, but to have it be "federal matter" was even more uncomfortable. But what could she do, deny the request of federal agents? "Oh, okay, gentlemen. I'll be right back."

Frazier looked at Wiley over his shoulder. "Miss? Miss? What the hell is wrong with you? Do you have any home training?"

"Home training? You slammed the damn door in my face without saying a word!" His voice was low, but the anger was evident.

"You should know better than to walk and text at the same time. What, do you expect the world to part for you because you're texting? And that lady has a name."

"I don't know her damn name."

"Her name is Ellen," Frazier replied calmly.

"And how do you know that?"

"Oh, I don't know. Call it a hunch, a skill picked up from years of experience. Or the simple fact that it's sewn on her T-shirt."

The look of stupidity drenched the face of the young agent. His ire that was slowly climbing suddenly crashed down. How could he miss such a thing? He was supposed to be an investigator. "You really love flashing those credentials of yours around, I see," Frazier asked.

Ellen managed to move the couple without any hassle and usher the agents to the booth. They sat opposite each other in a dual-seated booth with the table in the middle. Wiley reached for the menu and began looking as his appetite suddenly picked up. Frazier pulled out photos of Brice and Fray from their files and inquired about them to Ellen.

"Do these men look familiar to you?"

"No, I'm afraid not."

"You never seen them before? Sometime recently perhaps?"

"No, I haven't. I just got here about five minutes before I saw you two. Maybe the server for this table can help you. She has been here since we opened. I can get her for you if you want."

"Yes, that would be fine, thank you." Frazier smiled.

"So what's the plan, boss?" Wiley couldn't have said it with any more contempt than he just did. "Are you going to harass every staff member about two guys that don't even have a case anymore?"

"There is a reason why I am so good at what I do. Why else do you think my résumé is so impressive?"

The manner in which Frazier responded to all of Wiley's cynicism further infuriated him. "This case is as dead as they are. I don't know what you're thinking about."

"Of course, you don't. Because that would make you me." Frazier smiled at him like a professor proving how much more he knows than his pupil. "But we both know that can never happen."

The server started to go over to their booth until she was pulled aside by the Ellen. She informed her that the two men at her table were FBI. A feeling of serious concern took hold of her, which prompted her to run in the opposite direction in a back room. Ellen went after her to explain the situation.

With her voice low but anxious, she stood in a corner with her back against the wall. She motioned Ellen toward her vigorously with her hand. "What do they want? What did they say?"

Ellen took her by the shoulders to calm her. "Relax. They just wanted the person who was covering the table earlier. That's all. It could've been anyone. It just happens that you are the one who had table 9."

"So they didn't call for me by name?"

"No. But they did show me pictures of two guys and asked me if I'd seen them before, and said something about them being here earlier. Maybe they skipped out on paying the bill." She chuckled a little.

"Oh . . . oh." First relief, then slight anguish washed over her face, as she suddenly realized the nature of the meeting.

Ellen let her shoulder go. "What happened? When I came in, there was some strange feel going around. But I was late, so I was rushing to get here. I haven't had a chance to find out anything. What happened earlier?"

"I'll tell you in a minute." The woman ran a hand down the front and side of her uniform in an attempt to tidy herself up. "Come on, let's go."

Ellen brought her over to meet the agents. "Gentlemen, this is Ursula. She is the server for this table." Ellen took her leave as she noticed here manager signaling her over.

"Hello, Ursula. My name is Kyle, and this is Norman."

"Special Agent Norman Wiley, Miss—I mean, Ursula." Out came the wallet and credentials.

Ursula hesitated. The introduction on a first-name basis was much easier to handle. But when the term *special agent* appeared, her nerves got on edge.

Frazier picked up on that. Holding a hand up in a calming gesture, with his other arm draped across the back of his seat. "Don't worry, you're in no trouble. Just want to show you these pictures and ask if they look familiar."

"Yes." She gulped. "Those are the guys that killed each other in the parking lot over there."

"And you served these gentlemen this morning. Is that correct?"

"Yes."

"Did you see anything unusual with these two? I mean, when they were in here?" Frazier continued.

"They seemed normal. They came in together, ate together, sat, and talked afterward for a while like everybody else, then left."

"So there was absolutely nothing unusual about them whatsoever?" Frazier squinted with his head tilted, expressing his suspicions.

"No, sir," she answered with finality but nervously.

"What did they have?" he pressed.

"I . . . I don't remember."

"How big was the tip? You know tax evasion is a federal crime, don't you?"

Suddenly a look of sheer fright came over Ursula's face. Wiley sat with a puzzled look as he witnessed Frazier go from asking friendly questions to interrogation. Little did he know, Frazier was not referring to the tip she received today, but also her willingness to cut corners on her taxes illegally to yield a greater return. She looked around the diner, scanning the crowd swiftly. She sat right next to Frazier, speaking in a low voice.

"Okay, okay. They tipped me fifteen hundred. But I need this money. My—"

"Your little brother is in trouble. He was arrested for auto theft. You raised him after your mother abandoned you both for a guy and moved to Paris. You never met your father. Your last name is Vance. It's been just you two for three years now. He's fifteen and you're twenty-one. The rent is due, and your car is in the shop. Is that about right?" Frazier ran her down calmly.

Ursula sat speechless. Her mouth wouldn't work. She nodded in shock to hear someone know so much about her. And to hear a federal agent make mention of her corner cutting on taxes scared her to no end.

Frazier continued. "Your brother, Jackson, has been in trouble before. He gets in trouble often, actually. And so you cut corners on taxes so you two can save up and move somewhere else for a chance at a better life."

"How do you know all this?" she asked. Her shoulders started to tremble.

"I'm a federal agent. It's my job." Frazier had an amused look on his face.

"So are you going to report me or arrest me?"

"No." He waved a dismissive hand. "Just want your attention. I may need your assistance at a later date on a case you might be able to help me with."

Ursula breathed a sigh of relief. "Okay, but how do you know I will be able to help you?"

"I have a hunch."

"What do you need from me?"

"Two things. I want you to think back to this morning. Tell me everything about these two guys. What did they order? Who ordered what, who paid the bill, the cost of the bill, how much of the fight you saw—everything."

She spilled the beans. There was no point in trying to conceal anything. She actually did remember what Brice and Fray ordered. She just wasn't prepared to tell them everything for fear they would start digging in her background. But to no avail. They clearly proved they knew quite a bit. She felt relieved to know they weren't after her. Ursula was the spitting image of her mother: long legs and a small torso, with big ears. But her hair wasn't long enough to cover her self-consciousness. She didn't have much of a figure. Being taller than most girls as a kid earned her many unflattering nicknames, such as the Big Elf, Jack-O-Lantern, the Greek goddess of reject, and various other harsh names. But she had a spirit that could not be broken. It was clear in her eyes. Frazier admired that about her.

"And the second thing you need from me?" she asked.

"Well, Special Agent Wiley and I are starving." He smiled again.

The exchange between Frazier and Ursula really baffled Wiley. He wasn't sure what was going on. He just sat there, confused and quiet. He was, however, very amazed of how much insight on Ursula's life Frazier knew.

By appearance she was just another server at a restaurant. She still was, except Frazier knew the back story of her life. She stood up like a typical server does with notebook in hand, took their order, and headed back to the kitchen.

Wiley watched her go, maintaining the bewildered look. As she rounded the corner, he turned back around, pointing a finger on the table. "What just happened here?"

"We ordered food. Do you not remember?"

"You know what I mean. What's with you and Ursula?"

"She came over, told us about Brice and Fray, took our order. She will serve our food, and you will tip her. What else are you talking about?"

"Seriously? Seriously? You're not going to let me in on anything? You're just going to keep doing as you see fit and not let your partner in at all?"

"Well, there first has to be something in order to be let into."

"You know what, forget it. This better be one of those rookie hazing things. But end it quick, man. This is a serious case we got here." Wiley's annoyance meter was reaching maximum level.

"But I thought you said this case was as dead as they were. Did you not say that?" Frazier retorted.

"Yes, I did. But you're so hell-bent on it still—wait a minute. Did you say *I* was going to tip her?"

"She works hard. I hear she's got a kid brother in trouble she's taking care of. I hear she wants to make a better life for them. Surely you don't mind helping her get closer to that better life. As you can see, she is willing to work for it."

Wiley sat back in his seat, shaking his head in disbelief. Frazier's attitude toward him was really wearing him thin. He would play along, but only for a little while longer.

Frazier looked back at him with the kind of look that suggested that Wiley was off in his assessment. He gave the impression that it was all in his head, and nothing was being held from him.

Frazier abruptly pulled out his notebook and started writing. Wiley continued to stare until their food arrived. Ursula placed their orders in front of them. She continued to serve them as if nothing ever happened. Frazier acted likewise, being extremely polite when asking for extra condiments and refills.

Frazier requested the check before they were done eating. He then handed it over to Wiley and continued to enjoy his meal, still not looking at him. Wiley rolled his eyes, reaching in his wallet to pay the check and tip Ursula. She accepted it graciously, taking the bill.

Wiley found he could no longer play this game. He followed Ursula as she went to take care of the bill. She turned the corner to retrieve something and was startled by Wiley standing right there when she turned back around. She nearly dropped a plate she had in her hand.

"All right. Enough games. What is it with you and Special Agent Frazier? Where do you to know each other from? Is this some kind of a gag at my expense to make me look like a fool? Tell me now. Don't play games with a federal agent."

"Honestly, Special Agent Wiley. I do not know that man. I have no idea how he knew so much about me. I'm just a girl trying to make a life. I'm nobody special. I don't know how he knows so much. It's freaky." The look in her eyes and tone in her voice told him that she was innocent.

He suddenly felt like a jackass, trying to intimidate a young woman. But apologies were something he never cared much for. Instead, he nodded his acceptance of her answers.

"Aren't partners supposed to communicate or something. I hear it's something like a marriage almost?" Ursula commented.

"Not with this one. He's acts like a . . ." He trailed off from badmouthing his partner. "Never mind. You take care, all right. Get that kid brother under control. I don't want to see his name come across my desk. And if I find proof of you and tax evasion, I'll nail you myself."

He returned to find Frazier still absorbed in his plate. The veteran never even acknowledged his partner's return. Wiley moved to say something then shut his mouth, shaking his head. He would confront him later. But not here and now. This area already had one knockdown drag-out fight. Wiley felt that at the rate they were going, there might yet be another one. Then he noticed the fragrance of vanilla in his pancakes, and hunger pains took over.

CHAPTER 6

MURKY WATERS

FRAZIER LEANED FORWARD, practically holding both evidence bags to the windshield to catch a good light. In each hand, he held an evidence bag with a blank sheet in it. They drove down the street as he scanned them meticulously, searching for anything that could give him some answers.

Wiley remained silent as he glanced back and forth from watching the road in front and looking out the driver's side window. With each passing moment of silence, he grew more and more agitated over the complete dismissal of his presence by Frazier. After about a minute and thirty seconds of complete silence, Wiley decided to break it.

"So, are you going to tell me where we're going or what?"

"I need to pick up a car. Just keep heading north, I'll tell you where to go."

"What does this car have to do with the anything?" Wiley pressed.

"It has to do with me getting home and parking it in my driveway."

"So I'm taking you to get *your* car?"

"That's right."

"What about the case?"

"What about it? The trail is cold. I'm going home."

With a scowl, Wiley couldn't take it anymore. Confrontation time. "Let me ask you something." The tone was deliberate and aggressive. It sounded more of a statement he wanted to make instead of asking a question.

Frazier, still looking at the bags, responded, "Go ahead."

"Do you have a problem with me or something?"

"Or something."

"What?" Wiley frowned.

"You said do I have a problem with you or something. What is the 'or something'?"

With a deep breath of building irritation, Wiley shot back, "You know what I'm talking about."

"Why do you ask?"

"Because you're supposed to trust your partner. You don't just keep them at arm's distance on everything. Plus, you're rude and disrespectful."

"I'm afraid I don't follow."

"You handle all the evidence, do most of the talking, and make me drive you around. You don't fill me in on what you're doing or looking for. And you talk to me like a child that doesn't know any better."

"Correct," Frazier replied.

"Correct? Correct? What the hell do you mean correct?"

"Your assessment. It's correct."

Like a slow heat of water in a pot, after a while it starts to boil. Wiley was at that place now. His teeth gritted, as his hand gripped the wheel. "Now, I'm afraid *I* don't follow. I believe I may have heard your response unclearly. So please, explain yourself."

"Well, about us being partners. Partners are on the same level. We clearly are not." Frazier's tone was even and absolute. He never bothered to look at him while he spoke.

The beautiful, sunny day suddenly seemed to turn dark, at least through the eyes of Norman Wiley. Wide eyed, with raised eyebrows, he leaned his head toward Frazier as if straining to hear something he couldn't believe. "Excuse me. I don't think I heard that. What did you just say?"

"Honestly, I don't think you're smart enough for this case," Frazier remarked.

That did it. Fire and brimstone poured out from the driver's seat. It was a good thing no one else was on the road at that very moment. Because Wiley abandoned all attention and directed it all to the man sitting in the passenger seat.

"What! Not smart enough! Let me tell you something! I graduated with a degree in criminal justice, with a three point nine GPA, a master's in forensics. Graduated top of my class, and I passed the bureau exam with a ninety-one percent on my first try! Don't tell me I'm not smart enough! You know nothing about me! Who the hell do you think you are?"

Frazier stopped chewing his licorice root, keeping it in the side of his mouth. Still holding the evidence bags in his hands, he dropped his head slightly to look over the brim of his glasses. In a calm and relaxed voice, he asked Wiley to pull over.

Still steaming, Wiley looked Frazier right in the eye, neither man concerned with the road as they stared down for about five seconds. Wiley finally glanced back at the road and obliged to pull over. Frazier politely asked Wiley to turn the car off for a second. The request was obliged as well. The key was turned rather aggressively.

He leaned his back against the door, with his arms folded. The look in his eyes was pure rage—rage at the insults, the blatant disrespect, and the lack of willingness to notice, much less care to address it. Huffing and puffing through his flared nostrils, the young agent awaited an apology at the least, a clarified response at the most.

Frazier sat still, looking over his glasses when he spoke. "On the contrary, young man. I know a hell of a lot about you. Only child of a privileged family. Your father, George, owned a sheet metal manufacturing business. He went to a junior college in northern Oregon and nearly flunked out because he was a degenerate gambler."

Wiley seethed with anger, sitting there listening. Frazier, not the least bit intimidated, went on. "He shoplifted and sold the items to pawnshops to get money to feed his habit. However, his father was golf buddies with a local judge. He grew up carefree and compensated for his litany of idiotic choices, up until he dropped out of school because he impregnated someone. But that someone was not your mother, whom he was currently dating at the time, was it?"

Frazier paused, as if expecting an answer. But he wasn't. He did it for theatrical reason. Then he went on.

"It was indeed, in fact, your aunt, who was later discovered to not be pregnant with his child, but with another man's. Your mother, Janice, came from a single-parent home of her, her sister, and their mother. Your maternal grandfather died during basic training in the army. The government took financial care of them due to the freak accident that the commanding officer himself botched. As a result, your mother never had to work." He paused again before continuing. "You come from a family of loafers."

Still unmoved and getting increasingly more enraged at the mention of his parents, he fought every inclination to lean across and clout those glasses right off. But Wiley opted to go with the stare instead. Frazier continued. "When you were eight, you burned a hole in the living room rug and urinated on it to put it out. You then went and gave it to a homeless lady on the street and told her you made it extra warm for her.

"When you were thirteen, you told a girl that had a crush on you to meet you behind the school bungalows. She wasn't very attractive and had zero self-esteem. Nervous as a deer drinking water during hunting season, she went tentatively. The only thing that drove her forward was your assurance that no one would know about you two. You gave her your word. You met her halfway and walked her the rest of the way with her eyes closed. Trusting you.

"She was startled by the sudden gust of air from a vent you had her standing on, blowing her dress completely over her head and getting stuck. Adding insult to injury, you had all your friends there to watch and laugh at her. She was so embarrassed her parents had to check her out and have her homeschooled.

"When you were fifteen, you befriended a foreign exchange student named Nadeem, from Yemen. The poor bastard was bullied for his hygiene and his funny walk. But you befriended him on a dare, didn't you? Just to see if you could spend a week around him without throwing up. Until one day, the dare revved up. You had to drink sour milk then stand in a closet with him for a minute. He thought it was some American game and was more than happy to play it with his friend. But you weren't his friend, were you? No. Friends don't do that. A friend wouldn't turn toward him, grab him by the collar, and throw up in his face."

There was the slightest of change in Wiley's demeanor as he listened. But only the slightest. He covered it so quick a person would have been hard-pressed to see it.

So Frazier pressed on. "When you were nineteen, you had an affair with a married woman, the mother of your best friend, Ed Randle, a man that was later your best man, as you were his. You even made several failed attempts on his wife and both of his sisters. You thought to use money to bribe them, considering they were in tough spots for cash. But their integrity overruled your treachery.

"You got that degree you boast about not because you earned it but because you had an ace in the hole—a very smart and impressionable young lady to do your work for you. She was a genius, in fact. You used your charm to manipulate a young lady that was sweet on you, again. You even outsourced her intelligence to other people for money. Some were friends, some were just clients. They paid *you* to have *her* do *their* work."

Wiley held up a hand and shook his head with his eyes closed. "Wait a minute. How do you know this?"

Frazier continued, completely ignoring the question. Still holding the bags in hand, looking over the brim of his glass. "She was under your love spell and would do anything you asked of her. But you didn't love her at all, did you? No, of course not. She was a commodity. An asset."

"How could you possibly know this?" True bewilderment showed on the young agent's face. "I've never met you in my life. How do you know this about my past?"

"You made some pretty good money off of her," Frazier said, still ignoring the questions like they were never said. "You were near failing out of school, then decided to search for the most academically gifted people you could find. It just so happened that she was very impressionable and had no experience in dealing with snakes such as yourself."

"So what, you went digging in my past now? Like you did with Ursula, the server? That's a violation of privacy, you know. I could have you reported."

"Go right ahead. As long as you tell them how you were able to obtain copies illegally of the federal board exam."

Realization and fear washed over Wiley's face. "I don't know what you're talking about. I didn't do anything illegal. You think I'm a fraud? I'm not!"

"That would be the logical thing to say. However, you and I both know otherwise. I'll tell you what you are. You're a mosquito. You feed off the blood of others. That's what I think you are."

Wiley couldn't hide the look of shock. He tried to cover it up by scratching his nose, no longer able to the look Frazier in the face that never changed. Frazier never raised his voice. He stayed even keeled, authoritative, and in control. His facial expressions showed no emotional changes. He was well-known for having one hell of a poker face.

Wiley's chest that was once puffed out with anger and venom deflated. The look of fire in his eyes was extinguished as if a great flood ran through. His straightened postured position became curved and slumped. He started to open his mouth to say something but was unable to find any words. He snapped his mouth shut, letting out a deep, slow breath.

Ready to abandon the conversation, he turned, putting both hands on the steering wheel. He slowly turned the key and started driving north as they were before. Frazier said nothing else. He just simply stared with an unreadable look over his glasses, until he was tired of looking at the man. He rolled down the window and spat out his licorice root, a symbolic gesture of his feeling toward the agent sitting to his left.

"Keep going straight until you see Dunbar Street. Make a right, then a left on June. Take June down a quarter mile and a slight right on Mont Avenue."

Wiley followed the directions wordlessly. His head spun on the in-depth knowledge known about him deep in his private past. Doing the background checks, none of that was asked of him when he joined the bureau.

They pulled up to a junkyard. A hubcap rolled past the agent's car, bringing attention to the direction in which it came from. A car was being pressed. The sound of crushing chassis, windows breaking, and tires blowing out overwhelmed the sound of the pressing mechanism. Men laughed and yelled obscene jokes at each other in the hot sun.

They drove down an aisle stacked with various modes of transportation, some already crushed, some not yet. It was incredibly well organized for a junkyard. Scrap cars were kept together, as was trucks, motorcycles and scooters, motor homes, and boats.

The soft dirt road was thick enough that broken glass couldn't take root against a solid surface enough to flatten any tires driving over it. Glass would sink a little bit into the tire thread, but not enough to puncture. This leeway allowed one to drive right over a glass shard and have it sink or crush under the weight, not damaging the tire.

They drove the long aisle and made a right. The lane was shorter but no less dressed up with junk. Broken toilets, refrigerators, air-condition units, even big-screen televisions were broken down and stripped for parts. A few men tipped their caps as the federal-issued Lincoln rode through the lane. Frazier nodded in return. Wiley was oblivious due to the head swirl he had.

They made their way through the maze of scrap and expanse. Frazier requested that Wiley wait in the car when they finally reached the foreman's office, a request that saw no protest. Wiley replayed some of the most intimate moments in his life, now believing Frazier actually knew everything about him. He gasped, eyes grew as large as silver dollars. Realization hit him in the stomach like a cannon ball fired from a pirate ship.

"Oh, shit. He knows," Wiley muttered to himself.

He turned the key, preparing to leave. Frazier had been so cryptic he wasn't sure if he did know the full truth. He could've simply asked around about his actions as a youth. Wouldn't be hard to do for a federal agent. But the stuff he mentioned earlier was so random it was scary.

He put the car in drive, with his foot still on the brake. But if he took off now, there was no telling what Frazier might try to dig up, realizing there was something to hide. He thought better of it, putting the car back into park and turning it off.

He shifted uncomfortably in his seat, glancing at the junk and scrap in the yard but really seeing none of it. He only saw his life pass slowly in his memory. Ten minutes seemed an eternity, when Frazier finally emerged from the office.

The owner walked out right behind him with a hand on his shoulder to steady his descent down four steps with a cane in the other hand. He was an older gentleman, looked to be in his late sixties or early seventies. He wore tan slacks and dark-blue suspenders. His back hunched slightly, and his knuckles showed wear from years of being a mechanic and owning his yard. He labored painfully down each step. He had a full head of gray hair that slicked back into a ponytail.

Once reaching the bottom, he rubbed his knees. "Damn these knees. I'm getting too old for this shit, Kyle."

"I hear, Will. I hear you. I feel like that on most days myself. Especially with this new case that just came across my desk."

"I don't know how you do it for as long as you have."

"I could say the same for you. I should have gone into your business. There's a benefit to it that I don't have in mine."

"Yeah, what's that?" asked the older man.

"You have less trash to deal with," the agent replied jokingly.

Both men laughed, apparently old friends. The yard owner nodded over to Wiley. "How's the kid doing?"

"Greener than guacamole," Kyle replied, shaking his head.

Will also shook his head with a grin on his face. "You never had much patience for people. Don't know how we managed to be friends all these years."

"Well, Will. It's because we don't really like each other as much as we pretend to." Will doubled over with both hands on his knees, his cane suspended horizontally in one hand, as Kyle leaned a hand on his back as they both laughed. Will had the kind of laugh that makes you want to join in even if you don't know what the laughter is about. Frazier clearly followed suit in this case.

Kyle Frazier and William Benson. Best friends. As close as brothers for over thirty years. They were best men at each other's weddings. Will was there for Kyle's, and he was there for all four of Will's. Benson stood up still chuckling, and Frazier glanced over his shoulder to see if Wiley drove off.

He was pretty hard on him earlier. Dropped some heavy bombs on him. His smile faded a little. It wasn't a look of regret of any kind. It was more of a side glance that said he asked for it. He turned his attention back to Will, noticing the serious look on the older man's face.

No smile or smirk in sight. A look of compassion and genuine concern took shape. Frazier was taken aback for a second by the serious look. A small smirk maintained as his head reared slightly backward. Eyebrows slightly frowned.

"Kyle. Are you all right?" Benson asked.

The smirk maintained. "Yeah, I'm all right. Are you all right?" A small chuckle emerged again but was extinguished with the look on Will's face.

"You know what I mean, Kyle. Today marks the . . . anniversary, as some would call it."

The smirk evaporated, as realization set in. "I'm fine, Will. I'm fine."

"Are you sure, Kyle? This really isn't—"

"I said what I said, Will. Face value, remember?" The abrupt caught off gave Will the signal to let it go. That sentence clearly didn't need to be finished.

A loud crash brought them both out of the moment. They turned and noticed a car fell on the ground from being placed improperly on a stack. Shards of glass flew in different directions, even cutting a few guys' arms as they covered their heads and faces. Will turned around, furious.

"Goddammit! Joe, you numb nuts! How many times have I told you?"

Will stormed off, slamming the cane with each step in stride, cursing and yelling. Knowing Will like he did, Frazier let him go handle his business as he went back to handle his. He walked over to a covered-up car. He carefully removed the cover, clearly in no rush.

Wiley sat chewing his fingernails and paused when he saw the car fully unveiled.

It was the exact same make, model, and year as the one Brice and Fray was driving, just a different color, with small differences. Theirs was pearl white, whereas this one was royal blue. Theirs had stock rims, while eighteen inches as opposed to fifteen were on Frazier's. Theirs was silver colored instead of dull chrome, with tinted windows and a single light spoiler in the back.

Frazier got in and drove off. Wiley followed behind, still uninformed on what to do. Frazier drove about a quarter mile heading west when he finally stopped and signaled Wiley to pull up next to him. He rolled down the passenger-side window.

"End of the day, kid. Tomorrow is a new one." With that, Frazier sped off like a high school jock showing off his engine power for his girlfriend.

Wiley shook his head, snarling his displeasure. As if it wasn't painfully obvious to him already, he realized with finality. Things were not going to go well between the two of them.

CHAPTER 7

SPECIAL AGENT NORMAN WILEY

AFTER A LONG, tumultuous day, Wiley went back home. Daylight savings on the West Coast in the summer afforded the benefit of a bright sun close to near eight o'clock in the evening. Living as close to the beach as he did gave him a little more time, affording him the beautiful benefit of watching it set on the great horizon.

Thoughts ran through his mind as he navigated his way up a series of hills, making multiple turns. With his right hand on the steering wheel, his left arm rested on the door panel with his thumb tapping his lower lip. His speed wasn't enough to kill an unassuming person walking across, but it was enough to clip the wing of a pigeon that didn't get out the way fast enough.

The winding roads were narrow but wide enough for two cars traveling in opposite directions. If a car happened to be parked on someone's curb, one car would have to yield, allowing the other car free run. But Wiley was in no mood to yield. One turn he hit at a decent speed going uphill, while another car was coming down. The turn had an obvious blind spot and a caution sign indicating a safe speed.

The ominous, looming enigma of dirt origin known as a mountain was ever present on his left. Driveways were filled with cars parked for the night. Most homes on the south side of the mountain had no curbs or front gates. Forks in the road with signs pointing in opposite directions can make for a confusing trip to people unfamiliar with the surroundings.

Thoughts of confusion, anger, and fear swirled through his mind. Wiley blew uphill at a speed doubled over what was recommended. A car came down at a controlled speed, having to slam on the brakes to avoid collision. Wiley didn't slow. He didn't even acknowledge the other person. Just drove on by.

He approached the halfway point to his house, where video cameras were present. The first camera set off a signal to alert the other cameras. Continuing to make his way up hill, he passed the second camera about twenty yards from the previous one. He finally reached the top of the hill, where stood a ten-foot-high steel security gate. By the time he reached the gate, the security would have already opened it.

The security gate and guard shack were posted approximately fifty yards from his front steps. Of the fifty yards, twenty was all low-cut well-kept grass with a strong color of green. Two trees reaching over fifteen feet were placed on separate sides of each other in the middle of the grass. A large water fountain encased in stone spouted water in intervals from bottom to top in a circular form. A row of freshly groomed flower bushes on each side of the sidewalk paved the way toward the front door.

A stained-glass reinforced door was the main entrance to the house. It had no doorknobs and no keyholes. It opened as a sliding door, monitored by a camera. Before driving home, he went back to the bureau to pick up his own car, a silver Mercedes of an updated model.

He exited the car, walking past the spouting water fountains and up a flight of seven steps. He went to the front door panel where a traditional doorknob would be. In place of a knob, there was a waterproof sensor screen the size of a standard man's wallet. The screen didn't require to be touched to read. He waved a hand over it, and the door unlocked. The sensor was able to read the print, like a grocery store scanner.

Anyone not programed to enter simply could not get through the door. The same system was set up for the backdoor as well. He entered and was immediately greeted by two dark-brown Great Danes named Arm and Hammer. The massive dogs jumped around excitedly at the return home of their master. He reached down, returning pleasantries, then left toward the living room.

The dogs followed close behind him as he made a right turn past a spiral staircase of about twenty-four steps leading upstairs. He walked through a hallway of nearly twenty feet in length, paved with marble flooring. On the walls were professional pictures of a model posing in various different background settings.

He reached the end of the hall where the living room was carpeted. He removed his shoes and advanced. The dogs knew full well the places where they were not permitted. And this room was one of them. They lay down on the hard floor in unison on their bellies, resting their heads on their paws.

There are a number of words to describe the overall price of his living room. Expensive just doesn't cut it. The carpet, Alpaca, was roughly twenty thousand dollars; the couch and love seat, lamb wool, two thousand dollars for just the covering alone; the coffee tables, golfer wood, six thousand dollars; and the curtains and window shutters, eight thousand dollars.

With a deep sigh, he sat on the couch, propping his feet up on a matching all-white ottoman. He reached for the remote to turn on his seventy-inch flat-screen plasma television. He aimlessly flipped through channels, reflecting on the events of the day. The dogs were lying quietly, when suddenly they raised their heads and sprinted toward the front door. The door opened, and in came the model from the pictures, his wife, Marla.

She carried all the attributes of most models: tall and slender, with sandy-brown long hair pulled back into a ponytail and a low-pigment skin tone. She wore a one-piece off-white V-cut sleeveless blouse and shorts set. The length of her shorts stopped a quarter of a way from her hips, exposing extremely long shaved legs. The dogs greeted her customarily.

The litany of shopping bags she carried in her high heels made it look impossible for her to greet her two four-legged home-welcoming agents. Nonetheless, she showed tremendous balance squatting down and returning pleasantries with the great hounds. She looked down the hall and noticed the television was on.

She called out to Wiley. But he didn't answer. She called for him again, and still no answer. Given the attitude of the dogs, she knew it wasn't an intruder. And she knew the maids wouldn't be sitting there watching his television. So she made her way down the hall.

She found Wiley sitting there, flipping through channels, and not really watching anything particular. Still in his FBI standard suit and tie, she noticed that something must have been bothering him. She removed her shoes, dropping down three inches in height, and sat next to him on the couch.

She folded both legs under her, then turned to face him. Resting her chin on one palm with an elbow propped up on pillows, the other hand moved to smooth out his tie. "Tough day?"

"A tough day would be an understatement," he responded flatly.

"You want to talk about it?"

"The case is classified." He continued looking forward.

She gave him a glare that brought him out of his brooding. He noticed it quickly the second he said *classified*. "Well, not so much as it being classified. I'll tell you about a case. You know that. But there's something else on my mind."

"Like what?" she asked.

"Do you remember Linda Wells?"

"Linda Wells. Linda Wells." Her eyes searched the couch, as if it was going to yield the answer for her. "Oh! The brainchild. How could I forget?" She giggled a little. "Yeah, why?"

"What do you remember about her?"

"Are you serious? What do I remember? Norman, are you all right?"

"Just tell me." His voice displayed annoyance as he continued to stare at the television.

"Well." She spread her arms out wide, glancing around the room. "Do I really have to talk about what I remember? Because I can surely look at what I know."

He sighed, dropping his head. "Do you ever feel any shame about her?"

Marla laughed. "Shame? Honey, we're rich because of her. I feel no shame in being rich. Why are you asking about Linda Wells all of the sudden?"

He turned toward her with a serious look. "My new partner knows a lot about my past. And I mean, a hell of a lot. He started running things at me that I did when I was a young kid. And the kind of stuff that only one or two people know about. People I haven't seen, heard of, or spoken to for years."

Marla shrugged. "So. What's the problem? He knows some of the dumb juvenile stuff you did as a kid. Just because he knows a few things about your past doesn't mean . . ." Her eyes grew big with understanding.

His look was even as he watched her wide eyes. Goosebumps rose on her arms. "Oh no. What did he say about her?" Marla's hands began to shake.

"Nothing. He never mentioned her."

"What? He didn't mention her? Not at all?"

"No."

She settled some. "Then what's all this talk about Linda for?"

"Well, he already knew so much about my past. I'm just wondering if he knows about her too. He ran down practically my whole life. From my parents, to my childhood, all the way to college."

"Did he mention anything about me?" Marla asked nervously.

"No. But I wouldn't put it past him."

Marla found her heart pounding. This agent could ruin everything they worked so hard for. Or sort of worked hard for. Her tone grew anxious. "But I have a role in this too."

"Yes, I know."

"You have to leave." She reached over, touching his hand, and earnest look on her face.

"What?" The agent frowned.

"He's getting too close to you. You have to leave, quit."

"You can't just leave the *bureau*."

"If he knows about you, then he knows about me too. And that means he knows how we got our money. We can take our money and go to another country."

"I can't just leave, Marla. I'm a federal agent, for crying out loud. What the hell kind of reason am I going to give anyway?" He went into a mocking tone. "*So, Director Russell, sir. I don't think this is really for me, so here's my two-week notice.*' Please." His flippant tone wasn't acknowledged by the nervous model.

"Exactly! That's exactly what you do. You go and tell him this isn't for you. And we use those two weeks setting up to move to Costa Rica."

"I'm sworn in, Marla. I just can't. Besides, I think he's just worried about me."

"But he may start fishing and find out that we were part of that thing in Florida."

"When I first got to the bureau, that's the first thing I looked into. All the fall guys were taken down to satisfaction. That case is closed. That was genius work on our part. Cannot, *will not*, be traced back to us."

Norman and Marla started a pyramid scheme for low-income households in debt. They set up a false debt consolidation agency using a census to identify low-income for high-debt families. They had a guy at the post office that would notify them of credit card debt mail being sent to homes from the census.

Their post office guy would take one credit card statement that came in the mail and bring it back to them. Provided that it was only one statement, people wouldn't get too bent out of shape regarding it. They would likely assume that the mail was simply sent to another address by accident or lost in the shuffle of mail at the post office.

Once the statement came the next month, the people would deal with it. Norman and Marla didn't want anything to do with the accounts. They only wanted the information. The plan was to take those that were in the middle of the pack of increasing debt and outstanding debt. They would have people set up phantom calls and send fake documents to back up their claim as being a debt consolidation agency, offering to lump all their debt into an affordable sum. People leapt at the opportunity. To keep the real companies at bay, they would send them money orders covering a quarter of what was owed under the fictitious name of a company.

Interest would continue to build, but a payment of any kind prohibited them from going to collections. For those that got leery about it, they offered the consolidation plan for a six-month quarter term.

In the meantime, all the letters from the companies were intercepted. False statements from Norman and Marla were sent to the people showing a decrease in debt, per their agreement each month. Once the six-month term was complete, they changed the name of the company, claiming to have been bought out. They severed all ties to these homes and made off with their lump sums.

In a six-month period, Norman and Marla managed to pull in over two and a half million dollars. They filtered their money through offshore accounts that built interest controlled by the stock market. They had a hacker that was able to control the fate of one business in a particular market, so they put five hundred thousand of their money in the rival market. Their hacker sabotaged the business in that market, awarding them to rack up an additional million and a half.

The business that was sabotaged was a hospital in a third world country. They altered the shipping manifest of medicines and vaccines, forcing the people to go to local small clinics where they shipped some of the materials to. The rest they sold on the black market.

They operated out of Florida with made-up identities. Only a select few people knew who they were. Wiley's best man, Ed Tillman, was their guy in the post office. They worked close with him and two other people from college. They spent all of college, and three years afterward, setting up that operation. One friend went into law as an attorney. Another hired the fall guys and paid them to stand in front of things.

Ed left the post office before the Florida scam came to a bubble and moved to Iceland with his wife when she told him about a one-time affair between her and Norman. He forgave her but cut off all connection with his former best man.

Gretchen's background had no noticeable blemishes, which allowed her to become a lawyer. She got away scot-free with her money and moved to Israel. The hacker, Paul, covered up his tracks under a false identity as well. He was still at large, making money off scams. Norman and Marla had to back away from three of his proposals because he was getting too greedy.

As a result, the fall guys from Florida were sentenced to twenty years for major crimes. Norman and Marla moved to California under the umbrella of her becoming a super model. Norman wanted to join the bureau so he could be informed if any more movement was going to come on that score. He was pleased to find out later that none had.

"Like I said, I think he's just worried about me. Mostly centering on my rise to becoming a federal agent. He thinks I'm a slacker."

"How does he act toward you?"

"The guy's an asshole."

"He didn't mention anything at all about Florida, right?" She licked her lips nervously. "Because there's no way he could know about Togo in West Africa."

Wiley smirked. "Please. Nobody cares about that dump. Who would've thought a country as poor as *that* could make us so much money?"

"Excuse me?" Marla arched her eyebrows.

"Oh, sorry. You thought. It was your idea to choose them. Of course, I recognize your eye for business." Wiley schmoozed.

"Thank you." Marla nodded with a self-satisfied smile. She dug in her purse to retrieve her ringing phone. It was her agent calling with a modeling job. She jumped up in excitement and rushed out the room to go upstairs.

The dogs watched her leave, lifting their heads, but stayed put. Norman Wiley sat there admiring his two-thousand-square-foot living room. The walls in the room were littered with portraits of him and Marla, whereas the hallway was all her.

They didn't believe in photo albums, where most people keep a book log of past events for memorabilia. Those were typically hidden. Instead, they exploited their lives in the open. There were pictures of them visiting various countries, making purchases of exotic cars and riding in their boat, skydiving using a still picture caught from a GoPro, spelunking, horseback riding on their own horses, eating at fancy five-star restaurants, and riding elephants on safari.

He scanned the pictures, admiring the life he had on the backs of other people. The idea of Frazier telling him he wasn't smart enough really stuck in his craw. The work he orchestrated with the census project was a stroke of genius. At least in his mind it was. It made him more money than he could ever dream. The fact that he benefited on the misfortunes of the unfortunate meant nothing to him.

It's a dog eat dog world. He removed his coat and tie and headed over to his minibar in the corner. He ran his fingers across a costumed plaque. A credo, if you will, engraved in stone sitting on top of the minibar. It was his mantra. Whenever he needed a pick-me-up or a reminder of what life was, he resorted to this stone. It read, "*Take what you can, give nothing back.*"

He signed at the bottom, depicting the phrase was a quote from him. Signed, "*Lord Norman Wiley.*" The ego of this man clearly knew no bounds. He had made a lot of money by purposely denying men, women, and children in poor countries the most important thing they should have: medical care.

The events of the day didn't weigh on him half as much as what Frazier said to him about his life. His stomach was in a knot. He couldn't bear the thought of losing everything. He would definitely face criminal charges if found out. Anxiety began to take hold of him. He threw back a glass of scotch, coughed two times, poured another one, and threw back another one.

There wasn't much he can do about it at the moment. But he would be damned if he lost everything because some washed-up special agent was really good at Google and hiring private investigators. But what was he going to do to stop him? He stopped in midpour. The feeling of arrogance came over him like a flood. He finished the pour for the third drink.

He smirked to himself, now sipping instead of gulping. A thought hit him. One thing he paid close attention to in the police academy and FBI training was how to write up a report. If push came to shove, meaning Frazier threatened to ruin his lifestyle, then he might have to meet with an unfortunate accident with a paid homeless person.

The thought made him chuckle. He headed back to the couch and leaned his head back, closing his eyes. With a devilish grin on his face, he brought the entire subject matter to a close in his mind. Wiley didn't want to have to do it. It was extremely risky, but dog eat dog. He recalled the engraving of his mantra: "*Take what you can, give nothing back.*"

Marla returned from her conversation excited, informing her husband of a job she was offered.

"Honey! This is the big one! The one I've been trying to get for a long time! This is the modeling tour of the century. The tour takes me not only to various states here but also to the Philippines, Brazil, Cambodia, and Syria!"

The grin left his face as he raised his head to meet her excited eyes. "That's a lot of travel, honey. How long will you be gone?"

"Five months." She was sill excited as she answered.

"Five months!" Wiley's sprang up.

"I know it's a long time, honey, but this is my *dream* tour. It means a lot to me. I could go down as one of the most famous models of all time with this tour. Please don't stop me from going, honey. *Please.*"

Out came the bashful eyes, the childlike, innocent look. Both Norman and Marla could be cutthroat about their ambitions. Just a second ago, he was even thinking about having his partner killed to protect his lifestyle. He robbed people of their already low income for his own personal gain, sending them further into a spiral of bad finances.

Many of those families turned to drugs, alcohol, prostitution, and theft, both the adults and children alike. He robbed poor countries of life-saving medicines and pain alleviators just so he could get richer. Say one thing for Norman Wiley, say he was a heartless piece of trash. Except for when it came to Marla. She was the light of his life.

Sensing the apprehension, Marla straddled him, rubbing her fingers through his hair, trying to entice him. He loved her so much it ached. He finally relented. "All right. If it'll make you achieve your ambitions, I'll support you."

She kissed him hard, excited like a schoolgirl. "Thank you, thank you, thank you, honey!" She jumped off him and ran to the dogs, rubbing them, getting them all riled up. Then she started for the hallway again.

"Hey," he called over his shoulder. She stopped and turned back to him, still grinning from ear to ear. "When are you leaving?"

"Tomorrow. I have a lot of packing to do."

"Wait, tomorrow? Damn that's short notice." He turned in his seat to look at her.

"But it's a once-in-a-lifetime thing, honey. I may never get this chance again. You already said I could," Marla replied, smile still present, accompanied by whiney tone.

"Yeah, I get that. But damn."

"Honey." Marla knew him better than anyone. She knew what buttons to push and make him tick. She played on the knowledge by disarming him with the mantra. "Take what you can . . ."

"Give nothing back." A smile found its way to his face. "Speaking you leaving tomorrow and will be gone for five months, I think I need to take what I can."

She smiled seductively. "But what if I give nothing back?"

"Well, then I'll just take." He chased her down the hall as she playfully screamed, running from him upstairs toward the bedroom. The excited dogs were a slight impediment to his sprint, making it even more fun because they gave her a slight head start and he was going to have to catch her.

The dogs followed them upstairs, up until he slammed the door shut in their faces. The lay down on the floor again with their heads on the paws.

CHAPTER 8

SPECIAL AGENT KYLE FRAZIER

I T'S ALWAYS A good thing to get to know your neighbors. People have the tendency to feel a little safer around their home when they have a cop on their block. And it's a whole different level of comfort to have a federal agent living there. Frazier made his way home on the complete opposite side of town where Wiley lived.

His house wasn't as extravagant as his younger counterpart. A three-bedroom, two-bathroom, with a fair-size front yard. His garage faced the street, while he had an alley behind his backyard. The alley was closed off and gated. Only residents were able to access entry. His home was located two blocks from a university, a university in which he was an alum.

He pulled up in his driveway and exited the car. As he walked up to his front door, he was greeted by a neighbor out walking her dog.

"Hello, Kyle. How are you?"

"Doing just fine, Jessica. Yourself?"

"Oh, I'm all right. Just walking little Missy here."

Missy was an all-white toy fox terrier. She wagged her little tail in excitement at him, then her attention was quickly taken away by a fleeting squirrel running up a tree. For such a little thing, she nearly jerked Jessica's arm out of the socket, barking excessively. But that didn't deter her from her annual flirting with the special agent.

Jessica Sloan was a divorcee of over eight years. Her children were all grown and out of the house. Her hair was cut shorter than usual. The brunette-colored hair came down just below the ears. She wore glasses that weren't prescription. She was going for the studious librarian look since she found out that he wore glasses and was a big reader as was she.

She wasn't an unattractive woman by any means. He even entertained a cup of coffee with her on a few occasions. She was the head of the superintendents division in her branch, a very intelligent lady. She also knew her way around a kitchen. For as long as he'd known her, she always had a pleasant way about her.

She was a real catch by any man's standards. The problem was, she was clingy. For a man with a gruff demeanor such as Frazier, that marked the equivalent of oil and water. In order to get to his house, he had to drive by her home being that he lived in a cul-de-sac.

Every day when she got home, she looked out her window to see if his car was in the driveway. If it wasn't, she would sit in a spot where she could see when he pulled up. She would rush and get Missy to go for a walk, regardless of the fact that she had a sitter that walked Missy an hour before she got home from work.

Some days he was just too tired to stop and talk. But he was never rude or dismissive. He would simply make it a brief chat. Some days he'd spend some time visiting with her outside before he went in. She relished their conversations and just plain being around him.

After weeks of rehearsal in the mirror, she decided today would be the day. She worked up the nerve to ask him out on a date. She knew dressing up would give away some sort of intention. So she dressed comfortable in white shorts and a lime-green T-shirt. She wore a firm bra, a rather constricting one, in an attempt to draw his interest.

She checked his body language and decided not push it today. She could tell he was tired. "Tiring day, huh?"

"You have no idea. Got a real troubling case that just came across my desk," Frazier replied.

"Oh, you mean that parking lot case? It's all over the news."

The agent nodded. "That's the one."

"What happened out there?"

"I can't disclose that."

"Right, of course. I'm sorry." Jessica blushed in slight embarrassment.

He chuckled. "It's quite all right. Look, I would love to stay and chat, but I'm exhausted."

"Yes, of course, you are. Well, if you need anything, you know where to find me. Anything at all. It doesn't matter the time." She blushed again.

"Thank you, Jessica. Have a good night."

"Good night, Kyle."

He turned and walked into his house. She stood there transfixed, watching him, wishing she was on the other end of that door, greeting him with open arms . . . and open legs. She shook her head to snap herself out of that last thought. She looked down, only to see Missy looking at her with her head cocked.

"Oh, come on, old girl." She tugged at Missy. "I shouldn't have gotten you fixed. At least then you could relate."

Entering the front door to his left stood a mannequin model, a place for him to put his coat, tie, hat, and shoes. Frazier hated wrinkles in his coats and creases in his shoes. He took his time placing said items on the mannequin, smoothing out his coat with his hand. Every room in his house had a minimum of three three-foot-tall plants, plants that he took great care of.

He grabbed a squeeze bottle and sprayed the plants closest to the door. He made his way from room to room, caring for his plant life. As a result of the greenery he kept, a certain serenity was felt throughout the house whenever he entered. Often he thought of retiring and just sitting in his home, breathing the oxygen given off by his healthy fern.

He placed his keys in an African-camel-boned keyholder box on the coffee table before heading toward his home office. Of the three rooms, one room was his actual bedroom. Another served as his gym. And the third one, the biggest one, was his office. Inside the office was his personal library of well over three hundred books.

Frazier fancied himself a proponent of literary works and also ancient history.

He traveled to various parts of the world where he heard there was an ancient library. He paid good money to have some translated for him to read. He was big on studying cultural practices, religious beliefs, rivalries, legal and economic systems, education, and even lineage in hierarchy.

A seven-foot-high bookcase on the northern side of the room stood vertically against the wall. His order of organization was alphabetical. He believed the old civilizations, in some fashion, still played a significant role.

Origins were what interested him the most. Books on civilizations such as the Egyptians, Assyrians, Babylonians, Persians, Greeks, Romans, Mayans, Inca, Olmec, Phoenicians, Georgians, Etruscans, Minoans, Sumerians, and various other ancient civilizations hold space in his library.

He was never really big on artifacts. He studied enough of culture to learn that some artifacts, such as talismans, medallions, even small statues, had been known to carry a curse or two. Besides, one would need a warehouse to store such items of invaluable prize.

But he was a big fan of ancient art. In this very office, against the southern and eastern walls, were paintings and depictions of structures in operating function and populated—structures such as the Babylonian Hanging Gardens, the statue of Zeus at Olympia, the Oracle of Delphi, the Temple of Artemis, the early completion of the Great Pyramid of Giza, the Ziggurats of Ur, and also the Tower of Babel.

The brutal battle grounds included the Battle at Thermopylae, led by the Spartan king Leonidas I against the Persian Army; the Battle of Siler River (Gladiator War), led by former gladiator Spartacus, against the Roman Republic; the Battle of Kadesh; even the invasion on Egypt by the ancient Sea Peoples.

Along with the study of ancient history, his library was loaded with books on psychology of the criminal mind. Many of the authors were either professors or criminals themselves, telling their stories. Frazier had always been enamored in what makes a mind tick. His diligent study was one of the reasons why he became so accomplished as an investigator.

In the west wing of his office was where he kept all his awards as an investigator, from both as a detective and a special agent. Over nineteen awards in plaques and laminated certificates dressed the wall neatly and chronologically. Frazier had managed to achieve an 89 percent completion rating in closed cases, fourteen foiled sting operations, three successful hostage negations, and the arrest of five international crime lords, among his list.

His wall of fame at home mirrored the one in his office. However, he kept the originals at home. The ones at the office were replicas. Though he had a wall of over nineteen awards, the things he kept on his desk stood of more importance to him.

Next to his computer sat a picture of his family—a portrait of him, his ex-wife, and his daughter at an airport in China. He walked over to sit at his desk, reaching over to pick up the gold-trimmed custom-made frame.

A look of sadness and longing covered his face. He reached into a desk drawer and pulled out a whisky bottle and a shot glass. He removed the top with his teeth and slowly lowered the top on the desk. All was done with his left hand. In his right, he still held the picture. The symbolism was if he had another chance to hold them again, he would never let them go.

Never taking his eyes off the picture, he sat the bottle on the desk. He slightly tilted the bottle till the neck touched the rim. He began to pour. His daughter was eleven years old in the picture. Both of her little arms wrapped around his waist, with a huge grin on her face. He towered over her, with his left hand resting on her back.

His wife stood at his right side, always his right. Her right hand affectionately rested on his chest. Her left hand draped comfortable across his left shoulder. She fit naturally in the nook under his right arm.

He cupped his right hand on her right shoulder, an obvious display of oneness. They both grinned from ear to ear, smiling for the camera. The young girl wore a white-and-orange-flowered geisha girl outfit. Her mother wore a similar outfit the color of blue, with green flowers. The patriarch of the family donned a shaolin white gee.

In the distance behind them rose a mountainous temple surrounded by a sea of beautifully laid greenery. The ability to see the tops of a near innumerable count of trees blotted out any visual of the grounds below. On that trip to China, he accidentally walked into the ladies' room in a restaurant because he misread the writings. Three women beat him with their sleeves to get him out.

His wife and daughter laughed hysterically. His wife was able to read it fluently and purposely sent him to that room to watch the outcome. On another occasion, he got even with her. While showering on a chilly day, she relished the hot water, staying in the shower longer than usual. He and his daughter snuck in and dumped a bucket of cold water on her back, then ran out, stifling laughter.

Two days after that, their daughter tempted a barracuda at a local aquarium. Behind them on the narrow walkway was a mud trail. The barracuda attacked the glass, forcing her to jump backward and fall into the mud trail. The parents laughed, while she folded her arms and pouted.

At night, they all huddled up and slept on a futon. They ate and saw sights together, gathering as many memories as they possibly could. The picture he held in his hand was the epitome of love and happiness. That trip to China was the best trip he ever took his family on.

Joy filled his heart as the memories flooded his mind. Transfixed, the sudden sound of splashes on the floor and drops of liquid landing in his lap snapped him out of his thoughts. "Dammit." He cursed, turning the bottle upright, realizing his drink had overflowed. What's more, whisky wasn't in the bottle.

He replaced it with V-8 juice a week ago. His daughter committed suicide in college, and Frazier spiraled out of control because of it. He sank deep into depression. He turned into a heavy chain-smoker and alcoholic. A few occasions, he dabbled with cocaine. His wife was able to influence him to give at least that part up. She was unsuccessful with alcohol and tobacco.

She would replace all the drinks in the house with V-8 juice. She imported licorice root from China to help him quit smoking. None of it worked. He became hostile and standoffish but never physically abusive. He made life miserable for her and often blamed her for being too lax in her relationship with their daughter.

She eventually fell out of love with him, stating being exhausted. She remarried and moved to another state for a time, completely severing all ties with him. He drove her away with his actions and demeanor.

When she finally left, he made the conscious effort to maintain putting V-8 juice in his liquor bottles and chewing licorice root. It was Art Russell that helped bring him out of oblivion. They joined the bureau together from the same unit with the police. Art was propelled to his position once Frazier declined becoming director.

He always loved the job, but he loved his family more. He sat the picture down and went for a towel to clean himself up. It had been ten years since he lost his daughter and eight years since his wife left him. But it never got any easier. After drying himself, he headed over to his library. He often wondered why he had such a hard time moving on. His daughter would certainly want that for him.

It killed him to think of what in her life made her so unhappy. He never got that sense from her. And he was a detective. He made a living off reading people. She wouldn't want him alone. She would understand her mother had to seek happiness. And she would want the same for him.

He blamed himself for her suicide. He was usually too involved with casework, which prompted the sabbatical. He blamed his wife for not seeing it and telling him. He blamed his daughter for being so weak that she would take her own life. He pushed the last thought aside, for it was only grief and loneliness that filled him.

The accomplished, brilliant, valiant, fearless Kyle Frazier was actually afraid of being alone. It bothered him so much that he feared letting anyone in, for they might also leave him. She never said as much, but Jessica gave off the vibe that she would never leave him. Her husband had left her unceremoniously. So she had a clear understanding of abandonment.

He started to strongly consider her as a suitor. He thought, *She's a nice-looking woman with a good head on her shoulders. She's thoughtful and caring. And most of all, available.* But she was clingy, which gave her the desperate feel. He contemplated taking her up on the offer and inviting her over for company. Then he thought better of it. He still hadn't been able to open up to her, like she had with him.

He knew all the details of her ex-husband, her kids, her career, her personal likes and pet peeves. Even her goals and aspirations. He only let her know just enough to keep her interested in wanting to know more. He shook the thought of her and went over to his library.

He thought of the case—the blank sheets, the two men, the scene—and he pondered the purpose. With an outstretched index finger, he scanned the *M* section, looking for something in particular. He found the book he was looking for regarding the cultures and beliefs of ancient Mesopotamia. He sat down, putting on his glasses in his reclining reading chair. The he propped his feet up and began to read.

CHAPTER 9

THE CAFÉ

B RANCHES ON PALM trees slightly swayed from side to side from small winds going by. Hummingbirds hovered near flowerbeds as they reached into tall plants for their food. Pinecones and berries covered the ground on this warm Saturday afternoon.

The clinging of cups landing on tables was drowned out by the voices of many different conversations. Well-trained dogs lay at the feet of their owners on a leash, as squirrels sprinted up trees and across telephone poles. Creativity and postproduction were clearly on display. Screenwriters, poets, and executives typed away on laptops, swiped fingers across phones, and even a few still wrote in notebooks.

Servers tended to their tables, pouring hot coffee or teas, along with whatever pastry or sandwiches one desired. Laughter and some friendly banter filled the outdoor area. With all the friendly conversation going on, a table in the center of the coffeehouse appeared a little different. The main reason was because the patrons at the table brought their own personal portable chairs to sit in.

Three women—Leah, Tina, and Tracy—sat at this table, drinking coffee and conversing like the rest of the patrons. They appeared to be having a friendly conversation, laughter and a few high-fives between them after certain remarks. They were seated at a small circular table just big enough to have coffee and an appetizer but not big enough for three entrées. The server, a young man around nine-teen years of age, came over to attend to these women.

"Afternoon, ladies. Welcome to the Swinging Palms Café. My name is Darwin, I'll be your server today. Can I start you off with anything?"

Leah spoke first. "I think I'm good with just coffee, black. I'll add the cream and sugar in myself."

Tina answered next. "I might want to try your cinnamon roll with the yellow glaze, and the white herbal tea, please."

Darwin nodded and smiled at each woman as he jotted down their orders on his notepad. He then turned to Tracy. "And for you?"

"I think I'll take you." She sported a devious grin.

Darwin blushed, unsure he heard correctly. "Excuse me, ma'am?"

"You heard me, cute stuff. I want *you*. I have a Jacuzzi at home with your name on it. But of course, you aren't allowed in without the owner present as well."

He tried to work his mouth to respond but was at a loss for words. Leah and Tina laughed at the flustered young man. Tracy, on the other hand, did not laugh. She appeared serious, giving him a las-civious look, biting her bottom lip. She sat cross legged, leaned back in the chair, looking at him from under her newly done eyebrows. Her eyes trailed below his waist, then back to his face.

Uncomfortable would be an understatement. The woman was twice his age but not hard on the eyes. She had short cropped brown hair along the sides, with bangs in the front that laid over the right side of her face. Her tight-fitting polyester shirt revealed the com-plete effect of her being braless. His eyes jumped from her breast to her face, then to Leah and Tina.

"Well, Darwin, are you interested in *evolving* today?" Tina purred.

Throughout Leah's life, she was viewed as the classic good-ie-goodie. Observing the awkwardness the young man was in, she spoke up. "Now, now. I'm sure she's just kidding." She chuckled, giving Tracy a look, trying to get her to be less inappropriate.

"I'm not kidding," Tracy responded. "I like younger men. And I want you to come home with me so I can teach you things you only heard of or read about. Doesn't that sound like fun?"

Darwin had a sheepish look on his face, still not sure how to respond to such an open and aggressive older woman. But she was right. With Darwin being a virgin, he had only heard of this kind of interaction. This was like something out of a movie. His mind drifted to the experiences he could have with her. Then a thought hit his mind, a reminding thought. "That's very flattering, ma'am, but I have a girlfriend."

Tracy wouldn't let up. "That's my point. You have yourself a little *girlfriend*. I'm a woman. She will like you. Maybe even love you. But I will have you entranced. Come home with me and you will leave a new man. A better man. With a new name."

"What's wrong with my name?" he asked quizzically.

"It's not the name I would give you." Her predatory eyes roamed him.

Leah no longer thought it was funny. She began to get uncomfortable with the encounter. She jumped in with a clear tone of annoyance. "And what name would you give him, since you don't like the one his mother gave him?"

"That depends on him," Tracy replied, "on how much he can handle, then how much is he able to dish out." The eyes of seduction never left him. She stared at him the entire time.

Leah didn't see the comedy in it anymore. She at first thought it was a prank to mess with the young guy. Then, being a staunch equal rights supporter that she was, a thought came to her. What if the roles were reversed? One could consider this a serious sexual harassment situation if an older man was talking to a young woman like this. "You're really serious. This is harassment!"

Tracy ignored her. "Well, what do you say? Do you want to have a life-altering experience or what?"

Tina finally chimed in. "Oh, leave the young man alone. You're scaring him."

"That's all right. He can be scared. Some of the best things in life are scary. But when I release him, he'll feel like a conqueror?" replied the seductress.

Leah and Tina spoke in unison. "Release him?"

"Yes. Release him. Prisoners have to be released," Tracy remarked.

That rose Leah's ire. "Prisoner! What is wrong with you? I have half a mind to hire a lawyer and consider filing myself against you for harassment and attempted imprisonment against his will!"

Tracy waved her hand as if Leah was a mere fly bothering her. "It wouldn't be against his will. He would let me do it. Beg me even."

Tina decided to end the charade, turning to speak to Darwin. "I think we are fine here, Darwin. Here is your tip. Have someone else bring the bill." She reached into her purse, pulled out fifteen hundred dollars, and put it in his hand.

"Oh, wow! This is too much! I . . . I can't accept this." He started to hand it back to her when she stopped him with both of her hands enclosed around his, pushing it back.

"Yes, you can. You seem like a nice young man. Nice people deserve nice things," Tina remarked.

"I would like a nice young man like you to become *my* nice thing," Tracy quipped.

Leah turned an exasperated look at her. "You just can't help yourself, can you?"

Darwin's eyes followed the women as each one spoke, then brought them back to Tina. "Thank you so very much. But are you sure? Are you sure about this much?"

Tina chuckled. "Yes, I'm sure. It's perfectly fine. Now go on, get away from this crazy lady."

He turned and jetted away.

"You missed out! I could have made you into somebody!" Tracy called out after him.

Leah rounded on her in a harsh yet hushed tone. "My goodness! I can't believe you just harassed that poor kid like that. Have you no decency at all?"

Tracy responded nonchalantly, "What's the big deal? We're both adults. I made an offer. He refused. End of story."

"But it was the *way* you were talking to him. I don't know any man that would be turned on by a woman saying she would have to release him."

"Then you obviously don't know many men." Tracy chuckled, tapping Tina on the shoulder with the back of her hand.

"It did seem like you wanted to degrade him in ways that are not very pleasant. You must be into S&M or something," Tina added.

"Oh, absolutely," Tracy responded. "Most dominatrix wear leather. Me, I prefer suede. It's easier to get off."

Leah continued to rant in her prude nature. "Do you get many men to fall for that bit you just pulled? It's deplorable."

"Oh, honey, you have no idea. Let me put it like this. Some people have a room of . . . fun. I have an entire house."

Leah gasped, covering her mouth with one hand, with the other hand landed on her chest. "And all these men willingly participate in this?"

"Not all. I have drugged a few guys that wouldn't necessarily agree with it. But hey, momma gets what momma wants."

"You what? You're sick!"

At that last comment, even Tina was taken aback. "Honestly, that is a little over the edge."

Tracy shrugged. "There is nothing better than being in complete control. And that includes the other person not wanting to give it. But in the end, they always turn out supremely satisfied. So you see, it's a win-win."

"But that's illegal!" Leah realized she was raising her voice. She looked around and lowered her voice while dipping her head. But the heat didn't drop from her tone. "I'm surprised you're not in jail right now. It's, that's . . . rape."

"Not when you're a criminal prosecutor, with judges and police in your pocket, especially when you already have a few high-ranking individuals on your latest and greatest film sessions."

Tina shook her head. "Some women just don't deserve to have power."

"Only the ones that are afraid to use it," Tracy retorted.

The conversation at the table got pretty intense, especially between Leah and Tracy. To the outside eye, the conversation would not appear to be what it was. Leah was disgusted, outright disgusted with not only the words coming from Tracy but more importantly her mind-set. Tina wasn't a big fan either, but she wasn't quite as disturbed as Leah. That was until she learned that Tracy drugged people.

A completely different server came to the table, a woman much older than Darwin, closer to the age of the three women at the table, which was in the midthirties. The server thought to speak then thought better of it. The mood at the table was thick with tension. She brought the cinnamon roll and coffee and placed them on saucers on the table.

Two women cut hard glances at each other. She looked at them, then looked at Tina. Tina shook her head slightly, gesturing with her head for her to leave. The server turned on her heels and walked.

Heat boiled in Leah's eyes at the thought she was just having. "I have a little brother around his age. And if you ever touched him, there's no telling what I would do."

"You wouldn't do a damn thing," Tracy responded, sounding greatly annoyed. "I can't stand high and mighty like you. You probably couldn't get even a toothpick up that tight ass of yours."

"Excuse me!" Leah fired back.

Tracy reiterated, "Just because you don't like to have a good time, you don't want anyone else to. That's a *you* problem, sister-girl. Clearly you haven't had any plumbing done on you pipes in a while."

Leah gasped then responded in a defensive tone, "I do like to have a good time. I just don't believe in the other person feeling like a slave in ancient Rome. And my plumbing or pipes or my tight ass and whatever I can or can't get up it is none of your business."

Leah was the picture of a prude. Her brunette hair was wound up in a tight bun. A white dress with flowers on it in splattered print exposed her frail shoulders. She looked like a third-grade teacher from the fifties.

Tracy leaned back in thought with a smirk on her face. "I would have loved to live in Rome at that time. I read about the annual orgies they used to have. It was as common as going to a movie today. Now that's living."

Tina shook her head at them. "You two are something else."

No longer able to stomach Tracy's view of depravity, Leah turned to Tina. "And what about you? Do you agree with her point of view?"

"I think you both make good points. No, it's not okay to drug anybody. And I don't think you could get a toothpick up your ass either." She and Tracy broke out into laughter. Leah glowered at them.

Conversation with other patrons continued, completely oblivious to the three ladies at the small table. A dog lying on the floor wagged her tail slightly, then turned her half-asleep blinking eyes in another direction. A man in the corner slapped a hand on the table while holding a phone to his ear. He let out a burly laugh, disturbing a studying student next to him.

Darwin happily counted his money in a secluded corner in the back. A sudden gust of wind blew palm tree limbs, causing a rustling sound of comfort for patrons sitting outside.

Tina reached in her purse, still chuckling to herself. She pulled out her phone to check the time. "All right, it's a quarter to three."

Leah never touched her coffee. As soon as Tina called out the time, she dismissed the entire conversation. Tracy sat up straight in her chair, erasing the smirk from her face. She and Tina both opened the backs of their phones and took the chips out.

They put the chips on the ground and stomped several times, completely ruining them. They then handed their phones to Leah, as she headed to the restroom. Four small windows lined the walls that retracted outwardly. They might have been big enough to fit a toddler through. She cut the mesh screen with her keys, then tossed out the phones. They landed in a thorn bush below.

Tracy pulled out a big bill to pay for the cinnamon roll and coffee. She flagged the server over with the payment in her hand. She came over very cautiously, on account of how uncomfortable it was earlier around her. Tracy handed her the money, then dismissed her with a rather arrogant wave of the hand.

Such a gesture would offend most people, but there was something stern in the looks of the women's faces that made the server just want to get the hell away from them. Conversing was over. They moved purposely, as if on assignment.

The fifteen-hundred-dollar tip Tina gave to the Darwin was all the money she had on her. Leah found that she had fifteen hundred on her as well. She took it out and rolled it up with a rubber band. She walked over to a fake plant placed on a counter in the coffeehouse and put it in there. Tracy had fifteen hundred on her as well. She took it out of her purse and put it in an envelope Tina handed her. She sealed it, then walked over to where a woman was sitting working on her computer, the one with the dog lying at her feet.

The lady on the computer appeared extremely focused and a bit agitated with what she was reading and typing. She would type some, grunt in displeasure, and then erase it. The cycle was more than a few times. More than likely, she was a scriptwriter or author of some sort. She noticed that Tracy was down low greeting her dog, but she didn't see her slip the envelope in her opened computer bag.

"She's so well-behaved," Tracy mused, petting the dog. "I appreciate good behavior." The dog lowered her head as Tracy scratched her ears.

"Yes, she is," the woman responded, not really paying attention, still typing.

Tracy rose up, leaving the dog alone, and walked back over to her table.

Tina took hers and Leah's wallet, then headed toward the trash. She removed her earnings and gold bracelet and dropped them in the trash, along with the wallets.

Leah pulled out a small spray bottle of all-purpose cleaner. She sprayed and cleaned the table with napkins from a napkin box at the table. She took the half-eaten cinnamon roll to the trash as well but left the full cup of cold coffee on the table. In a plastic bag, Leah placed the spray bottle and used napkins inside. Tossing those in the trash also.

Tracy returned to the table and stood at the spot she was sitting. Leah did the same thing, waiting for Tina to return. She returned, and they all sat down. As if in debutant school, they all sat up straight, interlocking their fingers on top of the table. Unreadable looks were etched across their faces. A long moment of silence was broken by Tina first.

"By the way. My name is Tina Wilson."

"I'm Leah Washington."

"Tracy Collins."

A long pause between the three of them occurred. Their eyes scanned back and forth at one another. Suddenly, quicker than a hiccup. Leah snatched up her coffee cup and smashed Tracy right in the forehead. But it didn't break. The cup was made of hard ceramic designed to prohibit constant replacement due to unexpected cracks or breaks.

The blow sent Tracy falling backward in her chair. Her arms flailed as she was unable to uncross her legs in the fall, banging her head on the floor. Leah moved to follow up but was grabbed on the wrist and spun around to encounter a bone-crunching pie face with a saucer. Tina grunted with the effort of bashing the saucer into her face, trying to break the nose.

Success. Leah's nose gushed like a geyser, snapping her head back, sending her through a table. Miraculously, she maintained a grip on the handle of the cup. Plates, saucers, silverware, and napkins flew up in the air.

As much as people like to think, they are willing to help in a rough situation. When it comes down to it, they are all out for themselves. Instead of reaching down to help Leah, the people that were sitting at the table she crashed into ran.

Tina made her way around the table, following up on Leah with a stomp to the wrist with the hand not holding the cup. The hit forced her attention to grab the wrist with the other hand, dropping the cup.

Tina dropped down on her like a falling tower, with the saucer still in her hand. She made contact to the side of Leah's head, instead of the nose again. An instinctive slide to side did the trick for this, evading a repeat hit to the nose.

The jarring hits of ceramic dishes made the sickest sounds one could think to hear. The first hit stunned a few people that happened to turn and look as it occurred. And those that were aware of the first sure enough saw the second. People began to file out quickly, wanting no part in it.

The manager came from the back room, heading over to break up the fight. In a desperate attempt on her back, Leah hurled the cup at Tina, who was getting in position to mount and pound her. But in her disoriented state, she released the cup into a throw, with Tina no less than three feet from her face.

The cup sailed past her, clocking the manager right in his eye. The so far near-indestructible ceramic he spent a lot of money for just caused him a great amount pain. All heroism left him in that instant. He clutched at his eye and ran out with everyone else.

Tina mounted Leah, with saucer still in hand. Leah, already frail, was disoriented and unable to block or buck Tina off her. She covered her nose with one hand and attempted to shield with the other. Tina gripped the free hand, the throbbing hand, and moved to slam the edge of the saucer down at Leah's throat.

A miscue in aim landed the hit on the collarbone instead. Leah screamed in agony as Tina struck again to the side of her ear. Stars began to appear in Leah's vision. If she was to fall unconscious while Tina was hitting her, she would be unable to block or evade any uncontested hits.

Her arms began to go limp. Her head rolled back, exposing her throat. Tina saw the opening she wanted and paused. She was going to take her time and measure up the final fatal blow.

A chair to the side of the head sent her flying off Leah, shoulder first, to crash into a stand of dishes. The stand fell on her, sending spoons, forks, butter knives, and dishes falling on the floor, shattering—all except for the coffee mugs.

A few stragglers stayed to watch the goings-on of the fight, from what they thought was a safe distance. That ended the second a number of shards of broken plates flew in their direction. They ran away with lightning speed.

Tracy stood dazed on unstable legs, holding a folding chair in her hands, a goose egg on her forehead and a glaze in eyes, until she saw a half-conscious Leah lying on the ground. Every impulse screamed at her to lie into the supine Leah with everything she had with that chair. She decided instead to unleash on Tina.

The folding chair Tracy held had a metal back and side frames, sturdy black mesh knit for sitting, and a cup holder net on the side. She made her way over to Tina on the floor, who was slowly attempting to stand. Holding it with both hands in front of her like a Samurai warrior, she brought the chair up then down with a scream.

The noise gave away her position, allowing Tina to get her arms up to block the oncoming hit to the face, catching everything on the forearms. She screamed out in pain from the sickening thud but did not drop her guard. Another Samurai hit contacted the forearms again, followed by another scream. But the guard was still up.

The next hit landed right on the ribs. A crack was heard, sounding like a finger snap. The guard dropped to comfort the snapped rib. Tracy turned it into a baseball bat swing motion, landing right on the elbow of the arm comforting the rib.

Metal versus bone. Metal wins. Tina's left elbow shattered. She wailed in agony, the sound a yelling spoiled toddler makes when they don't get their way. Nerves shot all the way up to her neck. Tears welled up instantly. Through instinct or nerve reaction and force, she rolled three complete turns away from Tracy, holding the elbow.

Tracy, with fire and brimstone in the eyes, turned her gaze to Leah on the ground, just stirring faintly. The Samurai aimed again. This time the chair went all the way behind her arching back, touching the back of her legs. She lifted up on her toes, with huge eyes focused on landing the hit.

The little spat the two had earlier might have had some bearing on the focus of the hit. Whatever the case, the intent was clear. Murder was in Tracy's eyes all the same. Like a slingshot pulled back, Leah's knee cocked back and exploded into Tracy's right kneecap, bending it backward into hyperextension.

Tracy dropped the chair as her leg buckled unnaturally backward. The hit was sudden, shocking. That shockwave shot through

Tracy. She crumpled, holding the knee. She screamed like she was getting attacked by a pack of wolves.

Leah staggered up, still dazed. Blood drenched the front of her formerly pretty white flower dress, a limp left arm from the broken collarbone. It's one thing to break a nose and have it look as if it's going in different directions. It's another to have it caved in. That was what Tina did with the saucer. Leah's blurry vision made it hard for her to find Tracy. But her screaming on the floor made it easier than finding a crying baby in the woods at night.

But she went over to Tina instead. Scrawny as she was, a punch to the bigger Tina wouldn't mean much. She wiped her watered eyes and blood from her vision with a spare napkin on the floor. She noticed Tina curled up in a ball, gasping for a breath, holding her damaged ribs. Leah leaned down with both hands on her for support, one hand on her thigh, the other on her shoulder.

Using both gravity and inertia, she rammed a sharp knee to the small of Tina's back, hitting her right in the spine. Tina arched her back, completely ignoring the ribs. Her body folded backward in contortion. Her eyes snapped open, her mouth made as if she was going to scream loud enough to break every window in there. But no sound came out, the ultimate indication of true physical pain. She was unable to cry out.

The energy it took to land the blow was tremendous. Leah struggled to stand up, clutching her collarbone. As she missed her throwing target earlier, Tracy did not. Another ceramic cup belted Leah right in that mangled nose, as she stood over Tina's contorted body. Bullseye. Either the force or the pain sent Leah from her feet. She landed flat on her back on a pile of broken dishes.

One would have to believe the pain sent through her body sent a shutdown to her extremities. She didn't move a hand to comfort the nose as she fell. Her left arm stayed extended all the way until she hit the floor. Her right arm stuck in position over her collarbone.

Though patrons exited the battleground, they never fully left the scene. As much as one hates to admit it, nobody turns down the opportunity to see a fight. They stood outside behind the railing at the entrance. The sounds of gasps and groans murmured among the onlookers.

A moment of pause occurred, and people wondered if it was over. Tracy began to pull herself up on tables. Unable to stand, she put every bit of her weight into leaning on the table. It turned over on top of her, sending her back to the floor. She finally got hold of a chair stable enough to hold her struggle to rise.

Tracy sat in the chair for a second, grimacing, rubbing her knee with labored breath. She glanced at Tina then did a double-take to something she saw resting on the table next to her. Tina lay incapacitated on the floor, still contorted and breathing weakly. Not much fight appeared to be left in her, with her eyes closed, lying down on her side. Her right hand clutched her shattered elbow, with the left arm lined up against the broken rib.

The saucer that wouldn't break sure broke this time—right on top of Tina's head. Ceramic shards flew in different directions as a gash opened up on the side of her head. The break of a ceramic dish made a different sound than a glass one. It was deeper, sounding more like a thud. The sound caused the spectators to cringe, gasp, and look away.

Tracy attempted to stand, but the lame leg wouldn't allow it. She collapsed back to the ground. She took a few moments to grimace before pulling herself back up.

Leah got up slowly, unaware of her location. She found herself near a counter and used it to climb up on. Blood ran on top of the counter like a pitcher of water slowly pouring over it. She reached up to touch the source. The flattened nose with broken vessels. Her breath caught when a hand grabbed her by the hair.

The tight bun in Leah's hair unraveled as Tracy gripped it, yanking her head backward. With great force, she slammed her face into the countertop. The hit snapped her head back up, while Tracy had a death grip on her. Long hair draped over Tracy's hand as the tight bun worked loose.

A second slam. Leah's legs started to wane. Her arms weren't even up to defend herself. Hobbling on the left leg and bracing herself on the counter with her left arm, Tracy tried to still herself. She was hurt. She was tired. But she was determined.

Even the knot on her forehead the size of a tennis ball wouldn't stop her. The third and final slam carried a scream of rage with it. The blood-smeared countertop was already a gruesome sight. As if a water balloon filled with tomato sauce, Leah's face seemingly exploded on impact.

The puddle of blood spilled from her nose plastered a face-paint-like feature on her. Her arms that once flailed hung limp, as did the rest of her body. She slid off the countertop face-first, leaving a paint-like trail on the counter wall to the floor where she lay on the floor dead.

Adrenaline took hold of Tracy just enough to complete the job. The killing blow Leah sustained caused even the strongest stomachs to turn from the onlookers. A few excused themselves around the corner to the bushes. Others turned away, crying and screaming. But once again, no one wanted to go in.

Tracy gathered herself, huffing and puffing from the exertion and battle, wincing in pain. She grabbed a long shard of broken ceramic from the floor, staring at Tina. The grimace in Tina's face told the story. She couldn't defend herself; very little movement came from her save for small ragged breaths.

Tracy closed in on her. Slowly. Sloppily. Painfully. But surely. Tina lay, unable to move. The back injury was serious, so serious that she completely ignored the bleeding knot on the side of her head. Her eyes filled with terror when she caught a glimpse of Tracy coming closer with a shard in her hand, and she had no way to defend herself.

She got to within a foot from her and stopped. The knee was killing her. The grimace on her face was a clear indication of that. She limped her way to stand right next to Tina's head. Her idea was to land on top of her and slit her throat with the shard.

The problem was, the bad leg was right next to her shoulder. So she had to turn and fall on her first, then finish the job. But unexpectedly, Tina gripped the closed laptop the writer was using earlier, slamming the point of it on Tracy's throbbing kneecap. She dropped like a sack of potatoes off the back of a wagon. Hard and fast.

As a result, she landed next to Tina and not on her. Tina's legs were not able to work. But here arms did. She rolled over on top of the screaming and writhing Tracy. In her abrupt meeting with the ground, she dropped the shard. Blood pooled on the floor as she lay on her face, clutching the destroyed knee.

Leah was frail. Tracy was the tallest of the three. And Tina was the heaviest. Not in the sense of obesity, but she clearly outweighed Tracy by a good fourteen pounds. She used every bit of that weight to lie across Tracy's back, trapping her arms under her.

Tina held her head down, ramming the shard into Tracy's cheek. Once. The shard cut but ricocheted off a little. Twice. It broke through her cheek. The shard cut the side of her tongue. The muffled scream was horrific.

On the third stab, Tina pressed all her weight into it, dragging the shard through her cheek, splitting both face and tongue apart. Tracy thrashed unsuccessfully. Tina made it halfway through when she looked up and saw Darwin making his way over to stop her.

He moved tentatively and stopped cold when he met Tina's murderous eyes. When she spoke to him earlier and gave him the biggest tip of his life, she looked different. Albeit not beaten up, but different. She was a little cute in his eyes, a bit more weight than he liked in a woman, but not hard on the eyes at all.

It could have just been the fact that she gave him such a generous amount of money that made him see her as attractive. Or the fact that she was nice to him, while the other one was frightening him. But she didn't look nice at that at the moment.

She looked vile and menacing. Her eyes held heat the likes in which he had never seen. She glanced over to her left and saw a broken table leg with nails sticking out from it. It must have broken off when one of the tables was crashed through. It lay about three feet in the opposite direction of her prey.

She left the shard in Tracy's mouth, then started crawling arm over arm to it. Legs sprawled out lifeless behind her, but her eyes held to his. He backed away slowly then stopped with wide eyes. No words could form from his mouth, but it shot open.

Tina's mouth and eyes both snapped open as she froze in her tracks. Blood drained from both sides of her head like the pour of liquid. The corner of a wooden table leg stuck on the top of her scalp. Four one-inch nails connected to each corner of the wooden table legs. And all four pierced Tina's brain. She dropped lifeless on her belly, propped up on her chin.

Darwin looked from Tina to Tracy. Back to Tina, then back to Tracy. Shock wasn't a strong enough word to describe his feeling. More like ultra-shocked was is closer to his true feeling of witnessing the madness.

Tracy happened to find one of the other four legs that belonged to the shattered table. She managed to grab it right in front of her, when Tina gave her a reprieve. She had grabbed it and rolled onto her back in one full motion, burying it in Tina's head. All energy left her after the effort. But not her charm. Lying on her back, she rolled her head over to look at Darwin.

The poor guy was frozen stiff. She lost so much blood she looked paler than a jug of milk. She attempted a smile at him, which looked grotesque and deformed from torn facial muscles. Earlier, her eyes told him that she was lively, maybe a little too lively for his taste. Her eyes fixed on him, still wearing the distorted smile. But the eyes no longer had anything else to say.

CHAPTER 10

FAMILIAR

FOUR MONTHS HAD passed since the parking lot incident. Frazier still hadn't let up in his abruptness with Wiley. They had worked small cases that were kicked to them from local police departments—cases involving internet fraud, antitrust, destruction of government property, wire taps, and copyright matters.

Each case they were handed was solved and closed in record time. Wiley began to admire the process of investigation that his counterpart employed. The man just knew how to get the job done. Wiley showed some promise as an agent, but he wasn't in Frazier's building, let alone his league.

Not many real challenges came their way. Not since the parking lot case a few months back. Frazier was bored with the cases. They were too easy for him. An hour ago, they just finished wrapping up an election laws case. Frazier let Wiley type up the final report.

Wiley sat at his desk, working, while Frazier leaned back in his chair deep in thought, occasionally tossing a tennis ball against the wall and catching it, carefree of the noise it produced. Director Russell entered the office with another case for them.

"Frazier. Wiley."

"Yes, sir." Wiley stopped typing to respond to his commander in charge.

"Just got a call." He held up a file.

Frazier didn't stop tossing the tennis ball against the wall as he offered a quick quip. "Let me guess. An extortion case. A bond default. No, wait, don't tell me. Impersonation, right?"

Russell smiled as he as he turned a file over and over in his hand, glancing back and forth between the two. "No. This is something much more interesting than that. Guess again, hotshot."

"All right," Frazier replied, still at it with the tennis ball. "Exotic animal smuggling ring. Haven't had one of those in years."

Wiley was mildly interested in such a case. Having never experienced one and being an animal owner, such a case was intriguing.

"Wrong again. This is more interesting than even that. In fact, it's right up your alley."

Wiley asked, "Is it bank robbery, sir? A hostage situation?"

Frazier grew annoyed as he threw the ball a little harder, partly due to boredom and mostly because of the constant ass kissing Wiley spared at no expense to Russell. But Russell didn't seem to mind. Often he would tell Frazier he knew he was doing it.

Many other agents did the same thing. Russell wasn't the type that demanded it, but he wouldn't turn it down. And if a man thought so little of himself to kiss ass, he would leave him to his own devices. He even confessed to liking it a little. Because he sure wasn't going to get it from Frazier.

"Russ, come on, man. What is it?" Frazier uttered.

"There was a brutal fight at a coffeehouse about two hours ago. It happened in broad daylight, in front of a lot of people."

Frazier caught the tennis ball and froze. He slowly turned to look at Russell and saw him standing there grinning. He asked the questions with anticipation. "Two guys again?"

Russell shook his head. "Three women."

Frazier's eyes lit up, then he scowled. He turned completely in his chair and held out his hand. Russell handed him the file and stood there with his hands on his hips, waiting. Frazier skimmed through the file, then slammed it shut in his hands. He looked up at Russell, who then held out an inviting hand toward the door.

"Happy hunting."

Frazier snatched up his coat from the hanging rack, still holding the file. He stormed out with a determined yet excited look on his face. Wiley caught on, equally intrigued, trailing behind him.

The coffeehouse had the usual yellow crime scene tape around the area. Crowds gathered across the street, looking at the commotion. Police and medical investigators were everywhere. News trucks started to arrive the same time as Frazier and Wiley did.

Wiley learned a thing or two with each case. He found that it was incumbent to speak to the crowd of witnesses and not just the cops on the scene. Clusters of people stood around talking, exchanging various frantic views of the story. Police took statements, trying to keep control of the disturbed crowd.

Wiley stepped right up between and in front of the two cops standing there taking notes, cutting them off as if they weren't even there. "All right, ladies and gentlemen. I'm Special Agent Norman Wiley of the Federal Bureau of Investigation. Can someone tell me what happened here?"

"Well, look at what we have here. It's Mr. FBI himself."

Wiley, who paid no regard to the cops at all, had no way of knowing who was just speaking. But the voice did sound familiar. He turned to look. It was none other than officers Green and Burns.

Burns responded to his partner, "Well, I'll be damned, Greenie. It's Wyatt Earp himself."

Wiley didn't appreciate the sarcastic jab, especially from someone "beneath him" in rank. He responded in kind. "You see this?" He flashed his credentials a foot from their faces. "This means I own your asses. Keep your little sophomoric jokes to yourselves or else. Understood?"

In their first encounter, the two cops were clearly upset by the blatant level of disrespect they received from the agent. But this time, they just relished the fact that they could make him upset.

Burns fired back sarcastically, "Whoa. You hear that, Greenie? He just hit us with the 'or else.' What are you going to do now, Wyatt Earp? Are you going to buffalo us like the Old West?"

During the days of Wyatt Earp, he was known for hitting criminals or unruly patrons that didn't comply in the back of the head with his gun. It was called getting buffaloed. Burns made a play on the "or else" threat laid out.

"You know what, I just might. And guess what else?" Wiley retorted, with a smug look. "There's not a damn thing you could do about it. Because *I'm* the federal agent, and you two are the beat cops. It's as simple as that."

Burns glowered. Green stared angrily. All remnants of mocking and joking left them in a heartbeat. Before the two could leave or even come back with a witty retort, Wiley went at them again.

"You know, I'm not sure if you ever actually looked at these credentials. Or maybe reading is a little difficult for you. Here, get a closer look." This time he put it three inches from the faces, pointing at the words as he read them aloud. He spoke with long, dragged-out words, as if trying to explain something to a small child. "It says Federal. Agent. Norman. Wiley. Do you see this picture? That's me. Do you know what this means, Green? Do you know, Burns? No? Okay. I will tell you. It means you are beneath me. I am the cream of the crop. You are the backwash in the bottom of the drinking bottle. When I speak, you no longer are entitled to. Not unless I say you can. Is that slow enough for you to understand?"

"You son of a—" Green lunged forward, grabbing the collar of Wiley's coat. Wiley did nothing. He simply stood there with a smug smirk on his face while Burns pulled him away. Burns yelled over his shoulder as he rustled his partner way.

"You'll get yours someday, Wiley! And I can't wait for that day!"

Wiley simply readjusted his coat and straightened his tie. He went back to talking to the people with no regard to how he just looked in front of them.

Frazier did his patented wait and read routine. He noticed many people quickly respond to Wiley, willing to give their testimony. A few times he had to slow them down and ask them to speak one at a time. *Amateur,* Frazier thought to himself. *Always have to write things down verbatim. At this rate, he'll never get through this process.*

Continuing the scan, he noticed a lady sitting off to the side alone. She had a dog leash in her hand and a very bewildered look. He also noticed a server wearing a T-shirt from the coffeehouse, with an extremely distraught look on his face, both close to each other in proximity but still had plenty of space between them. They weren't speaking or even glancing at each other.

The dog lay at the woman's feet, performing a scan of her own. Her head rested on her front paws, but her eyes continued to move. Occasionally the head would lift up if someone got too close, then went back down when she felt comfortable enough. Frazier felt the dog and the owner must have been pretty close to the action for the dog to be as skittish as she was.

He checked out the server. The young man looked as if he didn't know which way was up. Even at a ten-yard distance, Frazier could tell the young man had been crying. He rolled down his window and called out.

"Hey, Wiley. Come here a second." Wiley held a finger up without turning, continuing to collect notes.

"Special Agent Wiley. Come here please," he said it with a more forceful tone. The call of his title snapped his head around. Wiley turned back to the crowd and told them he would return and that no one was to go anywhere. He got back to the car on the passenger side and leaned down to the window.

"What do you want?"

"I feel like teaching you something. Are you interested in that, Special Agent?"

"Teaching me something?" He scoffed. "All right, I'll bite. What is it?"

"Get in the car." The head gesture preceded the request.

"I'm in the middle of an investigation. These people were just about to give me—"

"Get in the car," he cut him off abruptly.

Wiley glared at him for a moment. He slammed his notebook shut then walked around to oblige. Reluctantly, however. Once in, he glared again then raised his hands. "Well, what do you want?"

Frazier looked at the crowd as he spoke. "Look at the crowd. What do you see?"

"Honestly, man. We've done this song and dance before. I don't have time to play your little games. And quite frankly, I'm not in the mood."

Frazier calmly repeated himself. "What do you see?"

Wiley reacted in the most petulant of manners, rolling his eyes, smacking his lips, and slumping his shoulders all at the same time. But his response was curt. "I see witnesses."

"What else? Does anyone stand out?"

"Like I said, we've done this before. What are you, getting senile or something? I'm out of here." He moved to step out while opening the door. A firm restraining hand clamped down on his wrist.

"On more occasions than I can count, you botched the investigation process, thereby giving us a much harder job to do. If you were to pay attention—close attention—you may learn a thing or two. But then again, intelligence is the mark of learning something and adapting to it accordingly. Something you display little of."

Wiley yanked his hand away. He'd been here before. Upset by some shot Frazier threw at him, throwing him off his game, he decided to throw a sarcastic jab right back at him.

"Oh, I get it. Don't go out there and cover bases with the people who are clear witness. I should just sit here and play eeny meeny miny moe." He pointed his finger at the crowd in mockery. "Oh, what great knowledge you have, Obi One."

The two didn't like each other. No mystery there. Oftentimes, Wiley would be a smartass just because. It was just simply his way, and he couldn't help himself. Frazier felt that about him the first time he saw him. Since then, he made it a point to throw shots at him whenever he acted like a jerk, which was quite often.

But when on a case, he was in teaching mode. Not so much to make Wiley a better agent, but to verbally refresh and sharpen his own skills. Similar to studying for a test, when reading the answers out loud to hear yourself learning. Often Wiley acted as if he knew everything, which was infuriating. And wrong.

But what was more infuriating was when Frazier didn't take the bait. He continued to look at the crowd, ignoring the jab. "Take that guy you were just talking to with the coffee mug in his hand, standing close to the news crew. He obviously wants some press. He's an attention seeker."

"And, your point is . . ." He rolled his hand as if beckoning for the punchline.

"The point is, he wasn't even there. He's holding a coffee mug at a coffeehouse where a horrible spectacle just occurred. And now he's talking to the press. No sign of being shaken up or anything. He's holding the mug in his left hand, but he's right handed."

"And how do you know that, Sherlock? Did you research his background too? Or did you teleport here earlier and actually *see* the whole thing?"

Frazier, still ignoring the little slights, went on. "Look at him grip the mug. It's still got liquid in it. Most likely someone else's. He gestures with it with slight movements. Plus, the reporter is on his right side. He holds it left handed so the people watching the news can see where he is at the moment. And he hasn't even taken a sip. If it was his, he would've. I bet he picked it up and was carrying it around, looking to get interviewed."

"The mug could be empty for all we know," Wiley protested. "You have no proof that something is in that cup."

"You should know. You were talking to him. You never noticed he was holding it the entire time. He walked over to you, spoke to you, and never took a sip. You were too busy taking open-book notes like a teacher's pet."

Wiley could do nothing but stare. No one had ever been so curt with him before. And he didn't like it. Not one bit. But Frazier went on.

"There are about five people over there that are all talking about what they witnessed. Take notice of the reenactment they are doing. They're a decent source of information, but they're not the keys."

"All right, old wise one." He made it a point to mark his advanced age by saying *old* instead of "*oh* wise one." "Where are the keys?"

"Those two." Frazier pointed at the server and the lady with the dog.

Wiley never paid any attention to them away from the crowd. With further observance, one could conclude that they knew something. Their body language indicated they might have witnessed something traumatic up close. All of Frazier's points were valid. But he wasn't going to tell him that.

"I see them," he responded flatly.

"What do you see about them?"

"Look, enough with the quizzes. We have an investigation to conduct. If you know something, spit it out."

Frazier finally faced him with an unreadable look. He continued looking at him as he pulled out a licorice root and started chewing on it. Then exited the car, still eyeballing him, and walked toward the two people off to the side.

He stood in the middle of the gap between them. The dog lifted her head, wagging her tail when he spoke pleasantly. His tone seemed to relax her as her ears lifted. He looked side to side at them, deciding whom to speak to first. He decided, whichever one looked at him first, that was the one he would speak to first. So he spoke in the open to both.

"Hello. My name is—"

Wiley, not one for subtleties and patience, walked right next to Frazier and cut him off, flashing his ID. "I'm Special Agent Norman Wiley. This is Special Agent Kyle Frazier of the Federal Bureau of Investigation. We have some questions or you."

Frazier rolled his eyes. Both people turned and looked at them. Wiley put his credentials away and pulled out his notepad. "So when did you two get here, and how much did you see? And don't leave anything out. That's obstruction."

Frazier snatched the root from his mouth and gave him an annoyed look. He was never the type to show up a colleague in front of the public. He believed it showed incompetence and dissention. But he just couldn't take Wiley's method any longer. He pulled him to the side by the upper arm, not angrily but stern enough to make a point.

"Take a walk." He blocked the line of sight from the two behind him to see what he was saying. Frazier stood about an inch shorter, but that wasn't a deterrent at all standing in front of the taller Wiley.

"Don't ever put your goddamn hands on me again!" Wiley threw his arm away, knocking the hand off him. Venom spilled from his tone through gritted teeth. He didn't actually yell, but he raised his voice loud enough to be heard. "If you ever touch me again—" He caught himself, realizing that he was about to threaten a federal agent, and in front of civilians, no less.

Frazier boiled with rage. He wanted to choke him out right then and there. But there was a time and a place. He played it cool for the public. They just witnessed a brutal violent display. The last thing they needed to see was the federal government having a spat in the open at the very same crime scene.

"Special Agent Wiley." His tone was measured yet cool. "I'm sure the people you were speaking with would be interested in continuing their civic duty and finish giving you their report. I can speak with these two here."

The young agent continued to stare directly into veteran's eyes. He looked as if he wanted to add to the trauma of the patrons by throwing a punch right there on the spot. Frazier made no further provocation.

He reluctantly stepped back, keeping his predator gaze, and went back to the crowd. Frazier turned back to the two people and spoke calmly.

"I apologize for that. I understand you've seen much today. Is there anything I can get you two?" They both shook their heads in response. "As you now know, my name is Kyle. May I have the names of the people I'm speaking with?"

They glanced at each other, debating who was going to speak first.

"My name is Yvonne Marsden."

"My name is Darwin Dane."

"Yvonne Marsden, *A Winter Comes Twice a Year*. Didn't you write that novel?" Frazier asked.

Her somber mood evaporated. She brightened up, smiling with a teeth-showing smile. "Yes. I did. Did you read it?"

"Did I read it? I love that book. I have a copy of it in my library at home."

"What did you think about it? Please, be honest."

"You have a good way of engaging the reader. I really found myself caring about the characters. It's all about creating a good visual for me. And that's what you did. I do feel you could use different ways to say the same thing. No offense, but some of the words became a little redundant.

"Some big words could have been said differently with smaller words to pinpoint the meaning. Also, a little too much detail of wardrobe for my taste. I appreciate the roller coaster the main characters went through. But all in all, I loved it."

She listened thoughtfully, nodding as if taking mental notes. "Thank you very much for that input, Special Agent. I will take that advice and apply it to my next work. I appreciate your support."

"Please, call me Kyle. And don't mention it. I'm a fan. In fact, here's my card. As soon as you finish your next book, call me. I'd like to purchase an autographed copy from you."

She beamed with excitement. Frazier completely disarmed her from earlier. She took his card. "Absolutely Speci—I mean, Kyle."

"And who is this beauty we have here?" He leaned down toward the dog.

The dog perked up, wagging her tail, licking her tongue out in welcome. "This is Hanna."

He scratched behind the dog's ears, earning him a pleasant growl. The tail wagged with lighting speed as he smiled at her. He then turned to the other person. "And, Darwin. Who is the science extremist that named you?"

"My dad." The mention of the word *extremist* brought a smirk to his face. It just so happened that Frazier was spot on.

Darwin felt a little more relaxed after watching the interaction with Yvonne and the dog. He felt more comfortable in speaking to this federal agent regarding the horrific witnessing.

"How old are you, son?"

"Nineteen, sir."

"When is your birthday?"

"April 7."

"Ah, last month?" Frazier raised an eyebrow. "Well, happy belated birthday."

"Thank you, sir."

"Kyle."

"Oh, thank you, Kyle."

He smiled at him chewing his root, then turned his attention back and forth between the two. "So what did you see?"

Yvonne spoke first. "I saw them when they first walked in. I was typing on my laptop, when one of them asked me if the cinnamon rolls in here were good."

"Did you get her name?"

"No. I saw the ladies enter with their own folding chairs. I thought that was strange, but hey, aren't we all in our own little way?"

"You right about that. What about you, Darwin?"

"I was their server. I didn't get any names, but one of them was hitting on me. At first, she talked about inviting me into her Jacuzzi, which isn't a terrible thing. I love Jacuzzis. Then she started talking about me being her prisoner. That part freaked me out."

"Prisoner?" Frazier frowned. "Are we talking S&M or something?"

"I'm not sure. But she had this hungry look in her eyes. Like she wanted to flay me or something. Talking about how she would rename me and make me into a . . . somebody."

"Did you agree to take her up on her offer?" Frazier knew the answer. He just wanted to poke a little fun as he said it with a smirk.

"No, sir!" Darwin exclaimed. "I told her I had a girlfriend. She didn't seem to care about that. The other two ladies stepped in on my behalf. One in particular."

"Which one?"

"The one in the white flower dress. Or used to be white." His face turned solemn at the last part.

"So what happened next?" Frazier had a way of pressing without pressing.

"One of them gave me a large tip—the biggest tip I ever seen—then told me to leave and have another server bring the order to get away from that freaky woman."

"So flower dress tipped you and told you to leave?"

"No. It was the other one. She was a little heavier than the other two. But not fat."

Yvonne spoke in. "That's the same one that asked me about the cinnamon roll."

"How much was this big tip?"

Darwin raised his eyebrows and took a deep breath. "Fifteen hundred dollars."

"That's so crazy," Yvonne chimed in. "I found an envelope with that exact same amount in my bag."

Frazier weighed the amount in his mind. "Fifteen hundred you say? Both of you?"

They nodded their heads. He chewed the licorice root and dropped his head in thought. "Anything else you can tell me? Before the fight?"

Darwin shook his head. Yvonne thought about it, then answered, "I did hear them talking about him when he left. The one in the flower dress seemed to be a real prude. She was outraged how the other thought. There was mention of her actually drugging men she brought home to have a good time with them."

"Drugging them, huh?" Frazier didn't show any sign of amazement.

"Yeah. She was unapologetic about it. The two of them argued for a while, with the other one speaking sparingly. I recall because I was thinking about making them characters in one of my books." Her face changed to somber. "But not now. Not after what I've seen."

"Anything else?"

"One of them used my computer to hit the other one. When they started fighting, I just grabbed Hanna's leash and ran. They were so close."

"My manager tried to get in there and break it up," Darwin remarked, looking off in the distance. "But he got caught in the eye with a coffee mug. They rushed him to the hospital."

"All right. Thanks for your cooperation so far. You too are very helpful. Now, if you please. Tell me everything you saw about the fight. Leave nothing out."

They told it all—every hit, counterhit, failed attempt, every cause of area damage, and every scream. He had a full picture of what went down. He wrote down nothing. He sat in a chair in the middle of them, crossed his legs, and chewed his root, resting one arm on top of a folded one across his chest.

Wiley finished up his rounds. He made his way back over to Frazier, Yvonne, and Darwin, still sizzling with heat for Frazier, but he had to put that aside. He showed up right at the end of the story. But he wanted to hear all for himself.

"All right, so go over all that with me now. Walk me through it." He got ready to take notes.

They looked at him, then back to Frazier. The veteran shook his head, rising from his chair. "Thank you, Yvonne, Darwin. Go home now. Or go do something fun. Watch a comedy, play a game. Something to try to get over this terrible event." They both nodded.

Wiley started steaming as he tapped the button on his pen, scowling at Frazier.

The two witnesses got up to leave. Yvonne gathered Hanna's leash and turned to walk away. Frazier stopped her. "And, Yvonne, I'm serious about that autograph copy." She smiled broadly and left.

CHAPTER 11

ONCE AGAIN

WILEY HALTED FRAZIER to stop, barring his path. "Tell me everything. Don't leave anything out. And if you ever try to embarrass me like that again, we may just have to step outside."

Frazier simply stepped around him without a response toward the coffeehouse entrance like he wasn't even there. The acknowledgment he gave that he indeed heard him was the response he threw over his shoulder as he walked. "We're already outside, sparky."

The two agents lifted the crime scene tape and walked into the coffeehouse. It was a complete mess. Tables and chairs were in pieces, dishes shattered, inventory racks tipped over, as well as blood everywhere. They observed the scene as they circled around the inside area, taking note of splatter patterns of blood on the walls and countertops. Frazier used his foot to move over broken pieces of coffee mugs and plates as he walked through.

He walked over to the bodies of the women, quickly making out Leah from the description Darwin mentioned about the white flower dress, although there wasn't much white left. She lay facedown in front of the counter, in enough blood to nearly fill a kiddie pool.

Tracy was lying on her back with her head rolled to the side. Her right leg looked unnaturally loose. But the cause of the puddle of blood near her face was enough to make the strongest stomach turn. A ceramic shard jotted from the side of her jaw. The point of the shard daggered the tongue to the other side of her mouth.

Tina was seen lying on her belly, with her chin propped up on the floor. Long trails of blood ran all over the back and sides of her head. The culprit, a table leg lodged on the top of her scalp. A sickening sight. At least that death was a quick one.

Frazier pulled the licorice root out of his mouth and knelt slowly, suddenly not feeling like chewing anything on the side of his jaw for obvious reasons. Wiley put a fist over his mouth, scanning the various cuts, bruises, and knots on the women. He put on a pair of gloves before making his way to Leah.

He turned Leah over slowly and nearly lost his lunch. Her long hair soaked in blood plastered to her face. Her nose was completely smashed inward and sunken in. Her cheekbones were also flattened a little. It looked as if she was tied down on her back and had an anvil dropped on her face from a good height.

He shook his head, disgusted at what these women did to each other. He stood up and looked around the scene, taking it all in. Wily noticed that Frazier started doing that strange thing he did at the parking lot—the investigative trance. His eyes closed. He stood still as a pillar and quiet as kept. Wiley decided not to say anything to him because he saw it before. He wasn't sure what exactly he was doing it for, but he let him have the moment. It really didn't matter to him anyway.

For as much as Wiley didn't like Frazier, he couldn't argue with the man's results. He got the job done. Wiley walked around the scene, observing patterns of blood splatters, touching it, and rubbing it between his thumb and index finger with his gloved hands.

Quicker than before, Frazier snapped out of his trance. He weighed the report from Darwin and Yvonne on the fight. In his mind's eye, he saw it all unfold as it was told to him. But that wasn't what he was focused on. There was a revelation he was after. He looked around semifrantically for something in particular. Or some things in particular.

He turned over a table and found one in the far-left corner, the second at a few feet from the first, in open view. The third was right in front of the counter on the floor. Surprisingly, none of them were damaged in the fight or marred with blood. He picked them all up with gloved hands and set them on the counter to look at. Wiley watched him collect the items then went to stand next to him as he opened them.

"Three purses? Why are you looking at three purses?" he asked.

"We have three women." Frazier gestured an open hand toward the sprawled bodies of carnage then brought the hand back over the purses. "Three purses."

"There were plenty of women that was in this coffee shop. How do you know these belong to them?"

"I don't. But if you can find another purse, by all means bring it over here too."

Scrounging through a woman's purse is usually an arduous task due to the litany of items one would have to move. But with these three purses, no such problems. They were bare. Everything gone, as if the purses were brand-new. Frazier checked the side compartments and inner zippers. In the inner zippers of all three were the places he found what he was looking for.

He pulled out a blank sheet of memo paper. The exact same size of the pure white paper they found during the parking lot case. Wiley's eyes grew wide as recognition came over him.

"You've got to be kidding me," he muttered.

"I wish I was. But you see it as clear as I do right here."

"So it might be safe to say that if we visit their homes, we would find these same blank sheets too. Am I right?"

"If? Oh, we're going." A look came over Frazier's face of an idea. He held up a finger, turning around, looking until he found what he wanted across the shop. He made a mad dash toward it.

"What is it now?" Wiley made no effort to conceal his annoyance.

Frazier went over to the trash can. He turned it over, footing his way through the trash on the floor. He found them. Three wallets. He opened them, looking for a long shot. Nothing.

"Dammit."

"What about cell phones? Surely they had phones with them," the young agent threw in.

"Right. Yvonne was near the entrance. She said she never saw them leave." He looked around again. "Check the bathroom."

Wiley entered the women's bathroom. He turned over trash cans and looked behind toilets and under sinks. Nothing out of the ordinary. He lifted the back plates on the toilets to see if anything was stashed in the water. Also nothing.

He craned his head back in frustration when he noticed something out the corner of his eye. The windows. Why didn't he notice them before? One had the screen cut. He headed over and looked out. Below, he saw a thorn bush.

He walked right out and turned the corner without saying a word to his partner. *Let's see how he likes not being informed,* he thought to himself. But no objection came. He noticed three cell phones stuck in the bushes. He fished them out carefully and opened the backs of them, looking for the chips. Nothing.

He sighed in exasperation then walked back into the shop. Upon entering, he saw Frazier had the three destroyed chips in his hand.

"Find the phones?" The veteran had a matter-of-fact tone when he asked.

"Yeah, I did." He threw them down on the ground in frustration, shattering them.

Ever since the parking lot case, Wiley had been on a mission to prove he could be as good as an investigator as his counterpart. Or better. It pissed him off to no end that Frazier always was two or three steps ahead of him and kept him out of the loop most of the time.

"You realize that you just destroyed evidence, right?"

A dumbfounded look came over Wiley. He let his emotions cloud his judgment. That very point was reiterated by Frazier. "Letting your emotions get the better of you is what makes you a subpar agent."

Wiley's face turned red with rage. "Subpar agent! I'm getting sick and tired of your mouth. This is the last time you disrespect me. The next time you talk to me like that, I'm going to—"

Quicker than a hiccup, Frazier closed a four-foot distance. The speed in which he arrived in Wiley's face shocked him, his words choked off. It took all the steam out of him. If an attack was coming, there wasn't anything he could have done about it. Frazier's voice was cold. His eyes were colder. "What? What exactly are you going to do?"

Wiley said nothing. His tongue betrayed him. He stared back at the older agent with heated eyes. But still no comeback. As quick as Frazier jumped in his face, he dropped the moment. As if it never happened, he turned back toward the view of the rest of the scene to comment on the visual.

"I have to say. These ladies meant business. I thought the brawl in the parking lot was bad. I mean, look at this." Frazier gestured at the turned-over broken tables, mostly turned over by people trying to hurry up and exit the fight; the broken dishes that weren't ceramic; the pools and splatters of blood; the napkins thrown about, also mostly due to the fleeing patrons; and the disfigured bodies on the floor.

Wiley stared at his back for a long moment, brooding, then decided to focus back on the case. He knelt down, glancing at each woman. He looked at them with a look of pity. Leah's face was hardly recognizable. With the table leg stuck on the top of Tina's head, little attention was paid to her face.

He squinted, looking from a semidistance. He cocked his head as he looked at her face. He couldn't help but think she resembled someone. He shook the thought as Frazier loudly waved the evidence bag so he could put the blank sheets in. He stood from the squatted position, frowning.

"I don't know why she looks familiar," Wiley murmured to himself but loud enough to be heard.

Frazier spun around, reading the expression on his face, but said nothing. He then went back to observing the bodies. "Three women. Three fatalities. Three blank sheets. And nothing else on their person. The exact same MO as the parking lot case. Like I said months ago, this case is not closed."

"All right, Sherlock. So what's the next move? Or is this the part where you walk away and simply ignore my presence again?"

"How old are you again? I swear sometimes you act like a little child, and one that hasn't even gone through puberty yet." Frazier glanced up. "The press is here. We tell them nothing of the blank sheets. Nothing of the correlation between this and the parking lot case. The details of this stay internal."

"So what do we tell them then?" the young agent asked with a tone of bitterness.

"We tell them nothing. We give them nothing to spin. If it was local police, I wouldn't care. But not with us."

"Yeah, that's fine. I think I'm good with that." The smug look of approval came over Wiley's face as he nodded his agreement. Anything that separated him from those he deemed beneath him suited his being.

"Oh, well, so glad to have your approval. Far be it from me to have the track record I have and have to do anything that you weren't *good with*." He walked out the coffee shop, leaving Wiley with gritted teeth and balled fists.

Outside was pandemonium. Police continued to hold back the press and new spectators. News reporters began to connect this public display of violent altercation resulting in multiple deaths with the one in a parking lot months ago.

The words *serial killings* and *cults* started to get thrown around. As the agents walked out the coffee shop, they were immediately approached by a reporter that snuck her way past the police barrier with a voice recorder in her hand.

She walked alongside both of them as they did not stop walking toward their car. Frazier never looked at her. He continued to chew his licorice root, looking down as he walked. Wiley walked closely behind, following Frazier's lead, also not making eye contact with her.

"Excuse me, gentlemen. I'm with KLPN, the *Daily Catch*. My name is—"

Frazier didn't break stride as he cut her off. "Your name is Gina Samuel. You're looking for a story that can boost you to senior editor. Hank Brown now holds that position but is retiring soon. You need something concrete and hard hitting to get considered."

She paused, shock on her face as they walked on. "How did you know that? How do you know my name?"

In an abrupt change of direction, Frazier turned around and walked back to stop right in front of her. "You are single by choice. You left your boyfriend of four years the day he was going to propose. You're too ambitious to be tied down. You don't want kids, and you can't stand pets."

Shock plastered her face. "How did you—"

"You are an only child by legitimacy. Your mother had a daughter two years older than you that she gave up for adoption because she was the product of infidelity, a drunken mistake at her former friend's bachelorette party. Your father ultimately forgave her when she volunteered to put the child up before they married."

She lowered the recorder in her hands and stared at him. She couldn't even form a question, just stared with her mouth agape. So he went on.

"Her name is Kellen Winslow, your sister. She lives in Tulsa, Oklahoma, with her husband and two boys, Harris and Gregory. They're seven and five. You're nephews. She's a schoolteacher. Her husband, Paul, is an electrician."

Her jaw hung like a net ready to catch flies. "You . . . how . . . ?"

"Your parents own a convenience store the same small town in North Carolina you grew up in. They are happy with their humble living down there. They wanted you to eventually run the place, but you have more ambition. You're ashamed of your hometown. That's why you hide your accent."

"How do you know all this about me?" she said it with wide eyes in amazement and somewhat fear.

Wiley jumped in, not wanting to play the quiet background. "It's what he does." The comment sounded lighthearted enough. But the look he gave said otherwise.

Frazier ignored the remark. "You want a scoop? A good scoop or two?"

Gina nodded, still unable to put a sentence together.

"Then go buy some Raisin Bran." He gave her a grin, put the root back in his mouth, and walked off.

She stood there still holding the recorder, watching him walk away. She wore a white skirt, a navy-blue blouse, and navy-blue heels. Her long black hair was wrapped up in a ponytail. She was still taken aback by her encounter with the enigmatic agent that seemed to know so much about her.

He was correct. She hailed from a small town in North Carolina. Her parents do own a convenience store that was passed down from her grandparents. Her father told her it was her role to take over the family business. But she wanted more. Marriage? Children? Pets? A small little convenience store? She thought not.

She was brought out of her thoughts by the other agent. "Gina, right?"

So perplexed, she shook her head no while answering. "Yes."

"If it's a scoop you want, it's a scoop you'll get. Anonymously of course."

"Yes. Of course." Suddenly shaking out of her stupor, she lifted the recorder to his face in expectation.

"But not now." He brought up his hands to push down the recorder, glancing back over his shoulder to see if Frazier was still there. He saw him speaking with a few officers on the scene. At a time like this, he was still joking and robbing elbows with the local police. Wiley sneered in disapproval then turned back to her.

"I'll give you a call. I'll give you the story of your career."

"Here, let me give you my card. Just give me a second while I get it out of my purse." She rummaged through her things, but Wiley was impatient. He kept turning over his shoulder to watch Frazier and snarl at him. He didn't even notice a single blank sheet of paper fell out of her purse.

She managed to catch it in midair and put it back in. By the time he turned back around, she finally found it. "Ah, here we are." She handed him the card. He took it quickly from her hand and glanced again. "I take it your partner would have a problem with this conversation we're going to have."

He turned around, fixing her with a deadly glare. Her eyes widened as her breath caught in her throat. She got the message. "I'm a federal agent. You see this?" He held up his credentials. "That's me.

You don't want to piss off a federal agent, especially this guy." He pointed at himself in the picture. "You better not say a word of this. Understood? Or so help me. Or shall I say, so help you."

She cleared her throat as he abruptly walked back over to Frazier, talking with officers Green and Burns. The heavy-set Green in his all-black uniform stood pointing in an opposite direction of the crime scene. Frazier stood at his side, twirling the licorice root in his mouth, following his finger.

Burns, an equally heavy-set man, stood on the other side of his partner. All three watched the direction as if trying to follow a story. Green was telling a joke, a very funny one. But they couldn't let the crowd see them burst out laughing like nothing ever happened. So they pretended to have a discussion.

Wiley walked up behind them. "All right, so what are we looking at? Anything to do with this case?" He started to reach for his notepad.

All three turned to regard him. All three men wore a small smirk on their faces. Two smirks faded to a withering glare. The third remained. Wiley widened his eyes, glancing at all three. He turned his palms up with a shrug and lightly jotted his head forward as if requiring an answer.

"Well, what?" he implored.

Frazier, still smirking, patted the two officers on the shoulders. "Why don't you guys go have a good night? And be safe out there."

Green and Burns walked away, glowering at the obnoxious agent without a word. The sound of their batons and keys at the hips jangled as they turned and walked off. Wiley watched them go, then turned his attention to the still-smirking agent.

"And what was that all about?"

Frazier shrugged his shoulders, holding the root in his mouth with one hand. "Well, I don't think they like you very much. You know, on account of you being an insufferable asshole and all."

Wiley turned to stand in front of him. That was it. That was the last straw. His eyes were hot. He felt steam rise from his head. His chest heaved, and his faced frowned deeply. "Who the fu—"

"You. That's who I'm talking to. That's who I'm looking at. And that's who I'm tired of," Frazier cut him off but didn't make a show of it. His words were sharp and aggressive enough.

Wiley stood stiff for a second, still holding his notebook and pen. He couldn't believe the nerve of this man. What did he just say to him? No one had *ever* talked to Wiley that way and got away with it. He slowly put his pen and pad back in his black suit coat pocket.

Wiley closed the distance, with his fists balled up, aware of but no longer caring about the raising eyes in their direction. "Call me an asshole one more time." His voice was cold and deadly. His eyes told the story. There was going to be another brawl right here, right now, in front of the already traumatized witnesses of the previous ones.

And like anything, the negative gets the attention. No one saw or paid attention to Frazier lifting the spirits of Yvonne Marsden when he commented on her work. No one saw him lighten the mood with the two officers. But if a fight looked as if it was going to materialize between two special agents, then all eyes wanted to see that.

Frazier regarded him calmly. "I don't like you, Wiley. You lack humility. You have no manners. You feel that credential means you can treat and talk to anyone in anyway. You've got no respect. And you think the world owes you something. I think you're an arrogant, pompous, self-serving little pip squeak." He held up both hands in front of him as if he was pushing something off. "Just for the record."

Wiley's blood boiled. He placed his right foot back a half step, ready to lead on his left and bring an overhand right. A quick glance to the right and he saw the horrified looks on the witnesses' faces. He turned his head a little more, then he saw Gina Samuels gesturing excitedly for her camera man to capture the moment.

He turned back to look at Frazier, only to see the same poker face he had got accustomed to seeing. He began to play it off as if they were discussing points of the brawl that happened earlier. It was convincing to the crowd. Many started to turn away, seeing nothing was going to happen.

Gina was not so convinced; she had her camera man keep rolling. Wiley continued to try to play if off more. "So you have to figure that one of them closed the distance with an angry intention like this. And then the reaction came. I mean, that's how it happens mostly."

Frazier jumped right in with the play. "In most cases, you're right. I'm sure there was quite a bit of distance closing between all of them. Let's head back. We've got a lot of work to do with this one."

They made their way back to the car. Gina kept her eye on them until Frazier stopped and turned and looked at her. She froze in her tracks. She placed a hand over the camera lens. The camera man lowered it, looking at her in confusion.

Two hours passed since the three women first walked into the Swinging Palms Café. Voices in the background were aplenty. Local police continued to move along traffic. Some of the witnesses started filing out after giving their testimony.

"What were you talking to the reporter about?" asked Frazier.

Wiley shrugged his shoulders mockingly, desperately wanting to give Frazier a taste of his own medicine. He then abruptly turned and walked away with a smile on his face. Frazier held the poker face at his actions. A man as analytical as him will not be outdone so easily. But he played along as they went to the car.

They didn't speak the whole ride back. Frazier was reading a book on ancient culture of the Celts. Wiley also was puzzled, in deep thoughts of his own. Aside from the haunting visuals of the three women, he kept trying to place where he might have seen Tina from.

The sounds of ringing phones, fingers slamming on keyboards, and multiple voices carried through the office as they walked in. In order to get to their office, they had to pass Director Russell's. He saw them out his window then quickly ended the phone conversation he was having with his wife.

He nearly leaped out of his chair when Frazier walked by and showed him an evidence bag with a blank sheet, as he kept walking past. Nearly seconds after entering their office, the door swung open with Director Russell entering.

"Talk to me, fellas."

"It was pretty bad, sir. The same MO as the parking lot. Those women really made a mess out of each other." Wiley spoke with a slight glee, being that he was the one to give the report. He looked over and saw Frazier sitting at his desk, wearing his glasses, looking over the old and the new blank sheets.

"How quick can we have their identification?" asked Russell.

"Any moment, sir. The medical examiner said he could get to us by the time we got back."

Right on cue, a man walked in with a file. "Kyle, here are the particulars you asked for."

"Thank you, Carl." Frazier took the file containing the identification of the three women. He lifted his head, peering at the file through his reading lenses, rather than over them. He read silently. Russell waited patiently. Wiley, not so much.

"Are you going to fill us in?" He leaned back in his chair with his arms folded and a slight sense of angst in his voice.

Frazier's eyes glanced up while he was still holding the file, then he returned back to reading. Wiley looked to Russell, gesturing his eyes back to the reading agent. Russell, still standing there quietly and patiently with his hands in his pockets, returned a slight head shake, telling him to let it go.

Russell was around the same age as Frazier, the same height as Wiley and just as thin. He wore black slacks and a white shirt with black suspenders. His black hair grayed on the sides, at the temple. He had no facial hair and had a strong square jaw for a thin man.

Abruptly, Frazier rose up and snapped the file closed. He walked out the office right past Russell and Wiley, unannounced. Wiley watched him go, then turned to Russell and held up his hands. Russell threw a thumb over his shoulder.

"I think you better go after him."

Wiley couldn't take it anymore. He had to voice his complaints. It's natural for people to have differences and voice their concerns. But the rant that Wiley went on was outright snitching, similar to an eight-year-old rambling to a parent or teacher.

"He does this all the time, sir. He doesn't fill me in on anything and just acts like I'm his driver or something. He talks to me in a manner of conduct unbecoming of a federal agent. He disrespects me. Tries to show me up. And on top of all that—"

Russell held a hand up, silencing him. "Kyle Frazier is the best federal agent we have in the entire bureau. You know full well his record. Plus, he's saved the lives of many men and women in this department alone, including yours truly."

He pointed a finger out the window behind Wiley. "Not to mention all the mitzvahs he's done with the general public. The one's *we* serve. He's an honorable man. So what if he's a little unorthodox in his approach. He's earned the right. Especially after . . ."

He trailed off from revealing something he shouldn't. Wiley sat in his chair, getting admonished by his superior. But his eyes lit up with wanting to know what the *after* was. Russell righted himself and continued.

"The point is this. And I'm going to make this plain and simple. He's is not the man I am prepared to hear get badmouthed about behind his back. You hear me? Now, you do what he tells you to do. If you can win him over, and I have no idea why he doesn't like you, but if you can somehow, he can make you a damn fine agent."

Wiley dropped his eyes to the floor. The look of defeat etched his face. He tried to rat on Kyle Frazier, the most decorated and beloved agent in the bureau. No one felt the same as Wiley did about the man. He didn't speak to anyone else the way he spoke to the young agent.

It infuriated him. And now he realized that he was all alone with the man that virtually ran the bureau. Even the director himself acted as if he walked on water and healed the sick. Russell wasn't done.

"I'll tell you something interesting, Special Agent. It was Frazier that requested you as his partner."

Wiley frowned up his face, rearing his head back as if he was just attacked by a foul odor. "What? Wait, what?"

"That's right. I don't understand it either. But if there's one thing I know about Kyle Frazier, it is that he won't let you know a thing until he's damn good and ready. I know, I've tried. But he's a good man and a great agent." He folded his arms in a stern visage to make his next point clear. "So I don't want to hear about you not following his orders. He is your lead. Learn from him, and do what he says to do. It might even save your life once. It will certainly save your career. I can promise you that. Now, get out there and catch up with him." He gestured with his head.

In a somber voice and head lowered, he responded, "Yes, sir."

CHAPTER 12

DUE DILIGENCE

THE TWO AGENTS went to the homes of all three women. As expected, they found nothing. All three homes were spread out in different directions. They were all swept clean with no trace of being lived in. The same as it was with Walter Fray and David Brice.

Tina Wilson: A gemologist. Single, in her early thirties. Made a pretty good living compared to the standard salary a gemologist receives. She brought in five figures due in large part of the expeditions she was a part of to study ancient ruins in the Middle East.

She was in the middle of her two other siblings. Her parents died five years ago in a freak boating accident off the Gulf of Mexico. Her older sister Barbara was a social worker living in Texas with her husband. They had no children, opting for pets instead. Her younger brother, Cameron, was a linebackers coach for the University of Auburn Tigers football team in Alabama. He and his wife were expecting their first in another six months.

Not much to say regarding any illegal actions for Tina. Just traffic infractions—five parking tickets, all paid; two moving violations, one for running a stop sign in a residential area, the other for changing lanes in a right-turn only, crossing the solid line. Both were dealt with in traffic school and paid.

Since her home was swept bare, the next thought was to stop by her lab. Fortunately for the agents, that was her garage. Also swept bare. They noticed the grass in her front yard was freshly cut. Not much vegetation was there, except for one fichus tree in a wooden bowl in front of her door.

Her neighbor, a woman in her early seventies, was in her yard, gardening. She wore a straw hat and sky-blue gloves, holding a small rake in her hands. She wore yellow scrubs top and bottoms, with a white long-sleeved shirt underneath it. She noticed the two agents exit the garage.

"Hello. Do you fellas need any help?" She spoke cheerfully yet suspiciously.

Frazier removed the root from his mouth and smiled. "Hello, ma'am. My name is Kyle. This here is—"

Wiley interrupted the introduction. "Special Agent Norman Wiley of the Federal Bureau of Investigation." He flashed his credentials. "My partner, Special Agent Frazier and I were investigating Ms. Wilson's residence." He pulled out his notebook and pen. "We'd like to ask you a few questions, miss. Your name?"

She placed her wrists on her hips, turning her hands away from her yellow scrubs. She scoffed and turned to Frazier. "Does he always approach people like that?"

"I'm afraid so," Frazier responded with a wry smile at her reaction.

She looked back at Wiley. "What can I do for you, young man?"

"Your name, miss." He kept the pen touching the notepad, looking at her with eyes that screamed authority and a tone to match it. "And it's Special Agent Wiley."

She folded her arms and tilted her head, no longer concerned about the dirt and mud getting all over her yellow scrub top that already had a fair amount on it. A frown found its way to her face.

She clearly didn't like his attitude. And coming off the way he did, who would? She looked at him for a moment, then to Frazier, then back to Wiley.

"My *name* is Elsa Bowers. And that's Mrs., not Miss, *Special Agent Wiley*." She spoke with an even greater authority than his voice or eyes could muster. A familiar tone, a tone well toned throughout the ages, the *mom* tone. "And I don't care what profession someone has. That doesn't give them right to show a lack of respect for their elders."

Frazier stood quietly watching this woman of strength put this young punk in his place. She drove his thought home with her last comment. Wiley seethed. He clinched his jaws, looking as if he wanted to rough the woman up. But he just stood there holding his pen and pad, saying nothing. So she went on.

"Now, I have your names. You have mine. We have each other's attention. So what can I do for you?"

Frazier kept the grin on his face as he placed the licorice root back in his mouth. He glanced at Wiley to see how he was going to handle it. This woman wasn't going to take anything from him and was not going to be shy about telling him that she wasn't.

"How well did you know Tina Wilson, Mrs. Bowers?"

"I've known Tina for six years now. Since she moved here. Why?"

"And did you speak with her often?"

"I speak to her—wait. What do you mean *did*? Has something happened to Tina?" A look of true concern on her face replaced the scowl she had when he was speaking.

"Just answer the question Mrs. Bowers," Wiley pressed.

"You said *did* I speak with her often, not *do*. What's going on? Is Tina all right? Tell me." Her voice became grave and insistent.

"I need you to answer a few questions first for us, ma'am. We—"

Frazier jumped in with a soft and sympathetic voice. "I'm sorry to say this, Mrs. Bowers. But Tina died today."

She gasped, bringing her gloved hands toward her face, then noticed they were still on. She yanked them off and covered her mouth with her hands, tears welling up in her eyes. She kept one hand over her mouth, while the other hand moved to lie over her heart. She spoke through a shaky, teary voice.

"How? What happened?"

"She was killed." Frazier's tone carried genuine empathy.

"She was killed? Why? By who? Tina is not the type of person to get . . ." She trailed off from saying the word *killed* again. Tears ran in abundance down her cheeks and across her hands. She turned her head away from them to compose herself.

Wiley shot Frazier a hot glance, a glance that said he thought they weren't supposed to say anything. Frazier didn't bother to look at him. He kept watching Mrs. Bowers gather herself. It further infuriated Wiley that he wouldn't even look at him. He started to turn and say something, until Elsa turned back around.

"Do you know who killed her?" Her voice was still shaky as she wiped her tears away.

"She was involved in a brutal triple homicide, a fight that clearly went way too far. At least, that's all we can gather at the moment. We're still investigating," Frazier answered.

"That's insane. Tina isn't the type to fight. She has a little temper on her, but who doesn't? Are you sure it was Tina? Tina Wilson?"

Wiley jumped in. "Let's talk more about this temper."

Frazier continued to ignore him and answered, "Afraid so, ma'am. That's what brought us here."

"But you guys are FBI. What's the FBI doing here instead of police detectives?"

"The manner of this unfortunate occurrence falls to us."

"You said triple homicide. Who are the other two people?"

"Now that, we cannot disclose. At least not at the moment." Frazier pulled the licorice root out of his mouth and pointed upward.

"Right. Right. I'm sorry." Tears began to roll again. "I just can't believe it." She turned around with her head lowered.

Wiley hated being ignored. He raised his voice slightly. "Mrs. Bowers. We are trying to investigate this case. I need you to answer a few questions for me before we can answer any more of yours." He glanced at Frazier with that last part.

"Now. Did you, or did you not, speak with Tina Wilson often?"

Elsa turned around, infuriated with him. Still with tears on her face, but rage filled her eyes. She gathered herself, lifted her chin, and looked at Frazier. "Special Agent Frazier." She pointed at Wiley. "I understand you have a job to do, and you are doing your due diligence. But you partner is too disrespectful for me to cooperate with. I will, however, gladly answer any questions you may have."

Wiley boiled. "To not cooperate with a federal agent is a serious offense. I could lock you up for that."

She continued to ignore him. As did Frazier. He responded to her, voice still sincere and assuring. "Please, Mrs. Bowers. Call me Kyle. And once again, I'm sorry for your loss."

"Thank you. And call me Elsa."

Wiley slammed his notebook shut. That brought Elsa's eyes toward him. "I'm not breaking any laws, Special Agent. I said I will not talk to *you*. But I will gladly talk to this special agent." She gestured an opened hand at the veteran.

"Say, Norman. Why don't you head back to the car and check the lead on the next person. I'll be there soon."

"No. You're not dismissing me like some schoolchild."

"It might be best, Norman." Elsa spoke up. "I was a high school principal for twenty-five years. And you are acting just like one of my kids from school right now. Not like an agent for the FBI."

"It's Special Agent Wiley!" he roared.

She simply looked at Frazier and turned a thumb at the petulant younger agent. "See what I mean? I would have held him in detention for that outburst."

"I agree. Special Agent Wiley, will you please give us a minute? I'll fill you in on everything."

Wiley stood there for a long moment, staring at Frazier, then looked at Elsa, then back to Frazier. "Fine. I'll head up the other lead." He huffed, turned around, and stormed off.

"Your partner needs to grow up," Elsa commented.

Frazier waved his licorice root nonchalantly. "Never mind about him. When was last time you saw Tina?"

"Two days ago."

"Was she behaving strangely?"

"Not at all. She was in a rush. But she typically was all the time. We would talk whenever she came back from one of her digs. She would show me some of the gems and stones she found. She sure loved those rocks. I used to joke with her about being married to a rock. She just laughed it off."

"What's the last thing she said to you? Can you recall?"

"We talked about the next dig she was going on to some old ruin in Turkey. That's it. She was so excited about it." Tears began to well up again at the remembrance of Tina's exuberance over her work. "I'm sorry."

"No, don't be." He placed a comforting hand on her shoulder. "I understand. I won't bother you with anything else. I'm sorry for your loss, Elsa. Try to hang in there. We'll get to the bottom of this."

She nodded then turned and went into her house. Frazier made it back to the car. Wiley sat there, still steaming. He made no effort to hide the irritation in his voice.

"Well?"

"Now we go to Leah Washington's home."

"You said you were going to fill me in on what you talked about with her."

"And I will. After we investigate Leah Washington's home." He arched his eyebrows and gestured forward with his licorice root. "Now, will you please drive?"

> Leah Washington: A publicist, also in her early thirties. Recently broken up with her boyfriend a year ago, a colleague. The year-and-a-half relationship fell apart when she took a promotion and became his superior. She had a son in her freshmen year of college but put him up for adoption so she could focus on her career. The father,

a senior, had no knowledge of a child. Due to a regrettable, drunken, one-night stand at a party.

She had no connection with the boy and requested that he never finds out about her. All she knew was that his name was Kevin Paul. He lived in Casper, Wyoming, with his foster parents, Mark and Rachel. His foster father, Mark, owned a construction company. Rachel was a regional manager for Whole Foods.

A two-hour drive north of the previous residence landed them at Leah's house—a two-story home painted bright yellow, with white lilies and red tulips as a flowerbed in front of the house. There was a white picket fence and a white-painted security door in the front. The neighborhood was seemingly upscale.

Aside from the kitchen and bathrooms, every room was carpeted. The carpet in each room was a matching bright pastel color of walls in every one of the five rooms in the house. But it was not furnished at all, just like the others. Except they didn't find a blank sheet anywhere in the house. Frazier began to get frantic and disturbed at not finding one.

They made their way to the garage and found it swept bare. Except it wasn't a garage to park a car or even store items. The garage was converted into a theater. Not the kind of theater to watch movies, but to watch and conduct plays and performances. A number of light bulbs behind lenses riddled the ceiling for lighting.

There was a small stage lifted up on a three-step platform. Four rows of six wooden high school auditorium–style seats. There were no windows, no curtains, but there were places that could have easily had a large curtain on stage and a few along the sides. But all was empty, except for the blank sheet sitting on top of the stage, as if on display. As if the blank sheet was the show. Up until this point, it was hard to argue that it wasn't. It sat near the front of the stage, under a slightly bigger light bulb than the others were in the place.

Frazier had a mixed feeling of relief of finding another blank sheet, then quickly suppressed it with dread at not knowing what it meant. Wiley maintained an incredulous look, all the while trying to be the first to put it all together in his mind.

Frazier didn't exactly go into trance, but he stood for a long moment, twirling the licorice root in his mouth, frowning. Both hands rested on his hips, drawing back the black trench coat.

"What was she, a director or something?" Wiley asked.

"I believe so. Maybe even a performer. Most likely drama."

Wiley stepped up onstage, inspecting the walls for any cracks or clues. "What makes you think that?"

"Just a hunch."

"Speaking of hunches. What were you talking about with Elsa Bowers?"

"That has nothing to do with a hunch."

"It's a segue, Frazier. I want to know what you two talked about."

"That's a terrible segue." His pose hadn't changed as he glanced around the room.

"Kyle!" The voice was forceful. And being in the closed-off garage/auditorium amplified it.

Frazier stopped twirling the root and turned to look at him with a most unreadable look. His tone was flat, but his attention was razor-sharp.

"I think you intended a different tone."

"What did you two talk about? I want to be filled in," Wiley asked, still raising his voice, chest heaving with anger.

Frazier stared at him for a long moment. "Before we headed out to Tina Wilson's house, Russell told you to do something. You remember what that was, don't you?"

Wiley only stared, knowing the answer. But then a sudden realization of surprise came over him. Frazier wasn't even in the room when it was said. How could he have possibly known? Unless it was already prediscussed. The chest heaving slowed. His frowned-up face began to soften.

"I thought you'd remember. Let me paraphrase what he told you to do. Just in case you forget again. Shut your damn mouth and do what the hell I tell you to do. Is that about right?" In most cases like this, Frazier would unceremoniously walk away from him like he didn't matter. But this time he stayed there, looking at him. Waiting.

This time, it was Wiley that walked away without a word, feeling defeated and angry at the same time. He went to the car and sat there waiting. Frazier took a look around again before leaving.

The stage was finished wood. The walls were painted burgundy. It seemed a symbolic message in contrast to the bright colors of the house and the drab colors in the theater.

He ran a hand along the base of the steps, feeling the smoothness while deep in thought. He sat down on the stage and looked outwardly at the chairs facing it. A thought hit him. He collected the blank sheet then walked out to check the last house.

> Tracy Collins: A criminal defense attorney in her midthirties. Not committed to anyone exclusively in a relationship but involved with more than seven men platonically. She grew up raised by her uncle Gerald, older brother of her mother, Gloria. Her mother had her at seventeen. The father, Oliver, was eighteen. After Tracy was born, they left her with Gerald while they fled the country against criminal charges.
> Gerald was strict in raising Tracy. He was always on her about her studies, manners, and public etiquette. They moved around a lot on account that he was a coronel in the United States Army. As firm as he was with her, she never felt he was unreasonable. He still found time to take her to the movies, play board games with her, even played tea parties with her as a little girl.

The house on record in which she resided in was swept clean with a blank sheet as well. There was nothing of notice in the place. She lived in a four-bed, two-bath house. Nothing fancy. Her front yard had artificial grass and small stones. It sat on the corner of a street, as she had never had any connection to her neighbors. No one knew anything about her other than she kept to herself. She turned down block party invitations and refused to participate any neighborhood meetings.

It was a dead end to any insight of her personally, until Frazier remembered a conversation he had with the server, Darwin Dane, at the Swinging Palms. He said she mentioned having a "pleasure house" instead of a room.

In her senior year in college, Uncle Gerald died in combat. He left her all his inheritance. She sold all his houses but kept one—a small one-bedroom, one-bath, stand-alone house. He used it as a storage unit in which she sold all the contents from it but kept the home, a home in which the two investigating agents were on their way to.

They arrived there close to nightfall. From the outside, the place looked about as homely and normal as any other. Both agents exited the car. Wiley spoke first.

"This doesn't look like much."

"Looks can be deceiving."

"It looks like some start-up house. The kind you find in a piss-poor neighborhood." He glanced around, frowning. "Actually. This is a piss-poor neighborhood."

"We still need to check it out."

Wiley gave a devious smile. "You just want to see what she's got in there, don't you? Get your jollies off, huh?"

Frazier only moved his eyes at him with his head facing forward, then back to the door as he made his way there without a response. He pulled out his lock-picking tools and opened the door. To their surprise, a second wooden door was there, a sliding one. They looked at each other for a quick second, then slid the door open.

The windows were lined with a mock picture film, the illusion of a kitchen or a bathroom, perfectly seen from a distance outside and disregarded as such. The smell of sweat and incense wafted through the house. The inner walls all were knocked out, expanding the place to just one loft. A bathtub, a toilet, and a sink sat in the far back left corner. Clearly, it was formerly a bathroom, which was now completely open, with no privacy to speak of. They surveyed the contents in the place.

"Whoa. This chick was a freak," Wiley commented with a hint of enthusiasm.

"No argument there."

"I mean look at this." Wiley tapped everything he spoke on with his pen. "She's got a sex swing, shackles for hands and feet on the wall. And check this out. Looks like some kind of locking device, like the kind they used to behead people in old times. It latches around your wrist and neck while, I guess, you bend over and take what you got coming to you." He chuckled to himself.

Frazier leaned forward, looking at a glass case on the wall. "She also has an array of tools." He pointed a lazy finger at the case. "Whips. Chains. Handcuffs. Tasers. Gags. Ridged paddles. A number of scented candles." He turned his head, raising his eyebrows and looking away. "And various other . . . orifice-plugging devices."

Wiley came next to him to get a look. He tilted his head at one item with interest. "Wow. Never seen one like that." Frazier turned back to see what he was commenting on. When he saw it, he also tilted his head then turned away to further investigate.

They turned on the light switch to find that it turned on in different colors—the colors of red, light green, or yellow in a dim tint. Frazier noticed a cage big enough to hold a silver back gorilla. It sat in a dark corner, where no light could reach it.

Frazier pulled out his mini flashlight to observe. He noticed a figure inside, a moving figure. He came closer and saw it was a man, naked, with his hands tied behind his back. He sat Indian-style and was blindfolded, with earplugs. But otherwise, he looked quite comfortable with his head leaning back against the cage.

He came closer when the man rose up and called out, "Mistress Tracy. I've been a good boy sitting here just like you said. But please, oh please, treat me like a bad boy again."

Frazier opened the cage to get a better look at him. Wiley grabbed him aggressively by the arm and yanked him out.

The man shouted joyfully, "Yes! Yes! Thank you, mistress. Thank you." He ran over to a table he obviously knew was there, willingly bent over it, spreading his legs apart with a big smile on his face. Showing no interest in trying to break from his tied hands and blindfold, he called over his shoulder, "Mistress, I would like the maximum if you don't mind. Please, mistress. Please."

Frazier and Wiley looked at each other then back at the man. Wiley holstered his gun then yanked off the man's blindfold and earplugs. The man turned around, about as excited as a spoiled kid on Christmas morning. The smile vanished when he saw the two agents standing there.

"Who, who are you two? Where's Mistress Tracy?" A concerned look etched his face then turned serious. "If you've done anything to here, I'll . . ." His words trailed off. His eyesight began to focus from being blindfolded. The man was in his midfifties and balding. He had no athletic build to speak of at all, but he was thin by most accounts, save for a small potbelly.

Wiley crossed his arms over his chest, while Frazier took a step forward to get a better look at him. "Goodness gracious, sir. You sure pulled the wool over everyone's eyes."

"You know this guy?" Wiley frowned in disgust as he asked.

"Why, this here is state council member Winston Bolton, responsible for proposition nineteen."

"Wait. You mean this is the state council guy that is leading the crusade to ban all adult entertainment? Claims that all nudity in movies, plays, books, cruise ships, beaches, and compounds should be abolished?"

"That's the one." Frazier nodded with a smirk on his face.

"The guy that paraded his wife and two daughters around to every public speech to show moral solidarity?"

"Once again, the same one." The smirked stayed etched.

"But that guy had commercials and pendants made with the slogan 'Making morality the only reality.'"

"And to think, here we find him locked up in some pleasure house, as a clear willing participant in . . ." He gestured both hands around the room in opposite directions, then moved them up and down at Bolton in his tied-up denigrated state. "Well, this."

Bolton stood up straight, tone frantic. "Look, gentlemen. Let's work something out. You guys are cops, right?"

Wiley scoffed. "Cops? I'm Special Agent Wiley of the Federal Bureau of Investigation. And this is my partner Special Agent Kyle Frazier."

"Please, Councilman, just call me Kyle."

A look of fright came over Bolton. "Look, I didn't break any federal laws, did I? I know this looks bad. But . . . but . . ."

"Enough with the *but* talk, Councilman. We saw the *butt* you had in mind." Wiley laughed at his own quip.

Frazier just looked at him with a straight face. Bolton dropped his head, feeling ashamed.

"Set him free, will you?" Frazier gestured with a head nod to Bolton. Wiley walked over to him to untie the knot. He stopped and lifted a finger at Bolton before going behind him.

"Now don't go bending over the table again, you understand? In fact, stand straight up. Keep your feet together. Stand straight as a pole. Although from the looks of it, standing poles seems like an issue for you. More like a crooked tent in the backyard on uneven ground." He laughed harder at that joke.

Bolton looked down at himself, feeling an even greater wave of shame as he rubbed his sore wrists and moved to quickly put on his clothes. "Listen, gentlemen. Perhaps we can work something out." He talked as he put his pants on. "Whatever you want, just name it. I have a lot of connections."

Frazier spoke in a playful, sarcastic tone. "Now, Senator, you wouldn't be speaking of bribing the feds, would you?"

Now dressed and buttoning up his shirt, Bolton licked his lips in an anxious manner. "No, no, no, not at all. I'm just saying . . ." He sighed in resignation. "Please. The people can't know about this, especially my family. I'm not trying to bribe you, but I'll do anything to keep this quiet."

"You're a pig, Bolton. A hypocritical pig. But you have the right to express yourself any way you please on your own time. Honestly, I could give a damn about your time or the law you're trying to pass. However, you will answer some questions for us."

"Absolutely," he answered eagerly. "Anything you want to know."

Frazier looked at Wiley, who understood the cue. He pulled out his pen and notebook as Frazier started asking questions. "Where did you meet Tracy Collins?"

"I met her at a fetish convention."

Wiley tilted his head with a smirk. "A fetish convention?"

"Yes. A convention where people meet and disclose their . . . sexual fetishes and desires."

"But wouldn't that be abolished if your prop nineteen law passes?" Frazier asked.

"It's completely anonymous. Plus, the membership fee would increase to maintain such anonymity."

"Ah, I see," Frazier responded. "This has nothing to do with a moral compass. This is an economic ploy. You're really nothing but a capitalist."

Bolton tucked in his shirt and shrugged, looking from one agent to the other. "Aren't we all?"

Frazier asked a question in response, "How long have you been here?"

"Since this morning. My wife thinks I'm in Utah, gathering votes from the Mormons. Please don't tell her."

"And how long have you known Tracy?"

"I just met her last week."

"You said the convention was anonymous. But you know her real name. Why is that?"

"Because she knows mine. She made me tell her in the heat of, you know. She wanted to know so she could rename me."

Wiley jumped in. "And what name did she give you?"

Bolton looked down in slight embarrassment before answering in a low voice, "Piddling."

"What? Speak up. I didn't hear you," Wiley chided.

Bolton rolled his eyes with a deep sigh, speaking up. "Piddling."

"What the hell does that mean?"

Frazier answered, "It's a synonym for *small*."

Wiley chuckled. "Well, it's fitting."

Frazier smirked a little before asking another question. "What else do you know about her?"

"Next to nothing. That's the beauty of the convention. We don't know anything that the other person doesn't want to disclose."

"And did she disclose anything to you?"

"Nothing of consequence."

"Answer the question, councilman. And do not lie!" Wiley roared.

Bolton shrank back at the verbal attack. "She only said that she drugs people that don't come willingly. I said I'll come willingly *and* take the drugs."

Wiley's patience was at an end. He took a step forward with the look in his eye that said he wanted to throttle the degenerate, hypocrite politician. Sensing the threatening motion, Bolton stepped back, bringing an arm over his face in an attempt to block an inevitable strike.

Wiley was stopped short by a vice grip around his wrist. He looked down at his wrist, then back up at Frazier, and yanked his arm back. Much to his surprise, the vice grip was still there. He yanked again, and still the same result. He turned to face Frazier with fire in his eyes and ice in his tone. "Let. Go."

Frazier maintained a mask of indifference as he decided, after a few more moments, to release the grip. The moment was tense. Earlier, there were many witnesses. This time, it was only one. And with the predicament they found him in, one can rest assured he wasn't going to be speaking to anyone.

Both agents stood face-to-face like two jocks in the hallway, waiting for the other one to move. Neither budged. Bolton took it upon himself to break the awkward silence.

"I think I'll be going now."

Frazier answered back, still eye to eye with his young counterpart. "Good idea."

Bolton uncomfortably shuffled around them in the narrow area and darted toward the door as soon as he had enough room. Just as he reached the door, Frazier called out to him, "Bolton."

The councilman paused as if he was just hit by a freeze gun, with his hand inches from the door handle. "Your mistress is dead. Never come back here again."

Bolton nodded and jetted out the front door. Frazier finally broke eye contact, only to watch Bolton leave and close the door. He then turned his glare back to the ball of fire standing in front of him.

Wiley shifted slightly on his feet, ready for a showdown. It felt like a long time coming. He licked his lips nervously, feeling a sudden tinge of fear. The vice grip was strong. Surprisingly strong. All bravado of believing he would win in a fight because he was younger went out the door as fast as Bolton did.

A quick smile found the face of Frazier. It quickly disappeared, leaving the mask of indifference again. Suddenly, as if he remembered something he forgot in the car, he did an about-face and walked out the door, leaving Wiley both extremely angry and equally relieved.

He gathered himself took one more look around and headed for the door. He was sick and tired of being bested. He wanted a way to even the score. Fighting was clearly too juvenile, and Frazier would never take the bait. Plus, Wiley began to doubt that he even wanted that anymore. He paused in midstride when a thought hit him. A sly smile etched his face. He nodded slightly to himself and walked out.

CHAPTER 13

DIVULGE

"I HAVE TO SAY, I'm surprised at this meeting. I never expected you to follow through." She held out her hand to shake.

"Right." He didn't return the gesture. He sat down, looking around in a paranoid manner. "Sit down."

"This isn't the kind of place I had in mind to meet."

"Well, we're meeting. And this is the place."

"I just thought we might meet at a café or restaurant."

"Are you that slow? You just named the two places that held the crimes. Good grief. Didn't they teach you nothing in broadcast journalism school?"

"Hey, you called me. I didn't come here to get insulted. And I'm a very accomplished and respected reporter. If you don't like it, you can find someone else. Someone not as good as me. I don't need this." She grabbed her purse next to her and moved to get up and leave.

"Wait." He held up a hand.

She paused in a crouched pose halfway to the chair and halfway getting up.

"You're right. I called you because you're the best. I would only trust the best with this anyway." He gestured a hand for her to sit down. She took the seat.

159

He knew he nearly crossed the line. That flippant tongue of his always got him trouble. But he did not apologize. Just a self-admission of a lack of tact. Far be it from him that he would actually admit true fault, let alone show remorse.

Clack. The sound of contact was made direct. The following sound was like a pipe being hit with a boulder for shaping. Hard and heavy. The ringing sound carried like a short echo. The sound was frequent. The occasional *clack* negated the sound of the ringing. But the sound of the thump from a short distance away also wasn't constant. Intermittent yet consistent at the same time. *Clack.*

She waved a hand in front of her face, staving off a small gust of dirt. The sun was at her back, bright but not hot. Slight breezes were the root cause of such a dirty disturbance.

"So why are we meeting at the batting cages?" she asked.

"Because I like baseball."

"I like mountains. But I wouldn't ask you to meet me on top of Everest."

He sighed. The sun was facing him instead. He wore silver-rimmed charcoal-gray-lensed sunglasses, a New York Yankees baseball hat, and a navy-blue buttoned-up polo shirt to match the hat. He sat with one arm draped across the top half of the bench he rested his back on. The other hand spun an envelope over and over on top a wooden tabletop.

He looked around, then settled his eyes on her. "You died your hair blond?"

She smiled with pride at recognition, throwing a hand through it near her left ear. "Yes. You like it?"

"You know what they say about bonds, right?"

Her smile faded, pride and confidence stamped out. A look of both hurt and anger took its place. "You're an ass. Do you always have to be so mean?"

"You asked if I liked it. I don't. I think it makes you look ridiculous. Truth be told, it makes it hard for me to take you seriously."

The anger surprisingly left and was replaced with a double dose of hurt. She worked her mouth in an attempt to respond but found no words. Suddenly, her eyes began to gather the slightest of mist in the corners while she stared at him. He noticed it and quickly moved on.

"At any rate, this is the perfect place to meet. I am, after all, on my day off. But let's get to it." He stopped spinning the envelope and held it up at eye level. "What I have here can make your career."

She blinked, wiping her right eye, pretending it was the dust that kicked up. She gathered herself. "I see. What exactly is it?"

"It's everything you want to know about the public homicide cases."

Her eyes grew large. "Wait a minute. You're giving me all the information that the feds have on the homicide cases?"

He maintained a serious look. "That's right."

"And what do you want in return?"

"Two things. Make sure it gets out to mainstream. Complete and correct as I give it to you. And of course, there is the small matter of anonymity."

"Don't worry. I never reveal my sources."

He grunted in a somewhat sound of approval, handing her the envelope. She leaned over and accepted it with a smile. "So, it's all here?"

"Everything. All the details from the parking lot, the evidence, or lack their off, all found during the follow-up, the identities of the suspects/victims, as well as the in-depth details of the café situation. There is a specific link between both of those occurrences, as well as all the participants. If you will."

"Participants? You mean these people did this as part of some cult or something?"

"That part is unknown at the moment. But what is known and significant is the evidence collected each time. So far it is still a mystery. But there is a clear connection."

"So what do you want me to do? What's the purpose of me getting this out?"

"The reasons are not your concern. But what *is* your concern is getting it out and the small matter of giving you a leg up in your career."

"Fair enough. And let me guess. You will call on me for a favor somewhere down the line, right?"

He looked at her meaningfully for a long moment, saying nothing. She could just make out his eyes in certain angles of the light. *Clack*. Another direct hit from the baseball bat. The sound of contact seemed to make his point very clear, that he virtually needed her for this deed for his own selfish reasons. It would most certainly boost her career to break a federally investigated story, with the details she had just been gifted.

"I may have use for you again."

"All right." She placed the envelope in her purse, rising up from her seat. "Well, thank you very much for this, Special Agent Wiley." She turned away, smiling.

"Gina." His voice was stern and direct. She paused in midturn, then turned back to him. He held out his hand in a manner of requiring something to place in it.

The smile faded when she saw that he wasn't smiling. She huffed, rolled her eyes, and handed him the tape recorder she hid in her purse. He placed it down on the table and put the hand back up again, beckoning for something else.

She looked at him with disbelief and began to turn again. "Gina Samuels." The voice was raised to a near roar. *Clack*. The sound filled the quick silence left after his voice.

"What am I supposed to do without it?" she asked.

"Not my problem."

She let out an exasperated breath and jammed her hand in her purse aggressively. She yanked out her phone then slammed it in his hand. A sarcastic smirk formed in the corner of his mouth.

She hefted her purse onto her shoulder and stormed away. He touched the screen on the phone, noticing it was also on voice record. "Reporters," he grumbled under his breath. He took out the sim card, then smashed it on the ground with a baseball ball bat he had lying near his feet.

He stood up, tossed the phone in the air, and sent it flying in dented pieces from the impact of the swing with the bat. He walked around to the other side of an empty cage, swiping his card before stepping to the batter's cage. He stepped to the plate, tapping his shoes twice on each side or the inside foot with the bat.

Setting both feet on opposite sides of the batter's plate, Wiley felt like a big-league hitter, hocking spit to the side, tilting his cap, and taking a few practice swings, readying himself. Right on cue, the ball released. He bit his lip, taking a mighty swing. *Clack.* Wiley stood there marveling at his hit. A sly grin appeared on his face, followed by a chuckle to himself.

He felt a sense of pride and accomplishment from the hit, but mostly from the play he orchestrated with the reporter.

"Let's see what you think about that," he said to himself, referring to the conversation when Frazier told him not to tell anything. He lined his feet up again, repeating the process. *Clack.*

CHAPTER 14

THE DOTS

"SO WHAT DO we know?"

"Right now, only this."

"But this doesn't give us anything to go on."

"You're right about that, Art. I'm just as stumped as you are."

Frazier stood in front of a wall in his office, looking at a timeline of all the evidence collected with the blank-sheet case. A pyramid design of the case locations was on display on the wall. On top sat a picture of the All Store parking lot. Underneath it on both sides were two other pictures—pictures of Walter Fray and David Brice.

They were set adjacent to each other. Right in between their pictures was the blank sheet of paper found in the car. Under those pictures were pictures of their homes with the addresses tagged and timed from when they visited. Under all of that was a picture of the Pots-N-Pans restaurant. Ursula was pegged with a yellow streak across it to signify not being a real concern.

The same was done next to her with pictures of the Callahans, Harvey Newman, and Lane Cooper. Continuing the downward slope in information intel of the design were photos of Tina Wilson, Leah Washington, and Tracy Collins at the Swinging Palms Café. Yvonne Marsden and Darwin Dane held small spots in the corner, connected with the café.

Dates, times, and address were also provided for them as well. Blank sheets being the common denominator were highlighted in on the wall next to each picture. He stood there observing intently. His left elbow rested on the back of his right hand. As his right arm draped across his stomach, he twiddled with the licorice root in his mouth.

FBI Director Art Russell sat back in Wiley's chair with his feet propped up on the desk, interlocking his fingers behind his head. "So this is really all we have, isn't it?"

Still staring intently with his back to him, Frazier answered, "Afraid so."

"So the only substantial evidence we have are these damn blank sheets."

It wasn't a question. Russell knew the whole story. He leaned back in the chair, throwing almonds in his mouth. Frazier didn't even acknowledge the comment. He was in deep thought as to what it all meant.

He was broken out of his thoughts when he heard Russell speak to someone entering the room.

"Wiley. Where have you been?"

Wiley suddenly felt a twist of anxiety seeing Russell not only in his office but in his chair, asking him where he was. The thought suddenly hit him that he was only saying it in just a form of small talk or greeting. It was, after all, his day off yesterday. It's not like he was missing for two straight days.

Frazier didn't take the day off. He rarely did. He spent two weeks setting up the timeline on the wall all by himself. But when he stepped out of the office for a second, Wiley quickly took pictures. He combined that with copies of the reports he'd written up and gave it all to Gina Samuels. The funny thing about resentment is that it allows no room for reason.

He found himself disliking Frazier so much he wanted to do something he knew would truly get under his skin. Up until this point, Frazier had been successfully getting under Wiley's skin with splendid regularity. After their discovery of Senator Bolton, the thought hit him on how to get back at him.

He was going to do the one thing Frazier appeared to be the most serious about. And that was not leaking anything about the case to the media, the exact thing he just did yesterday with Gina Samuels.

"I was just bringing some coffee on the way in, sir." He handed a cup to Russell, who took it gladly. He sat his cup down on his desk. Russell stood up from the chair then moved out of the way.

"Thanks, Norman." He pointed at Frazier, still in thought with his back toward them. "You didn't get him one?"

"You're holding it, sir." It was a lie. He meant for it to go to Russell the whole time. He passed by his office with the intent to step in and hand it to him, something to make him soften the blow the bureau would get for the info he leaked. Granted no one knew he did it, but it would have made him feel better.

But the feeling of knowing it would upset Frazier made anything that would come afterward worth it. Or rather, almost anything. Frazier continued to ignore the exchange.

Russell took a loud sip of his coffee, clearly having no intention of giving it up. He held the cup up as if he was giving a toast, raising his eyebrows to Wiley, apparently pleased with the taste. He took another loud sip. "What's on your mind, Kyle? What are you thinking?"

Still with his back turned, he answered in a bland tone. "Of a lot of things."

Wiley frowned as he sat down in his chair, holding his cup up to his mouth. He hated how everyone else was treated as if they were all on Frazier's schedule to know anything. Or more specifically, him. Annoyance spilled from his tone. "Can you give us something? Anything at all? We may even have some thoughts that you simply can't figure out on your own, you know."

He half turned over his left shoulder to look at Wiley, then turned back to the wall. He pointed at each mark with his licorice root. "Brice and Fray fought in the parking lot of the All Store around ten in the morning. They ate breakfast first, at Pots-N-Pans."

"Yes, Frazier. We already know that. Tell us something we don't know," Wiley commented.

"They live in completely opposite directions. They work in totally different fields. We found no link of a social circle they may be a part of. Yet they were riding together in this car." He pointed at the picture of the Mustang. "They didn't meet at this place. They were in the same car."

"That's got me baffled too, Kyle." Russell spoke while still enjoying his coffee. Frazier made like he never heard him. He continued like he was just speaking out loud.

"On the scene, two young medics pulled the knives out of Fray and Brice. With permission from these two officers. Bill Green and Tom Burns." He pointed at each of them, also on the board.

"What did we do about the medics tampering with federal evidence?" Russell asked. Wiley smirked at the question, waiting to see if Frazier had an explanation to offer the boss. He mentioned the same thing on the scene. It's a serious thing, tampering with federal evidence.

Frazier waved a dismissive hand. "They're just kids. They did what they were told."

Russell didn't press. He dismissed it as well. Wiley nearly fell out of his chair of how Frazier was allowed to get away with that. Russell put a hand in his pants pocket, still holding the coffee in his other hand as he asked more questions.

"What about the officers?"

"They got a pass in light of owing us later."

Russell nodded in approval. Wiley hid his disgust in his cup of coffee as he drank. "And who are those people there?" Russell asked.

"The Callahans. Doug and Shelly. Seem like good-enough people. They gave the rundown first. They even came in and issued their report formally. The background check we did on them came up clean. Doug served in the army. Shelly is a homemaker."

"And that kid there?"

"Lance Norris. Gave us the name Derek Cooper at first. An alias. He's trying to start up a website that catches public occurrences, then reports them. I have to say, he's got a hell of a business plan. But we can't allow this getting out before we can control it. When we placed a fake file in front of him, he sang like the opera on a Saturday night. He's also just a kid, and an aspiring entrepreneur at that."

"That file was fake? It was empty?" Wiley asked.

He turned around to answer, arms still in the same position. "Well, not empty. It was a list of recipes I had Sanderson's wife type out for me. There's a spicy venison stew she makes that's to die for." He trailed off in thought, tilting his head up with closed eyes blissful in memory.

Russell closed his eyes in remembrance as well. "Ah. I remember when she made that at the Christmas party last year. Damn, that *was* delicious." He smiled, then his eyes suddenly snapped open. "Oh, what about those chocolate dipped scones? Did she give you that recipe too?" he asked excitedly.

Frazier nodded, grinning. "And the chicken alfredo nachos."

Russell closed his eyes again and made the sound of a small whimper, as he recalled the dazzling array of flavors. He paused suddenly and opened one eye, noticing Wiley was staring at him. He cleared his throat and continued to ask questions. "And the server. The lady right there. What's her story here?"

He turned back to the wall and pointed at her. "Ursula Jennings. Honest, hardworking lady. She bust her hump to take care of her troublesome kid brother. They tipped her handsomely."

Wiley butted in. "Frazier did some freaky thing where he knew all about her. It was like some weird fortune-teller thing. Although, I don't believe in that sort of thing. You never told me how you knew so much about this random girl." He looked back at Frazier.

"And nor will I."

Wiley looked back at Russell with his hands spread as if he was looking at a father to say something to the difficult older brother. But he only shook his head and continued to ask about the case. "How generous are we talking about?"

"Fifteen hundred dollars."

Russell made a whistle in response. "That's a handsome ransom for a tip. I used to wait tables in college. The most I ever got was nine bucks."

Frazier half turned, grinning. "You must not have been very good."

"I was freaking horrible," he answered, half chuckling. "But more power to the young lady. What about Brice?"

"There was no one to speak with at Brice's house. His landlord was out of town. But we spoke with Harvey Newman, the hotel manager where Fray lived." He tapped his picture as he spoke the man's name. "But he gave us nothing we could use."

Russell looked intently, scanning the wall as Frazier went from picture to picture, explaining. Wiley turned his back to Russell in the chair so that he could roll his eyes at Frazier when he spoke. One of the more childish moves one can do.

Frazier went on to go over the particulars of the café brawl. "At the Swinging Palms, we have three women this time." He pointed at each woman. "Leah Washington, Tina Wilson, Tracy Collins."

"And there's no connection between these three women other than they were at the café together and beating the hell out of each other?" Russell asked, pointing only the index finger on his right hand, holding the coffee cup with the other four.

Wiley chimed in with a response. "That's right, sir. And even though they destroyed the chips for their cell phones, we were still able to get someone to retrieve their phone records. None of them ever called one another."

Russell nodded slowly in thought as he sipped more coffee. "And who are those people?"

Frazier took the reins again. "This is Yvonne Marsden, best-selling author. She was sitting not too far from them with her dog, Hanna."

Russell took a sip, chuckling. He leaned down toward Wiley, speaking low. "Who thinks to add a person's dog in a timeline? Sometimes Kyle be a real nutjob, heh?" He grinned, nudging an elbow against Wiley's shoulder.

Wiley returned the grin. Not that he thought it was funny, he just was grinning because the boss shared a joke with him.

"Perhaps I am. But when investigating a case, everything is relevant." He clearly heard the comment behind his back, but he didn't turn around to answer.

Russell's eyes grew large, raising his eyebrows as he looked down at Wiley. He tucked his lips, showing a playful mock gesture of a student getting in trouble with a teacher. Wiley returned a half grin. Frazier continued.

He pointed to the young man in the photo. "Darwin Dane here was their initial server. He spoke with all three women. He said they seemed to be having decent conversation until this one," he pointed at Tracy, "started talking about making him her sex toy and whatnot, renaming him and even drugging him if need be."

Russell's eyes went up as the cup stopped halfway to his mouth before slowly dropping it back down. "Drugging him? What kind of drugs?"

"He didn't say. He did say that this one," he pointed to Leah, "took great exception with the way she was talking. And this is the one that tipped him." He pointed at Tina. "Oh, and take a wild guess how much the tip was."

"Don't tell me fifteen hundred dollars too."

Frazier nodded. "And not only that." He pointed back at Yvonne. "She claims to have found an envelope in her computer bag. After, she noticed her computer was damaged from being used in the brawl. Want to take a stab at what was in the envelope?"

"Fifteen hundred for her too?"

"Indeed."

Gina Samuel was noticeably absent from the wall, a good thing too. After Wiley leaked information to her, he didn't exactly want her to hang for it. But that's only because he would hang for being the source. Also missing from the wall was Councilman Bolton. Frazier kept his word.

"And this house they talked about Collins having?"

"Wiley." Frazier turned completely around, gesturing his head.

It put Wiley in a spot. They gave their word they wouldn't speak on the councilman. But then again, he gave his word he wouldn't leak evidence. But not only did he leak information, he gave away the whole damn case thus far. Step-by-step. However, he felt no shame provided that he left it in Gina's hands to tell the world about the case. The way he saw it, he just merely passed over an envelope.

He went on to give details about the house they found. "It was like an underground adult store in there. To be honest with you, it was too much to actually state, sir. So I'll just say, you name it and it's there."

Russell gave Frazier a questioning look of confirmation. The look was returned with a nod. He looked back at Wiley and saw an expression on his face. "What is it? There's more?"

Wiley looked to Frazier, who gave him the patented poker face, then back to Russell. "Yeah, sir. There is. She had a couple of cages there. One had a person in it."

"Was this a dead person?"

"Not at all, sir."

"Oh no. Don't tell me it was a kid."

"No, no. Nothing like that."

Russell threw his hands up impatiently. "Well, spit it out."

"It was Winston Bolton, sir."

Russell frowned, looking down in thought. "Winston Bolton. The councilman?"

Both Frazier and Wiley nodded seriously. "What the hell was he doing in the cage? Was he kidnapped?"

"Actually, sir. We found him tied at the hands, naked, and blindfolded sitting Indian-style. He had earplugs, but when he thought he heard something, he called out for his . . . mistress to do more to him."

Russell shook his head with his eyes closed, as if trying to wake himself up from a long nap. "Whoa, wait a minute. Are you saying that Councilman Winston Bolton, the guy crusading over sexual morality, was into S&M with Collins?" He pointed at her picture on the wall.

"That's exactly what we're saying, sir. He even bent himself over a table, asking for something to be—"

"I get it. I get it, Wiley." He waved his hand, cutting him off. "How about that? Well, I guess the adult shop around the corner of my house is safe for a while. Let me tell you. There's more than a few items I bought there that really spiced up things with me and Mrs. Russell." He smiled devilishly.

"How charming," Frazier interjected. "But we gave him our word we wouldn't mention him. I'm sure he'll back off the crusade a little though." Frazier turned back to the wall. "At any rate, we have two live brawls, both resulting in massive damage and death. Plenty of witnesses and nothing in their homes that speaks of them."

He chewed the licorice root in thought. "We haven't found any connection of acquaintance they have to each other, but we know they all were doing well in their respective careers. We can't even find a freaking Facebook link between them." He walked to the wall and removed a tack holding up a paper, looking at it as he spoke.

"All we have is this damn blank sheet." He paused in midchew, and his eyes grew large as he gave the look of receiving a revelation. He turned back to look a Russell and Wiley. He counted off the numbers with his other hand.

"Two public brawls. Both ending in murder. Two for the first. Males. Three for the next one. Females. Five blank sheets found in their homes. One in the car, one in each purse." He turned back to the wall, still holding up the last number he counted. "What number is missing?"

Wiley answered, in an antagonistic tone. "Four. But if you count up the one from the car and the ones in the purses, there's your four. So what's your point?"

Frazier turned back around, ignoring the would-be vibe. "Five will get you ten. There will be another brawl. Except this time, it will be two males and two females."

Wiley didn't back off. "All right, hold up. If we use your math on this, it doesn't add up to come to this equation of four."

Frazier looked back and forth between him and Russell. "The two homes of the men had one each. The one in the car added up to three. The three ladies' homes had one each. The purses offset themselves with the number except for one thing. Collins had an extra sheet in her purse."

Russell raised his eyebrows. Wiley threw his hands up in exasperation and brought his chair upright from the leaned-back position he held. "What are you talking about? You held out that information?" He was furious. That's one piece of evidence he didn't know about to give to Gina Samuels.

Frazier ignored him. "I'm telling you, Art. This blank sheet thing is a mystery for the ages. Not sure how to crack this one."

Russell raised the cup like a toast. "I believe in you, Kyle. Nobody gets the job done like you."

Wiley couldn't believe this bit of information was hidden from him. All the more reason he felt good about leaking what he did. But he was brought out of his vengeful thoughts by something Russell said.

"Well, at least we have the element of concealment on our side. If the press got wind of this and spread it to the masses, we'd be in it waist deep, boys. We have to maintain full competence. Or at least the perception of it."

Frazier nodded once then turned back to study the wall. Wiley nodded then looked down at his hands folded on the desk, playing the role.

CHAPTER 15

NEWS

THE THOUGHT ALONE sends one into a myriad of emotions, when the desire is strong enough. Few things in life are better when it's good. However, when it's bad, few things in life are worst. But when it's good, it's good. It causes you to do things you weren't even aware you were doing. And once you realize you're doing it, you don't really care.

You make faces, throat moans, dance a little bit, and even smile. Definitely smile. That's what was happening at this very moment. His eyes rolled, his shoulders slumped as if all strength was sapped out of him. He couldn't exactly find the words to voice his pleasure, so he moaned. First low, then louder.

"Oh. My. God. Jessica, this Peking duck is terrific."

She smiled broadly. Proudly. And utterly relieved at the praise she received. "Thank you, Kyle. I'm so glad you like it. I added some special ingredients for you."

Still chewing and eye rolling, Frazier responded after he swallowed. "Well, I'll tell you what. That ingredient is damn sure special." He sat at the table with his cutting knife in his right hand, his fork in his left. He had everything you wanted in a full-course meal.

Pan-seared Peking duck, brown rice risotto with green onions, honey-roasted bell peppers with fresh parsley and almonds, fresh garlic bread, and Merlot red wine. For dessert, she made caramel-coated brownies topped with vanilla bean ice cream.

What was the occasion? Simple. It was a celebration. She was celebrating the fact that he finally agreed to come over her house and have dinner. She wanted to impress him. So far, mission accomplished. Still holding the fork in his right hand, he lightly pounded a fist on the table.

"Awe. The risotto is delicious. And the bell peppers. The bread is super fresh. Can't wait to try that dessert. Where did you learn to cook like this?"

She smiled, sitting across the table no more than three feet from him. "My brother is a chef in Seattle. I called him for all my recipes."

"Well, tell big brother it turned out perfectly." He wiped his mouth with the handkerchief he tucked in front of his shirt.

"How did you know he's my big brother?" She maintained the smile but was genuinely curious.

"Oh, just a hunch." He winked.

"Have you been checking up on me, Special Agent Kyle Frazier?" The smile remained, a pretty smile showing her pearly white teeth.

"Of course." He cut another piece of duck and ate it, not looking up at her when he spoke. "I check on everyone whose house I enter."

The smile slightly dropped. Slightly. "So you know pretty much all about me?"

Still looking down, cutting and chewing, he said, "Pretty much."

The smile left completely. "I'm not sure how I feel about that. It's kind of an invasion of privacy."

Noticing not only the tone but the mood changed, he paused in midmotion with the fork halfway to his mouth. A red bell pepper dangled lightly at the pause in motion. He met her eyes. She wasn't angry. She looked more hurt than anything. "I'm sorry. I didn't mean to upset you." His apology was sincere.

She looked down into her plate. "You could've just asked me anything you wanted to know. That's what normal people do. That's what getting to know someone is about. Communicating with them.

Not researching their deepest, darkest secrets without them being aware of it."

He put down his silverware and reached over to take both her hands in his. It was the most affectionate gesture he had ever given her. She suddenly felt a rush of excitement and was no longer bothered. She looked into his eyes—eyes that said he meant what he said and did what he meant.

"I sincerely apologize. I guess it's just an old habit of mine. Yet and still, it is no excuse. You're right. I should just ask you. But I did say pretty much. I don't know it all." His smile was broad. The disturbed mood melted away like ice in a bucket of boiling hot water.

They stared at each other for a long moment. The moment was broken when Missy stepped on the remote control in the living room. The surround-sound was turned all the way up because Jessica was listening to a program earlier when preparing the dinner.

She was startled then got up to rush over and turn it off. Frazier began to go back to eating, when he saw Gina Samuel. She was sitting at the report desk, doing her job. Behind her was a still picture of the All Store parking lot. The next picture was the Swinging Palms Café.

He paid her very little mind, eating what was on his fork. He was in midchew when he saw her pull out a blank sheet. He suddenly froze. He strained to hear what she was saying while Jessica turned down the volume, then turned it off.

"Jessica, turn that back on." She felt the urgency in his voice and saw it on his face. She quickly turned it back on. "Turn it back up, please." She obliged. He listened to Gina giving her broadcast report.

"Rules out the thought of a serial killer. However, with this new evidence surfacing, it's quite clear that these blank sheets are linked to the two cases, making it one case." A picture of Brice and Fray appeared on the screen, followed by the car they were in. She went on.

"Both of these gentlemen, identified as David Brice and Walter Fray, were seen driving in this car. After they engaged in their mortifying display of violence on each other, a blank sheet of memo pad paper was found in the trunk of their car. No other item was found.

It was swept clean like it was brand-new. Not even a spare tire or a piece of gum wrapper was found inside. Nothing except for this blank sheet." The screen showed a picture.

"A public display of despicable carnage such as this has been taken over by the FBI. Upon further investigation, the FBI went to both of the residents of these two gentlemen. They found the homes swept clean as if they were never lived in. A few of their neighbors spoke to the feds, admitting to seeing these people prior to their involvement.

"It is known that the two males live nowhere near each other. They work in completely different fields and are believed to have virtually no internet connection between them."

She went on to report everything—the place that Fray and Brice ate at, the tip they left, the cleaning solution they used, everything.

Frazier gripped the knife and fork hard in each hand. His eyes blazed with rage. Information regarding the case had been leaked. And he knew instantly who the faucet was. Samuels went on.

"The three women at the Swinging Palms have been identified as the Tina Wilson, Leah Washington, and Tracy Collins." A picture of each woman appeared. "After the carnage they caused, their purses were found with nothing in them but a blank sheet in each.

"The connection is clear. The FBI further investigated their homes that ultimately were the same empty shell of real estate the first two assailants had. No marks on the walls from hanging items. No scrapes from a moved refrigerator. Not even a piece of lint from a pulled-up carpet.

"None but a blank sheet of paper was found in various spots in the homes. These women, like the men earlier, are also not linked according to the investigation. After pulling their phone records, no numbers were alike. No mutual call or received numbers. Not even the numbers of one another.

"The only place that held items in it under ownership was one that belonged to Tracy Collins." She showed the picture again. "The home was found to be a sexual play pen for sadomasochism. The most stunning revelation was the person they found in the house."

A picture of Winston Bolton showed up. It was a picture of him at the podium of a convention, pushing his agenda of proposition nineteen. "Councilman Bolton was found stripped naked and bound at the wrists. He was blindfolded with earplugs. When he was approached by the two agents, he was said to think it was time for him to continue with his willing participation."

Jessica let out a small chuckle, covering her mouth. She glanced over at Frazier, and her smile quickly faded. The heat in his eyes told her that something was wrong with this update. Samuels continued.

"One would have to assume that the crusade of Councilman Bolton and the ballet of proposition nineteen no longer has the legs it once did. As for the blank-sheet case, we can only rely on the vigilance of the FBI to bring this thing to a close before another debacle occurs.

"You heard it here first. I'm Gina Samuels, KLPN."

Jessica didn't have to ask. She got the sense that Frazier had seen enough. She turned the television off and slowly turned to him. He did not meet her eyes but slowly sat back in his chair. He looked as if he was going to suddenly leap out of the chair and become a tornado of carnage.

Gina Samuel had laid the case bare for the world to see. All their evidence. All their casework. The identities of the people involved. Even the identity of the now-ruined councilman. His face was a mask of calm. The quiet before the storm. His chest rose and fell slightly.

She wasn't sure what was going to happen. A seemingly beautiful evening went to hell quickly. Nothing good ever comes from watching the news. She thought to slowly make her way back to the table and place a calming yet cautious hand on his right wrist, the one that held the knife.

As she made her way over to him, she began to realize that his eyes hadn't moved. They weren't fixed on her, but rather the direction she was previously in. "Are you all right?" she said it slowly and carefully.

He said nothing. He continued to stare, breathing evenly. But the grip on the utensils seemed to tighten. She asked again in an equally sounding tone and cadence as she did before. "Kyle, are you all right?"

His eyes found her, only his eyes. Then his head turned toward her. He observed the look on her face—the look of care, worry, concern, fear. A slow smile broke across his face, a genuine smile. Like there was nothing in the world that bothered him. "I'm fine, Jessica."

"You looked pretty upset when that reporter was talking. Is that the case you said you couldn't talk about?"

He started eating again. He might have been upset, but he wasn't going to let that disrupt the best meal he had in a long while. He can't cook, after all. His wife did all the cooking. And she left him some time ago. "That's the one."

"Is everything she reported true? About the councilman and everything?"

"Sure is." There was no reason in keeping it confidential now. The whole damn case just went viral.

"I would have never guessed. About the councilman, that is. The whole finding of the blank sheets had to be bizarre, wasn't it?"

He continued to cut and chew, sip his wine, cut and chew, and sip some more. He nodded, not wanting to answer with a full mouth. He looked her in the eye but no longer had the blaze of brimstone in them.

"Did those people really not know each other?" He nodded, still chewing. He had a few bites left to finish.

"And do you have any idea what the cause or root or whatever it is that makes these people do this?"

He paused with the last bite in his mouth. His eyes stared directly at her. She went rigid. Sensing she was asking too many questions, she held up a hand. "I'm sorry. I'm overstepping. I do that sometimes."

She really did. She was a big believer of giving people space and time. She was just so excited to have him over that she lost her wit. He finished chewing before asking her in a polite tone. "May have some of that delicious-looking dessert, please?"

She sprinted off, happy to comply. They sat and ate and talked for hours. She wanted to ask him to stay over but thought better of it. He showed no signs of wanting to anyway. He appeared unfazed by his mood when the news was on. They laughed and shared stories. He even played with Missy for a little while.

He knew Wiley leaked the information. And he knew why he did it. But it had been a long time before he enjoyed the company of another woman, especially one near his equal in intelligence. They talked about books, movies, food, and travel. He wasn't about to let Wiley have control over him by ruining his evening.

He walked home six hours later, around one thirty in the morning.

CHAPTER 16

CONFLICT

"WELL, YES, IT is great. But you've already been gone for a while now. No, that's . . . that's not what I meant. Of course, I want . . ." He let out a deep sigh, resigning to give up on a potential argument.

"All right, all right. You go ahead. Yes. Yes, I do mean it. What do you mean you want to hear me say it? I just said it. I said go ahead, didn't I?" His ire began to rise. He held the phone on the right side of his head with his right hand.

His left hand covered his eyes, massaging his temples with his thumb and middle finger. "No, I'm not happy about it, Marla. Because you've been gone for too long. Oh, well, excuse me if I miss my wife."

He stood with his back leaning against a high counter kitchen. His tones went from confused to angry to sarcastic, pretty much the scope of his overall personality. He eventually realized he was in a no-win situation, so he decided to at least let the conversation end peacefully.

"Look, honey. Of course, I support you in all you do. It was my idea for you model, wasn't it? Exactly. So, no, I'm not saying I want you to stop. And no, I'm not saying it's causing a strain on our marriage. I just miss you, that's all."

He sighed another deep breath then finally released the hand from his face. "I love you too. Call me next week after your shoot. I don't care what time it is. All right, honey, bye." He tapped the hang-up button on his phone, breathing deeply, holding the phone away from him.

"And thank you very much, Christina. You can't imagine how stressed out I've been." His maid arose from a kneeling position in front of him. She ran the back of her wrist across her mouth.

"Of course, Mr. Wiley."

"What was that?" He leaned slightly forward, eyes wide, pointing an admonishing finger at her.

"Oh, sorry. I mean Special Agent Wiley."

He relaxed his demeanor, grinning triumphantly. She stood there looking downcast, eyes shifting from the floor to his face a number of times. She suddenly leaned in to kiss him as he jerked his head back and turned it. "Hey, what the hell are you doing?"

"Sorry, Special Agent Wiley." She dropped her head shyly. "I just . . ." Her words trailed off.

He grabbed her by the shoulders, turning her around toward the door. He gave her a little shove, but it was enough to make her nearly trip in her heels.

She had no strong feelings for him. She was a refugee from a third world country, and he was her federal agent employer. Whenever she tried to explain to him the dire straits here family was in back home, he waved her off. She wasn't particularly fond of the "extra work" she did for him.

Quite frankly, she might not have mind as much if he was nicer. Or if it was at least satisfying. But he was incapable of doing either. She had no skills and no education. She was very shy. She hardly spoke. And if she did, it was just a little above a whisper.

Christina wasn't considered by many as a beautiful woman. She had clammy skin and a long flat nose. To her face, he said that her nose looked as if it was smashed in with a cast iron skillet. His wife, Marla, called her fluffy. Her sides overlapped the rim of her pants around the midsection. She had long stringy hair and a full set of lips, narrow eyes, and a dimpled chin.

Marla took great delight in playing the high school "mean girl" role with her. She hardly ever passed up on an opportunity to say something regarding the contrast of their looks. The docile Christina didn't have it in her to stand up for herself. So she took everything Marla said about her to her face. Graciously.

But if she knew what her husband did with her when she wasn't around, it just might be a double murder. Wiley cared nothing for Christina. He just wanted his needs met by someone he didn't have to go out and meet when his wife was away. The thing he enjoyed about the situation the most was the superiority he felt when doing it.

A woman of a lesser ilk than he, willfully bending to his every whim on command, no reluctance, no debate, no compromise, and definitely no rejection—that was the ultimate turn on for him. He always had to have control. The only problem was, he married a woman that was the complete opposite of that. However, he did that purposely as a balance. If his wife was completely subservient and docile, he would bore quickly.

The arrangement he had with Christina enabled him to light the fire of the "big man on campus" whenever the mood struck him. "Christina." She made for the door and stopped when he called her.

"Yes, Special Agent Wiley?" She had worked for him for three years. And he still made her call him special agent.

"Expect to stay late tomorrow." He offered a devilish grin.

She dipped her head in a reluctant bow and left out the front door. A soon as she walked out, Frazier stepped in right before the door closed.

Wiley's smile abruptly disappeared. "What the hell are you doing here?"

"We need to talk."

"No. No. What the hell are you doing in my house?" His ire was rising.

"Okay. I'll say it slower." He used hand gestures as if trying to convey his point to someone that spoke a different language. "You. And I. We. Need. To. Talk."

"Get out! Get the fuck out of my house!" He stormed over, pointing to the door. "How did you get here? How did you get past my security? How do you know where I live?" Then it dawned on him. Frazier knew all about Wiley's past—intimate things of his past.

He ran it down to him before. If he could find those things out, then finding out where Wiley lived and how to get past his security wasn't too far-fetched. Yet and still, he couldn't stand the man. And the last place he ever wanted to see him was in his own house.

He left the dogs in the backyard. But they still had a means to reenter the house. He was hoping they would sense his angst and attack. He wouldn't even pull them off if they did. As far as he was concerned, Frazier was trespassing. Federal agent or not.

The veteran agent looked determined, upset. The poker face had tales this time. No licorice root in his mouth, and no reading glasses resting on the bridge of his nose. But why was he here?

The thought hit Wiley. He saw the news. Gina Samuels did her job and did it well. The anger on Frazier's face brought the boil in Wiley down to a low simmer. He even felt a small smirk cut across his face. He finally got a one up on him.

Frazier took a few steps forward until they were virtually face-to-face. "You were the one that leaked the case details." It wasn't a question.

The smirk widened to a grin, to a full smile. He extended his head forward, raised his eyebrows, and pursed his lips. The he spoke in mocking baby talk form. "Aww, what de madder? Did I make a booboo? Did I spoil your widdle pwans? Did I break one of your widdle wules?"

Quicker than a flea can jump, he felt it—a sharp, gripping pain in his throat. He found himself gasping for air. Instinctively, he brought both of his hands to his throat, but it didn't help with the breathing. His eyes bulged then closed.

He coughed fiercely, trying to catch a decent breath in between. He doubled over, then bent on top of the counter he was just at. Frazier stood stoic, watching him scramble. The hit came so quick and sudden it didn't even look like he struck him. But he did. Wiley finally caught a few legitimate breaths, then opened the drawer at the counter.

He snatched out a meat tenderizer and turned to face Frazier. With fire in his eyes and a hand still on his throat, he stalked forward, ready to pound him like a slab of beef. He raised the weapon up around his right ear and swung a completely telegraphed swing at Frazier's head.

Frazier stood there, unmoving. Then, within a fraction of a second before getting hit, he dodged the swing. In one full motion, he caught Wiley's arm and tossed him aside effortlessly. Wiley put the force of hatred and rage behind it. If he had connected, there would be some explaining to do, followed by a plea bargain. But instead, he found himself hitting hard on the marble.

He got up with new rage, charging the intruder with another swing with bad intentions. Frazier caught the wrist in mid descent and held it there, frozen in time. His face was a mask of calm. Wiley's was a mask of a rabid dog.

He brought the other hand up to grab Frazier by the shirt, but that hand was stopped too. With both of his wrists caught in vice grips, Wiley boiled over even more. He thrashed, trying to free his hands, grunting, growling, and snarling. At first glance, he looked the stronger of the two. He was younger, taller, and appeared in better shape.

Besides the fact that he usually wore the standard federal white buttoned-up shirt and black blazer with a black tie, as mundane as the uniform was, he seemed to love it. Frazier wore virtually the same, except he always wore a trench coat in place of a blazer. But not today.

It was morning time, around seven o'clock. He wore his black slacks and white shirt. But no tie. His cuffs were rolled up and unbuttoned. His trench coat must have been in the car. Wiley was still in comfort clothes. He wore gray sweat pants for the easy access he just participated in with Christina. And he was shirtless.

After a few seconds of jostling, Wiley found himself effortlessly flung to the very counter he was at again. This time, sliding to the floor. He looked up in a mix of more anger and amazement. But anger took hold. He charged at Frazier, screaming like a medieval times Viking, with the meat tenderizer raised high above his head.

Frazier stepped forward, dropped to one knee, and shoved his right palm into the solar plexus. Wiley's yelling was cut off abruptly. He froze at the hit, as if he was shot with an ice gun. His mouth agape, his eye bulged.

Frazier applied a headlock throw, turning his body sideways. All in one swift motion. He tossed Wiley over his right hip, sending him meeting the floor again. Harder this time. The weapon skittered across the floor, in a corner opposite of them.

Wiley lay there, clutching his chest with both hands. A small whimper escaped as he tried to gather himself, rolling on the floor. Again. Wiley lived in his house for two years now. And he had never been so intimate with his floor until now, other than the times he was there with Christina.

Marla, the debutant she was, wouldn't be caught dead on the floor. She would crawl her dying carcass to a chair and throw her head back in a vanity pose before she ever lay on a floor. The floor was something he found exotic and enticing. Until Now.

He slowly made it to his knees, with his head down. He fixed his feet in a semi track and field start pose. The right foot planted behind him, while his left foot balanced on his toes. His right hand stayed across his chest, while his left made it to the floor for bracing.

Frazier watched the whole ruse with detailed calculation. He knew Wiley was attempting a full charge, an attempt to spear him in the gut with his shoulder. He stood stoic with his back straight, waiting for the futile attempt.

Wiley charged just as expected. This time he didn't yell like an idiot. He gave no grunt or verbal indication as to his charge. He used every bit of burst he could. He shot for Frazier's legs, intending to take out his bass, sending him to the floor for once, then mount him and pound him like a loose tile.

His charge was swift. But to no avail. Frazier brought his right palm down on the back of Wiley's head, just as his fingers came within an inch of grabbing. He dropped to the floor face-first, like a book off a bookshelf.

More shock than pain ran through his body as he lay at Frazier's feet. He craned his head, looking up at him slowly. As soon as they made eye contact, Frazier grabbed him by the scruff of his neck with a painful grip. He flung him to the opposite side of the kitchen to meet a stand of dishes.

The stand dropped on top of him with a loud crash. Every dish on it shattered on the ground. He angrily swung and kicked broken dishes off him and saw the tenderizer in the corner. He snatched it up and stood to his feet.

He suddenly felt in no hurry to get back up and rush at him again. He was hurt. The face-off looked as if the bully finally got his due. He stood there huffing and puffing. Frazier was breathing evenly. Once he figured there would be no more charges, he spoke.

"You wanted my attention? You got it." He pointed a finger downward. "This is the penalty for what you did."

"I'll kill you."

"There are a lot of bad decisions one can make in life. Leaking that info to the press is one of the worst you could've done."

"I'll kill you!"

Frazier continued to ignore the veiled threat. "It would have been better if you accidentally shot a priest, then pull the stunt you did."

"News about cases get reported all the time. What's the difference with case?"

"The difference is, I told you specifically not to leak it. And not only did you leak it, you gave her everything. Even Councilman Bolton. We gave that man our word he would be not be mentioned."

"*You* gave him your word. I didn't."

"I can clearly see that integrity is nothing you're accustomed to." He gestured a hand at a wet spot on the front of Wiley's gray sweats.

"What are you doing here, Frazier?" Complete annoyance was in his tone.

"I came here to hit you. And to tell you if you ever go against me in a case again, I will put maximum effort into hurting you."

"Fuck you!"

"No thanks. You're not my type. Perhaps we can call your maid back here. She should be halfway down the hill. You know she would turn around and come back. She's done it before. You know, with your wife not being back and all."

"Hold up. I just got off the phone with her. She's in freaking Alaska right now. How the hell did you know that? Are you tapping my phones? Do you have a bug in my house? And how the hell did you get in my house? How did you get past my security? How in the hell do you know any of the things you do?"

With expert precision, he ran off the answers to each question by counting them off by his fingers. "I didn't know *where* she was. I just knew she left town for a few modeling gigs not too long ago. You told me that." He held up another finger. "I'm not tapping your phones." Another finger. "I do not have a bug planted in your house." Another finger. "I asked your security to let me through. Nicely. Apparently, your staff doesn't like you very much. And to their credit, they asked to see my identification first." Another finger. "And I know the things I do because I seek to know them. When a man puts his mind toward his wants, things get achieved. I'm sure you can attest that. Right, Norman?"

A chill ran down Wiley's spine as he thought to himself, *He knows. Son of a bitch, he knows. But he can't know. He can't know about Florida. He can't know about West Africa. I used different names. No one could even get to me. I was a ghost to all those people. Everything he knows about my past is connected to my name. No. He couldn't possibly know.*

To his credit, he showed no signs of panic as his mind raced. Only anger. "What are you talking about?" he said it with disdain to further conceal the relay race his mind was having.

"I think you know what I'm talking about."

"No, I don't." His voice rose. "For once, will you just answer a simple fucking question?"

"You are an FBI agent, Norman. Not everyone is cut out for the bureau, but here you are. You work hard. There's no denying that. And you are flawed. There's surely no denying that. But you are a special agent. And that's nothing to sneeze at."

It was the only time Frazier remotely showed him any modicum of respect. Wiley was taken aback by it. He lost some of his rage. "What did you hit me for?"

"I found my temper."

"What? Wait, don't you mean you lost your temper?"

"No. To lose your temper is to go haywire. I stay in control. I have to find my temper. But usually when I do, bad things happen. I don't like you, Wiley. Just like your staff. But for different reasons."

He retightened the grip on the tenderizer. "What reasons?"

"Well." He paused in thought then shrugged. "I guess it's for some of the same reasons. You enjoy bullying those you deem less than you. Bottom line, you're an asshole. But you are a federal agent, and people have to respect that. So that makes you a federal asshole. But you already knew that."

"Oh yeah. Well, let me tell you why I don't like you."

"Not interested."

"Well, get interested."

"Wiley. You leaked federal information to the press that could hurt the bureau."

"How can it hurt the bureau?"

"You let key information on an ongoing case go public. We will be held completely liable for this now. If another incident like this occurs, the press will be more interested in pointing the finger at us for not preventing it, then the people involved. And how do you think the president will react? Provided he has no idea about the intricacies of this case."

Wiley put the meat tenderizer down and looked at as it lay on the counter. "I didn't think of that."

"Of course, you didn't. Because you don't think. You only knew that you were mad at me and wanted to do something, anything, to piss me off. Well, mission accomplished, Special Agent. And you also managed to piss off the rest of the country and the leader of the free world."

Petulant defiance took over the young agent. He started to see the major flaw he committed, then remembered he didn't care. As long as he could stick it to Frazier. "You know what? Get the fuck out of my house before I sic my dogs on you."

"Oh, you mean Arm and Hammer? They're out back enjoying a fresh six-pound ribeye. One a piece. They'll be at them for a good while."

"You son of a bitch!"

"Now. Russell wants us back at the office. We have a lot of damage control to do."

"Unless I hear from Russell himself, then I'm not doing a damn thing. Especially from you. Now, I'd like you to kindly get the hell out of my house and off my property. Or I will have to physically remove you myself."

Frazier looked up at the hanging chandeliers. He looked down the long hall of vanity and glanced back at the spiraled steps, the high ceilings, the marble flooring, the state-of-the-art sliding door behind him. He smiled and nodded as if impressed.

"It's a very nice place you got here, Wiley. Nice indeed. And your wife is beautiful."

Wiley only stared. He said nothing to the compliments. Offhanded or genuine, he didn't care. He just wanted to let all the frustration out on this man that he could muster. Frazier continued nodding, looking around. He turned his back to Wiley completely. A thing that further upset him.

He came to his house uninvited, fed his dogs without his permission, called him insulting names, and physically attacked him. "Frazier, this is the last time I'm going to say it. Get out of my goddamn house."

Frazier didn't turn around. He kept his back to him as he answered, "Are you going to grab me by belt and collar and throw me off your steps?"

That's exactly what he was going to do. He marched over to do just that. He grabbed the belt in his left hand and the collar in his right. But as soon as contact was made, Frazier spun around in a water-like fluid motion. He ended up behind Wiley with an expert sleeper hold on his neck.

He squeezed, cutting off all air.

Grabbing at arms to pull free, Wiley saw his vision narrowing. Suddenly, Frazier released him and walked toward the door. It wasn't an attempt to really harm him, just a warning at how easy it would be. Wiley stayed there, panting on all fours for a brief moment.

Then like a charging bull, he crashed into Frazier's back against the glass door. The industrial reinforced glass didn't break. This fight was a long time coming. This was what Frazier came over for. There had been many instances where both men felt like they just needed to get on with it and get it over with. Today was the day.

But one thing you never do is go over a man's house to fight. Unless you have zero respect for him, which clearly was the case. Wiley locked his hands around Frazier's waist and rolled him around on the floor. His old high school wrestling came back to memory. But he didn't pay enough attention to the glimpses revealing the expertise of Frazier's martial arts background.

The swift hit to throat was the first indication. The fluid maneuver and toss was another. Then the reversal followed by a choke hold was strike three. Three strikes. You're out.

Frazier gripped a single finger around his waist, and Wiley let out a howl. The next thing he knew, Frazier had a wrist contorted with him now lying on his back, yelling.

"Don't try to get up." Frazier's voice was cold and deadly. He wasn't panting for air like Wiley was. But the ever-defiant younger agent did the opposite. He tried to rise again. Only to be quickly floored again with a subtle jerk of the wrist. He screamed in pain.

"I said, don't try to get up."

"Ah! Fuck you! Ah!"

Frazier shook his head. "You just don't learn. You have no remorse, and no honor. You actually and truly think you are never wrong." His face turned sad briefly, then anger replaced it. "You truly have no regrets."

"Ah! What are you talking about, you crazy bastard? Let me go before I—ah!"

"You really are a remorseless man." The tone in Frazier's voice was low. He was talking to himself but loud enough to hear.

"I'll fucking kill you! I'll fu—ah!"

A look of resignation came over Frazier's face. He nodded his head. "Very well." He released the death lock he had on the wrist. Wiley curled up in a ball, writhing in pain on his cold marble floor. He was too hurt for embarrassment. He moved the wrist around, getting feeling back into it.

Frazier stood up straight from the knelt position he was in. "You have no remorse at all. Everyone is at your whim."

Wiley spoke through coughing bits. "What are you talking about?"

Frazier looked at him for a long moment without answering. "I'll see you at the office." He turned and left, coolly, casually, and fluidly.

Wiley made it to his feet after a few more minutes on the floor. He couldn't remember hurting his leg, but it did. He planted one foot, while the knee stayed down. He found himself near a wall, where he placed the hurt wrist on to steady himself. Pain shot through his arm like lightning.

He had to shift and turn the other way to use his good hand. He made his way up and looked around as if making sure no one else was there watching him get his ass handed to him. He straightened up and went out to the backyard where the dogs were.

"And where the hell were you two?" he yelled at the dogs. "I'm in there getting attacked by a trespasser, and you're out here eating!" He was genuinely upset. The dogs stopped eating, sensing their master was unhappy. They dropped their ears, with their heads lowered.

Wiley continued to take out his frustrations on his dogs. He snatched the bone away from Hammer and glared at him. Arm lifted his head and tilted inquisitively, then received a smack on the nose. "What are you looking at?" He snatched his bone also.

Both dogs cowered and began to shake. Hammer always lost control of his bladder when he was in trouble. As he did this time. Wiley smacked them both on the top of their heads, yelling and cursing. He was more upset that he was no match for Frazier than upset at the dogs.

Christina would most likely have received a very rough sexual encounter with him right now. But she was sent away. Virgil, his guard at the front, was too far from the door at the moment. He would punish him later for letting him in. Stan, his landscaper, was much smaller than him. He might actually beat him like a high school bully for lunch money, if he was there. But thankfully, he had the day off.

He would probably start a fight with Marla over something as petty as her makeup station taking up too much room. Despite the fact she already had an entire room specifically for her to go in and put her makeup on, all neat, organized, and color coded, completely out of his way, but she would hear about it anyway.

No one else was there. So that left the poor unassuming dogs. He took turns smacking them in the head, on the nose, on their cowering backs, while he let out his anger. He finally stopped. The terror and confusion in their eyes did nothing to bring him out of his mood. He was pissed off. And it had always been his MO to take it out on his lesser.

The dogs did absolutely nothing wrong. They didn't even have it in them to defend themselves against the vicious assault. They were overmatched. Much like he was against Frazier. Never would he have guessed that going up against the shorter, older agent, something like that could happen.

Frazier could have done this in a park or the bathroom at the office. He wanted to make a statement by coming to a man's house to impose his will—a tremendous psychological play on his part. And the message was well received.

For as much as he thought he wanted a piece of Frazier, it turned out that's exactly what he didn't want. He never thought he would have promptly, efficiently, and effortlessly gotten his ass whooped.

He went back in the house, got dressed, and drove to the guard in the front. He rolled the window down, wearing his sunglasses. Virgil, the gate guard, was an easygoing man. He and his wife had three kids. The eldest, his daughter Pam, was a senior in high school. She was recently accepted to Cornell to study political science.

Paying for his daughter to go to school was his sole priority and pride. His wife, Amanda, was hurt last year on her job. She had been unable to work since then. Their other two children, Terrance and Martin, were twin boys the age of fifteen.

Virgil always had a kind word and a warm face. He greeted Wiley as he drove up. "Hello, Special Agent Wiley, sir. You have yourself a safe and healthy day today." He smiled broadly.

"Virgil. You're fired." He rolled up the window and drove off.

CHAPTER 17

TO THE POINT

"Go! Go! Go! Go! Go!" went the chanting of over twenty agents looking for a reason to unwind. With Art Russell at the helm, the office would have occasional events to break up the mundane and stressful nature that normally was found in an FBI headquarters.

He stood among a crowd of people, cheering with money in their hands. He had his in his hand as well. A few agents farther back had to result to standing on chairs to get a view. Every office and cubicle was emptied.

Wiley made it the office to find the spectacle in progress. He stood on his toes, trying to get a glimpse of what was happening in the middle. He caught hold of one agent, asking him what was happening.

"Hey. What's going on?"

"A bet," he shot back. A sneer of disdain touched his face. He turned back to watch.

"A bet for what?"

The agent waved him off annoyingly. Wiley looked at him for a moment then walked around to find a spot to get a look.

"Let's go, Kyle!" Wiley heard one agent yell out with his fist raised and a grin on his face. Wiley's mood quickly became sour. He thought about what happened at his house the whole way to headquarters. He hated that man. But everyone else loved him.

He finally got close enough to see what was happening. A different Kyle was arm wrestling with another agent. Both men looked as if they arm wrestled before. Their hands were clasped and bound with brown straps. Wiley looked over and saw Frazier standing next to Russell, cheering like everyone else.

Their eyes met. Frazier didn't show any indication of a mood change. He simply went back to the spectacle, with his money in his hand. Wiley felt a rush of a strange feeling in his gut, the feeling one gets when locking eyes with the school bully: fear.

Russell had his arm around him, watching and cheering along. Wiley began to notice something familiar about the hand straps. He quickly remembered it was the same kind of straps that held the hands of Councilman Bolton when they found him. He immediately got angry. Frazier came over his house upset about leaking information, and here he was using a piece of identical evidence in this charade.

Still steaming from the prompt humbling he received, he stormed his way around people to get to him. But it wasn't easy. The cheering and jostling continued as the two arm wrestlers neared their breaking point. They were at a stale mate for a good while, both holding on to the table with their left hands, with their bodies leaning the opposite direction of the struggle for leverage.

Special Agent Harris Moore was losing strength. The position he held in pulling the other way changed. He now sat up in an attempt to shift his position so that his arm didn't break.

Special Agent Kyle Manning poured on the reserve strength he had to get the win. He leaned and leaned, jerking periodically, attempting to bring down his opponent's hand to the table. Success! He won the match.

A mix of cheers and groans showered the office. Money exchanged hands begrudgingly, while playful taunts were thrown at Moore.

"You're a pansy, Moore."

"Your mouth wrote a check your ass couldn't cash."

"Should've known better than that, Moore."

"You owe me money mothafu—"

"Hey!" Director Russell cut the surly agent off. "Get back to work." Everyone returned to their places, and suddenly the phones started ringing. The two participating agents rubbed their sore arms and bumped fists in a show of sportsman-like respect.

Russell turned back to Frazier, slapping his winnings in his hand. Frazier took it with a smile, nodding dramatically.

Wiley finally made it to them and began to say something until Russell cut him off.

"Wiley. In my office." He turned and stalked away, not waiting for a response. Wiley stared Frazier in the eye as he passed. He wanted to redeem himself. He just couldn't let a butt whooping like that stand with no receipt.

But for the time being, he had to see what he was being summoned for. He walked into the office. Russell stood behind his desk, hands on his hips, face in a stern frown, looking every bit the disapproving stepfather.

"Shut the door," he commanded.

Wiley complied. Russell lost all the jovial nature he had when Wiley saw him standing next to Frazier during the match. His office was nothing spectacular. A stack of files sat to the right of his glass-top desk. Pictures of his boat and beach house graced the west side of the wall. Plaques of bureau accomplishments graced the wall behind his chair. Various other pictures of he and Frazier and other people were draped across the west wall as well. He smiled broadly in every one of them. He was a man that clearly knew how to enjoy himself. But at that moment in his office, he had no desire to smile. He scowled like a high school principal.

"Put your ass in that chair." The chair sat directly across him at his desk. He didn't point to it. He stared at him with jaws clenched. Wiley obeyed without protest.

As rich as Wiley was, he loved being an FBI agent. It wasn't just because of the power such a title holds. He felt important and needed, conducting the cases he undertook. As a sworn member of the FBI, he really and truly felt special. He didn't want to mess it up. But he was starting to feel that it was too late for that.

"You want to tell me what the hell you were thinking?"

"I made a mistake, sir." His phone went off with a text.

Russell scoffed. "A mistake? A mistake? Referring to a Chinese person as Japanese, that's a mistake. Getting so drunk at the Christmas party, you xerox a copy of your bare ass, that's a mistake. Hell, calling out another woman's name while you're at with your wife, that's a mistake."

Wiley nearly snickered at that part. He did the same thing once. Except he said it very low and Marla didn't hear him call out Christina's name while they were role-playing. But he did his best poker face impression, so Russell went on.

"What *you* did, my friend, was violate federal penal codes."

Wiley's blood went ice cold. He only thought of getting back at Frazier when he told him not to leak any information. He never considered any serious violations.

"I . . . I'm sorry, sir. I never—"

"What? You never what?" Russell cut him off. "You never thought giving case information in its entirety to a news reporter was a bad idea? You never thought how much this compromises the bureau? You never thought . . . period? Speak up, man. What exactly is it you never thought?"

"Sir, I sincerely apologize for—"

"No. Go back to the part about you never thinking. That's what has my interest."

The young agent dropped his head in shame. "Did Frazier tell you this?"

"Kyle? You're asking me if Kyle told me this? I saw it all over the goddamn news last night! Everyone did. Can you imagine? Here I am, giving the Mrs. the old high hard one. And right when I'm getting close, some damn reporter throws the blank-sheet case up. I mean seriously. I didn't even get to finish, damn you. I couldn't. That makes me grumpy, Wiley. Very grumpy."

Wiley kept his head down then looked up and asked. "So Frazier didn't say anything?"

Russell threw his hands up in exasperation. "What the fuck, man! What is with this obsession you got with him? I'm talking about *you*! *You* leaked the information. *You* gave away the inner workings of our case. *You* did that! And no, he didn't say a damn thing. He didn't have to. Everybody here knows it was you."

Looking down while being berated, he finally gathered enough courage to look up and ask another question. "Did he say anything about this morning?"

"Did who say anything about this morning?"

"Frazier. Did he say anything?"

That was it. Russell's frustration reached a fever pitch. He could no longer take the obsession Wiley had with his friend. And being that he just screwed up royally, the last thing he wanted was for Wiley to pass the buck on Frazier. He lost it.

"I will shoot you, Wiley. I swear to God, I will reach in my drawer, pull out my gun, and shoot you in the fucking face."

Wiley held up his hands in protest. "Just hear me out, sir. Please."

"What?" he said it through grounded teeth.

"We had a fight. A fistfight. He came to my home and attacked me. He physically attacked a federal agent. And in my own home. Uninvited no less."

Russell looked at him for a long moment silently then burst into sudden laughter. "Man. You must have managed to really set him off." He continued chuckling as he spoke.

Wiley looked confused. 'Sir?"

"Kyle swore to refrain from 'finding his temper' as he calls it. He hadn't lost it to that degree in a number of years. For him to lay an ass whooping on you in your own home says that you really pissed him off to no end." The chuckling continued.

"I said we had a fight. I didn't say he won."

Russell shook his head, still chuckling. He sat down and leaned back in his chair. "My dear boy, Kyle is an eight Dan in aikido."

"An eighth what, in where?"

"Eighth Dan. It means degree of black belt in martial arts. And his art is aikido, a Japanese style of martial art. He's ascended to the level of grandmaster." He suddenly looked at him with a slight surprised look. "You're lucky to be walking. He must have been feeling generous."

Wiley thought back to the solid look he always saw in Frazier's eyes when they faced off, not knowing that he could easily ball him up like scratch paper and throw him in the waste basket. It made sense now. He couldn't get within striking distance of him without getting flung away like a dry dishrag.

"No, my young fool. Kyle didn't say anything to me. But I'll tell you who did. Councilman Bolton called me. He said something about being promised by the bureau that he would be left out of any reports."

Wiley bit his lip, mumbling a curse. He knew full well he dropped the ball on that score. Russell continued to school him.

"You realize he has friends, friends that can make things difficult for us. And let me be honest. If things are made difficult for me, they most definitely will be difficult for you."

"I understand, sir. But isn't there a rule or something against striking a fellow agent?"

Russell laughed. Resting his elbows on his desk, he gestured with his hands. "What do you think this is? The Boy Scouts? Oh wait, let me guess. You want to file a formal complaint. Is that it? Or better yet. You want to file charges." His tone was mocking and condescending.

"So he can just get away with it?"

"Do you want to file a formal complaint? Press charges? Or how about a sanctioned fight right here in the office for your rematch? I'll clear out all the desks and make a gladiator ring. How's that sound?" Another text went off.

"Cut the goddamn phone off, will you?" he spoke irritably.

"Sorry, sir. It's just my wife."

"Now. Do you want to take legal action against Kyle Frazier?"

"I might." He was suddenly getting upset at the prospect of the seemingly untouchable veteran getting away with what he did.

"Fine." He opened his drawer, pulling out a pen and paper. "Here you go." He passed them to him. "Write it out. I'll sign it and log it. But I must warn you. He will petition. And I will have to sign off on his petition on the grounds that you also will have to be placed under arrest for violating federal penal codes." He paused to let it soak in before he continued. "Keep in mind, Wiley. His record is spotless. He wouldn't see any real punishment. You, on the other hand, will be tried for a federal crime, a felony. Given your status as a sworn agent, your sentence will be doubled. You could be facing fifteen to twenty years of hard time."

Wiley opened his mouth to say something but found no words.

"So I'll ask you again. Do you wish to file a formal complaint? Press charges? Or just chalk this one up? The way I see it, you got off easy with just a beat-down."

Wiley slid the pen and paper back over to him. Russell nodded his agreement. "Finally. You make a wise decision."

A knock on the door brought their attention to it. "Yeah!" Russell called out. Frazier walked in, reading a large file. He had his head tilted up slightly, looking down through his reading glasses.

"Check this out, Art. I didn't notice it before. But every one of the blank sheets we found had no other fingerprints on them besides the victims."

"Right. We gathered that much. Considering we don't have a perp."

"You didn't let me finish. All sheets are accounted for. But check this out from a still picture we got outside the café."

The picture was of Wiley speaking with Gina Samuels. There they were speaking, and she deftly caught the blank sheet of paper from her purse and put it back before Wiley could notice.

Russell looked at curiously. "So what exactly am I looking at here?"

Frazier leaned over and snatched up the picture with a sigh of frustration. "What we have here is collateral against a hot-shot reporter that doesn't mind breaking treaties for her own benefit and an opportunity to save face with a *certain* man in office. Never know when you might need one of those."

Russell looked to the silent Wiley and smiled slowly. "Well, well, my boy. It appears that our mutual friend here has found a way to save your ass."

Frazier stood still looking down at Wiley, who found it oddly strange that he was unable to meet his eyes. He simply nodded, looking down. Russell continued, "Of course, this means, she has to be brought in for questioning. I'll send a police unit to bring her."

"No," Frazier spoke, still looking at the crestfallen agent. "I think a betrayer must be betrayed by another betrayer." He smirked from the corner of his mouth.

Russell pointed at Frazier. "I like the way you think, Kyle. Wiley, you will go and arrest her under suspicion of federal tampering."

Wiley was nodding his head when he realized how quiet it was. Both men were staring at him. He looked back and forth between both of them, his eyes ultimately falling on Russell. "Now?"

"Yes, now. The news station isn't far from here."

Simply glad that the venom was no longer flowing in his direction, he got up and left the office. He walked past Frazier, never looking at him.

Frazier watched him go, then turned back to look at Russell in his chair, and shrugged. "Was it something I said?" Both men broke out into laughter.

"So what do you think, Kyle? Think Bolton is going to give us hell?"

"Not at all. He has bigger fish to fry, especially with that broad-shouldered wife of his. I swear. From the back, she looks like she could play linebacker for the Oakland Raiders in 1988." They both exploded in laughter.

"I kind of don't blame the man. If I had that to go home to, I wouldn't know to either greet her or tuck my briefcase under my arm and take a knee." Russell pounded the desk with his fist, tears streaming down his face. He always found his own jokes funnier than anyone else's, especially the ones that made no sense like this one.

Frazier took a seat, as they went over the files some more. They discovered nothing different. No breaking revelation that connects. Both threw out suggestions but were both shot down by the other.

Frazier eventually sat back in the chair, removing his glasses, squinting with his thumb and index finger gripping the bridge of his nose.

In record time, Wiley reappeared with Gina Samuels back at headquarters. She was handcuffed, being led by her arm to an interview room.

They both observed the indignant look on her face with her head held high. She clearly regretted nothing she did. Frazier glanced at Russell, smirked, then walked out to meet with her in the interview room.

CHAPTER 18

DAMAGE CONTROL

FRAZIER CONSIDERED THE "old song and dance" approach he used on young Lance Morris. But he knew she was way too polished to fall for that trick. So he went for the jugular. He stormed in, snatching up a chair and slammed it right next to her. He forcefully turned her chair around to face him.

He huffed and puffed as if he just ran a ten-yard dash at full speed. She moved to cover her face as a reflex, with both hands cuffed. He sat there, paused inches from here face. She glanced over to Wiley, who now regained his bravado and stared back at here with his arms crossed.

Frazier brought the picture up to her face with her holding a blank sheet of paper identical to the ones involved in their case. He slammed it down on the desk then pointed to it. "Talk."

"Talk about what?" Her voice came out high pitched with fear.

"Don't play with me."

"I'm not." Fear still held tight on her.

"You already know what this is. So talk."

"I got that from him in all the evidence he gave to me." She pointed at the mole with his arms crossed. He only stood there, staring at her stoically.

Frazier didn't bother to look at him. His eyes stayed glued to her. "You're lying."

"No, it's true. He gave me all the information regarding your case. We met at the batting cages on his day off."

"When was this?"

"A week ago."

Frazier smiled mockingly. "Look at the date. The one in this picture was taken last month."

Her eyes darted nervously back and forth between the two agents, oftentimes landing on Wiley. "You can't do this. I've done nothing wrong. The right to free press is constituted. I want my law—"

Frazier held up a finger, stopping her in midsentence. "I want you to consider this real carefully. If you go the lawyer route, a lot of things will have to come out that you might not want to. And not just the powwow you and the special agent out there had either." He gestured his head at toward the door, never taking his eyes off hers.

"We're talking about your past. The citations you have against you for your overzealousness. We'll have to delve into your character flaws. And that can go as far back as your little . . . high school debacle."

"What do you mean high school debacle? There's nothing wrong with my character."

He sighed. "Do we really have to go there? I'm trying to give you a way out here."

"No. Let's. There's no character flaw. I did nothing in high school worth mentioning pertaining to my character and my professionalism. I worked my ass off to get to where I am." Her anger began to kindle as she challenged Frazier.

"All right. How about the time when you were caught with a boy in the girls' room? It was at a prep school in Westchester, California. You were trying to get accepted to a journalism program in Connecticut. But you knew such an action would destroy your chances. So you claimed sexual assault."

Wiley slowly unfolded his arms, taking an aggressive stance. The memory of when he was falsely accused of sexual assault came back to him. Her eyes darted his and saw fire. She thought he was her protection, provided that he was her source. But the look he gave her said otherwise. Frazier continued.

"You were pretty convincing in your report, even describing a certain direction his genitalia turns when erect. The poor bastard had his full scholarship to Brown pulled. He was prosecuted to the full extent of the law and was sentenced to fifteen years in a federal prison.

"He was going to be the first in his family to go to college. His mother was sent to a mental institution for trying to smother him as a baby, claimed it was postpartum depression. His father had to quit high school and work two jobs because they had him young. The poor guy busted his hump to make sure his son saw him at every science fair tournament.

"But you were the one that pressured him into going in the bathroom. He repeatedly turned you down. But the ever-ambitious Gina Samuels gets what she wants, doesn't she? You told him that if he didn't do it, you'd make up a bad rumor about him. And when the school counselor, Abigail Summers, came in, you did just that. He never thought you would lie on him if he did what you wanted."

Tears flowed down her face. She felt pure guilt ever since that day. She tried her best to suppress it with her work ethic and success. But she knew what she did and did nothing to reverse it.

"Lonnie Fisher. That was his name. Why did he deserve that, Gina?"

Her head dropped in memory. "He didn't. I . . . I was so scared. But I didn't think he would get in that kind of trouble." She sobbed through her words, making it hard to fully understand her.

Frazer scoffed. "What exactly did you think was going to happen? You said he raped you. And it was a lie. You had plenty of time to change your story. When Ms. Summers brought you into her office, you could've said something. When the police interviewed you, you could've said something. We he was in court and you had sat there and watched him, you could've said something.

"When he was stripped of his future, sentenced to prison, labeled a sex offender, and then sexually offended himself for fourteen years, you could've said something. But, hey. At least he never saw that fifteenth year. The poor bastard went and cut his own throat with a license plate. But you knew all this, didn't you?"

She didn't know. She wailed in remorse. "Oh, I'm so sorry, Lonnie! I'm so sorry!"

Frazier watched her with cold eyes, offering no comfort at all. "You don't want that to get out, do you, Gina?"

She shook her head, looking down at the table, still sobbing. "No."

Wiley's phone went off again.

Frazier kept looking at Gina when he spoke. "You might want to get that. Never know if it's important."

"No, it's fine."

Frazier continued to go at her. "You don't care who you have to step on to get what you want. Special Agent Wiley here," he pointed a thumb over his shoulder, "made a terrible mistake by leaking information to you. He gave you everything you needed. But even if he didn't, you were going to run with some semblance of the story anyway."

She looked up from her sobbing, but her eyes were still watery. "What?"

"You were going to take this blank sheet in this photo," he pointed to the picture, "and shape the news as you saw fit. Am I right?"

She wanted to protest, but she had the feeling that any lie would come back on her. He seemed to know an awful lot about her anyway. She dropped her head again, unable to meet his eyes and nodded. "Yes."

"Answer me this, Gina. What did Agent Wiley offer you in return?" He left off the *special* part and turned to look at Wiley as he spoke.

She suddenly stopped her sniffling enough to answer a question truthfully without any cause for lying. "Nothing. He said I would owe him."

"Is that so?" He was still looking at Wiley.

"Yes. I was suspicious at first, but then—"

"But then you realized it didn't matter. As long as you could break this story and gain favor for that spot, you didn't care how you got it. You didn't think it all the way through. Just like Agent Wiley here."

Silence. No one else said anything. Frazier got up out of his chair and walked out without saying a word.

Wiley finally spoke to her. "What the hell did you mention the councilman for?"

"You said you didn't care." They both spoke in antsy, hushed tones.

"You're a damn idiot. But that should go without saying."

"Don't call me that!" she shot back.

He rubbed his hands through his hair, taking a deep breath, shaking his head. His eyes were wide as he looked off in the distance.

"So what now?" she asked.

"We're fucked, that's what."

"Am I going to go to prison?"

He took a deep sigh. "I think we both are."

Frazier walked back in soon after. "Gina Samuels." He paused for affect, a long pause. Her lips quivered as tears streamed down her face. "You're free to go."

"What?" she asked, confused. She knew for sure she was going down. "What do you mean I'm free to go?"

"I mean that if you would rather go to prison, keep running your mouth."

She got up, eager to leave. She then noticed that her hands were still cuffed. She held them out in front of her, for him to see. Frazier turned to Wiley and nodded. Wiley walked over and freed her. He gave her a stern look but said nothing. She didn't want to meet his eye.

She stopped in front of Frazier, standing beside the door. She motioned to say something then stopped, when she saw the poker face he gave her. She opted to simply rush out of there as fast as she could.

Wiley pocketed his cuffs and walked over to Frazier. "What was that all about?"

Frazier looked him in the eye, put a licorice root in his mouth, then walked away without a word.

Wiley stood there, dumbfounded at the ordeal. The whole thing made no sense. Nothing added up at all. Frazier walked back in and spoke to him.

"She will report nothing else regarding this case. If you give her anything else, she will reject it. She will make a public apology to Councilman Bolton on air, claiming that she received false reports and falsely reported. Bolton will regain his sponsors and become a catalyst for federal funding in any capacity the bureau requires. He will personally call Art to indebt himself to us.

"We now have a top-notch reporter to spin whatever story we need her to. Her career will take a huge leap because Art will call her bosses and tell them that she will be working in conjunction with the federal government, thereby have the ability to receive stories that others cannot.

"She will be deemed untouchable. Bolton will be grateful. The blank-sheet case will lie dormant with no new developments, and we can go about business as usual. Everybody wins."

"What about me?" He wasn't sure he wanted the answer.

Frazier answered, "To release you now would cause an investigation to take place. That would leave us vulnerable. *Incompetence* and *gross negligence* are words that would be thrown around. And we would have a media frenzy. Something we can ill afford. *You*, my special ed agent friend, will keep your job per my request to Russell. You will never jeopardize the bureau again. And if you are really smart, you will never try to piss me off again."

He looked Frazier right in the eye as he spoke. Wiley didn't shy from the look, but he didn't challenge either. The thoughts of earlier still played fresh in his mind. Frazier could have pulled a bully move and tried to force him to answer, the typical "Do you hear me?" or "Do I make myself clear?" But his point was made, and they both knew it. No need to rub it in.

It was something that if the roles were reversed, Wiley wouldn't hesitate to do. Frazier turned and walked out, leaving the young agent standing there forlorn. Given the entirety of the morning, a wise person would simply want to move on. But alas, that wasn't Wiley's way. He gritted his teeth and stormed out the office.

CHAPTER 19

FALSE MOVE

"AND MAKE DAMN sure we don't get another accident like the one we had yesterday. I'm going to be covering poor Jared's medical bills for six months."

"It was an accident, boss," a man yelled back from a distance.

"You were the accident. I knew I should've used a rubber that night."

Laughter broke out among the men. Even the one that received the intended insult. The constant noise of crunching and compacting drowned out the sound of a car approaching.

The man turned around when the car came to a stop not too far from him. His smile didn't stay as wide as when he made the joke, but it didn't exactly go away when he saw who exited the car.

"What can I do for you, young man?"

The young man was wearing fresh black slacks and a buttoned-down white shirt, a jet-black tie around his neck, and no jacket. As hot as it was, who needed one? He wore dark sunglasses that still allowed you to see his eyes when the sun hit them right. He had his wallet at the ready rather than in his pocket.

He flung it open ceremoniously, revealing his identification. "Special Agent Wiley of the Federal Bureau of Investigation. You're William Benson, is that correct?"

"Last time I checked."

"I need to ask you a few questions." Wiley's text went off again, but he ignored it.

"So ask." Benson leaned with both hands on his cane in front of him.

"I wanted to talk to you ab—" *Clank!* "Abou—" *Clank!* "About your relat—" Grinding and crunching distracted him from continuing.

"Speak up, son." Benson spoke clear and loud without yelling over the sounds of the junkyard. Through the years, he developed the perfect tone for speaking over it.

"Perhaps we should take this inside."

Benson cupped a hand over his ear, feigning to be unable to hear what he said. "Eh?"

Wiley raised his voice to a yell, "I said we should go inside and talk!"

Benson lowered his hand, smiling. He turned to walk toward his office. He took each stair up carefully, laboring on his cane and the stair rail. They entered the office and shut the door. The noise wasn't completely drowned out, but it was muffled enough to speak and hear clearly.

He gestured for Wiley to sit down as he strolled around his desk to take his place. The older gentleman sat down gingerly, a look of clear discomfort on his face, easing himself into a chair. He propped the cane up against the wall behind him, rubbing his ailing knees.

The office was a trailer and not exactly a small one. A kitchen with a sink, refrigerator, and electric stove sat farther away from his desk on the left of him. To the right of the desk was a bathroom with a standing shower. A washer and dryer was tucked away in a closed closet. There was a nice-sized closet space for his clothes and a forty-inch flat-screen television mounted on a wall in front of the bed.

All the windows had venetian blinds in between a thin layer of glass. It negated the possibility of getting dusty, or damaged, from constantly looking through them. He was a collector of classic car models. There were rows and rows of wall shelves littered with models of various years near the door.

On his wooden desk sat a laminated plaque signed from the mayor in 1987 for best entrepreneur. His desktop computer sat to the right of him. To his left sat a huge three binder of orders for the business. He reached in one of his drawers, pulling out two glasses and a bottle of whiskey.

"Drink?" he asked as he poured himself some.

"No, thank you."

Benson shrugged and threw his back with practiced regularity. Completely unfazed by the strong burning sensation such a drink carries, he made no face of discomfort. It was as easy as drinking a glass of water. He poured some more in the other glass.

Wiley took on an irritated tone. "I said I didn't want any."

Benson froze with the bottle in his hand as he looked at Wiley for a second. "I heard you the first time." He put the bottle down, scooped up the glass, and leaned back in his chair, holding in his hand. "This one's for me." He threw it back as easily as he did the first.

He slammed the glass down on the desk like a drunken cowboy in an old Western tavern, then poured two more drinks. "So, what can I do you for, Special Agent?"

"How well do you know Special Agent Frazier?"

A picture in an eight-by-ten frame faced Benson. He leaned over, spun it around for Wiley to see, and then leaned back again. It was a picture of him, Frazier, and Art Russell on a boat in fishing gear. They stood side by side in a row, holding a seven-foot-long white sturgeon.

"Took that last year. Known him for over thirty. I was the best man at his wedding. And he was at all five of mine. Each time he said it was the last time. But he was there every time I asked him."

"Five weddings?" the agent asked with surprise.

Benson shrugged. "What can I say? I'm a hopeless romantic. I fall in love easily." He knocked back another drink.

Wiley struggled with the concept of one, let alone going through it four more times. But that was beside the point. He pushed the thought away, refocusing on his reason for being here. But why was he here? What did he hope to accomplish? He knew from the second he saw Benson and Frazier talking after the parking lot case that they were close. Yet and still, he sought to gather as much information about Frazier as he could, looking for a weakness to exploit.

"You said you were at his. When was he married?"

"Well, that's more of a question for Kyle." Benson tilted his head in curiosity. "Why do you ask?"

"I would like to know."

"Oh, I don't remember the day. I do know it was summertime. It was hot as hell. I sweated clean through my damn tux. The sun beamed down on us like the end of times. I thought I was going to be reduced to ash."

"But when was it?" His phone rang, on vibrate. But he ignored it.

"Like I said, kid. I don't remember." He poured himself another drink. "And I think you really should be asking him about this."

"It's Special Agent," he remarked testily. The phone continued to ring, yet he still ignored it.

"Right. Special Agent." He gestured with a glass in his hand as he spoke in a mock grandiose tone. "How could I forget? I beg your forgiveness."

Wiley's jaws clenched at the response. But he wasn't going to take the bait completely and risk Benson shutting down. He still wanted to find out more about him. "Did Frazier have any children?"

Benson looked over the rim of the glass as he took a much slower drink. "The Frazier you know—does he look like father material?"

"That's not what I asked you. Give me an answer."

He took another sip. "I gave you an answer."

"No. You answered a question with a question."

"Why exactly are you asking me about all of this?" Benson's look was not curious. Now it was guarded.

"I have my reasons. You see that there? That's an answer. Now give me mine."

"Look, kid. You don't just start asking a man about another man's life. It's no one else's place to say. Better to just ask the man himself. It's the decent thing to do."

Wiley's anger flared, not just because the man was being evasive, but it's that he was being invasive with him, a federal agent. Plus the fact that he kept calling him kid.

"If you call me kid again, I'll haul your knock-kneed ass in for obstruction."

Benson put down the glass. He sat up at attention, bringing a hand to his forehead to form a salute. "Oh, forgive me, Special Agent Wiley, sir."

"Don't you dare mock me, old man. I'm a federal agent. You're a civilian. You answer to me and act how I want you to."

"And why is that?"

"I have the credentials that prove I am your superior. You can't get any higher than the federal government in this country."

Benson sat back with a thoughtful look, hands shaped in a steeple form. "I see. So with that, you only answer to the federal government itself. Is that correct?"

"Correct."

"And they are the ones that pay you, correct?"

"Correct."

Benson pursed his lips. "Let's explore that theory. When I need my staff to do something, I ask them to do it. And guess what? They do it. Because they work for me. Since I control their finances, they answer to me. Now, let's look at you. You are paid by the federal government. I, as a business owner, pay more taxes to the federal government. And those taxes are mostly dispersed to pay your salaries. So in essence, *you* are the one that answers to *me*. And *you* are the one that should act the way *I* want *you* to."

Wiley had nothing to come back with. As much as he wanted to, he just didn't have anything. He scowled in an attempt to intimidate the older man. But to no avail. It was already bad enough he was humbled by Frazier. But he would be damned if he would take it from a friend of his too.

Benson noticed the look in his eyes and put up an imploring hand. But there was no fear in his deliverance. "All right, take it easy. No need to get all fired up and shoot your pants, kid. Sorry, Special Agent," he said the last part with a hint of disdain.

Wiley spoke through gritted teeth, slowly rising from his chair. "You know what, you old piece of shit? I've had just about enou—"

Benson cut him off. "What are you doing here? What do you want? You're not going to intimidate me, young man. And you're not going to get any information about my best friend, who happens to be your partner that you have a problem with."

Benson put the bottle and glasses back in his drawer, slamming it shut. "I mean, honestly. You want intel on Kyle Frazier. And you come to me? Goodness man. You couldn't win any money on Jeopardy, could you?"

Wiley kicked the chair behind him down. All sense of composure was gone. He reached over the desk, grabbing Benson with both hands by the collar, face snarled, eyes of brimstone. Suddenly his eye caught something on a trunk behind Benson. He never saw it from the seated position he had opposite the desk.

"What's that?"

Benson tried to turn around to look, but Wiley's younger stronger arms wouldn't allow it. "I can't see. Let me go, you son of a bitch." He struggled to get free. But Wiley wouldn't let go. He stared at Benson with malice. Then slowly and maniacally, he smiled.

He released him aggressively, shoving him back in his seat. He walked around to get a better look. On the trunk sat a blank sheet of paper identical to the ones found in the case. He pulled out a pair of tweezers and lifted the paper, carefully looking at it.

"Well, look at what we have here." The maniacal smile remained.

"Look at what?" Benson clearly had no idea what he was talking about.

"Oh, nothing. Just this a little piece of incriminating evidence. That's all."

"What? Are you touched or something? Incriminating of what?"

"Too late to play dumb now, old man. I got you red-handed."

"What the fuck are you talking about?" His eyes were wide with confusion.

"I'm talking about . . . William Benson. You're under arrest for terrorism and conspiracy to commit murder."

"Wait, what? Hey! Get your goddamn hands off me! Ah!" Benson struggled but was overpowered.

Wiley slammed him hard against the desk, wrenching his arms behind him. Benson yelled in pain. He was hauled to his feet and shoved out the door, with Wiley holding him. Benson nearly fell down the steps, walking without his cane.

He was aggressively placed in the back seat as his staff watched on. All of them, to a man, loved the old curmudgeon. He would yell, curse, and call them names, but it was all an act.

William Benson was beloved by his staff. He paid them well for the hard work and the risks they took daily. He gave them great benefits, retirement plans, and investment options. He knew all twenty of his employees personally. He knew their wives, their children, and all their birthdays.

He played the role as surrogate father to more than a few of his guys. His secretary, Jennifer Graham, was due the standard six-week maternal leave. He gave her a year with her normal pay and allowed her to work from home in a minimal capacity. He thought it was only fitting, provided that her husband was currently in a war oversees.

He'd been in business for over thirty years and had only one failed robbery attempt. It was foiled by one of his staff, which happened to be working late. The culprit was seen coming out of Benson's office late at night. Benson's safe was broken into, but all twenty-plus thousand dollars was recovered and put back. Every penny.

That same hero was working hard labor with a sledgehammer in his hand. He was an ex-con that had no skills but a desire to do better. Benson not only gave him a chance, but he gave him something far better: respect, responsibility, and purpose. The same man turned and saw his boss handcuffed and thrown in the back of a car. He motioned as if he was going to come over. Benson shook his head. And the guy stopped. Reluctantly.

Brian Anderson had every intention of using that sledgehammer to protect his employer, mentor, and surrogate father. Even if that meant using it on a federal agent. Benson knew this full well and called him off. For he knew it would only go bad. All bad.

But being treated with such disrespect as he had, he knew it was still going to go all bad anyway. But not for him.

CHAPTER 20

ONE TOO MANY

"HAVE YOU LOST your fucking mind!" Frazier roared as they faced off in the office.

Wiley had never seen him this upset, not even when he came over his house and attacked him. The sight pleased him to see such emotion. He knew Frazier wouldn't hit him at headquarters. Too many people were around as witnesses if an internal investigation were to occur.

He spread his arms out mockingly, with a smirk. "What? I'm investigating the blank-sheet case. Your man there had this identical blank sheet in his office. The same sheet you've spent hours analyzing."

"You dumb fuck! There are countless sheets like this!" He held the paper up in a plastic bag. "Paper manufactures print metric tons of this shit! Just because he had it in his office doesn't connect him to the case!"

"Gina Samuels had a sheet like that. And you all but made it seem like she was the figure head behind it all."

Frazier growled, a loud growl through gritted teeth. "She wasn't a part of it, and you know it. That's why you went to her in the first place." He was furious. He looked as if he was ready to swing a ball and chain into the face of this smug agent.

"What? Oh, just because he's your friend he should be exempt from an investigation? But you can bully a reporter, a female at that." He wanted to dig that last point in, implying a cowardly act on his part. "But I can't bring a guy in for questioning because he's a friend of yours?"

"Question him for what?" Frazier asked, teeth still gritted.

"That's what I intend to find out." His phone went off again.

"The work we did with Gina Samuel was in part to help clean up your mess. No, wait. Let me use the more appropriate term—your fuck-up."

Wiley scowled. His shame was laid bare. But he recovered quickly with a comment of his own. "You're a hypocrite, Frazier."

"A hypocrite," he repeated.

"Yes, a hypocrite. This is because that old man is a friend of yours. And no other reason." Wiley's phone went off again. The vibrating buzz made a loud sound. He ignored it, standing there with a light smirk on his face. Frazier, in contrast, stood there with blaring nostrils.

And then, just like that. As easy a light can be turned off with a switch, Frazier cooled. The poker face of indifference reappeared then formed into a small smile as he turned and walked away.

It baffled Wiley at first. Maybe even scared him a little. He suddenly felt himself grow angry watching him leave. He followed Frazier into the room where Benson was.

"Can't seem to keep your dog on a leash there, eh, Kyle?" Benson chided.

"You know how these damn rat terriers can be." He started uncuffing Benson. "Bark all the time, but dumb as shit."

Wiley let the insult pass for the moment. He stood there watching how this was going to play out, his arms folded across his chest, looking in disdain.

Benson rubbed his freed wrists and glanced at his captor standing by the door. "You know, out of the partners you've had through the years, that one's the most dangerous."

"Dangerous," Frazier repeated.

"Yeah. Lack of intelligence can be very dangerous. Like your old partner, Clark Hammond."

"You got that right." He gestured with his head at Wiley, continuing with the inside joke. "Or maybe about as dumb as that old secretary you had before Jennifer came along. What was her name?" He looked off to the side, rolling his hand in thought, then snapped his fingers. "Bernice."

They both shared a laugh. "Oh, yeah. Bernice. She was as useless as Chapstick on a scuba diver." They laughed hard. Frazier slapped the desk in delight.

"Hey!"

They both turned to him, still chuckling.

"I've had it with you two! One time too many, Frazier. One time too many. And you too, old man. I'm sick of both of you."

Benson and Frazier looked at each other. "Ooh. We really pissed him off, Kyle."

"Yeah, you're right. He's even more upset now than he was earlier today."

Wiley took a step forward and stopped when the door opened behind him. Director Russell walked in. "Will, on behalf of the bureau, I want to sincerely apologize. Please forgive this careless, stupid, unjustified action." He shot a hard glare at Wiley, who lowered his head in shame. "You're free to go."

Wiley's head came up as he protested. "But wait, sir. He had a blank she—"

"Shut the fuck up!" Russell seethed, speaking through clenched jaws and gritted teeth.

"Go easy on the kid, Art. From the first time I saw him, I could tell he was as green as artificial grass. I don't want nothing drastic done to him. But he better not come by my yard again, federal agent or not. Do you know he was seconds away from Brian laying a sledgehammer over his head?"

Frazier whistled. "Brian? I take it he wasn't close to you."

"Thankfully not close enough. About thirty feet from us. I'm afraid if he was something like ten or eight, I don't think I would've been able to stop him."

"All the same, we apologize. Agent Wiley will never set foot on your yard again. I'm sure of it." One would have thought that if Russell gritted his teeth any more, they might just shatter.

Wiley's phone went off again. He tried to ignore it. Frazier glanced over at him. "You might want to check that out. It's been doing that quite a bit I lately.

"It's fine."

"Get it," ordered Russell, looking like he was on the brink of smashing his fist through Wiley's face. Noticing the demeanor, he stepped to the corner and checked his messages.

Thirteen text messages and eight voice mails—all from Marla. Nothing substantial at all. She was really just thanking him for being so supportive and understanding of her. She gave him the usual song and dance about how she missed him and couldn't wait to see him again.

He listened to the voice messages next.

"Hi, honey. Just got off the plane to Alaska. The flight was great. I can't believe they tried to put me in coach. But I straightened that out quick. Anyway, talk to you soon, bye."

Next message: *"Hi, honey. Just got to my hotel room. I'm super tired. I've been modeling all day—"*

He cut it off, turning back to a waiting infuriated director. "It's nothing, sir. Just my wife letting me know she made it to her destination." He didn't bother to check the other voice mails.

He leaned over and extended a hand to Benson. "Will, I'm sorry about all this."

Benson accepted the handshake. "Don't worry about it, Art. Who do you think I am? Some tight ass looking to file a lawsuit? Please."

"We're still on for fishing next month?" Russell asked.

"Absolutely. If we could get Kyle over here to not drop the damn rod again."

Frazier spread his hands. "Hey, it was either me or the rod going overboard. And I can't swim. You know this." All three men laughed.

Wiley snared at them while twirling his phone in his hands. Art noticed him, and his smile faded. "In my office."

Wiley complied. He waited in a chair like a troubled youth waiting for the principal to come. Russell walked in after a while, shutting the door calmly behind himself. He wasn't half as furious as he was earlier. He seemed more collected but still upset.

"You know, when I first started, I made a lot of mistakes, stuff that could've gotten me fired. I never did anything without due cause, though. So explain to me. What possible reason do you have bringing William Benson in for?"

"He had a blank sheet, sir. I just figured it as due diligence to question him. We pulled a similar stunt on Gina Samuels, didn't we?"

"I would think you could clearly distinguish the difference between the two. In essence, all it is, is a piece of damn memo pad paper. Technically, anyone who has that paper could be looked at for this. And at the same time, you can't look at anyone."

Wiley nodded his understanding. He knew full well of the difference and the reason. He always had a way of letting his pride get the better of him. Russell went on.

"I understand there's a beef between you and Kyle. I don't understand what the problem is, though. And I certainly don't understand why he continues to stand in defense of you. I was set on firing you and filing charges myself, for espionage."

Wiley's eyes flashed with fear. He knew that there would probably be some kind of backlash. But espionage? His breath caught in his throat. He wanted to apologize profusely. He opened his mouth, but nothing came out. His phone went off again.

"Close your mouth, Wiley. I said I *was* set on it. I didn't say I'm *about* to do it. Kyle talked me out of it."

Wiley snapped his mouth shut, seemingly relaxing a little. But only a little. The simple fact that he was that close to going to prison was wiped away, all because of the one person he couldn't stand.

"But I do have to slap you on the wrist. You're suspended for a week, without pay."

Wiley simply nodded his understanding, feigning being upset about the punishment. As long as he could still be an FBI agent, he could deal with a suspension. Missing the money didn't bother him as much. The man was worth more than four million from his scamming days. He expertly suppressed the urge to smirk, looking down at the floor.

"And it starts now. Get out of here, Wiley. Go home."

He walked to the door then stopped and turned around. He wanted to say something about Frazier. As if reading his mind, Russell spoke before Wiley got a chance to.

"If you have anything to say to me about Kyle . . ." He ran his index finger across his throat, a symbolic gesture of decapitation that Wiley understood full well.

But he only responded with, "Thank you for being lenient, sir." And then he walked out before Russell could go on another tirade.

He walked by the room where Benson was taken. He and Frazier hadn't left yet. Benson sat there, resting both of his hands on top of his cane. Frazier was leaned back in the chair on the two back legs. They laughed and talked like best friends at a Christmas party. They both caught sight of Wiley walking by and stopped talking, but smiles were still on their faces.

Benson leaned in, mouthing something silently. Both man started laughing anew. Wiley could only scowl as he passed, seeing them through glass to the room. When he was out of sight, he squeezed his phone as it went off again. It was a call from Marla. She clearly wanted to talk about nothing he was interested in, so he swiped the Ignore button.

The thought of not having his money reentered his mind. So he checked his offshore account when he got in the car. He smiled knowing that's one thing that couldn't be touched.

CHAPTER 21

FOUR

"Ah! Ah! Ah!"

"I mean, honestly. Does he really have to make all that noise?"

"Just ignore him. He's minding his own business."

"How can I ignore him? You could hear him yelling across the street, I bet."

"Doesn't bother me."

"Well, it bothers me. I can't focus. Look at him. All he's trying to do is draw attention to himself."

"It seems to be working. You can't keep your eyes off him."

"Please. He doesn't move me like that one bit."

"Then go say something if it bothers you that much."

"You know what, I think I will."

Some people just simply feel they have the right to say the way things should be in life. And Gretchen Berg is one of those people. She once walked by a mother with her eight-week-old child in the hallway. The mother had the baby in the car seat, covered up for warmth.

In a carpeted hallway, the mother placed the car seat on the floor, patiently standing around. Gretchen Berg walked by and glanced at the child in the car seat. She continued to walk toward the elevator, pretending not to pay much attention to the mother other than a snarling glance.

She eventually couldn't help but come back and say something to the mother. She told the mother it wasn't right to have a baby on the floor in a public hallway while she just hung out. It made her look neglectful. She said a real mother would hold her baby rather than lay them out on the floor like a dog.

The nerve of this woman.

To no surprise, the mother responded with great offense, and the situation escalated until the husband walked out of the restroom, clearly the reason why the mother was in the hallway. The husband picked up child, and they walked away.

It wasn't until then that Gretchen realized the mother had both of her hands bandaged up pretty good. The family was heading into the doctor's office to get her hands looked at. The mother was physically unable to hold the sleeping child in the car seat.

With Gretchen having no children of her own, she clearly didn't know the rule of thumb with sleeping babies. And that is, you don't wake sleeping babies. Quite often, Gretchen would do such things. She had approached gardeners about the sounds of their leaf blowers being too high for her to sleep off her hangover.

She'd gone as far as asking children at a park to keep the noise down so she could read her book. And this case was no different. She weeded through objects on the floor as well as people in her path toward the source of her irritation. The man, Dan Barnes, saw her coming.

She walked up to him, waving her hands as if to flag down a taxi. "Excuse me, excuse me."

The man stopped what he was doing, wiping his face with his towel. He pulled out his earphones. His size was massive as he towered over the smaller Gretchen. But his demeanor was not aggressive when he spoke to her.

"Yeah?" he asked.

"Yes, hi. Um, you are making an awful lot of noise over here, and it's pretty distracting."

His kind demeanor died. His face screwed up as he looked at her. "Distracting to who?"

"Well, it's distracting to me. I can't focus on what I'm doing with all the noise you are making, yelling and slamming down weights and everything."

He gave her an incredulous look. "You're in a gym, lady."

"I'm well aware of that. But you really don't need to make all that noise. I'm sure other people feel the same way."

Dan Barnes looked to his left to ask another man. "My man, am I bothering you with my workout?" The man shook his head, continuing to do his routine. He asked another guy behind him doing preacher curls. "My man, is my working out bothering you?" The man shook his head also. He asked a woman who walked right by them. "Excuse me. Is my working out distracting to you?"

She shook her head no and chuckled. She clearly heard everything Gretchen was saying and thought her ridiculous. Doug turned back to face her, giving an exaggerated shrug. "I guess it's just you then."

"Well, yes, it is me. I just don't think I should have to be subjected to hearing you yell like some *lumberjack* while we're all trying to exercise."

"Lady, I am a lumberjack, owned my company for five years now."

She thought he was being sarcastic, until she saw the seriously offended look on his face. She blanched beneath his withering glare and turned and walked off without further word. She went back to the treadmill she was at previously, next to the woman she was first talking to.

The lady watched the whole thing but couldn't help but say something. "That went well." She smiled.

Gretchen never felt bad about approaching people. She never cared whom she offended because she always thought she was saying it nicely. But the way she said the word *lumberjack* was meant in a demeaning way. She turned the treadmill back on and said nothing else.

Doug was even louder this time. He was upset beyond the reason he was there in the first place. One of his staff got hurt at work. The man had a shard of wood break off and shoot straight through his leg. The injury would clearly have him out of commission for a while.

Doug was good friends with the man. The guy was a good worker. So he told him to put a rush on the work because of the mass orders they needed to fill. He blamed himself for pushing so hard. With each rep, grunt, and yell, he was forgiving himself. It was starting to work until little miss "*distraction*," came over and messed up his vibe. Not only that, she insulted his profession. She made it sound like barbarian work.

Elliot Allen, the second man Dan Barnes asked the question to, came over and said something when he finished his reps, chuckling. "The nerve of that lady."

"Tell me about it."

Elliot reached in his backpack, pulling out two bottles of water. He took one and offered the other to Dan.

"Appreciate that." Dan accepted it.

They both gulped simultaneously. Both men were around the same size, not cut lean but bulked massively. Their arms were the size of low-back pillows in width. They both wore tank tops and basketball shorts. They mirrored each other by bringing the bottoms of the bottles down at the same time.

Elliot looked down at Dan's waist, then back up to his face and smirked. "Seriously?" He pointed at his waist. "A fanny pack?"

"Hey, it's convenient. All I need in here is my driver's license, my keys, a few dollars, and some gum." He pulled out two sticks of Wrigley's Spearmint and offered one to Elliot.

"Thanks." Elliot took it. "I'm about to work some chest right now. Want to spot me?"

"Yeah, all right."

They walked over to the classic bench press area—bar and bench. Elliot began putting plates on each side, along with the already forty-five-pound bar. Each side of the bar held a weight poundage that Elliot steadily added to.

He put on a pair of forty-five-pound weights, followed by a pair of thirty-fives. The total amount came up to 205 pounds. Dan pointed at the bar with a mirthless smirk. "Really?"

"Just to warm up," Elliot responded.

Dan nodded, seemingly approving of the answer. "What's your max?"

"Not sure. I got up to three fifty, six years ago. But that was when I wasn't focused on strength training. You?"

"Four twenty."

Elliot shrugged, nodding approval as he sat down on the bench. "Say, throw two more tens on there for me."

Dan obliged. He put one on each side while Elliot lay down and grabbed the bar with two hands. He took three short, hard breaths, then lifted. He lifted 225 pounds with the greatest of ease, rising and falling gracefully as the bar lightly touched his chest and sprang back up to his full arm extension. Dan stood a foot away from his head, ready to intervene if needed. He counted silently in his mind with each completed repetition.

Seeming entirely unfazed, Elliot began to talk. "Are you a movie fan?"

"Yeah. Big time," Dan answered.

"Give me your top five movies of all time?"

Dan gave a whistle sound. "Wow, I don't know. There's so many."

"Just give me the five that you just can't ever get tired of watching." If Elliot was starting to feel any fatigue or strain, it wasn't evident in his voice or rhythm. He was already nearing rep nine, and no slowing down.

"Give me yours, first."

"I'll start from five to one. Then you give me yours." He slowed the rep up to match the number he called out, pausing at the top to mention the name of the movie, reaching rep ten to coincide with the five movies and fifteen reps of 225 pounds.

"Yeah, all right."

"Number five, *The Sin City*. Number four, *Mr. & Mrs. Smith*. Number Three, *Rocky*. Two, *Die Hard*. And number one, *Braveheart*."

With that last name, he hung the weights back up on the rack at fifteen. He still didn't look labored, but he might be the type that knew his limits.

He sat up from the bench and walked around to the head side, while Dan changed positions with him, nodding his head. "Not bad. Not bad. Now, my list."

He put his gloved hands on the bar and lifted it off the rack. Likewise, he pressed and paused while he ran off the names. "Number five, *Master and Commander*. Number four, *Beverly Hills Cop*. Number three, *Total Recall*." He paused to look at Elliot. "The classic one with Arnold, not that garbage remake one." He went back to pressing. "Number two, *Usual Suspects*. And number one, *Gladiator*."

Elliot always favored *Braveheart* over *Gladiator*. He had no problem arguing over it as well. "Don't tell me you're one of them."

Dan paused and looked at him, with the bar in midair. "One of who?"

"One of those that think the *Gladiator* is better than *Braveheart*."

"Well, I did say it was my favorite movie of all time."

"I'm just wondering if you simply slipped up and forgot to put *Braveheart* on your list."

Dan continued pressing. "Nope. Because I gave you mine after I heard yours. *Braveheart* was good, but it was no *Gladiator*."

"You're right it wasn't. *Braveheart* was way better."

Dan stopped and put the weights back on the rack. His count surpassed Elliot's by two. He lifted seventeen and clearly had enough to keep going. But the topic of his favorite movie was being approached, and he had to deal with it.

"Tell me exactly, what makes *Gladiator* better?" Elliot asked.

"You first."

"They were fighting for a cause in *Braveheart*—freedom of tyranny, brotherhood, leadership, war . . ." Elliot spread his arms. "What more do you want?"

"I'll give you that *Braveheart* is a good movie in its own right. It's just not better than *Gladiator*."

"Give me specifics." Elliot took another gulp of his water.

"A commander of the most powerful army in the world set to take rule. He's double-crossed by a usurper, sent to slavery, and his family is murdered. He ends up embracing the life of a battle animal, with the intent to get revenge. I mean, honestly." Dan spread his arms this time. "Are you not entertained?"

"It's not a matter of being entertained. It's a matter of being impressed. And *Gladiator* doesn't impress me. William Wallace? He rode into a man's bedroom on a horse and smashed his face in with a ball and chain. You can't get more badass than that."

Dan finished his water in a few more gulps. "Hey, walk with me over to the nutrition store over there. I need some more water. And I will be more than happy to explain to you how Maximus the Spaniard was more of a badass."

The nutrition store was placed in a corner of the gym. There was where they sold protein shakes, protein bars, fat-burning capsules, T-shirts, tote bags, towels, and water. They walked by the cardio area where rows of recumbent bikes, stair steppers, treadmills, and elliptical machines were. Gretchen eyed the two gentlemen walking by bickering over movies, as she sped up her pace to a fast walk on the treadmill.

"Look at him. No regard for anyone else."

"Why are you so worried about him? You asked him to stop, and he did."

"That's not the point. Guys like that always think they can just do what they want. He even walked by this way to taunt me."

"I think you're overreacting. He didn't even look at you. And you and I both heard the conversation. They were talking about movies."

Gretchen continued to give a side glance at Dan and Elliot at the store. Their conversation continued, while Gretchen seethed. "I have had a rough week. I just want to get my workout in before I have to do what's next on my agenda."

"You know, if I didn't know any better, I'd say you have a little thing for him."

Gretchen scoffed but kept watching out the corner of her eye. "Good thing you don't know any better."

Dan and Elliot walked back by the cardio area, still in conversation. Gretchen hid her face a little as they passed. She turned to watch them go back to the free-weight area. As her eyes followed them back, she met the eyes of the lady on the machine next to her.

Gretchen nearly missed a step on the conveyer belt and had to hold on to the side rails. The other woman laughed. Gretchen laughed it off as well, with wide eyes at the near misstep. "Whoa."

"So what's the real reason you wanted to go over there? To complain about his distracting you, or to get a better look at his bulging biceps? Wondering how strong he would wrap you in those arms."

Gretchen responded, "I went to over there to simply ask him to keep the noise down. We're all trying to work out here. We don't need to hear all that animalistic grunting and yelling."

"Well, there is a time and a place for animalistic grunting, isn't there?"

"Can't argue with you there." They both laughed. Gretchen glanced at the two gentlemen having their spirited debate. "But I can't help but notice how cute he was up close. What about the other one? You think he's cute?"

The woman looked over, still maintaining her mild speed walk. "He's cute. But I'm married."

"Oh. Well, can you just go over there with me and be my wingman?"

"Don't you mean your wing woman?"

"It's a general term, if you think about it. It really doesn't have a gender connation to it. Some try to make it that way, but they don't have to. Just like an actor and actress. An actor is a role-player. It really doesn't require a gender distinction. Some feel it does, but it really doesn't."

"You know, I agree with you on that. Just like a model. It's general. A model is male or female. Even animals sometimes. But all the same, my husband is in law enforcement. He can get pretty high-strung at times."

"Oh, come on. You don't have to maintain any connection with the guy. You're just there for support. It would feel awkward to walk up to him now after how I came at him a while ago."

"Oh, all right."

The woman slowed the treadmill down to cool down, then stepped off. Gretchen didn't bother. She hit the stop button and immediately stepped off, tightening her hair in its bun. Gretchen was not a bad-looking woman. She was athletically built and short. She wore matching gray tights and an athletic top.

The woman next to her was tall and petite. She was slender built like a model, with long hair tied into a ponytail. She wore black tights and a pink athletic top. She wiped the sweat from her neck then draped the towel over the arm of the treadmill. She turned to Gretchen.

"All right, I'll go over there with you. But you're going to do all the talking."

Gretchen smiled. "Deal."

They made their way through the clutter of people walking by, trying to get from one workout station to the next. They closed in on Elliot and Dan, and as the two were still bantering.

Elliot was up in arms in his discussion. "Are you kidding me? The cinematography of *Braveheart* was way better. From the landscape out on the range, to the ratty outfits the Scottish wore under. And the plot was more interesting."

"What? More interesting?" Dan frowned.

"That's right. Tell me what the plot is then. Because obviously I'm missing something," Elliot responded.

"All right. A great Roman general is decreed to be the next emperor. The night he is named successor, the son who was passed over kills his father and assumes the mantle. The general is arrested and set to be executed. He escapes to find his family is killed and his home destroyed by the new coward emperor because of the threat he poses to him.

"The general ends up a slave and is forced to fight in the gladiator games for Rome. He embraces the life and vows vengeance on the emperor. His second-to-none skills and defiance earn him favor over the Roman crowds, thereby tying the hands of the emperor. He had to fight impossible odds and always won. He got his vengeance but died due to the coward playing dirty.

"But he died fulfilling the wishes of his mentor and former emperor. He wanted to give Rome back to the people. And he did by getting rid of that piece of trash."

Elliot smirked. "Okay. I'll bite that the story is interesting. But the execution in *Braveheart* was much better."

Dan crossed his massive arms. "Oh, please elaborate."

"A nation under the tyrannical rule of the British has only a select few that are willing to fight. One boy learns his father and brother died trying to fight the tyranny. He vowed to stay out of all of it and just live a simple life. Until his wife is killed for fighting off a rape attempt by British soldiers.

"He goes ape shit and says no more bowing. He sets out on a path to kill as many Brits as he can under the guise of freedom. His legend grew and inspired many Scotts. Of course, he gets double-crossed and dies a martyr."

Dan yawned. "Oh, please. Talk about not being creative with a plot."

"It doesn't have to be creative. Because unlike the guy in *Gladiator*, William Wallace actually lived."

"Did you even see *Gladiator*?"

"Of course."

"So are you saying you would take William Wallace over Maximus in a fight?" Doug asked.

"Now that's a different discussion. We were talking about which is the better movie. Now you're talking who would win a fight."

"It's clear, we can't come to any common ground between the two movies. So let's look at the characters." Elliot sat down on the bench, preparing to resume his reps. Dan stood at the head of the bench after adding thirty-five more pounds on each side, bringing the weight to 295 pounds total.

"I would still go with Maximus, straight up in a one-on-one fight."

Elliot sat back up quickly after lowering himself slow. "You can't be serious! William Wallace was no joke."

"But he always had a crew. Maximus had to go out and fight four and five guys by himself."

Elliot put his hands up apologetically. "Hey, all I'm saying is—"

"Hello again," Gretchen cut into their conversation. She spoke to both of them but was focused on Dan. "Sorry to interrupt, but we just wanted to come over and say hello."

"Thought you already said hello. In your own little way." The tone in Dan's voice spoke volumes of how he felt about her last approach.

"I'm sorry about that. Just been having a rough week."

"Yeah, me too," Dan responded.

"I second that," Elliot replied.

"Here, here," the woman threw in.

Gretchen went on. "Listen. I'm not the shy type as you can tell. I speak my mind on things I want. I think you're hot. I would like to get to know you, in a biblical sense. No strings attached. I honestly don't have much time."

"So what does that mean to me?"

"I would like to apologize to you for my behavior earlier, in the steam room, perhaps."

Dan looked at Gretchen, actually looked at her this time. A smile crept across his face. "Fair enough. I don't have much time either. Let's go."

The two headed over to the sauna, leaving Elliot standing there with the tall woman. She watched them go and grinned, turning her eyes back to the gawking Elliot.

Her smile stayed as she lifted her left hand. "I'm married."

"I see. Well, I think you're beautiful anyway. He's a very lucky man."

She thought for a minute. She couldn't remember the last time her husband said she was beautiful. She clearly was and tried to look her best for him. It also didn't hurt that her profession required it. He was always so wrapped up in his achievements in his career, even after everything they'd been through.

Elliot looked at her, tilting his head. "Do I know you from somewhere?"

She rolled her eyes. "One of the oldest lines in the book, I see."

"No, seriously. You look strangely familiar."

"We really don't have time for this, you know."

"Yeah, I know. You're right. What time is it anyway?" Elliot asked.

"About a quarter to five." She looked at her watch.

Elliot grunted. "Well, I need to finish my sets."

"I'm about to do legs anyway."

They went on with their workout routines, now only spaced five feet from each other.

She couldn't deny that there was a certain attraction she had toward Elliot the moment she saw him. She sat on the leg press machine, glancing at him as he hefted heavy weights on the curl bar. She watched as his muscles bulged and veins flared.

Her husband was not puny. But he wasn't the specimen that Elliot was either. She never actually considered stepping out on her husband, until she laid eyes on Elliot. He finished his reps, dropping the weights with a thud.

Moments passed. Dan and Gretchen met back up with Marla and Elliot. All four stood in a semicircle. Gretchen tied her hair back into a bun again as she spoke.

"What time is it?"

"A little past a quarter to six," Elliot answered.

The other three grunted in response, standing in a circle of four. No one said anything for ten seconds, standing there with eyes shifting from person to the next. Dan broke the silence. "Ready?" They all nodded.

"All right. I'm Dan Barnes."

"I'm Elliot Allen."

"I'm Gretchen Berg."

"I'm Marla Wiley."

CHAPTER 22

ANOTHER ONE

WHEN SOMEONE HAS a day from hell, the first thing they want to do is bury it. The countless number of distractions one uses to achieve this burial is subject to the individual. Being a late night, Wiley sought to such distractions by a burial of his member.

In a small guest room in his house, Christina howled a sound of ecstasy mixed with agony. Wiley had required her to do this times before. She never protested but hated that he had to be so animalistic about it. It always left her sore for days and forced her to walk awkwardly.

Wiley was never considerate of her. He could have done number of things to ease this situation for her. He could have had her leaning over the bed so her chest would have something soft to fall upon. He could have slowed his rhythm, used more controlled tenderness. Hell, he could have even used more lube.

But it was never Wiley's way to be considerate of anyone. Sweat ran down his forehead onto her back as he had her bent over a bedpost. He vigorously thrust, with his hands wrapped around her throat. Christina searched her mind to enjoy it. Perhaps then she could open herself completely. Perhaps it wouldn't hurt so much.

But she couldn't. Mostly because she had to force herself to enjoy *him*. It had nothing to do with his appearance. She first thought he was attractive. But his attitude and smug nature knocked him down a good four or five points. But what was she to do? She had no skills and came from a foreign country where life wasn't much better there either.

She would have been forced into doing this for a means of simply live, not just an extracurricular thing in addition to cleaning households. The agency she came from only employed refugees. There was no union to air their grievances to. She never felt brave enough to deny him. And he was a federal agent. She feared deportation.

In most cases, particularly in this one, she had to literally grit and bear it. He slammed her face in the bed, cutting off her breathing against the gold orb on the bedpost in her stomach. He gripped tighter as he neared climax.

The final four thrusts were the worst of all. She hated this part. It felt as if she was being impaled by spring-loaded tree log. She tried to brace, readying herself for it. But nothing ever had. The more she screamed, the more it excited him. It always did. Sometimes she would increase her screams, knowing it brought him to fruition sooner, just so it could be over with.

But that failed to maintain working because he would be aroused again shortly and go at her harder than before. It was best to let his energy wane with time rather than have him complete too soon. On the forth thrust, he yelled like Tarzan—literally like Tarzan.

It was apropos to the role-playing he had them do. She was a jungle native that never wore clothes, and he was Tarzan himself. He released the grip around her throat. She had gotten good at holding her breath. She inhaled deeply, only to have another surprising gasp as he finished with thrust number 5.

He backed away, wiping the sweat from his face with his Tarzan sash.

"Woo! I needed that. After the day I had . . . let me tell you. I'm sure you needed it too, didn't you, Christina?"

"Yes, Special Agent." Her voice was hoarse, a little above a whisper.

He took off his Tarzan costume and handed it to her to wash. "This whole room needs to be cleaned up and incensed. I don't want Marla having any idea what's going on."

"Yes, Special Agent."

"And, Christina, keep your clothes off."

"Yes, Special Agent."

He went downstairs, walked passed the dogs, and headed toward the kitchen. He walked past the front door when he heard a knock. He stopped and turned to look, making sure he wasn't hearing things. The knock came again, this time more forceful.

Wiley, still naked, went over to the monitor to see who was at the door. His heart pounded that Marla might have come home early. But she wouldn't knock on her own door, so he suppressed the anxiety. The knock came a third time, just as forceful. He reached the monitor just as the knock came.

His blood boiled in recognition of the person. "Frazier." He growled in a menacing voice. He thought to open the door and quickly punch Frazier in the face. His muscles tensed at the prospect. Then he noticed he was naked. He ran to the laundry room and put on some boxers and sweat pants. Frazier didn't knock anymore, as if he knew Wiley saw him there, debating if he should open the door.

In short time, Wiley had on his sweats pants and a T-shirt fresh out of the dryer. He opened the door, snarling. Frazier stood there with a strange look on his face. He removed his glasses with one hand on the side of the brim. Before he could speak, Wiley yelled in his face.

"What the hell are you doing here again? I told my guard to not let anyone in, specifically you!"

Frazier completely ignored his anger and spoke calmly. "We got another one."

"Another what?" Annoyance dripped from his voice.

"The parking lot. The café. And now," he held up a blank sheet of memo paper, "the gym."

"I'm suspended, remember?"

"No longer." He tossed Wiley's credentials at him that were caught between his hands and his chest.

Wiley cooled only a little. He stared at Frazier, receiving nothing in return. Finally, he decided to get in gear and do his job. "All right. Let me get dressed. Wait here."

"I'll be at the guard shack."

Wiley closed the door and walked upstairs to where Christina was cleaning the room. She heard him come to the door and stand there. She froze, hoping he didn't want to start a second round. She felt his eyes staring right through her. She turned her head slightly to see him out the corner of her eye, trying not to look obvious.

She saw that he was not looking at her at all. She let out a small sigh of relief, but only small. He had done that before. But this time, he looked really disturbed in thought. She wanted to ask him if he was all right. For all the ways he treated her and forced her to do things she didn't want, she still held a small level of concern for him.

Dust kicked up in her face, prompting a hard sneeze, the type of sneeze that comes from the toes, the type that make you double over uncontrollably. She reactively put a hand over both sore areas to mask the shot of pain. She paused, attempting to collect herself and take a breath.

He stood there looking in the corner with one hand on his hip and the other twirling his bottom lip. He jumped in gear, as if a thought finally came to mind. He left the room and went to his closet in another room. Christina continued to clean, saying nothing. Fear gripped her that Marla might come home and see her like this.

For all of Marla's beauty, she had a real ugly streak. Christina was often more terrified of her than him. Wiley passed back by the room, fully dressed in standard special agent attire—black slacks, white collared shirt, and black blazer. He was fixing his black necktie when he leaned in and spoke.

"Christina."

She jumped. He was stealth in his return. "Yes, Special Agent?"

"You'll stay in this room tonight. I'll be back. I got another case to deal with."

"But it's my night at the shelter."

"Say what?"

"The children's homeless shelter. I volunteer there helping feed the children, wash, and provide clean clothes for them. I stay overnight and help feed them breakfast in the morning. There are shifts, and no one else to take mine. I promised them."

Still fixing his tie, he shrugged. "Well, not tonight. I need you here."

"But there's no one else to cover me. It's my duty. Who will care for them?"

"Not my problem. I need you here. You volunteer for them, but you work for me."

Christina dropped her head and voice. Her body seemed to deflate like a balloon. "Yes, Special Agent."

"Good." He nodded, making his way downstairs and outside. He walked to a car near the guard shack, where Frazier waited in the passenger seat. Anger flared in him. Not only did this guy come to his house at night, but he expected him to drive too?

He stormed over to the passenger side and yanked on the door handle. It was locked. The handle gave with no resistance. As a result, Wiley staggered back on his heels, arms flailing, trying to find something to grab a hold of.

He finally caught his footing and righted himself. Frazier never even looked at him. The windows were down as he spoke, looking straight ahead.

"I haven't been up here at night before. I think it's only fitting that you're the one that should drive down a hill that you're familiar with. I wouldn't want to get us crashed. We already have a tragedy we're headed to."

Wiley wanted to explode. He stood there a long moment, staring daggers at the passenger. Once again, no return came his way. Frazier just continued to patiently look straight ahead.

Wiley made a point around the front of the car to the driver's side, staring at Frazier the whole time. As soon as he got in, Frazier leaned over and turned the key in the ignition. "You made it up here. Why can't you make it back?"

"We're late, Wiley."

The angry agent continued to stare as he put the car in drive. He signaled the guard over, as he leaned out the driver's side window. Wiley turned his eyes back to Frazier as he spoke. "Hey, Alexander, you're fired." Then he drove off.

Halfway down the hill, Frazier spoke in the silence they rode in. "A man has to lose his job because he let me in?"

"He lost his job for not doing as I said."

"And that is?"

"Not to let you in."

Wiley drove scary fast down the hills at night, twisting and turning like a street race, running virtually every stop sign. Frazier continued to look straight ahead. "Do you have to drive so fast?" His tone was flat, nonchalant even.

"You're the one that said we're late."

Frazier sat quiet for a second before speaking again. "You realize she doesn't like it."

"What?" Wiley frowned in confusion.

"Christina. She doesn't like being your sex slave. And I'm pretty sure your wife wouldn't to be happy about it either."

"First of all, you mind your own business. Don't speak on wife. And don't speak on anything I do in my own house." Venom dripped from every word. He remembered the last time Frazier was there, and it burned at him for rematch.

"What's the second of all?" Frazier asked, still looking forward.

"What?"

"You said *first of all*. When you say first of all, you have to have at least a second of all." The little dig caused Wiley to swerve. He lost focus on the road momentarily, only to have an oncoming car honk their horn at them.

"Oh shit!" Wiley struggled to regain control. He ran across a rose bush on someone's front yard coming down the hill. Frazier showed no semblance of fear. He simply held on to the door panel with his right hand, with his left braced up against the roof, still looking forward. They rode in silence after that little scare, until they reached their destination.

The usual was scattered all over the crime scene. Witnesses, new arrivals, police, medics, and reporters littered all through the parking lot of the Fit Pit gymnasium.

The usual yellow tape sealed off the entrance. The two agents rolled up, and Wiley started to exit the car. He paused, glancing over at Frazier and saw him scanning the crowd. He settled himself back down and started scanning as well. "So who looks good to you?"

Frazier flipped a licorice root in his mouth, completely ignoring Wiley, exiting the car. Wiley sat there watching him in exasperation that turned into to bottled rage. He opened the door then slammed it shut.

Wearing his long black trench coat, Frazier stepped right under the yellow tape into the gym. A beat cop noticed and ran over to him.

"Hey, pal! Get back over across that line." He stepped in front of Frazier, putting a hand on his chest. He saw Wiley come through and said the same to him. Frazier didn't say a word. He looked down at the hand on his chest, twirling the root in his mouth.

Wiley walked up and did his favorite thing in the world to do, throw his weight around, flashing his credentials. "Unless you want to get busted down to meter-maid man, you better keep your nose out of federal business."

The cop blanched, pulling his hand back as quickly as if it were on a hot stove. "Sorry, sirs. Just doing my job."

"And a fine job you're doing, Officer . . ." Frazier looked at his name tag, "Preston. What precinct are you with?"

"The Fifteenth, sir."

"Ah, the Fifteenth. I will call Captain Dunn in the morning and inform her of the display of excellence her officers show. I'm sure she will take it as a personal compliment. This will go in as a good mark in your jacket from the federal government."

Officer Preston's eyes widened. "Thank you, sir. That's generous of you."

Frazier nodded and smiled. He paused, holding up a finger as if a thought struck him. "Oh, and, Preston."

"Yes, sir?"

"She doesn't mean it when she says she could wait another year before you propose. She would rather you at least propose now, then marry her a year later. You know, give you both some time to plan. That's the irony of it. It's not exactly a lie, but it's not all the truth. She just wants something a little more concrete."

Preston looked genuinely shocked. "Uh, sir. What are you . . . ?"

"Suanne. She's a good girl, Preston. Don't run her away. Bad enough she doesn't think she deserves you. And she loves you with all her heart. But, come on. To string her along for four years then telling her you could marry her any day if you wanted to, not the kind of thing a woman wants to hear."

"Wait. How do you . . . ?" He looked at Wiley, then back to Frazier. "How do you know all this?"

"Just a word from the wise, kid. Tomorrow is not promised today. The biggest difference between time and money is you can only get one of them back. Take her to that skating ring she loves so much. There's nothing better than a woman getting a proposal by the man she loves in her favorite place."

Officer Preston was dumbfounded. How did Frazier know so much about this man's personal life? The guy had been contemplating marrying his girlfriend but wasn't sure if he was ready for it. But something about the way Frazier talked to him pulled him in that direction.

He felt resolute. Decisive. Motivated. He was going to buy the ring tomorrow when he got off his shift and propose that very next night at the ice skating ring. One could see the wheels in his head turning as he considered how his woman had been so patient and never forthcoming about her feelings in favor of his.

He looked Frazier in the eye and no longer cared how he knew. He simply felt relieved to have help to get pushed in that direction. He took one of Frazier's hands in both of his, shaking it vigorously. "Thank you, sir. You're right. I'm going to make Suanne Mrs. Preston."

Frazier returned the shake with a genuine smile, clapping him on the shoulder. Preston walked past Wiley like he wasn't even there, making Wiley upset as he nearly bulled by him, grazing his shoulder.

He turned back to Frazier with his hands arms spread out wide, ready to take it out on him. But Frazier wasn't looking at him either. He looked around and let out a deep, slow breath as he took in the scene. Wiley stopped next to him, raised his eyebrows, and put his hands on his head.

The facility was large. Rows of exercise-specific sections were grouped together. They entered the door to the left, and there was an area where various classes were held, blocked off by glass with hard wood floors and an abundance of mirrors. It was clearly used for aerobics and whatnot. The room next to it was slightly smaller.

Instead of open space, the room was littered with spin cycle bikes. In the room next to that one was a slightly smaller area, with not as many mirrors as the one for aerobics, but still a few. A number of sand-filled punching bags hung for the steel planks across the ceiling.

A small rack hung on the wall holding jump ropes, boxing gloves, and punch mitts. Kick pads rested on the floor against the wall under the rack. A set of blue fall mats sat off in the far corner of the entrance. To the right of the mat stood a five-foot-tall Wing Chun dummy post.

Three-foot-long wooden pegs jotted from the center of the post in an upside-down triangular shape. Although the post itself was wooden, the exterior was incased in cushion. The post saw regular use only by those with familiar knowledge to its purpose.

A skilled practitioner of the Wing Chun dummy post could perform a series of fluid movements to mirror a near dance. A series of strike and block combinations in close quarters prove invaluable in real-life application. However, the grace of the techniques, the balance, timing, even the post itself become nothing of any use to those with no concept of the knowledge required.

Next to that room was the general store. All the various goods and supplies needed for gym etiquette can be found in that store. On the other side of the wall of the store were the main offices.

The steam room, sauna, and swimming pool were on the east side of the gym. In the middle was where all the equipment was. Rows of tall windows were facing both the north-side and the south-side entrance. All cardio equipment and machines were on the north side. Treadmills, ellipticals, stair climbers, recumbent bikes, and various other cardiovascular stimulating machines lined the entire north wall from end to end.

Machines that allowed to work on specific muscle groups in a safe and controlled manner were located in the second row behind the cardio equipment. The desire to work on arms, legs, back, chest, hips, and core were all found there.

Then there was the "big boy" section, the free-weight area. The bench press, curl bars, kettlebells, dumbbells on racks, weight plates on racks, medicine balls, weight belts, weight bars, and even resistance bands occupied the last row headed back toward the south-side entrance.

Blood splatters made their way over to the far end of the cardio section. Three treadmills had specks on conveyer belts, as well as a few more on the bottom half of the machine. The strength machines appeared unaffected due to the fact that they didn't go as close to the free-weight area as the cardio section did. Dumbbells were spread about on the floor, with the rack turned over.

The free-weights section began at a wide berth from the strength machines, with thick black mats in between. The mats continued throughout the section, finally ending within three feet from cardio machines. One treadmill was tipped over on its side, with a pool of blood gathered where it previously sat.

Four people lay dead near the southeast side—two men and two women. One man, with massive arms and blood-soaked tank top, wore a black fanny pack around his waist. Frazier walked over to him first because he was the closest to them. He put on his gloves, squatting near the man. The man was lying on his left side as Frazier approached.

A puddle of blood seeped alongside his head, forming a wet pillow. Frazier stepped around the man and stopped short at what he saw. He straightened, rolling his eyes as if wishing he hadn't seen what he did.

"Uh."

"What is it?" Wiley stepped close, still pulling his gloves on. He caught sight, not wavering as Frazier did. He stared, tilting his head as if to decide if he was looking at what he was looking at. "Damn. That's pretty bad."

The man on his side had deep abrasions on his knuckles, a wider pool of blood on the side he was facing, and a myriad of scratches on his arms. But the thing that stood out the most was a curl bar shoved in the place where his nose was supposed to be.

The curl bar went about a yard long. It curved in two places in a waving patter. The ends were the size of a soda can in diameter. No weights were on the other end, while the other end submerged deep into his face. His eyes locked open as if he saw the plunge coming and couldn't do anything about it.

Frazier looked closer and saw the imprint of the wide-diameter end on the back of his skull. "This impact had to have come from someone standing over him." He moved over to a woman, about five feet from him. She was short and athletically built.

She hung limp over a weight bench, bent backward. Wiley looked at her, narrowing his eyes. Frazier walked over and put a hand on the center of her chest. He brought his hand across the both sides of her breasts, then back to the center. Wiley couldn't help but seize the opportunity for a wise crack.

"Should I leave you two alone? I could have them turn the lights down low, or are you the type that like to see everything?"

"What are you talking about?" He continued to go about his inspection.

Wiley held up pleading hands. "Hey, I have my share of fetishes, I must admit. But necrophilia is not one of them."

Frazier turned his head to look at him, standing near his shoulder. His face was not one of anger or indignation. He shifted the root in his mouth as he chewed. "Took quite a while to stop sniffing glue when you were a kid, huh?"

The smirk on Wiley's face vanished. He did indeed develop an addiction to sniffing glue when he was eight years old. He continued to do it until he was thirteen. His face went slack as he put his hands down. Frazier turned back to the woman.

"If you know anything about the female body, you know that one breast is always going to be slightly bigger than the other. But look at this." He pointed. "Not only is the right breast bigger, but her chest is shifted."

"Shifted?"

"This whole left side is caved in."

The poor woman had her right leg bent back unnaturally. Her hair hung free, touching the floor. Her arms hang free, spread out wide with the backs of her knuckles touching the floor. She had a fair share of cuts and bruises on her face and head. Blood seeped from the corners of her mouth. The indication was that some must have spit out.

Free-weight plates scattered all over the floor told the story of the struggle. Most likely the men might have jostled quite a bit. The other man involved had similar-size arms. He lay on his weight bench as if he was getting ready to do a set. The only problem, the weight bar was on his neck.

"How much is that on there?" Wiley asked.

"Looks like nearly three hundred pounds."

The man had more than a few bruises on his face. He clearly took a pounding from the other man on the floor. A mass of shattered mirror in larger chunks and tiny pieces littered the floor near a wall.

Frazier shook his head in shame. "Unbelievable that these people would go to these links. A fight is a fight. But to leave all this destruction and brutal means of killing in their wake . . ." His words trailed off as he walked over to the last victim/culprit.

Wiley moved in to get a closer look at the man on the bench. Something about his face seemed vaguely familiar. He shook his head, unable to place where he might have seen him from. Frazier brought him out of his thought as he called him over.

"Wiley. You might want to take a look at this." Frazier's face was grim. "Then again, you might not," he muttered under his breath.

Wiley came over, pulling his gloves up and letting them snap. He stopped short when he saw the last person. He froze in place. He stood there staring, mouth agape.

His hands began to shake as he took in the sight. With a voice not much higher than a whisper, he spoke. "Marla."

CHAPTER 23

THE VIDEO

W ILEY STAYED THERE, stroking his wife's bruised and bloodied face for some time, before he allowed the coroners to take her. He cried so hard and loud that he found himself with no more tears left. He sat in his chair in the office with a blank stare, facing the desk.

Director Russell was much more compassionate than their last meeting. "Wiley, I'm terribly sorry about your wife. If you need anything, leave of absence, counseling, you name it."

Wiley didn't respond. His white shirt, coat, and tie were stained with his wife's dried bold. Frazier had taken the wheel back to headquarters this time. He gave him some tea from West India to calm him. It did, a little. The fact that it was so flavorful compelled Wiley to finish it.

Back in their office, Frazier placed more evidence on the big board. In addition to Marla Wiley, he put up the pictures of the other three people—Gretchen Berg, Elliot Allen, and Dan Barns.

Russell moved over to stand next to Frazier at the big board after releasing a firm sympathetic hand from Wiley's shoulder. "So what's the background on this people?"

Frazier stood facing the board, with one hand in his pocket and the other hand holding the licorice as he chewed. He looked over the board for a moment, quietly. Rather than speak, he handed the file to Russell to read over.

Gretchen Berg: No children, unmarried. A small business owner of a dance school. With a staff of nine people, the school taught many types of dance, such as contemporary, modern, tango, ballroom, and tap. Belly dancing had begun to make a strong start as of late, as was ancient Middle Eastern marriage dancing.

She was the elder of two children. Her younger sister, Haley, was an office manager at a medical clinic in Santa Clarita, California. Their parents, Kirk and Audrey, married of twenty-seven years and worked as accountants in Santa Clarita. Gretchen lived in Valencia, California, with her six cats.

Her small business proved quite lucrative. She managed to shell in over eighty thousand dollars a year, mostly due to the myriad of shows her school participated in.

"Crazy cat lady, huh?" Russell chuckled at his own quip. Frazier didn't bite. He maintained a focused demeanor as he chewed the root, continuing to survey the board.

Elliot Allen: Owner of a construction company. Unmarried, with four kids. All boys and two different mothers. His oldest boys—Jackson, age ten; and Grant, age nine—lived with their mother, Sherry, in Houston, Texas. Sherry was a social worker and engaged to a musician named Jerad Gray.

His other boys—Leonard, age eight; and Phillip, age seven—lived in Newark, New Jersey, with their mother, Sandy, a real estate agent for the corporate market. She recently married an engineer named Aaron Morrow.

He was seemingly one to rock the boat. The mothers of his children were also sisters. Needless to say that the involvement both women had with Elliot caused a rift between them, prompting them to have to live completely apart.

Elliot was third in a line of five. Two older sisters, Maggie Allen and Drew Frederickson. The eldest, Maggie, was never married, in her mid-forties, a dentist, living in Harrisburg, Virginia. Drew, the second-eldest sister, lived in Tuscan, Arizona. Divorced, high school principal with twin eleven-year-old daughters, Laura and Carey.

His two younger siblings, brothers, Morris and Fred Larson, were children of his mother remarrying. They worked together, running a small convenience store in Alhambra, California. All five siblings were close in communication. His stepfather and mother, Horace and Fiona, retired and gave the business to the younger sons.

Elliot was the man that Wiley thought for a brief moment he knew from somewhere, the same man that thought he recognized Marla. Frazier remembered Wiley mention it and turned to regard him. Wiley still sat in his chair, in a shocked state.

Frazier let the thought drop, returning his attention back to the board.

Dan Barns: A lumberjack. Owner of his own woodyard in Alta Dena, California. His girlfriend left him a month ago when she found out he impregnated another woman. No siblings. Raised by his foster parents, Joe and Lily Fisher, in Lawrence, Kansas. His foster father, Joe, was a plumber. Lily was a mailroom supervisor for the United States Parcel Service.

Russell turned another page in the file. "What's this?"

"The medical examiner came across something in her study that was interesting. Thought you might want to know."

Russell read the highlighted section of the report. "They found traces of Barns's semen in Berg? That is interesting. So they decided to have themselves a go before killing each other?"

"Wouldn't be the first time something like that happened. It happened quite a bit, as a matter of fact, during Roman times."

"Goodness, Frazier. You and your study of ancient history is beyond me. What is it you love so much about studying history as deep as you do?"

"One can learn much from the past to influence the future. Besides, it adds a new wrinkle in the pattern."

"Such as?"

"Well, from what we understand in all these cases, it appears the people are total strangers. How they end up here is beyond me. But these two total strangers have a one-night stand, then go back out and kill each other." He shook his head. "Something is not right."

Russell threw his hands up in the air. "Well, that's the understatement of the year, Kyle. Nothing about this whole damn thing is right."

A knock at the door announced an agent entering. He stopped in his tracks, giving Wiley a sad look, as he clapped him on the shoulder. Wiley sat still, oblivious to the sentiment. The agent handed a file to Frazier then walked out.

He took his glasses off the front of his shirt collar and put them on. After reading the short report, Frazier looked anything but pleased.

"What did it say, Kyle?" Russell noticed the look.

"I can't believe we didn't have this bit of information from the beginning." He slapped himself on the forehead with his palm. The first and only show on lack of control he displayed in a long time.

"What is it?" Russell became seriously interested.

"Well, it appears we missed something in our investigation. Jamison ran a bit of information for me that he thought would help with this case. I'm not sure if it does or not, but it is an avenue I apparently failed to address. Or even explore."

"Well, what is it?"

He handed him the file. "Read it for yourself."

Russell read it then looked at Frazier with a bewildered look. "Bank accounts? Off-shore bank accounts? Investment holdings? You have a list of all their financials. So what?"

"Look at the balances a week before their arriving to their respective crime scenes."

He looked at them, then back to Frazier, his face a mask of bewilderment. "They've been closed. All their accounts are empty. Even their otherwise off-shore untouchable accounts."

Suddenly, Wiley snapped his head up. He had over four million dollars on one of those accounts. He might have loved his wife, but he damn sure loved his money. He and she worked very hard at coming up with the right cons. He finally spoke.

"What? Empty? As in there is no money in the accounts?"

Frazier chewed his root, looking over the brim of his glasses as he turned halfway to look at him. "Afraid so."

Wiley started to panic. He looked around his desk, like he was seeking something. But he never used his hands to probe for anything. He simply sat there, shifting his head back and forth. "Oh shit, shit, shit."

He stood up quickly, walked over, snatched the file from Russell's hands, and started reading. Frazier and Russell shared a look then went back to watching the nut crack before their very eyes.

"Oh, shit!" Wiley threw the file on the desk and jetted out the door. He immediately called the off-shore account in Costa Rica. The phone continued to ring because they were closed. Wiley paced back and forth like a caged animal, hanging up the phone in frustration, only to dial the same number again half a second later.

"Come on. Come on. Come on." All traces of mourning disappeared. Russell thought the poor guy snapped. Frazier, on the other hand, eyed him suspiciously. Wiley finally walked out and got in his car. Russell moved to go after him but was stayed by Frazier's hand on his arm.

"Let him go. He'll be all right."

"Kyle, he might try to hurt himself."

"He won't. He would never do that."

"You're sure of this?"

"I'm sure of this."

Russell relaxed a little, then shrugged. "Well, he's your partner. You would know." He walked away and left Frazier standing there, nodding his head slowly in his own thoughts.

Another agent came to the office, handing him a disc. "Here it is, Kyle. Digitally mastered like you requested."

"Thank you, Anna." He observed the faraway look in her eyes as she tried to look down. She was clearly distraught, having seen the video of the brawl in the gym. "That bad, huh?"

She looked back up at him. "It's awful. And I've seen awful before, but this is something different."

Suddenly intrigued, he asked, "Different how?"

"Just, just see for yourself." She turned and walked away.

Frazier watched her go, observing her uncomfortable demeanor. He had worked a case or two with her before. Once, they found a kidnapped victim tied to a tree, naked, with barbed wire wrapped all the way around them.

She had a strong-enough stomach for that. So he wondered what he was going to see in the disc that would make her utterly disturbed. He patted the disc case in his hands a few times, then went over and inserted it into his computer.

Just as he did, Wiley came back in. He still looked disheveled. His hair was a mess, tie turned sideways. His eyes carried a defeated look. He was still wearing the same stained clothes. So he clearly didn't go home to change. Frazier didn't bother to ask him anything or even look up at him. He pressed Play on the computer.

"Is everything still there?" he asked.

Wiley plopped down in the chair. "What?"

"Is everything still there?"

"Still where?" His voice was hoarse and exhausted.

Frazier, still looking at the computer, answered him calmly, "Your house. All your furniture and belongings."

"Oh, yeah. Wait a minute. How did you . . . ?" He trailed off when Frazier finally looked at him. The man had a way of simply knowing. It no longer surprised him, but he was still caught off guard for half a second.

"I called Christina. She said everything was still there. I didn't tell her about Marla."

"Of course not. You can hardly believe it yourself."

"I just don't get it. What the hell was she doing there? She was supposed to be in Chicago by now." His face betrayed the look of crying, but no tears came.

"Did you check all your messages? Maybe she told you she was in town."

Wiley reached in his pocket and pulled his phone. He noticed there were a few more voice messages than he last checked.

"*Hi, honey. We had a last-minute change in plans. I will be back in California tomorrow. I'll be shooting in San Pedro. We have a hotel lined up, but I'm going to get me a workout in tonight at the Fit Pit. I hope you're being safe, honey. I love you.*"

Wiley lowered the phone slowly, looking at the desk. "She's been leaving me messages all this time. I could have answered any one of those calls and spoke with her. I could have talked her out of going to the gym. She would be home with me right now."

"I'm terribly sorry about that, Norman. But I doubt it would have prevented anything, or even delayed it for that manner. She had a blank sheet in her car."

"What? I'm so sick and tired of these fucking blank sheets!" Wiley roared, pounding his fist on the desk. "When does this end!"

"We have been trying to figure that out for the better part of a year. I know you want to be in the loop with the investigation. But I don't know if you want to see this video."

Wiley rubbed both hands on his face, collecting some resolve. "If my wife is on there, then I want to see it." He brought his chair next to Frazier to see the video.

Frazier pointed to the treadmill where Marla and Gretchen were talking and walking. They saw Gretchen glance over to the free-weight area and walk over. Marla continued to stay. Her fast walk became a jog. Wiley felt a pang of longing at seeing his recently deceased wife in motion.

The video cut to where Gretchen approached Dan. They were talking a little bit before Elliot came over. No audio was available. Shortly, Gretchen walked back to the treadmills. Dan and Elliot continued their workouts but appeared to be engaged in a spirited debate.

The video cut back to Marla and Gretchen at the treadmills talking. Wiley wanted to reach out and touch the screen but resisted the urge. Frazier sat there watching with the patience of a college professor observing a midterm project.

Dan and Elliot walked by the treadmills, still engaged in their conversation. Gretchen followed them with her eyes as Marla continued on with her cardio. When the men walked back past the treadmills again, Gretchen and Marla stopped what they were doing and walked over to talk to the men. Wiley leaned forward a little to try to lip read what was possibly being said.

Dan and Gretchen headed away toward the steam room. Marla and Elliot stood there talking for a brief stint. They eventually moved on to their respective workouts. The video cut away to Dan and Gretchen in the steam room. The mass of steam made it hard to get a clear visual.

So when the door opened, it was easy to miss. What was noticeable was Gretchen's feminine frame straddled the massive size of Dan in a seated position. Spouts of steam flowed, giving glimpses of Gretchen leaning her head back in ecstasy. A large spout of steam blocked the field of vision.

Half a moment later, the two figures were seen again. Dan had Gretchen pinned against the wall, bodies writhing. Wiley squinted when something caught his eye. They snapped open wide.

"Zoom in."

"Why?" Frazier asked.

"Just do it!"

Frazier complied.

Wiley's mouth dropped. In that moment, Wiley noticed. It wasn't Dan that had Gretchen against the wall. It was Marla pinned by Elliot. A wave of steam showed the figures of Dan and Gretchen on the other side of the room. But Wiley only saw his wife entangled with Elliot.

Noticing the need for some semblance of decency, Frazier tapped a button on the computer. The scene skipped. It cut away to all four standing in a semicircle back near the weights. He eyed the distraught husband. There were no words. Wiley sat still, frozen in time. A minute passed before he spoke.

"Why?" His voice cracked. The tears that dried flowed anew.

There was no room for anger at her betrayal. The thought of him being a hypocrite in that regard didn't even enter his mind. Sadness held his only emotion. Frazier began to play the rest.

A conversation among all four occurred. They all turned and looked at the clock on the wall, then faced each other.

Frazier leaned forward. He saw something. He skipped it back a bit then played it again. He did that about four times. Wiley didn't know what he was looking at. At the moment, he didn't care.

"There. You see?" Frazier pointed at the point the four people made. He was never good at lip reading, but he saw it on their faces as clear as day.

Wiley said nothing, still reeling from the steam room revelation.

"They are introducing themselves," Frazier added. "After all that time of talking and . . ." He trailed off, being sensitive to not speak on the previous scene. "They never knew each other's names."

Following the introduction, Marla threw a reverse spinning heel kick right into Elliot's face. Her long legs cleared the distance of a yard's length. He stumbled backward, slipping on a loose five-pound weight on the floor, hitting the dumbbell rack hard.

Within half a second of the kick Marla delivered, Gretchen squeezed water from her bottle into Dan's eyes. The slight distraction was all she needed. She bent down and picked up the weight Elliot slipped on that slid to her feet. She flung it like a Frisbee, hitting Dan above the lip right where a man's mustache grows.

Though it was a devastating blow, a man the size of Dan wouldn't go down that easy. Sensing that very notion, Marla heaved an eight-pound dumbbell with two hands for extra zip. The weight hit Dan square in the forehead. He also found himself falling backward, hitting the floor with a loud thud.

Gretchen leaped on Marla like a velociraptor. Her arms extended with her hands fixed in a clawing position. Her nails were half an inch long, filed and sharpened. Her legs were bent, using her knees to lead the way. She crashed with impact against the taller, slender Marla.

Both women met the ground, with Marla getting the worst of it. Gretchen immediately started slashing at Marla's pretty face, like an attack in the woods of a horror movie. Some of the slashes found purchase; most found forearms and elbows. Marla blocked whatever she could, unable to get a real look at where the strikes were coming from.

Gretchen used her knees to squeeze her ribs. She swung wildly, not attempting any precision. She swiped and screamed, looking like a little Tasmanian devil. It was hard for Wiley to watch. His face took on the look as if he was sucking on a sour lemon.

Right in midswing of her flurry, Gretchen was lifted by the scruff of her neck off Marla. The vice grip around her neck felt like an iron manacle. She found herself unable to move. She only held on the arm lifting her, looking like a scolded kitten.

She was flung effortlessly into the recumbent bikes, knocking two of them over. The impact also knocked over the nearest treadmill. A hit like that was sure to crack a rib or two. The powerhouse that flung Gretchen away was Elliot. He stumbled slightly, still reeling from the kick he received.

He bent down to grab Marla by the throat. With one hand he heaved her up. Her feet suspended at least three feet in the air before slamming her down on her back. Wiley gritted his teeth, unable to do anything about a past event he was currently watching.

Elliot followed up, lifting Marla again in the exact same fashion. He delivered another choke slam that saw her head pounce off the mat like a ball. Relentlessly, he reached down a third time. Her arms now limp, unable to reach out for defense. She was clearly dazed. The next slam was sure to break her skull.

As he lifted her to the full extension of his arm, he was spear tackled in his side by a Bison, better known as Dan Barns. The impact folded Elliot's body to form the greater than, less than symbol in mathematics. Elliot released his grip on Marla, thereby letting her fall to the floor limp like a towel dropping from the shower bar.

Both men crashed into a strength machine for squats. The machine was massive. Already weighing over a ton, it had plenty of heavy weights on it. It might not have been as painful if the machine tipped over. But it didn't give.

They lay there rolling slowly and painfully, while Gretchen finally got her bearings and went back over to mount Marla again. Marla appeared unresponsive. Gretchen brought a hand up high to deliver a catlike swipe with her clawed hands. She stopped at the height of her swing.

She glanced over at a weight plate of ten pounds. She leaned over and grabbed it. Huffing and puffing with blood running down her neck from the crash she took, she raised the weight above her head with both hands. She let out a shrill scream before bringing the weight down on Marla's head.

The scream brought Marla back to coherency, and instinct alone forced her to dodge to the left, avoiding the killing blow. Gretchen slammed the weight into the floor, smashing her fingers in the process. Marla cracked her in the side of the head with an elbow that sent her off.

She rolled over twice, landing near a weight bench. Marla got to her hands and knees, just trying to find a second to collect herself. She was the only person trying to stand. She got to her feet then found herself doubled over, falling to the floor. Dan threw a dumbbell, hitting her square in the stomach, unprotected.

He was still lying on his back when he threw it. Had he been at least on his knees, he might have been able to hit her in the head. He threw the fifteen-pound dumbbell with ease. A hit like that guarantees internal bleeding. Marla coughed blood, confirming the notion. She clinched at her stomach, unable to draw a breath.

Dan started to make it to his feet when a vice grip locked on both of his ankle. He was yanked forward to fall flat on his belly and face. His left cheek bounced off the floor, causing teeth to fly. Elliot found renewed vigor. He jumped on Dan's back, trying to administer a choke hold.

Lying in his belly, Dan managed to block the massive arm from getting around his throat with a massive arm of his own. Elliot delivered a series of rib punches, trying to get his opponent to drop his guard. Elliot reared back, preparing for a crushing deciding rib shot.

Dan reached and found a forty-five-pound plate near his head. He swung it backward, hitting Elliot on the side of the head. Elliot fell backward with his arms locked out straight and frozen stiff. Dan didn't bother getting up. He scurried over on his belly to Elliot, sticking a straight right hand to his mouth.

He took the hit square. His head snapped straight back unnaturally. Not the typical hit that sends someone's nose and eyes facing upward, this one saw his head slide back like a ball-bearing drawer.

The neck was clearly broken to some extent. Not to the point of paralysis, because he reached and grabbed the back of his neck instinctively with one hand when he hit the floor. The other hand went to cover his face for another blow. And as sure as the sun rises, another blow came directly to the guarded hand.

Even Frazier hand to grimace at the angle in which Elliot's head snapped back. Wiley was staring at Marla, stirring off to the side as Dan rained blow after blow. He didn't want to allow Elliot any time to regroup. He rolled on his side to generate more force in a short distance.

At that moment, Marla stomped on Dan's thick neck. If it wasn't for his muscled neck, the stomp would have killed him for sure. His head bounced against the floor. But he was enraged with adrenaline. He took the stomp and knocked her from her feet, swinging a tree trunk of an arm.

He got up and stood over her. He put two hands around her thin neck and lifted her up so fast he had to turn his body to stop her from flipping over him. He kept his left hand around her neck and his right hand between her legs. With the greatest of ease, he lifted her above his head. He tossed her into the mirror on the wall.

Wiley jumped, putting both hands on his head. He might not have been able to stand it if the audio was available. She slammed hard against the mirror, falling to the floor with shards of mirror falling on and around her. Marla at least had the wherewithal to put her arms up to cover her head a little. Glass shards stuck into her arms, and a few stuck in the side of her face.

Dan stalked over to her like a mighty predator in the jungle. Gretchen jumped on his back, swinging the mirror shard wildly. She got him one good time in his broad right shoulder. He reached back, grabbing a lock of her hair, and flung her to the ground.

As soon as she landed, he brutishly stomped on her stomach. He grabbed her by the hair and flung her away. She glided through the air, landing backward across a weight bench. Her head and feet hit the ground simultaneously upon landing.

The brute walked over and picked up a fifty-pound medicine ball. Her head laid back, her arms splayed out, and her legs spread apart and straightened, he stood between her legs, looking at her for a moment. A position he was no doubt in recently, but under different pretenses. He watched her breath pull raggedly.

He raised the ball above his head with both hands, arms extended. The ball lifted until it seemed to have reached its apex. Without remorse, he brought the weight down on the left side of her chest. It was more of a very hard toss, than a hammer.

Gretchen's body jerked from the force, then her arms and legs went limp. A stream of blood ran out of her mouth. Dan stood, taking a deep breath, when a forty-five-pound weight bar crashed across the back of his head. A dent is guaranteed with a hit like that. Dan fell over Gretchen's lifeless body on the weight bench.

He clutched the back of his head, rolling over and over until he was several feet away from her and Elliot. But Elliot didn't let up. Dan finally stopped rolling and ended on his back, appearing to be screaming in pain. The lack of audio provided the assumption.

Elliot stepped above him with the bar in his hands. He held the weighted bar like a broom about to sweep up the trash. He snarled and jammed the end of the weight bar into Dan's nose instead of his opened mouth. Dan's body went rigid. His arms fell away. Elliot glanced around when he noticed Marla still lying by the mirrors.

He limped over to her with blood running down his head and arms, holding the back of his neck. She noticed him coming. She willed herself to stand for defense. Already knowing she died, Wiley balled his fist up so tight he cut his palms with his own nails. She stood in front of Elliot defiantly. Elliot looked her up and down, then glanced behind him to see if Gretchen was still moving.

When he turned back, he caught a foot coming right at his head. Fool him once. He threw her foot away, causing her to spin around uncontrollably. He caught here in a bear hug and squeeze. The mass he carried compared to her slender form was sure to crush a number of ribs. Her arms were locked by her sides, while he thrashed her around like a rag doll.

Her eyes bulged, clearly losing breath. Elliot stopped swinging her, when he felt the fight start to leave her. He buried his head into her neck to apply more pressure. In a last attempt of defense, she bit his ear, the whole ear. She yanked her head once and spit it out. Elliot released the hold, grabbing the ear hole with one hand, shoving her away with the other.

She bounced off the wall and landed on her stomach. The fall didn't look so bad to Wiley, but he gritted his teeth angrily. Elliot turned round and round, holding the earless side of his head. Blood spouted from the wound like a busted sink. His hands couldn't stop it from gushing. They drenched his fingers to the point they couldn't be seen anymore. Only red liquid.

Marla managed to sit up and scoot back against the wall. Elliot charged her like a raging bull, but she kicked a shard of glass in his path. He slipped on the shard, landing face-first on the metal dumb-bell rack. His arms gave way, and he landed on the floor, twitching.

Marla was the only one alive. Wiley felt a sense of pride to see his wife fight so hard and be the last one living. Then the memory of him holding her lifeless body in his arms came back to him. She sat there panting in exhaustion and pain. She tried to stand up, only to collapse on the floor. Her right leg gave in when she tried to put weight on it. That was when Wiley saw it. A shard of glass jotted out of her leg. She nicked an artery. If she pulled it, she would bleed out.

"Leave it in, Mar!" Wiley screamed frantically at the video. It was a moot point, but the husband in him had to say it. She scrawled over to the treadmills and lay on her side. She pulled the shard and tossed it away. She didn't bother to cover the leg to attempt to put pressure on the wound. She simply lay down on her side and breathed her last.

Wiley's heart sank. Knowing your wife had died is one thing. It's a whole other thing to watch it. He leaned back in his chair, with slumped shoulders and eyes wet. Frazier leaned forward and closed the laptop with one hand.

"I'm sorry you had to see that."

Wiley said nothing in return. He stared at the floor, reliving the horrible visual. A knock came to the door. Morgan, the lab tech for the bureau, peeked his head in.

"Excuse me, Kyle. Is this a bad time?"

"No. Come in, Morgan. What do you got?"

"I have the lab results. Here are the two of yours right here."

The bureau required a mandatory blood test every six months. Many agents had to go in areas where they could be exposed to something that could be contagious or grievous. Even Director Russell had to comply. Morgan stepped in through the doorway.

"I'll just leave the results on the desk."

Frazier reached out for the envelope. "No, that's all right, I'll take them."

Morgan turned and left after handing them over. Frazier opened to look at his first. He lifted his head slightly so he could see through the lower half of the spectacles. He grunted, then put it down.

"I have your bloodwork results here, Wiley. Would you like me to read them to you?"

Still looking down, entranced, Wiley gave the slightest wave of the hand to go ahead. Frazier nodded and did the same thing, reading Wiley's results. His eyes opened wide, dropping his head to look over the rim.

"What does it say?" Wiley asked flatly without looking up.

"Here, you should see for yourself." Frazier handed him the results.

Wiley took the file weakly, letting his arm drop without effort before reading it in his lap. His eyes slowly grew wider and wider. He sat up straight, bringing his eyes to Frazier's.

"Results are not satisfactory, I take it?" Frazier spoke, looking over the brim of his glasses.

Wiley tried to work is mouth but found it difficult to form the words. "I . . . I . . . I got . . ."

"You got what?" Frazier furrowed his eyebrows, leaning back slightly away from him.

"I got syphilis, hepatitis, gonorrhea, *and* the clap."

Frazier looked at him for a moment. "You're a nasty son of bitch."

"This is not a joke, Frazier!"

Frazier shrugged. "I'm not joking. That's a lot of stuff, man. You're nastier than public bathroom."

Wiley's left eye started to twitch noticeably. He rubbed it, trying to stop the annoyance. All thoughts of Marla seemingly became distant. Wiley could grieve the loss of his wife, but he could always use Christina as a mind detractor. But that's after he got cures for all these aliments.

Then the thought hit him. *Christina*. He sat up straight again with a look of recollection on his face. Frazier sat there quietly, observing the various emotional changes the young agent was going through. Wiley noticed and tried to reform back to the look of the grieving husband.

"You know, Frazier. I'm going to go home. I need some time."

"Of course, Norman. Take all the time you need. I'll let Art know."

With that, Wiley got up and left.

CHAPTER 24

SWEPT

NEARLY A QUARTER mile from his house, Wiley slammed on his brakes. They say that most car accidents happen when you're closest to home. Wiley just about proved that theory. He honked his horn, screaming obscenities at the U-Haul guy. The guy simply rolled his eyes and drove on.

He was in the right after all. The guy was coming down the hill, about to stop. Wiley cut his left-hand turn short, nearly hitting the truck head-on. He found himself blinking uncontrollably on his way back home. It was part of the reason why he almost hit that truck.

When he reached the top of the winding hill to his security gate, he was stunned to see the gate was wide-open. The guard wasn't there. No reason for surprise, because he fired the last one. But even the guard couldn't leave the gate open. It closed automatically.

He drove in, and his mouth dropped. He stopped his car on a dime as he took in the scene. In the light of night, he could see that his water fountain was gone. The ground in which it stood was a caved crater with a pipe sticking out. He also saw that his pristine rose bush aisles leading toward his door were uprooted.

He got out of his car and stood looking at the rest of his yard. Even in the dark, he could see U-Haul tracks all over. He had a greenhouse off to the side that housed a number of rare plants collected from various continents. Marla liked to use the greenhouse as a place of serenity when her modeling gigs stressed her out.

The plants were all missing. So was the greenhouse. There was no shattered glass, so the assumption of the whole house being taken was evident. Wiley ran up to his front door to find that it was unlocked. He pulled his gun, anticipating an encounter. Slowly, he slid the door open with his little finger, crouching low.

He got in. His first clear view was of the stairwell. Nothing there. He stepped in carefully not to give away his position with any noise. Holding the gun in both hands, he peeked down the hall and saw nothing. His eye twitched again, causing him to rub it and lose focus.

He rubbed it with his left hand, still holding the gun in his right. There wasn't a sound in the place. Then it suddenly hit him. There was nothing in the place, absolutely nothing in the hallway. No pictures of Marla modeling. No pictures of his dogs, Arm and Hammer. Nothing. And where were his dogs anyway?

He went to his living room at the end of the hallway. The television, stereo, minibar, furniture, even the carpet was gone. The expensive drapes on the windows, the standing lamps shaped as elephants, even the two-hundred-pound Greek mythology statues. All gone. Neat and swept clean as if they were never there.

In his haze, he completely forgot the blank-sheet case. The houses of every one of the victims/assailants had their homes swept clean just like his. But he remembered calling Christina while she was still here. Or was she still here? He dropped his guard, no longer feeling that anyone was still around.

He called to Christina. "Christian! Christina!" Nothing but an echo answered back. The noise was magnified in a vacant house in the dark. He even called for the dogs, whistling. "Arm! Hammer! Come here, boys!"

He raced from room to room. The kitchen was empty. The pots and pans were gone. Cooking utensils, measure cups, towels, dishes, all gone. The refrigerator, stove, oven, microwave, coffee maker, all represented by empty spots.

He went to the laundry room, already knowing what to expect. Not only was the washer and dryer gone, but so were the shelves. All the clothes and blankets in every room were gone. If Wiley wanted to sleep in his house, it would be on the hard marble floor.

Even the vanity pictures Marla had of herself modeling in the hallway were now gone. So too were the photos on the wall in the den dedicated to Wiley posing with his FBI credentials.

His heart sank, staring at those bare walls, walls that looked like they were never even touched. Not a nail, double-faced tape, or even a tack looked like it touched that wall. He had well over one hundred pictures in there.

He went to the backyard to see what happened to the dogs. Was he going to find them out there dead? Was the backyard going to be a mess? Whoever did this, the dogs wouldn't have allowed them to come back there and take them away. They would have torn them apart. Perhaps he would find the dogs and the mangled bodies of the people responsible.

He went back to the yard, gun at the ready. Nothing there. The dogs were gone. Their food and water bowls were gone. His hardwood deck was waxed. If he ran across it and tried to stop on a dime, he would slip and fall on his back. Either that or break into a split.

The garage door was stuck wide-open, showing him the emptiness. He never used it for anything other than storage. But that storage held some nostalgic things—a few swimming trophies from when he was a kid, a few karate trophies from Marla when she was a kid, various gifts they received from family and friends, and a few souvenirs they accumulated in their travels.

He stomped his foot and dropped his shoulders like a petulant child. The barbecue pit he had put out back was gone. It cost him ten grand to put that pit out there. It was custom-built and cooked three times as fast as normal pits. He cursed and whined. If there was anything at all back there to kick, he would have.

His fruit trees were picked clean of all fruit. Lemons, peaches, apples, plums, and apricots were all gone. He thought he heard a noise from inside the house. His attention snapped back. He spun around, pointing his gun, slowly making his way through the house.

After clearing every room and closet downstairs, he made his way carefully upstairs. The stairs were made of marble. Sound would not give away his approach if the carpet was still on. He stepped lowly, looking over his shoulder and back in front of him behind the point of the gun.

He checked and cleared every room. Finally, he headed toward the bedroom at the end of the hall. Every room was vacant, but not to his surprise. He half thought to find Christina dead in this room. That would at least give him some understanding. His biggest fear was to be alone and irrelevant.

Sweat ran down his face. He tried to slow his breath. He never fired his gun, except for target practice. He always hid behind his credentials, both as a cop and especially as a special agent. He stepped into the room. The door was wide-open, as were they all.

Christina was not there. Nothing was. And it looked like nothing ever was. He thought it was a dream. He hoped it was. His eye began to twitch again. Both eyes this time. He rubbed them with both hands.

"Feels like a needle, doesn't it?" a voice called out.

Wiley turned around, pointing his gun. He could only make out a figure in the bedroom doorway in the dark. If the man would take another step inside, his face would be illuminated by the moon shining through the window.

"Freeze!" he called out.

The figure in the doorway seemingly put his hands up. "Don't worry. It should pass in about . . . any minute now," the man replied.

"Who are you?" Wiley asked, squinting.

And just like that, the twitching stopped. Wiley opened his eye and used both hands to aim for a more precise shot. "I said, who are you? What are you doing in my house? Do you know who I am? I'm a goddam federal agent."

"Now what's the purpose of asking a question then answering it on your own?" the man answered.

Wiley cocked the gun back. "Last chance, asshole."

The man stood silent for a second, then stepped into the light with his hands still up and a slightly amused look on his face.

"Frazier? What are you doing here?" Wiley asked, but he didn't lower the gun.

Frazier chewed the licorice root. "The twitching eye is super annoying. But the next feeling is the worst part. The feeling of paralysis. You'll still be alert and coherent. And all facial expressions and thought recollections will be unaffected. In fact, you'll also find your memory to be a bit sharper than it already is."

And just like a puppet with its string cut, Wiley collapsed in the middle of the floor in a heap. His right leg bent awkwardly underneath him. His left leg stretched out in front. His arms splayed out wide, dropping the gun out of his hand. The gun slid away to a far corner.

Frazier leaned up against the wall and flipped the light switch. He crossed his arms over his chest and his feet at the ankles. He wasn't wearing his glasses or chewing his root.

Wiley lay there motionless except for his head, mouth, and eyes. "You bastard! You poisoned me!"

"Drugged, actually," Frazier responded calmly.

"For what? What the hell are you drugging me for?"

"We need to have a conversation. You want to be informed. You have questions. Well, I think it's high time you got some answers." He got off the wall and walked over to Wiley.

The agent lay there, panting nervously as Frazier knelt down and pulled one of his arms, dragging him to the wall like a hunter dragging his kill. He propped Wiley's back up against the wall, adjusting his head until it stopped trying to tip him over.

"There. That should do it." Frazier had a satisfied smile on his face as he stepped back. "Just this once, I'll go down to your level." He sat down in front of Wiley. He drew his knees up toward him, wrapping his arms around them, locking his hands together. He sat looking at Wiley, saying nothing.

"What did you drug me with? I can't feel my arms and legs," Wiley frantically asked.

"In ancient Mesoamerica, there was a civilization called the Olmec. It was an area inhabited by what we would now call South Central Mexico. They were considered to have a very advanced culture. You can still find huge stone heads in the jungles in some parts. But also, you can find the tatami leaf."

"The what?"

"The tatami leaf. It went by another name at the time and was used for many cures. They used it for fevers, male pattern baldness, and also momentary paralysis for surgery."

Wiley's eyes went wide with fear. He tried to work his mouth to say something but suddenly couldn't. Frazier noticed this and put up a hand of assurance.

"Oh, no, no. I'm not going to perform any surgery on you. What do you think I am? A savage?"

"I know your ass is mine when this shit wears off," Wiley remarked, though he knew he was no match for Frazier in a fight. Frazier knew it too. He didn't rise to the bait. He simply smiled then went on with what he wanted to say.

"Every clove of the leaf cuts off a portion of the body. But it always starts at the feet. One clove affects the legs. Two affects the waist. Three affects the upper torso. And four affects the arms and neck. But it has a nice taste to it. Don't you remember how good that tea was I gave you?"

"And how much did you put in that tea? Four?" Wiley asked.

"Six."

Wiley's eye grew large again. Facial expressions were the only bodily function he could control.

Frazier held up a hand again. "You'll regain full control of your body in fourteen hours. But that's not what's important. What is important is why we're here."

"Why are we here? Why are we here? You're the reason why we're here, asshole. We're here because you drugged me." Anger was seething from Wiley's every pore.

"No. We're here because of you. You brought this on yourself. You did this. All of it." Frazier pointed angrily as he spoke.

"What?"

"There's a reason you were recruited to the bureau. A reason you passed the exam on the first try. A reason you finished so high in your class in the academy." He paused for a second, ceremoniously spreading his arms. "Say thank you."

"What the fuck are you talking about?"

"Rita Miles." Frazier's face was stoic as he answered quickly.

"Rita Miles?" Wiley frowned. "What about her?"

"You went to college with her. You had a thing with her. You used her. You caused her to kill herself."

"No, I didn't have a thing with her. She had a thing with me. I was her privilege. She was nothing without me. And believe me. I've had much better. Just because she was a weak loser that killed herself doesn't mean she has anything to do with me right now."

Frazier was silent for a long moment, face unreadable. He appeared to not even blink, up until the point he spoke again. "She was my daughter."

CHAPTER 25

JIGSAW

WILEY HAD NO control over any other part of his body from the neck down. But his breathing increased. He knew what he did to Wiley's daughter. He knew what became of her. And he knew he was the sole reason for her demise. She left him the suicide note on his pillow in his dorm.

> *I thought you loved me. I would have done anything for you. I regret ever helping you. This isn't fair. You did this to me.*
>
> *Rita*

The words of that letter stuck with him for all about a minute, after her death. Wiley suddenly recalled them word for word at this very moment. Frazier gave him the ultimate poker face. His breathing was even and controlled. Wiley couldn't even see rage in his eyes. That, above all else, was frightening. Frazier finally took a deep breath before talking.

"Rita was my only child. I'm sure I don't have to tell you that she was a genius. Ever since she was a little girl, she had the knack for noticing progress. She could tell which trees would yield the best fruit. She had a photographic memory and even started reading at three years old."

Wiley continued to stare directly at the disturbed father, understanding the man must be hurt over losing his daughter but still wondering what she had to do with him today. But he only stared. He let him continue to talk.

"When she was nine, I taught her how to play chess. By the time she was eleven, she could beat me on a timer. She had an IQ of one hundred and forty-nine. Besides her brilliance, she had a kind heart." He looked off to the side, remembering his daughter. He grinned at the visual he held. "And she was beautiful."

He looked back to Wiley still propped up against the wall. The grin faded. "But like I said, I don't have to tell you these things."

Wiley spoke calmly so as not to make Frazier snap. "Frazier, I'm sorry about your daughter. I truly am. But what does she have to do with me, right now?"

Frazier looked at him like a dog questioning a sound. "Wiley, she has everything to do with your entire career."

"Wait, what? What are you talking about, Frazier? No more ignoring me. No more ancient civilization crap. Spit it out, damn you."

Frazier looked at him for a moment, unmoved. He nodded as if ready to finally reveal a secret. "All right. I'll tell you what I know. I know how you made all your money. And I mean, *all* your money."

Despite the fact that Wiley was sweating, he suddenly felt ice cold. Frazier let it sink in, then went on. "I know all about Florida *and* Togo."

Wiley never had asthma, but suddenly he felt as if he was about to have an asthma attack. He tried to still his breathing but found it extremely difficult. One thing he always hated was letting Frazier see that he had gotten to him. At that very moment, he didn't care for concealment. At first, he was nervous. Now he was flat out scared.

Frazier shifted positions. He extended his legs, crossing one foot over the other. He leaned back on the palms of his hands and continued. "You found her in political science class. You noticed her genius and found out about her crush. You played on that, pretending to be in love with her. Now, I understand that the youth are lustful and seek to explore.

"She was of age and made her own decisions in that regard to you. But you used her for her genius. Now, using her to help you get better scores is one thing. I'm no fool. That sort of thing happens all the time." His face took on a dark look. "But what I have a problem with is the way you used her brain to line your pockets."

It would be absurd for Wiley to believe that Frazier didn't know already, but he played the odds by denying it. "No, I didn't. I made my money on my own. She had no hand in my success." His tone suggested that he was trying to convince himself.

Frazier scoffed. "Is that what you call it? *Your* success?"

"You're damn right I do. So the cat's out of the bag. You know how I got my money. Then you know that I masterminded the whole thing. She was long dead before I became successful." The words were insensitive. He almost felt like Frazier was going to hit him. But no. He stayed calm. He even smirked a little.

"It's amazing, Norman. The way you keep referring to your exploits as success. However, I promised you answers, did I not?"

"Damn right you did." Wiley spoke through gritted teeth.

Frazier leaned back with a deep sigh. "All right. Rita had a deep hatred for census. She felt that they could be used negatively to impact finances. Or more specifically, loss of finances. She developed and showed me a system to check out. I put our best people on it. We noticed that the system could work and work flawlessly.

"It was just a practice, you see. But I felt it was best to pocket the testing just in case. Lo and behold, the exact same system showed up in Florida some years later. I thought it was a joke until I read her letter she left for you. It was balled up and thrown away. Not burned or even shredded. When she said 'I should have never helped you,' I immediately knew."

To Wiley's credit, he maintained a poker face himself. But his insides were flipping like a circus acrobat. If he would've only just destroyed the suicide letter, he wouldn't be in this situation. Frazier continued.

"You were smart enough to follow her instructions by not using your names in anything. Only a select few knew who you were, and they could easily be dealt with. It was a brilliant scheme she devised. So imagine my surprise to the very same scheme being used after her death. It wasn't hard to trace it back to you, regardless of how well you tried to cover your tracks."

Wiley knew that he could be facing serious jail time if Frazier was to report it. His thoughts began to race, then Frazier brought up the other moneymaker he had.

"And let's not forget Togo. It's bad enough for you to destroy people's financial lives." Frazier's face went from poker to cold, hard steel. "But you little piece of shit, you tampered with people's health resources. You crossed the line."

Wiley attempted to speak in his defense and found himself without one, other than for greed. So he fessed up. "Yes. I scammed my way to a lot of money. I had an opportunity to make something of myself, and I took it. I was in a selfish phase, all right. You got me. And yes, I used your daughter. But I didn't kill her. She killed herself. You know it, and I know it."

He paused, seeing if Frazier was going to snap. But he only sat there, still leaning back on his palms. He suddenly felt that Frazier might even kill him himself. He gulped in the silence. But his defiance wouldn't let him continue to look scared. "So what now? Are you going to turn me in?"

Frazier finally smiled, a complex smile of warmth and deviousness. It was as frightening of a smile that one could ever see. "Of course not. I am the one that guided your career to this point. But you also guided mine."

"What do you mean?" There was no moment where Wiley was more confused than at that moment.

"Well, you see, Norman. After my daughter died, I was a wreck. I dabbled in substance abuse and fell into depression, a little obsession as well. I drove my wife away. I grieved for the loss of my family because of you. My sanity as well. Truth be told, I died that day I found out about Rita.

"You asked me one time, why I don't address myself as an FBI agent. That's because I haven't been an agent for a long time. Since Rita. My track record in closed cases are remarkable, yes. Do you know why?"

He paused for effect. Wiley expected him to follow up on the rhetorical question, but none came. Right when he was about to respond, Frazier leaned forward with a wicked look in his eyes as he answered. "It's because I caused the crimes."

Wiley felt a stab of fear. Real fear. He stammered his words. "W-what do you mean?"

"Every case that came across my desk and went into the files as closed was because I orchestrated them. All of them from racketeering, kidnapping, hostage situations, embezzlement, narcotics violations, and even espionage. I caused it and solved it. Big or small, I solved them all. I caused them all. I even let some slip and fall to another agent as to not look suspicious."

He tapped a finger to the side of his head. "Genius, my boy. The apple doesn't fall far from the tree."

Wiley didn't see how it could be possible. But the eyes he was looking into showed that there was no lie in them. Frazier really did everything he said, somehow. Then it hit him. His voice was low. He didn't want to ask because he knew the answer already. "You orchestrated the blank-sheet case. Didn't you?"

Ever so slowly, Frazier nodded.

"You picked all those people on purpose?"

The slow nod continued.

Some of the anger that left Wiley returned a little with his next question. He knew the answer but felt compelled to ask it anyway. "You chose Marla, didn't you?"

The nod stopped, pausing to align hope. But it was false hope. The nod resumed.

"Why?" All the anger left the young agent at that moment. Only dread remained.

"Because everyone, every single person involved in this case, had contact directly with Rita."

"What? What do you mean?"

Frazier slid over to sit next to Wiley against the wall. If Wiley had any ability to reach out and strangle him, he would have. But he couldn't. And it frustrated him. Frazier pulled out his phone. He had taken a screenshot of the big board in the office. He leaned over, showing Wiley each person he spoke of by enlarging the picture.

"David Brice and Walter Fray. They were the first two that paid *you*, through Marla, for Rita's help. Brice was trying to get accepted in an entrepreneurship program and needed to create a legitimate business plan for acceptance. Fray, on the other hand, used all his parents' money to get into a top investment banking program, but he couldn't get the numbers right.

"Each paid you fifteen hundred dollars for her help. However, Rita never saw a dime. She never even met them. Rita was a genius. But she was naive. But of course, you knew that. My wife couldn't have another child. And I didn't want to adopt. Rita was desperate to have a sibling, a sister, more specifically. You did an excellent job instituting Marla as a de facto sister. She trusted Marla, and she loved you."

He slid a finger across the phone to the next screenshot. "Now what does the Ursula Jennings have to do with this? She spent a month at college with her. Noticing that she looked like a fish out of water, she was late to her own classes, showing Rita to hers. Ursula is a selfless human being, always sacrificing and looking out for others. The complete opposite of the likes of you and Marla. You already know of her family issues that subsequently drove her to drop out.

"So the fifteen hundred she got for a tip helped her move out of the dump she was staying in with her brother. She also managed to get a very expensive watch appraised and sold it for a car twice the value of its cost."

Wiley's face frowned in confusion. "What are you talking about?"

"Let's just say a very generous and gracious junkyard owner was willing to fix up a classic royal blue Mustang and trade it to her for the watch. But would you believe? That kindhearted owner ended up declining the watch, thereby allowing Ursula a chance to pocket the money."

"Benson," he voiced the recall. Frazier nodded. Memory tickled at Wiley. "I thought you said the car was yours."

Frazier shrugged. "It was. For that day. I arranged to have it delivered to her at work. Benson was to meet her at the restaurant and make her the offer. Provided she didn't have a car, she accepted."

He slid to the next slide. "Derek Cooper, a.k.a. Lance Morris. His brother, Kevin Cooper, used to have a thing for Rita when they were children. Kevin was unfortunately killed in a car accident. Drunk driver. Lance was much younger. But he supported her through her grief instead of the other way around."

He slid again. "Leah Washington. A classmate. Incredibly snooty and mean to poor Rita. Rita tried many times to be friends with Leah, but to no avail. All she got from her was down-talk for her lack of fashion sense. Until she needed a script for a play. Leah pretended to be her friend until Rita finished writing a good play for her.

"Well, the play was well received. And Leah was accepted into a prestigious acting school. All promises of bringing her along to watch her perform was broken off. But payment was still made to Marla when she learned that befriending Rita was a sure way to get her to do the work."

He slid again. "Tina Wilson. She spoke to Walter Fray about Rita. She went straight to you for help. I saw the strange look of vague familiarity on your face when you saw her. At any rate, she needed something and paid you fifteen hundred dollars for it. Not Rita, *you*. It was easy to get her to agree because all you had to do was tell Rita it would please you if she did the work."

He snorted a laugh that wasn't really a laugh and slid again. "Of course, you know the dominatrix." He pointed at Tracy Collins. "I guess I don't have to tell you she was a piece of work."

"I received no payment from her. What does she have to do with Rita?" Wiley asked.

Frazier looked up at Wiley. He noticed Wiley was telling the truth. He never met her. "No, you may not have met her. But your wife did. Apparently, you didn't know Marla and Tracy drugged Rita and had her participate in a dominatrix show. Something she was not apt to do, but with her trusting Marla as a sister, she believed the man she would be working with was you. She was wrong."

The thought lingered on Wiley. He never in a million years suspected Marla of such a thing. She always seemed so vanilla with him. He didn't love Rita. Their relationship was a sham. But even under the pretenses, the thought of her being unfaithful to *him* made it feel . . . personal, even though he was already conducting secret rendezvous with Marla at the time.

Frazier continued. "The young kid, Darwin, Rita used to tutor him. Part of a mentorship program. She needed to have a mentorship in her portfolio for college. She grew fond of the kid, as he excelled with her. She was the de facto big sister he never had. And he cried like a baby when he heard of her death."

He slid a finger again. "Yvonne Marsden, the author. Truth be told, I really am a fan of her work. But I'm more of a fan of her character. She was having trouble in her creative writing class. Rita and Marla were in the same class with her. Marla approached Yvonne with a solution. Yvonne figured out exactly what was going on and turned it down.

"She liked Rita. She knew the genius she was and whom she was friends with. She put one and one together, figuring out Marla was using her poor gullible friend. She tried a number of times to talk her out of being associated with Marla. But alas, Rita didn't listen.

"So Yvonne decided to distance herself from Rita and leave her to her own devices. I can't tell you how much I respect that." Frazier frowned as he shook his head slowly in reverence.

Wiley knew of Yvonne. He recognized her but gave no indication that he did when he saw her at the café. She might have been too distraught that day, because she gave no indication of ever knowing him either. But Frazier knew.

He slid again. "Gina Samuels. She sought to uncover the scam and expose it to the school council. She claimed to be an associate of Rita's. Rita told her in confidence that she helps people struggling. Gina managed to go around you and Marla and got Rita to help her with an idea for a story in her journalism course.

"Like I said, Rita was naive. She revealed the whole thing to her. Gina Samuels planned on taking that information in confidence and breaking the story for school news. The problem was, she would have had to include Rita's involvement. That would have been bad for Rita. She would have been expelled with a black mark on her record."

Wiley didn't know about this. He became curious. "So what happened? She's not the type to sit on a story. And I didn't hear anything of the sort."

"You're right. She didn't sit on it. She reported it and involved everyone. The report was submitted and kicked up to the superintendent. However, the super had to kick it to the head of the board. The head of the board is a friend of mine, a neighbor actually. Her name is Jessica Sloan. Jessica couched it as a favor to me." He relaxed his demeanor, smiled, and took on a condescending tone. "You know, Norm. You mind if I call you Norm?" Frazier didn't give him a chance to respond. "Jessica is a nice woman. She's always been a little sweet on me. But she would never impose on a marriage, mind you.

"But when Doreen left me, she upped her pursuit. As a matter of fact, she cooked an exquisite meal to impress me once. I was over her house eating it when I saw the product of yours and Gina Samuels's collaboration on the news."

Frazier leaned back against the wall, looking up in thought as he spoke. "I don't know. She seems like a good enough woman. Maybe I could have something with her. It's just been hard, you know. After my daughter dying, me going into serious depression, and my wife leaving me and all.

"It's just been hard for me to open up to anyone like that. But of course, I have you to blame for all that." He looked back at Wiley and brought his phone back up. He slid a finger across to the next photo. Wiley watched and listened, speechless.

"Dan Barns. Needed help and paid the money to an outside collector. You and Marla began to get smart and not collect money directly. I'll give you credit for that. Gretchen Berg needed much of the same thing. Now, you already know of the little fun they had in steam room. But what you didn't know is that Gretchen is actually your half sister. Another one of your father's famous moves.

"So I guess it was only fitting that the guy that killed her is the guy just recently . . ." he pumped a fist back and forth a few times, "killed her. If you know what I mean. Oh, and I forgot to mention. They have no blood relation whatsoever. But Dan is also your cousin on your mother's side."

Wiley's eyes snapped to Frazier's. The look he received showed he was hearing the truth. He never met either of them. They were his family. He knew a family reunion was coming up, and he was looking forward to meeting everyone. Being an only child, he longed for family.

Shock stained his face, as Frazier continued. "And this guy, Elliot Allen. He was the guy that participated in the dominatrix experiment with Rita and Marla. Of course, all under the influence of Tracy Collins. Plus . . . we know his involvement in the steam room."

Wiley raged. He tried to swing at Frazier. He pictured placing a well-placed left hook on him. He wished he could have swung a fist at Elliot. At Marla. At Rita even. But he still had no control over his limbs. They didn't even feel tingly. They were just useless. The thought would normally frighten a person. But he was too pissed off to be frightened.

He tried to thrash. His eyes grew large, then he shut. Large and shut. All in the attempt to get to his feet and attack. Frazier watched him contently. He fought for what felt like an hour but was actually no more than ten seconds. He ultimately surrendered. Rage turned to despair. He spoke in a defeated tone.

"And you orchestrated all this? What did you do this for? And what is the significance of a blank sheet anyway?"

"What, indeed," Frazier answered.

"What the hell does that mean, what indeed?"

"Well, one may ask, what's the significance of *you*? I know I sure have. Many times, in fact."

"What does it mean, Frazier?" Irritation spilled from Wiley's voice.

"Well, a blank sheet is a beacon of great potential. Some of the most innovative, beneficial, and creatively expressing things in the world started from a blank sheet of paper. On the flip side, a blank sheet is a piece of nothing. Something to step on, discard, ignore, or use dismissively. Usually, it's one of or the other, but you managed to use my Rita as both."

"So you just felt like putting all this together for what? Vengeance? Retribution? For sport? You destroyed all those lives to get back at me? To get back at them? To make them . . ."

His words trialed off, when realization finally hit. The eyes of content coming from Frazier became as steel. Frazier made them suffer at the hands of each other, but he made Wiley suffer by watching his wife die on film.

"You son of a bitch!" he roared. "I'll kill you! I'll fucking kill you! Wait till this wears off! You had to drug me, you a coward! You touched my family! I'll kill—"

His words were cut off with a sharp chop to the throat. He gasped with wide eyes and an open mouth. But there wasn't much else he could do to breathe. Frazier put a hand on his chest to keep him upright against the wall while he choked.

"You see that feeling you have right now?" Frazier's voice was cold. "That's about a quarter of the dread feeling I felt when you drove my little girl to the depths. She went home instead of meeting with another client of yours. She overheard the two of you plotting how much money you were making off of her.

"To hear firsthand that you two never cared for her, just the asset she was, was crushing. Then to watch you two have sex right after that conversation, laughing and mocking her, devastated her. That's when she decided . . ."

He couldn't finish the last part. His words caught in his throat. He no longer cried for his daughter's death. He only seethed. Seethed with hatred. The origin of that hatred sat in a heap against the floor next to him.

Wiley finally caught his breath, the anger not as pronounced. But it was still there. In between coughing, he managed to ask a few questions. "How did you do it? Marla would've never agreed to do this. How did everyone to go through with it?"

Frazier righted himself. He didn't appear delighted in revealing everything, like a serial killer explaining why they are the way they are. He appeared to have the sense of duty and obligation. Like it was a mission he had to see through.

"Well, as you know. I enjoy reading. Mostly history and ancient cultures. In our most recent historical memory, there was a piece of trash tyrant from Germany. He was very interested in mind control. However, the concept is much, much older than him. Many had coveted the skill throughout the ages. And one culture actually succeeded. An ancient civilization called the Sanxingdui figured it out, a culture in ancient China that existed over three thousand years ago.

"They had more than a few herb healers that found a plant high in their mountains that was viable for such a thing. The name of the plant is too long for you to understand, much less pronounce. They would grind up the leaf and put them in tea. Then whomever chewed the root had a controlling link connection to the person, a form of hypnosis, you might say.

"The root itself just strengthens resolve, enhances the senses, rather than dull them as drugs or alcohol do. How Marla could go along with this, you ask? Well, let me ask you something. Was she a tea drinker?"

The question hit him like a boulder in the chest. She loved tea. She would often bring back different tea leaves from other cultures on their many travels. It suddenly made sense. And that made it more terrible. Tears ran down his eyes. Frazier smiled.

"Now you're getting it," Frazier remarked. "You're the one that introduced her to tea in the first place, back in college when she was having trouble sleeping. You learned from a botany student what helps the best from sleeping, didn't you? You had her drink the tea and fall asleep in your arms, while you still had my daughter believing she was your only one."

Wiley closed his eyes at the thought of Marla. "Oh, Marla." He sobbed.

"Now don't get me wrong. I'm talking about magic or anything. There are many drugs that enable people to do various things they would never do in their right mind. That, and the secret cult of mind they joined."

"Cult? Marla wasn't in any cult." The defensive tone returned.

"I'm afraid she was. All those that drank the tea met with me. I wore a mask, mind you. But it was a cult for the 'successful.' People that want to strive for the heights and would do absolutely *anything* to achieve them."

It was a lot to process. Wiley couldn't imagine his wife being a part of a cult. Then again, she was hell-bent on the progress in her career. She often talked about doing whatever she had to do to reach the heights. *The heights*. That word rang in his head. He never paid attention to it until now. The sharpened memory from the tea was doing wonders.

Frazier cut into his grief with a question. "If you loved your wife so much, then why were you making Christina your sex slave?"

Wiley kept his eyes shut, not wanting to answer.

Frazier leaned forward and with a wicked grin on his face. "And just for the record, I orchestrated her as well."

Wiley's eyes snapped open. "What? Wait. You mean you paid her?"

"No, I didn't pay her. I arranged her arrival through an agency. One of Benson's former brothers-in-law is a supervisor for deportation. He has connections to send over refugees looking for work. Or shall I say, those looking for more respectable work in the eyes of society over here."

He paused, letting it sink in. Wiley's eyes went wide. "That's right, Norm. She was a prostitute, a prostitute for sixteen years. And not because she had no choice. She became a madam in Guadalajara at nineteen."

That killed Wiley. He always thought of Christina as a nice, wholesome little lady. She was always so timid and guarded. That was what he liked the most about her. He could dominate her timid ways, and she was virtually a novice sexually. But she was the complete opposite. Not only was she a working girl; she was a seasoned veteran.

"She ran a brothel?" Wiley asked.

"Three, actually. They called her the 'long winded.' I'm sure you can take a wild guess at the origin of its meaning."

There was no denying it. Wiley already received his blood results.

Frazier continued. "Naturally, a girl that active has contracted many sexually transmitted diseases. Most of them were taken care of quick with the required medicines. However, the clinic in which she received her meds from were connected to a supply chain with Togo, Africa. But once Togo no longer got their meds, neither could she get hers in Guadalajara."

The color drained from Wiley's face. His biggest scam came from rerouting vaccines from a poor third world country like Togo. He always believed they had no bearing on his life other than an opportunity to make a lot of money. Now to find that he was responsible for contracting a number of STDs from his own scam made him want to cry.

Tears began to well up in his eyes again. But it wasn't for the people that he prevented from receiving cures for their diseases or even Christina. It was for him contracting it in the first place. He always feared contracting something. He wore protection any other time in the past before Marla. But he rolled the dice with Christina.

Snake eyes.

"What the hell do you want from me?" Wiley asked in a fit of exasperation. "Why don't you just kill me? Kill me and be done with it."

"Because I don't want you dead," Frazier answered.

"Just kill me!" Wiley cried out. "You took everything from me!"

"Only after you took everything from me and all the other people you benefited from." The condescension returned. "But don't worry, I've made arrangements to right those wrongs. All the people that lost money to your Florida scam was paid back double, with anonymous checks, mind you."

Wiley's rage returned in his eyes. Right when he was about to roar, Frazier cut him off.

"Oh, and the medical supply chain is reconnected."

That really hurt. With the supply chain down, he was able to receive an excess of an extra twenty grand a month. The money linked directly to an account that Marla didn't even know of in the

Philippines. Right on cue, Frazier responded to the horror in Wiley's mind.

"That's right, Norm. Your account in the Philippines is emptied and closed." A smile crossed Frazier's face.

"You won't get away with this. I'll go to Russell. I'll go to the goddamn Senate if I have to! I'll get you back, you bastard! You won't get away with this!" Wiley spoke through gritted teeth.

Frazier casually rose from his seated position on the floor, dusting himself off in a theatrical affect. The place was spotless. One couldn't find a speck of dust, wearing a rubber gloved suit.

He arched his back with his hands on his hips, stretching until a small crack was heard. He let out a sigh of satisfaction as he looked down at Wiley. He stood in front of his motionless frame, save for his eyes. He squatted down a foot from his face, smirking.

"I already have."

He took his index and middle finger, then jabbed them in the left side of Wiley's neck. It was the only time during that sequence that Wiley's entire body shook. It jerked as if hit with a shock wave. His eyes rolled as he collapsed in a heap.

CHAPTER 26

ONSLAUGHT

WILEY WOKE WITH a start. Bright light shone in his face. He flinched and covered his face with his hand. In a slow realization, he found he could actually move his own hand. He wiggled his fingers to make sure he wasn't imagining it. He split two fingers of his hand to peek an eye through, scanning to see if Frazier was still there.

The room was completely empty. There was nowhere for Frazier to hide. Suddenly, the light beaming from the window felt brighter and brighter with every second he tried to feign being unconscious. He pushed himself up against the wall in a seated position, the same position he was in last night when Frazier had him paralyzed.

The memory of it forced him to jump to his feet. The forced motion alerted him to the splitting headache that was waiting for him to awake. He grimaced, rubbing two fingers on each hand to rub his temples. He opened his eyes slightly to notice that his clothes were changed.

He no longer wore his black slacks, buttoned-down white shirt, black necktie, or black blazer. He now wore a plain red shirt and gray sweat pants. His black dress shoes were replaced by a pair of all-white running shoes. He looked more like a hipster than a special agent.

He looked around the room and didn't see his gun on the floor. He felt his pants, noticing that he wore pocketless sweats. *Where is my wallet? My credentials,* he thought. He also noticed he didn't have keys. He grunted in anger, storming out of the room. Marla loved light. She had large six-foot-high windows put in upstairs. Without curtains, one could see through clear as day.

He paused, getting a good look at the missing fountain from above. At night, he thought it was just ripped out. But in the light of day, it looked as if it was expertly removed without disturbing much of the surrounding ground. No rubble or jagged rock was seen. It was neat and orderly.

He looked across the yard and saw that his car was missing. He rushed to the stairs, not bothering to look in any rooms as he ran past. He knew they were empty and was certain that Frazier was in none of them. He ran down the stairs, taking two at a time.

He didn't bother looking to his right toward the kitchen or his left toward the hallway. He remembered they were bare. Sound echoed off his shoes as he ran, confirming that nothing and no one else was in the house. The front door was wide-open. He rushed out and stopped on the front step. He looked around, finding only grass and ground.

He was alone. All alone. With no means.

Anger made him move. He was not sure what he was going to do, but he started walking down the hill. The twisting, winding road that he had never walked before seemed like an eternity to reach the bottom. A few dogs barked at him from their front yard as he passed.

The morning was hot. Sweat spots appeared through his red shirt. A flock of birds flew over him. One had perfect aim and timing, as his shirt now carried a white splatter behind his left shoulder. He cursed and continued to walk. At least he had on a good pair of shoes. His feet would not have been happy in the dress shoes he had on before.

The only thing in his favor was that no one came zooming around the corner. He reached the bottom and looked around. He didn't know what time it was, but not many cars were on the street. He had no car and no money to even catch a cab or a bus.

Headquarters was twenty-two miles from his house. He knew he could get there in forty minutes without traffic. But that was in a car. He even thought of trying to hitch a ride from someone. The chances of anyone picking him up in the city were slim to none.

He arrived at headquarters in a little over an hour and a half—sweating, dehydrated, foot sore, and hungry. But it was the anger that drove him on. After nearly two hours, he made it. The guard at the front, Nelson, had been there for over thirteen years. He was a heavy-set man in his midsixties.

He caught accidental fire during a hostage situation. The entire ordeal was too much for him to want to go back out into the field. He opted for a less aggressive role, such as door and equipment guard. He found himself much happier and safer for it. Frazier was the one that saved his life, pulling his wounded frame from the line of fire and patching him up until he received medical attention. The two had been friends ever since.

Wiley spoke with him maybe twice. Frazier spoke and joked with him often. Wiley would look the man off every time Nelson looked his way to say good morning. The thought was that Nelson was beneath him in rank, not a field agent, not an equal.

But he needed him now. He needed to get in. He walked up to the guard behind the desk, sweating profusely with labored breath. The man was watching a football game on his computer behind a bulletproof glass casing.

"Hey. Newman, right? Listen. I need to get in there. Buzz me in, will you?"

"It's Nelson." The guard didn't bother looking up.

"Yeah, whatever. Look, buzz me in."

"I'm afraid I can't do that."

"Don't play with me, *guard*. Buzz me in. I'm not in the mood." Wiley seethed.

"Sir. Only FBI can be buzzed in this way. If you would like to speak with an agent, you'll have to call that number." He pointed to a posting on the glass. The posting was a federal agent hotline with a list of specific crimes.

Taking a slow, angered composed breath, Wiley closed his eyes, holding a hand up and slowly forming a fist. His patience was clearly at an end. "Listen, old man. You know who I am. I'm Special Agent

Norman Wiley, sworn member of the FBI. Stop playing fucking games with me. Now is *not* the time!"

Nelson sat back in his chair, pulling out a bag of popcorn. He propped his feet up on the counter, crossing them at the ankles. He no longer cared to argue with the vagabond at his window. The show of blatant disregard set Wiley off. He pounded on the glass with his fists, yelling and cursing.

He threatened Nelson physically, threatened his job, threatened his family even. Nelson didn't bite. He was retiring in four months. All he wanted to do now was watch his Florida State Seminoles play. He turned the volume up, drowning out the petulant child that couldn't do anything to him at his window.

Wiley, already exhausted from the walk, fell into a new exhaustion, a mental one. The beating on the glass and screams of obscenities did nothing. He leaned against the glass, laboring for strength. Director Russell walked out, heading for his car.

Wiley perked up and ran over to intercept him.

"Sir!"

Russell jumped. He was reading a text on his phone and didn't notice Wiley until he was right in front of him. "Jesus, Wiley. You nearly gave me a heart attack." He clutched the left side of his chest, catching his breath. "What are you doing here?" He frowned. "Do you know that you have bird shit on your shirt?"

"Sorry, sir. Look we need to talk. Frazier has gone out of his mind. He—"

Russell held up a hand, cutting him off. "Wiley. You're no longer a federal agent."

Wiley blinked. "What? W-What are you talking about, sir?"

"I assumed Frazier went to tell you last night. Christina Reyes filed a report against you."

"What? What kind of report?"

"Sex slavery. If it was all simply role-playing and consensual, you got no problem from me, even if you are married. But we can't condone one of our agents engaging in such a heinous act."

"Whoa, whoa, wait a minute." Wiley's face screwed up in a mix of confusion and disturbance, holding his hands out in front of him, patting the air in little pushes. "Christina wasn't my sex slave. She was my maid. She worked for me. I paid her. That means it wasn't slavery."

"Did you have sex with her?" Russell was curt with his question.

"Well, yeah. But—"

"Did she ever approach *you* for sex? Was she ever the initiator?"

"Well, no. But that hardly makes—"

"Did you, or did you not, force her to break off a prior engagement she had to help the needy which she volunteers for, in order to tend to your sexual needs for the duration of your wife being out of town? And forced her not to refer to you by your name but as your slave master name? Special Agent?"

Wiley's face dropped. His eyes told the story. He didn't have to answer. He had no defense.

Russell shook his head. "You disgust me, Wiley."

"No. You don't understand, sir. It's Frazier. It's all Frazier."

"What the hell does Frazier have to do with this?" Russell's tone was hostile.

"Everything. He set up everything. He smuggled Christina over and connected her to the agency that delivered her to me."

Russell frowned. "Delivered. That's an interesting word."

Wiley waved his hands in protest. "No, no, no. That's not what I mean. He had her give me an STD, a number of them, in fact. She was a prostitute before she came to the agency. He set up the whole thing."

"You know, there's a thing about STDs. Don't have sex with the people that have them, and you won't end up with them yourself."

There really was no argument to be made with that statement. But Wiley felt he had to tell Russell everything about Frazier. "Sir. He set up the blank-sheet case. He orchestrated all his closed cases. That's how his completion rate is so good. He's a maniac, sir. He did all of this to get at me."

Russell squinted. "Time out. How could he have set up the blank-sheet case?"

"All the people involved were handpicked. All of them."

"And how did he do that? Our reports say that they had no common knowledge of each other. Didn't work or associate in any of the same circles. Not even social media, for crying out loud."

"He knew them, sir. Every one of them. He got them all to do that to each other."

Russell folded his arms. "And how did he do that? Did he wave a magic wand over their heads while they were sleeping at night?"

"No. He drugged them with a mind-control leaf, sir. It comes from the jungles or mountains or something like that. Then he inducted them in a cult that he ran. That's how he got them to meet in these places. They were instructed, under a drug."

Russell looked at him with an unreadable face. He said nothing, but his arms were still folded. Wiley took it as a cue to continue.

"Look, I know this sounds crazy. But he controlled those people to do that. Even . . ." His voice trailed off for a second, then returned softer. "My wife."

"So, let me get this straight." Russell held up a fist, pulling a finger up with each point with his other hand.

"Kyle smuggled Reyes in from another country, a prostitute, to be your sex slave and give you a number STDs."

Wiley protested. "She wasn't my sex sla—"

Russell cut him off, pulling another finger up for another point. "He handpicked all the people involved in the blank-sheet case, people that have no record of having any connection with each other, and drugged them with a leaf to control their minds."

"I know this sounds ridiculous, sir. But it's the tru—"

"There were no drugs found in any of their systems, yet you claim they were. Oh, and he's the leader of a cult. Is that about right?"

Wiley nodded anxiously. "Yes, sir. Absolutely. I know it sounds crazy, bu—"

"How did he pick these people anyway? By osmosis?"

"College, sir. That's how they know each other. He had a person on the inside change their records."

Russell paused. "All right, wait a minute. Now you're telling me that Kyle had someone change the records of the people involved with the blank-sheet case? As in changed their school attendance?"

Wiley nodded. "Exactly."

"And how did he do that?"

"He said he knows somebody on the inside."

"Inside of what?" Irritation mounted in Russell's tone.

"A superintendent, a woman that sat on the board. She had it changed to make it look like they went somewhere else."

Russell took a deep, restraining breath. "And why would she do that? Better yet, how can she do that?"

"I don't know how, sir. But she did it as a favor to Frazier."

Russell frowned, closing his eyes and rubbing his temples. "It's not possible, Wiley. You can't just change a person's college attendance and place them somewhere else. And why would Kyle go through all this trouble anyway? What is this underlined issue he has with you?"

Looking and sounding like a crazy person, Wiley spoke with wide eyes and labored breath. But explaining the reason why Frazier was after him to the director of the FBI was guaranteeing his arrest. He would have to bring up the legitimate cruelty of Rita Frazier as well as her cause for suicide. The biggest part, he would have to explain the census scam in Florida—the scam that earned him a lot of money from ripping people off. It was a federal crime that he thought he got away with. That explanation would also lead him to tell about the vaccine supply train he disrupted—another federal crime. He would surely be looking at near life in prison.

He couldn't do it. He wouldn't do it. He simply said, "I hooked up with his daughter."

"What do you mean *hooked up*?" Anger, in a slow boil, came in Russell's words. "Are you saying you used my goddaughter for your own gratification then threw her away like a piece of trash? Is that what you mean by *hooked up*?"

Wiley's eyes grew large, taking a half step back. "I . . . I thought Benson was her godfather."

"We both are. What's it to you?"

"Nothing, sir," Wiley blurted out with obvious fear in his voice. "Nothing at all."

"You little shit. You treat my little Rita like a whore and blame her father, my best friend, for giving you a hard time? And on top of all that, you claim him as a criminal mastermind? I should not only throw you in jail. I should beat your little snobby ass right here, right now."

The words were not an idle threat. The look in Russell's eyes showed he was seriously considering it. But he restrained himself and took a step back, composing his breath.

"Now it makes sense why Kyle was such a hard ass with you. I give the man credit. Had it been me, I would shoot your balls off."

Wiley backed up another step, holding his hands up in front of him. "Sir, please. You have to listen to me. Frazier is dangerous. He—"

"Get out of here, Wiley. At Kyle's request, he doesn't want me to lock your ass up. But I will if you don't get out of here right now."

"But doesn't that strike you as odd, sir? Why would he say that? Think about it."

"All I'm thinking about is the count of ten. That's what you have to get out of my presence. You're no longer an agent. I had Kyle collect your credentials and gun. Your status is updated as terminated. Gina Samuels reported you earlier as part of a sex slave ring.

"Councilman Bolton is heading the crusade against sex slavery in this country. He has a decent case, considering the way he was found in Tracy Collin's web. The revised report by Samuels cleared his standings with the people. He's seen more as a victim than a participant. And now a crusader.

"You were a disgrace to the bureau. I will not allow it to look like a disgrace. Now, that's all I want to say to you anymore." He started to count. "One. Two. Three."

"Wait, sir. I'm being framed. This is a travesty of justice. You have to believe me. You have to—" Wiley spoke in protest.

"Four. Five." Russell moved his coat aside at the hip, exposing his gun. He unclasped the button with his thumb, still looking Wiley in the eye. "Six. Seven."

As if it were possible, Wiley's eyes grew larger. He saw without a shadow of a doubt that Russell was serious. Each number was spoken with cold meaning. It's always scarier when someone is angry and resolute but not yelling.

"Eight." The gun came out. "Nine."

Wiley turned and booked, foot sore and everything. He ran like a pack of lionesses were after him out on the plains. He turned the corner so quick he clipped his shoulder on the wall. But it didn't slow him much. He kept going. Good thing Frazier gave him some running shoes.

CHAPTER 27

JUMP

WILEY CONTINUED TO run. Making sure Russell didn't send agents after him, he ran with his head turned, looking behind him. In his haste and fear, he crashed right into a family walking on the street—a husband, wife, son, and daughter. He knocked over all of them. They were standing in a huddled circle, looking at pictures the husband had on his phone.

The children, ten and nine years old respectively, hit the ground first with their parents falling on top of them. Wiley rolled over them, got up without saying a word, and kept on running. A police officer walking to his car saw it all. He called out to Wiley to stop.

Wiley looked back but kept running. The cop gave chase, but he was in no shape to catch him. Wiley didn't know that. He turned a few corners, then buzzed to enter a pawnshop. He hurried in, ducking behind the door. He waited to see if the cop was still following. All was clear.

"Can I help you, sir?" A woman's voice sounded behind him.

Still looking out from behind the security screen door, Wiley panted. "What?"

"Is there anything I can help you with?" Her tone was more forceful than the first time.

Wiley turned around and walked over to her at the counter. "I, uh . . . just needed to get inside for a second."

She looked at his shirt—bird shit and sweat stained. There was the smell of must and sourness. She leaned her head back a little, not in a haughty way, but in a way that made it clear that she caught a strong whiff. "Rough morning, I see."

He sighed. His shoulders slumped in exhaustion. "You have no idea."

She reached under the counter and came up with a cold bottle of water. "You look like you could use this."

"Yes." He snatched it savagely. Thank gratitude returned. He simply guzzled it with quickness. As soon as he brought the empty bottle back down, she had another one in her hand. He took that one as well, guzzling it just like the first.

He looked at her as if he expected a third to be there. But there wasn't, only a concentrated look on her face. "Sorry about the clutter. We had an influx of merchandise come in recently."

He nodded, looking around. "What's your name?"

"My name is Shelly. And yours?"

"Sp—" He caught himself. He was no longer a special agent. The thought pained him. "I'm Norman."

She didn't have a protective cage to stand behind like most pawnshops. Anyone could reach over and take what they wanted. He noticed she wasn't bad to look at. Suddenly ignoring his current state, he leaned in on the corner toward her. She leaned back.

He leaned a little more then found out why she didn't need a cage to stand behind. Arguably one of the biggest, meanest dogs he had ever seen charged the counter, barking and snarling. The dog was bigger than his Great Danes, Arm and Hammer. He let out a wimpy, girlish squeal with freight as he fell on his butt.

"Heel, Kane!" she commanded the beast. The dog obeyed immediately. "I'm sorry. My husband trained him himself. He isn't much for strangers. I suppose that's a good thing."

Still on the floor, Wiley looked up. "Yeah, I suppose it is." He looked to his left and noticed a rather large flat-screen television in the far corner. Its mounting brackets were on the floor next to it. He frowned as he looked closer.

"When did you get that TV?" he asked, pointing at it.

"Oh, that? We got that in this morning. You want to buy it?"

His eyes grew in recognition. "Buy it? It's mine. I own it."

Shelly frowned. "I don't recall seeing you come in this morning to sign it in."

Wiley stood up. "I don't care what you remember. This is my TV." He looked around, pointing. "And that's my stereo. And that's my home theater system." He spun around, finding various other items he had in his home. "This is all my stuff!"

"I'm sorry, sir. But it was sold to us outright. We own it all."

He whirled around to her. "No. This is my stuff. All of it! And I'm taking it back!"

The dog went crazy again. She didn't bother to settle him this time. The dog was a German shepherd and bull mastiff mix. He moved himself in front of Shelly, barking and snarling with bad intentions.

"Hey!" a man's voice came from the back. A door closed behind him. "What's going on?"

He walked to the front to see what Kane was going off about. A disheveled-looking man stood a few steps away from the desk. "That's enough, Kane. Go in the back."

The dog silenced and walked away. The man walked over to his wife, eyeing the man in the shop. Shelly stood there with her arms crossed and a not-too-pleasant look on her face. He directed his look back to her.

"What's going on here, Shell?"

"This man claims the new shipment is his. He said he's going to take it all back."

The man turned back to the disheveled person. "Sorry, friend. We own all this stuff. Fair and square. It was donated to us with no mention of a previous owner. Now, if this stuff truly is yours, you're welcome to have it all back. But only as a sale."

Wiley still steamed. How dare these people think they could hold his stuff? He eyed the man. "Like I said, it's mine. All of it."

"Okay, we'll see if we have a signed slip from you." The man reached a hand out. Shelly brought him the logbook. He slightly turned his head to her over his shoulder, still watching Wiley. "Is it all updated?"

"Yes, it is," she replied.

Wiley watched them both. His exhaustion had faded. Anger had taken up residence now.

"What's your name, friend?" the man asked.

"Norman."

"Norman, what? You got a last name?"

"Wiley."

The man paused. His look turned to curious. "Say, isn't that special agent that was on that parking lot case some time ago?"

Wiley's demeanor changed. It wasn't because the man knew him. It was because he remembered him being an agent. He then eyed the man suspiciously. "And who are you?"

"My name is Doug Callahan. You already met my wife, Shelly."

She snapped her fingers. "I knew there was something familiar about you. You look a lot different though."

"I had a rough night. But I still want my stuff."

Doug gave an apologetic shrug. "Sorry, Special Agent. But we already signed for ownership. It was from the orders of the federal government that we take it. Since it was free of charge, I didn't want to argue with that."

"You're a federal agent," Shelly chipped in. "Maybe you could talk to the signing agent that sent it to us. I have his name right here." She leaned over her husband's arm to see the name she put in. "Here it is. Signed over by a Ky—"

"Kyle Frazier," Wiley finished the name for her, with his eyes closed.

"Oh, good. You know him," she replied.

"Know him. Shelly, this is his partner. Don't you remember?" Doug asked.

"Oh, yeah. That's right." Recognition caught hold of her. "You're the one that made everyone call you special agent. It's a little vain, if you ask me."

Wiley was done. He was done with everything. He lost all his will to fight anyone or anything. He jerked the door open. "I didn't ask you." And he left.

The stuff that were sent to them would fetch them some good money. They were smart enough to put some good marketing signs up for a sale. They would no doubt be able to move virtually all the stuff by the end of the month. A lot of financial concerns would be settled.

CHAPTER 28

COME UPPING

WILEY WALKED IN a daze. He couldn't believe how everything came down on him. He wasn't a special agent for the FBI anymore. Being heralded as a sex slave master on his record, he would never get in law enforcement again, especially if they leaked the espionage claim.

He lost all his money and all his connections to recoup his money. He lost his benefits. He had a number of really bad STDs and no means of getting treatment for them unless he went to a free clinic. His lost his home. By now, he knew Frazier would have found a way to lock him out of it.

He was hurt, tired, and hungry, and his wife was gone. Things couldn't get any worse. He sat on a bench at a bus stop. He leaned back and slumped his shoulders. Suddenly, two uniformed police officers hauled him up.

"Well, I'll be a rotten banana on a brown tree," one cop commented when he looked at Wiley's face. "Look at who this is, partner."

His partner smiled broadly. "Oh, man. Talk about Christmas coming early."

Wiley got up lazily. It really didn't matter who these cops were until he glanced up and saw them. His eyes grew wide. It was officers Burns and Green. He tried to struggle but had no strength to break free.

"Uh, huh," Green whispered. "We got you now—slaver, espionage—and now we hear that you're hurting little kids? Let's go take a ride, shall we?" They walked him to the car, cuffed him, and threw him in the back seat. Literally. His head smacked the door panel on the other side, with his hands locked behind his back.

The family looked satisfied as they stood there watching the cops drive off, waving at them as they passed. Wiley had no idea how long they were riding. He didn't care anymore. He was too tired. He closed his eyes to rest. Shortly thereafter, he was hauled out aggressively and slammed into cold concrete.

He looked around and noticed it was an underground structure. No one was in there. Green and Burns had on black leather gloves. But for what reason?

They stood side by side, looking down at Wiley, uncontrollable joy in their faces. Officer Burns spoke first. "You know what, Bill? I think Mr. Wiley here is about to have one hell of a bad day."

"Yes indeed, partner. Yes indeed. I used to pray for this. To catch him slipping and be there when he falls," Green responded. "What's the matter? Don't you want to flash your credentials in my face? Talk down to me? Huh?"

Wiley now knew exactly what was about to happen. He scurried to his knees, still with his hands cuffed behind his back, pleading. "All right, look. Gentlemen, I was a jerk. I shouldn't have treated you two the way I did. I was wrong. I see that now. I—"

A stiff punch to the stomach delivered by Green cut Wiley off. He doubled over, coughing violently.

"Now, now, Bill." Burns placed a restraining hand on his partner. "That really isn't necessary." He leaned down and uncuffed Wiley. "There, that's better. Now the man has a chance to block. Makes for a longer beating when a man can block a little. If he can't, he may just be knocked out after the first face shot. Then the fun is over."

Wiley still tried to collect his breath. He glanced up, lying on his back. One hand was across his stomach, the other hand outstretched toward them. He spoke in between coughs. "No. Wait. Plea—"

Another punch came down on his chest. A punch coming downward to the chest when someone is down on the ground is a devastating blow. The air left him—all of it. Burns left the fist there on his chest, crouched on one knee, watching as Wiley gasped and wheezed.

"You had this coming for a long time, you pompous ass." Green spoke loud enough for Wiley to hear, as he coughed profusely. He hauled him up to his feet.

"No, please. I'm sorry. I didn't mean to—"

Green delivered a crushing punch to the side of Wiley's head. Wiley hit the ground like a sack of potatoes. He was out like a light.

"Goddammit, Bill! Why the hell did you knock him out?"

"I hate liars. The son of bitch had the nerve to say he didn't mean to. Bullshit. He always meant to." He calmed himself. "I'm sorry, man. I jumped the gun. Looks like I robbed you having some fun too."

"Don't worry about that. I'm a patient man. Kyle delivered. Not how we expected, but he still said we would get a chance at him. And there would be no repercussions for it. So we'll wait. When he wakes up, we'll continue. If he takes too long, I have smelling salt."

About fifteen minutes later, Wiley awoke. By the time Green and Burns were through with him, he wished he hadn't. Two more times they rendered him unconscious. One time, they had to use the smelling salt to bring him back.

They pulled up to the hospital and escorted him in. "Hey, need some help over here," Green called out in the ER. It wasn't an urgent tone, but when two cops bring someone in, staff usually jump to their feet to come over and help.

A resident came running over. She was tall and lean, close to her midfifties. Black hair with streaks of gray were pulled back in a ponytail. "What happened to him?"

Burns answered, "Found this guy stumbling out of an alley on Peach Street. Looks like someone worked him over pretty good. I'm no doctor, but I think the first thing you guys want to check is his head. He's been babbling some stuff we couldn't understand."

The doctor nodded, shining a light in his eyes then checked his chest, listening to his breathing. Then she called for help.

Wiley awoke on a gurney in the hallway. His vision was fuzzy. All he could make out were figures in bright-colored scrubs passing by him. His head came up, and the doctor that checked him in walked over to him, putting a retraining hand on his shoulder.

"Now, now. You lie back down. We haven't had a chance to get a scan of your head yet. You have six broken ribs. If you stir around too much, one of them might puncture a lung. We took a blood sample to determine your type. It wasn't hard of course, provided that you were bleeding all over the place."

He lay back down with a grimace and groan in pain.

"What's your name?" she asked him.

He coughed. It hurt to cough. He clutched his chest to collect a voice. It came out jumbled. His jaw was swollen, most likely broken. "Norman."

"Well, Norman. Someone really did a number on you. It's a good thing those cops found you and brought you in. Injuries like these would have you die in the street." She started writing something down in a chart. "What's your last name?"

"Where am I?" he asked incoherently.

She stopped writing and looked at him. "You're at Apex General Hospital. My name is Dr. Doreen Clayton. Now, what's your last name, Norman?" She went back to writing.

"Wiley."

She paused in midstroke. She didn't look up as she asked her question. "Did you say your name is Norman Wiley?"

"Yeah."

She still didn't bother to look up. She finished writing and closed the file. Her demeanor changed from concerned and talkative to strict businesslike health-care professional. "I'll be right back."

He watched her walk over to the nurse's station, pull out her cell phone, and send a text. Curiosity took him. He tried to get up to leave. He sat up too fast and heard a crack. Another rib. He screamed in pain, so much pain that it made him pass out.

He woke up, still in the hallway, with Dr. Clayton standing over him. She was talking to someone behind him that he hadn't bothered to see who it was yet. He was rolled onto his left side in order to breathe.

"I didn't think anything of it at first because this is the ER. We see all kinds of mysterious injuries in here. I'm conflicted. Part of me wants to cheer. Another part thinks it's gone too far."

She spoke low to the other person. She was staring across at them with her arms crossed. Her eyes glanced down, when she noticed him stirring around.

"Here, take these." She handed him a small cup with three pills. "They're antibiotics for the STDs you've contracted. You're going to need more doses to clear everything up. But you don't have any insurance to cover it, unless you can pay cash."

His voice came out in a croak. "Whom are you talking to?"

She glanced back up at the person on the other side of him. No smile on her face, no dislike in her eyes. Just a look of indifference. "My ex-husband."

A familiar voice spoke behind him. "Not sure he'll be paying cash either."

The voice. He knew that voice. A sudden pang of fear washed over him. His entire body went rigid. His eyes snapped open, and his breathing became short and rapid. He couldn't turn over to visually confirm whom the voice belonged to. But without a shadow of a doubt, he knew.

The person walked over to the side where he could be seen and stood next to Dr. Clayton. It was Frazier.

"My, my, my, Norman. Someone really put you in the hurt locker."

After everything Frazier had done to him, he wanted to be enraged. He wanted to be livid. He wanted to jump up and strangle this man. But he didn't have it in him. All he had left was fear of this man.

Kyle Frazier was cunning, brilliant, calculating, and effective. To sum it all up, the man was dangerous. Wiley soon realized he couldn't muster enough hatred to match what Frazier had for him. He felt deflated. Defeated. Devastated. He began to cry.

The former husband and wife stood there looking remorseless. It was their baby he drove to the brink and passed it. Doreen left Kyle because of the spiral to hell he went through. She didn't want to spiral that low with him, and she knew she couldn't help him. She wanted to change and start anew.

But that didn't mean that she forgave Wiley. She blamed him for it all. But Frazier had gone so dark she fell out of love with him. But the bond of parenthood still plagued her memory. And therefore, vengeance also had a special place in her heart.

They watched him cry. They didn't snicker, didn't taunt, didn't antagonize aggressively. Wiley looked up through watery eyes and saw two poker faces looking at him. They let him collect himself.

He wiped the snot from his nose with the back of his hand. He rubbed it on his dirty, sweaty, blood-stained shirt. He sniffed and held his broken ribs, coughing through pain.

"So what happens now?" he asked with a strained voice.

Frazier took note that not once did he apologize. Not one time. Frazier had made mention of it when he beat him up in his house before. He had him in a lock and remarked, "You really have no remorse." Though it mattered not. Frazier was already too far gone. The wheels were already in play.

But at some point, there might have been a situation where Frazier would at least set up a redemption plan for this man. But the apology never came. The time for reconciliation and/or redemption had long passed.

Doreen didn't take her eyes off Wiley while Frazier spoke. "You suffer, Mr. Wiley. That's what's next. You suffer the consequences."

"Haven't I suffered enough?" His voice was pleading. "You've taken everything from me. I have nothing left."

She looked at her ex-husband. She wanted to say something. But she didn't. Frazier kept looking at Kyle as he responded.

"Do we have our daughter back? Do we have our love back? Do we have each other back? Or better yet, how about an apology?"

Tears still streaming down Wiley's face. "For what?" The pleading voice remained.

Doreen's eyes snapped to Norman, iron rage showing in her look. Had he actually asked for what reason was an apology warranted? She replied, "For what you did to our daughter. For what you did to our family. For what you did to us!" Cool, calm collection was out the door with her as she spoke. The voice was low enough to not allow others to hear, but it wasn't exactly a whisper.

"I didn't believe Kyle when he said you wouldn't apologize. A small part of me—and I mean, a very small part—almost thought to ask him not to be as harsh with you. But not now. Now I see you got what you deserved. And maybe not enough."

"You want me to apologize? Okay, fine. I apologize. Is that what you want? Does that make you feel better? I have nothing. No wife, no home, no job, no money, and multiple freaking diseases. And no health coverage to take care of it."

What started out as pleading turned to defiance. "All I did was capitalize on my opportunities. Did I use Rita for a financial benefit? Yeah, I did. But who hasn't used someone to get ahead? It's unfortunate that she took her own life. But that was her decision. I didn't tell her to do it. You did all this to me because you're weak." His anger was kindled. He was defeated. He lost everything. So he no longer cared. "Both of you. Now I see where she got it from. You two are cowards. Why didn't you just come and fight me like a normal father would? You had to conceive this elaborate plan. Coward!"

He fell into a coughing attack, clutching his ribs, grimacing in serious pain. Neither Kyle nor Doreen moved to help him. They stared at him like a predator eyeing its prey through a glass case. Wiley finally collected himself, taking slow, steady breaths. He looked at them and saw the same unreadable look still hitting him.

"What? What are you going to do now? I just don't care anymore. I don't give a flying fu—"

"Shut up, you worthless piece of shit." Doreen spoke with the venom of ten vipers. "You shut up right now."

He complied then succumb to coughing.

She turned to Kyle. They looked at each other for a long moment. She finally turned and walked away without saying a word.

She headed over to the nurses' station, grabbed a chart, and walked away, reading it. Kyle watched her go then turned back to Norman.

"You need to rest." He reached a hand on the side of Wiley's neck and squeezed. Wiley's eyes bulged, his mouth opened, but nothing came out. He fell asleep.

CHAPTER 29

TIED ENDS

SIX MONTHS LATER.

The room was warm. On a night as chilled as this, it's wise that it was. The lighting had a unique mixture of not being too bright and well-lit enough as to not have to strain. Kyle Frazier lounged in his chair, reading one of his many books. He read every single night.

Nothing was more relaxing to him than reading a book before he closed his eyes. He propped his slipper-laced feet up on an ottoman, crossed at the ankle. The cushioned chair swallowed him in a "fit like a glove" fashion. He thumbed through the final pages and closed the book. Gently. Always gently. He never slammed his books shut.

He reached up and took off his reading glasses by the side of the frames. He squinted as he pinched the bridge of his nose with his thumb and forefinger. He let out a tired yawn. He got up and walked over to the other reading chair, one similar to the one he was just in, which was delivered a month ago.

He stood behind the chair, then reached down and ran his hands across a pair of shoulders. The touch of one hand was reciprocated by a hand reaching up and squeezing one of his. "You always read so fast," the woman commented as she looked up over her shoulder at him.

A smile crossed his face in response. "You know me. When I'm locked in, I'm locked in."

"I know that to be very true."

"What are you reading?" he asked.

"The book you got for me. *The Secret Lies of Truth and Dishonesty*, by Yvonne Marsden. I can't believe you got me a signed, autograph copy. I love her."

"Any good?"

"Oh, yes. She really does a good job of character development. That's what I like the most about her. I felt that in her previous books, she used too many big words to explain something that could be done with smaller, denser ones. Well, she did that in this one. And it makes for a much better read."

"It's a romance, right?"

"It has a little of that and a whole lot of drama."

"You women love your drama," he joked.

She slapped his hand playfully. "I'd rather read about drama than be involved in it."

He shrugged. "You got me there." He walked around her chair and sat down at his desk across her.

"Are you all right?" she asked with a frown of concern on her face.

"I'm fine," he answered her quickly. But assurance was heard in his tone.

"Are you sure?"

"Of course. Why, do you know something that I don't know?"

"I worry about you. I just wonder if you feel fulfilled. You know, after retiring from the bureau."

"Believe me when I say this. I feel like I haven't been an agent in a long time, way before I retired."

"What do you mean, Kyle?"

He sighed. "Nothing."

"Kyle."

"I'm fine, sweetheart. You have my word on that."

She huffed her dissatisfaction but resigned to say nothing else. She hated to see him appear anything other than happy. She sought to change the subject. "What were you reading?"

"The Bible."

She asked in a tone of genuine interest, "What part?"

"Philippians," he responded.

She closed her book and turned around to look at him excitedly. She put a finger to her bottom lip in thought. "Let me guess. The focus was moving forward from the past. Right?"

Frazier smiled. "That's right, my dear. Always been the scholar, haven't you?"

She beamed with the combination of his approving compliment and the fact that she was right in her guess. "That's because I know you so well."

Kyle looked her up and down in her nightshift. She felt it was too warm in there for a robe. The look on his face was mischievous. "Speaking of *knowing*."

She put her book down, returning the grin in understanding. "You know how much I love that Old Testament term."

"Yes, I know." His grin grew wider. "Tell you what. I'll give you to the count of ten. You better find a good place to hide." He covered his eyes with his left hand. The white-gold ring on his ring finger gleamed off the light. "One. Two."

She shuffled toward the doorway, trying to be silent. She placed her left hand on the door frame with an even brighter gleam, hitting off her elaborate diamond-studded ring and matching white-gold band on her ring finger.

"Three. Four." The count continued. "Oh, and, Jessica."

She froze.

"About that count. I lied." He made to chase her as she ran giggling like a schoolgirl.

A month after.

"You don't look like the type of fellow that travel in these circles, friend." It was a portly man wearing loose-fitting blue overalls, a dingy white shirt, and a pair of brown work boots that spoke. He had long black matted hair that flowed untamed over his head. If he was outside, the wind would blow it every which away. "Are you sure you're not a cop?"

"Yes. I'm sure I'm not a cop," the tall, slim man responded. He looked ill. He wore a pair of faded blue stonewashed jeans and a black T-shirt. His shoes were run over. They look like they used to be white.

"Because you know, it's entrapment if you don't tell me."

"Do you think I would be here as a cop? Think about it. And besides, at this point, it really wouldn't matter."

"You have a point there, friend." The man looked up as a van rolled to a stop. "Looks like the rest are here."

They were in an abandoned warehouse. Nothing but metal support beams and walls were in there. The emptiness carried echoes throughout a great distance. Out of the van stepped three more guys. One wore a dirt-brown suit. The other wore a black cut-off pair of shorts and a red T-shirt. The third man wore a pair of olive-green sweat pants with a matching color long-sleeved shirt.

The man in sweat pants opened the back door to the van. Two large dark-brown Great Danes sat in separate cages. They looked feral and hungry. They lurched at the sight of the slim man. They barked and thrashed, wanting nothing more than to get after him.

The cages rocked from their strength. They growled, snarled, and drooled. These dogs looked like they'd been battle hardened. Definitely starved. Once docile upon arrival, turned vicious and relentless. The echoes were loud enough to wake the dead. It's said that animals have a better sense of recognition than people do at times.

The suit spoke up. "Can we at least put a blanket over them so we can hear ourselves breathe?"

The man in sweat pants obliged, pulling out two heavy dark-green tarps, placing them over the cages. The thrashing ceased, but the muffled barking continued.

The man in overalls spoke. "All I have to say is, I'm not going back to jail."

Slim responded, "What is with you and this jail thing? You understand the details of this, don't you?"

Overalls answered, "Yeah, I do. I'm just putting it out there. For my own benefit, I guess."

The man in shorts didn't have much to say. He watched the others with rapt attention. Sweat Pants didn't seem bothered in the least bit. But Suit kept glancing at Slim, squinting.

Slim eyed him back with a harsh look. His face showed the wear of hard living. He clearly had slept in an alley or two. Craters and bumps covered his cheeks. And he coughed. A lot. Not a loud, resounding cough, but a low, catching one.

"See something interesting, friend?" Slim directed at Suit.

"I just feel like. Do I know you?"

"What are you, a dumbass or something? You know who the hell you know or don't know," Slim responded. "Don't go asking me if you know somebody."

"Oh ho!" Overalls laughed. "I always wondered why people asked that."

Suit tightened his mouth but said no more. Shorts remained silent. And Sweat Pants looked back and forth between the two during the exchange. The dogs continued to bark.

"Hey, guy," Overalls called over to Sweat Pants. "I've dabbled in a livestock trading. Bet you I get a good deal on those two beasts you got over there." He pointed a beefy finger at the dogs behind the cage and tarp.

"They're not mine to sell. They came with the van," Sweat Pants called back.

Overalls shrugged. "No matter. I'll just collect them after."

"I seriously doubt that," Suit commented.

"He's got a point," Shorts chimed in. "From what I understand, they're in this."

Everyone turned to regard his first words.

Slim shrugged in a manner that indicated that he clearly didn't give a damn about anything or anyone. "Whatever." He coughed.

Overalls looked around. The empty warehouse had no storage shelves or containers, just open space. "Well, anybody got the time?"

Suit looked at his watch. "I got a quarter to ten."

Shorts was first to empty his pockets—an empty wallet, a key chain ring with no keys and pin. The last thing, he would wait to pull out.

Overalls also dropped an empty wallet on the floor. A small rope gold chain rested on his neck. He took it off and tossed it on the floor.

Suit took off his tie and blazer. He folded them both neatly, placing them on the hood of the van. He then removed his watch and put it in the blazer pocket. His wallet was also tossed on the floor.

Sweat Pants left the single key to the truck in the ignition. Two keys, one a piece, rested in the key hole of each lock to the kennels.

Slim was the last to do anything. He looked around as each man removed their things. He had nothing to remove. All he had to offer to the situation was a cough. Once everyone had emptied their pockets, they all looked at each other without saying a word. The dogs continued to bark the whole time.

One by one, they turned their attention to Sweat Pants. Understanding the meaning, he walked over to the dogs. He removed the tarp and watched the savage display of aggression they showed to Slim.

Slim stood in direct line of the dogs. If their cages opened, they would head a beeline right for him.

He nodded to Sweat Pants. And he obliged by turning the key. All he had left to do was yank the safety lock bar off. Right before he did, he pulled the last item out of his pocket and tossed it on the floor.

It was semi-small-sized blank sheet of notebook paper, the same kind of paper that was part of the infamous federal case some months back.

Overalls tossed the same kind of paper out. It swung and swayed in the air a little until in settled on the floor.

Shorts pulled out the same thing. He opted to gently bend down, placing the paper by his feet.

Suit put his on top of his blazer on the hood of the van.

That left Slim. He watched them all discard the blank sheets of paper with a look of sheer hatred in his eyes. He coughed. But this time, the coughs grew violent. He collected himself after a time, then reached back and pulled his out of his back pocket.

He tore it in two pieces, then tossed them. Both pieces flew in different directions. One flew higher than the other. One dropped relatively quickly. The one that flew higher landed back on his shoulder before falling off to the floor.

Overalls spoke first. "My name is Andrew Garland."

Next was Shorts. "My name is Ronald Long."

Sweat Pants followed. "My name is Barry Oliver."

Suit said, "My name is Ed Butler."

Slim coughed again, much lighter this time. "My name is Norman Wiley."

Andrew Garland etched closer to Ronald Long. Barry Oliver noticed that Ed was walking toward him. Wiley coughed again then clapped his hands. With that, Barry Oliver yanked open the bar off. Arm and Hammer charged straight for their former master, Norman Wiley.

About the Author

E RIC DILWORTH WAS born and raised in Los Angeles, California. The youngest of four boys, Eric credits his mother for his desire to write. He credits her efforts to teach him to learn the dictionary at the age of four, prompting him to win two spelling bee competitions at ages seven and eight. Aside from his love of writing, Eric is a big sports fan, movie buff, and ancient cultural studies enthusiast. He is a devoted husband, father, and friend, with an equal devotion to entrepreneurship.

CPSIA information can be obtained
at www.ICGtesting.com
Printed in the USA
LVHW052101240220
648041LV00002B/221